Mot

Dau

Strength

Strengthen Me

A Healer of an ancient race, Brierly often thought about how using her powers would bring a swift and painful death if discovered . . . but the need to help felt stronger than even the safety of life. She stared grimly at the castle and the danger that lurked there for her on the morrow.

"If I am the last," she declared aloud, "I will be a flame to the end."

"A hauntingly beautiful story, rich in texture and language, with a fascinating mythos and well-drawn, compelling characters. Riveting!"

—Elizabeth Haydon, author of *The Rhapsody Trilogy*

"A well-paced plot and strongly realized characters make this a suitable choice for most fantasy collections."

—*Library Journal*

Tor Books by Diana Marcellas

Mother Ocean, Daughter Sea
The Sea Lark's Song

Mother Ocean, Daughter Sea

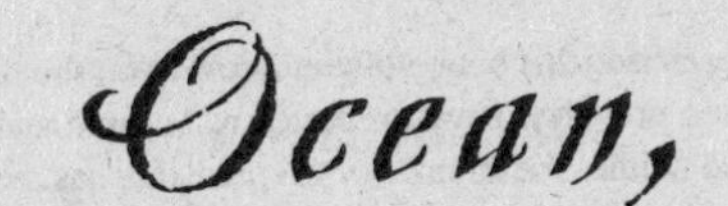

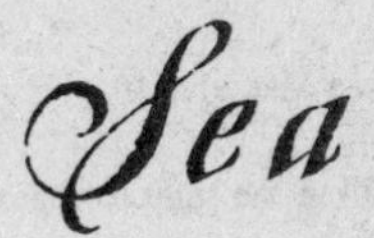

DIANA MARCELLAS

A TOM DOHERTY ASSOCIATES BOOK
NEW YORK

MOTHER OCEAN, DAUGHTER SEA

Map by Ellisa Mitchell

A Tor Book
Published by Tom Doherty Associates, LLC
175 Fifth Avenue
New York, NY 10010

www.tor.com

ISBN: 0-812-56177-5

Library of Congress Catalog Card Number: 2001034702

First edition: September 2001
First mass market edition: October 2002

Printed in the United States of America

10 9 8 7 6 5 4 3 2 1

To Tom,
my first reader and constant support,
and to all who believe in dragons

Northern Waste
Western Sea
Tellach
LIM
Eastern Bay
Efe
Himle
TYNDALE
Skelleford
Jarre River
Essenbai River
MIONN
Arlenn
Ries
INGAL
Flinders Lakes
Lowyn
Darhel
BRIDING
Iverway
Witchmere
Carandon
Savandon River
AIRLIE
Eury River
Tiol
Amelin
YARVANNET
North
Natheby
Farlost

1

When the second sun sets into the sea, the shadow of the offshore islands slowly climbs the coastland slopes, ascending the serrated pattern of the trees: one by one, each dark pine and everwillow passes from daytime green to silhouette shadow. The dying sunlight glances off the exposed rock of the mountain, warms the thin soil on the higher ledges, then shadows the ridgeline of topmost pine. Above Peak Willenden, a first evening star emerges in the east, a beacon for all wayfarers who wend their way home.

In the gathering dusk of the Companion's setting, Brierley Mefell made her way down the sandy bluff to the beach below, careful in walking on the uncertain footing of the path. The bluff stood the height of four tall men, steep and sandy, and was treacherous in the darkening nightfall. She descended to the beach with a final awkward step onto the sand, then sat down on a broad stone to rest. She put down her staff and bag, then rubbed the ache in her arm from the healing she had done that day.

A herder boy had run too quickly after his flock and had tumbled himself onto rocky ground, breaking his forearm bone as he fell. It was not a grave injury, but painful to a young and active boy, and a Calling had taken her to him today. With her witch-sense, through her hidden witch gift, she had healed his broken bone by taking his pain into herself.

It was her craft, that healing, and the pains of it were well accustomed and accepted. But she had not intended to return home this late.

Beyond the beach on which she sat, across a swirling pattern of cove-caught waves, stood a long row of large sea stones. Several of the great stones were large enough to be small islands, and were together the remnant of an earlier sea bluff now nearly eroded into the sea. Among their dark procession in the gathering gloom, Brierley's island home flickered with the white flash of breakers, beckoning with its promise of rest and sanctuary. Beyond the island's deep shadow, across a wide wave-swept bay and just visible above a northern headland, the tallest pinnacles of Earl Melfallan's castle stretched spidery fingers into the darkening sky. Beneath the headland, a distant fishing boat crept along the shore, weathering the point toward harbor and home.

The earl's castle was her constant visible reminder of the dangers of her hidden witchery. In all the Allemanii lands, the shari'a witches were proscribed as evil and forbidden to live, and so died a quick and agonized death whenever found. The Allemanii High Lords had a long memory, and had suffered greatly under witch's curse—or so they said in their histories. In the three hundred years since the Disasters, the tales of Witchmere's evil had grown with their telling, becoming a legend of trouble and pain, of domination and plague and oppression. Or so the Allemanii would have their history: the journals in her cave told a different tale, although her predecessors also wrote of times they themselves did not remember. Their warning of secrecy, however, was clear, for the shari'a proscription still existed, preserved in the High Lords' laws.

How long had the shari'a lived in these lands before the Allemanii came from over the sea? How had the Allemanii's search for a new homeland, far away from blight and war a thousand miles to the west, turned into the destruction of an entire people? The Allemanii themselves had felt uneasy with their answers, and so had crafted excuses for their triumph, tales of rightness and fate, of black evil and men's agony. She sighed softly. Who had the truth? Were the shari'a truly evil? Or did that evil lie in the Allemanii who had hated them? Who?

Who could give her answers? On all of Yarvannet's shore, Brierley knew of no other shari'a witch. She was alone, and often wondered if she was the last of her kind, the last of the shari'a everywhere.

Many years before, the fishing town of Amelin had welcomed a pale young woman and her infant daughter, and had believed her tale of a husband's fishing accident in a northern town and the need to escape memories. Jocater Mefell she called herself, but had no history before the ship plank touched down onto Amelin's wharf. Had Jocater left behind shari'a kindred in Duke Tejar's northern counties, or to the east in the earldom of Mionn? Brierley never knew: by the time Brierley was aware of herself, her mother had long since deliberately forgotten.

In time, Jocater had married a shipwright in the town, a widower of middle years who wanted someone to keep his house and give him the comfort of wife and family, a busy man who needed sons for his shop to replace the two lost to plague years before. For all Amelin knew, Alarson and his Jocater had lived contentedly: only the occupants of their house knew of the worsening strain, the disappointed husband, the too-strange and barren wife, the arguments, the hurt feelings, the mutual bitter regret about the marriage. The stirrings of witch-sense, rigorously denied, had tormented Brierley's mother all her unhappy life. Unable to cope with Alarson's emotions, she had finally fled from him into madness and a plunge off a high sea cliff that extinguished all pain, all need.

That night, as her mother lay in her death shroud, twelve-year-old Brierley had sensed Alarson's relief that Jocater was dead, a relief as keen as a twisted joy, however carefully he hid his joy behind the pretense of grief he showed to neighbors and friends. And that same night Brierley had left his house, never to return. A fine gesture, she thought sourly: he was glad I left. Two years later Alarson had drowned in a sailing accident, before the time Brierley needed to forgive him. She appreciated being spared the effort.

He's dead, she thought, and dug the end of her staff in the sand. Dead for years now. Why are you thinking about him? She scowled more fiercely and banished the memory.

She braced her hands on her staff and stood, then swayed as the night wind suddenly buffeted hard against her back, its fresh breeze swirling down the forested slopes. It whipped her pale brown hair into streamers, and tugged impatiently at her broad-brimmed hat. She braced herself against its push and blinked wearily, half-blinded by the squat bluish sun on the ocean's horizon. In this autumn season, both the Daystar and Companion began to move together to the other side of the world, bringing into the late evening the True Night, a time of star-filled darkness that grew steadily longer as the world changed toward winter. As she watched, the Companion's blazing arc finally vanished beneath the Western Sea, and the world seemed to grow colder.

She turned and studied the top of the short bluff behind the beach, wary of any observers who might have strayed away from the coast road to overlook her beach. The beach was blocked to both the north and south by a tall jumbling of rocks, and was accessible only by the steep descent down the bluff. In that isolation lay her safety, and she hid her small boat here among the rocks each day, concealing it from above, and took care that her use of it to reach her island refuge was never observed. In the gathering night, she saw no one above, and her faltering witch-sense confirmed that absence of mind and eyes. She was alone.

Brierley pulled her small boat from its sandy crevice among the sea rocks and hauled it across the sand toward the waves, resting at short intervals as she again checked the bluff tops. Finally, at the edge of the sea, she pushed the boat into the water and stepped aboard. As the boat slid into the water, she dipped her paddle into the sea, and slipped across the waves with long-accustomed practice and rounded the southern end of her island. She waited for the proper wave, then neatly guided her boat into a half-submerged tunnel. The sound of the waves thundered in the enclosed space, then quieted as she turned a bend into the hollow heart of the island.

Ahead, above a rocky platform carved from the island stone, the small square shape of her Everlight gleamed in the shadows, its mellow light repeated in moving patterns in the water below. It flickered as it sensed her approach, then flared in welcome.

"Good evening, Everlight," Brierley murmured as its love suffused into her mind, bringing promise of peace and rest, and a comfort of long familiarity. "I am glad to be home."

She stepped from her boat onto the ledge and tied its bowline fast to a stanchion, then reached up to touch the Everlight, reinforcing its bond with her. Once the Everlight had likely guarded the ancient caverns of Witchmere, the great capital of the shari'a, and had somehow come to this cave to guard a witch's home yet again. It had a mental presence, and it loved her, but the Everlight no longer spoke, if in fact it ever had.

"Ah, well." She sighed, wishing it could speak and tell her answers. She touched the Everlight in a second caress. The Everlight flickered in response, dancing its reflected selves into the gently surging waters of the entry pool.

She bent to retrieve her cloth bag and staff from the boat, then climbed the long stair above the landing. Outside the doorway to her cave, she took off her hat and hung it from a peg, then leaned her staff and bag against the wall below. She walked into the upper level of her home, a small space scarcely a dozen paces long but comfortable enough for a single occupant. The stone surrounding her reverberated faintly from the pounding waves, a blanketing sound that walled off all rumor of the outer world. Only here did she escape the harsh light of her witch-sense, a knowledge of the heart and physical pain, of motives and thought not her own. Only here could she heal herself after healing others, mending the damage to her body and mind. She stretched and glanced around the dimly lit cave, finding comfort in its familiarity.

She rubbed her aching forearm again and winced at the stab of pain, then crossed the stone floor toward her bed and table, drawing off her tunic as she went. She stepped out of her long skirt, dropping both to the floor. Dressed only in a linen bodice and petticoat, she bent over the wide table and replenished the oil in her lamp from a flagon, struck a match to light the flame, and then sat down in the single chair to draw off her shoes. Her lamp shed a golden glow over the wood and stone, fabric and leather of the cave, catching the polished shine of the carved oak bedstead in the nearby corner. The light gleamed on the worn flagstones that led downward to her bathing pool and pantry and, on the opposite wall, warmed the bright-colored leather of the books ordered neatly on shelves.

How many had dwelt in this cave? She had often wondered. Some of her predecessors had not left a written record and so left no traces, but all of the cave's contents, handed forward from witch to witch, were old, perhaps dating back to the Disasters three centuries before, when the shari'a had suffered their final defeat. A few of the oldest books had crumbled to dust when opened. She had not dared to disturb others, so cracked and ancient they seemed, and regretted the loss of their answers.

She counted her beloved books with her eyes, knowing many volumes well, others only begun, still others for the next year or the year after. On most of the shelves stood books of herb lore and healing, various histories, religious texts and hymnbooks, and the other books that had caught the interest of the cave's many occupants. In the center of the shelves, on the middle shelf on the far wall, stood a row of twenty-three journals, each carefully hand-bound in leather and brass, most timely recopied by later occupants of the cave and so preserved, five now too fragile for handling. Each was the record of a witch's life, speaking from years now long vanished into time. Through the journals, the twenty-three had preserved their knowledge and experience for those who might come after them, and had written to affirm a belief in the future of the shari'a, however forlorn that belief had been for a few.

On the table beside her lay Brierley's own journal, to be the twenty-fourth of such volumes, and was the compilation of what Brierley Mefell had learned and felt and known in her short life, for whomever might come after her to this place. If one ever did. She had seen the signs of too long an emptiness when she found the cave eight years before: it had been abandoned long enough to crumble a pile of witch's bones to dusty ruin.

She lifted a shawl from the bedstead and wrapped her shoulders against the chill draft of the cave, then opened her journal to a new page.

My dear child, she wrote, *do not despair. I believe that the Blood will continue beyond me, and that I am not the last. . . .*

She shook her head impatiently and began again. *Today I went to Natheby to watch the fishing fleet before my Calling to the herder boy. By the docks I spoke to a northerner captain named Bartol about the lands farther up the coast. He had many strange tales, but no hint of other shari'a—*

Or, rather, he had many tales of witches, each shrunken and evil and wishing men into death. In Allemanii minds, we have become creatures of the night, murderers of children, drinkers of men's blood, an evil concealed deep in the earth, within the boles of trees, or in any woman's heart.

At the end, he asked too pointedly about husband or father, glancing about for a protector against his intentions, and so I clouded his mind and slipped away. An unwise choice: I had misjudged him and he sensed what I had done. He raised a hue and cry throughout the docks, shouting "Witch! Witch!," and caused great panic among the wharfside folk.

She stretched and rearranged her shawl, warm in its woolen folds, then smiled ruefully.

I spent two hours among the wharf piers before the Natheby folk tired of the search and found more fun in taunting Captain Bartol. Duke Tejar's men are not liked here: it is easier to believe in a man's wounded vanity than a legend come to horrible life.

A foolish risk to ask about witches: I may end up undone by my wish to know too many things—

One thing I know: best to stay away from Natheby until Captain Bartol is safely gone home.

Her smile faded as she stared into the lamp's light. The flame flickered restlessly and the wick end crumbled ash into the oily pool beneath the flame, smudging the gleaming oil.

My child, be careful. The Disasters still live with us, and none of the Blood can walk openly in the High Lords' lands. Be vigilant, and take great care.

I wish I could meet you, my child. I feel alone. I wish . . . for many things I do not have.

Thora Jodann was content with the sea and the fisherfolk of this shore, and found her completion in simple things—a lark's caroling, the blue twilight of autumn, a fisherman's chant as he threw his nets. I wish I could find her peace, but it is lonely without you, my child, my hoped-for apprentice, so very lonely. When will I meet you? Will I ever meet you? And if I do, will you and I ever meet any other of our kind? Are we the last, you and I?

She stopped and bit her lip. *I am tired, my child. Forgive me. The Beast presses too closely tonight.* She shut the book and rose, then turned down the flame in the lamp and climbed into her bed.

Beyond the stone walls, the sea murmured ceaselessly, a varying rhythm of water and tide and seaborne life. The sea gave a cloaking sound to ward away the world, or perhaps some substance had been built into these walls to make a sanctuary for a witch gone beyond her strength. Or perhaps one need only believe in such a thing—

She closed her eyes, and listened to the crash of the waves and the surge of water in the channel nearby. As with the Everlight, the journals often took the cave's protection for granted: did only she wonder about such things? So many books, so many voices speaking from dusty years: somewhere on the shelves, surely, she would find her answers.

Against the darkness of her closed eyes, from deep within her mind, the Beast rose from a churning sea, beginning the ordeal that followed every Calling. As its terrible gaze fixed upon her, pitiless and knowing, Brierley found herself standing upon a beach of firm wet sand, her heart pounding, held motionless by that horrible great eye. She had healed today, using the gift: the Beast now came for her, to seize her if it could.

The Beast advanced slowly upon her through the breakers, coiling and uncoiling its serpent's limbs beneath a gas-bloated body, its stench of rotting flesh corrupting the breeze. As it neared her, its massive head swayed higher. It advanced still further, then roared as it struck down at her. *No!* she shouted, and darted aside from its terrible jaws. The Beast roared again, menacing her, wanting her, and filled her ears with the sound of its fury and need.

In her bed, she threw her hands to her eyes and pressed hard against them, covering the Beast with scintillating patterns that beat as frantically as her panicked heart. The Beast roared from within the sparkling light, heart-stoppingly close. She drew a ragged breath, then another, and willed away the Beast. *No!* The Beast's smell filled her nostrils, and its roar filled her ears: she felt its touch graze her wounded arm, and that coldness leapt into her body, seeking her heart.

No!

With that silent shout, she drew harder on her will to drive it away, denying the Beast. *No!* Baffled and roaring, the Beast began to retreat into the sparkling sea, and she shouted in triumph. Groaning, the Beast sank slowly downward into the waves and submerged, its single eye gleaming pallidly beneath the green water, then faded in the white splash of a wave. The sea waves ran up the beach, sighing in a final splash of foam.

Brierley lifted her hands from her eyes and took a deep breath, then another, aware of the sour smell of her own sweat, and of the light-headed dizziness that tipped the edges of her bedstead and doorway. She tried to breathe more deeply, shuddering as if the Beast's cold touch still lingered near her heart, and slowly warmed beneath her coverlet.

She touched her arm. The ache had vanished, as always, dispelled by the sympathetic magic of the Beast. Madness? Delusion? Her books did not say, but each shari'a witch who healed recorded a similar mental vision, always the same for its bearer, always inflicted after a Calling. For some, they saw a giant bird descending upon a crag, others a fiery worm aroused from its burrow, each time to be defeated by the edge of a ragged will. For some of those who continued to heal—and some did not—the record stopped abruptly from one day to the next.

Had they failed against the Beast? She suspected so.

She listened to her heartbeat as it slowed, then counted a dozen measured breaths. The sea air moved lightly through the darkened cave, chilling the sweat on her face and body. Beyond the cave walls, water crashed against stone, shielding her in a womb of sound. She shivered slightly and nestled under her blanket, rebuilding her warmth, then shuddered again with more than the chill of the cave.

Prescience? Already she felt the tug of another Calling, a dim vision of a future self bending above a sickbed, lending strength, risking the Beast.

Tomorrow. In Earl Melfallan's castle high atop the headland.

She sighed in dismay. As a prudent witch, she avoided the earl's castle as often as she could. It was a risk to come too close to lords, and such mistake might not be retractable. Should she go?

"If I am the last," she declared aloud, "I will be a flame to the end." Her voice echoed hollowly in the chill cave, and her smile turned grim. "Ah, brave words, Brierley," she told herself mockingly. "You'll be stubborn to the end that will surely find you."

She turned on her side and pulled the cover over her head, then listened to the sea, finding comfort in the sea's unending voice.

Mother Ocean,
Daughter Sea,
Strength unchanging,
Strengthen me.

The child's prayer repeated again in her mind, then broke into fragments of other memories and, finally, fell into dreams she would not remember.

Brierley awoke the next morning to the pale gray light of the Daystar. A wide crack above the stairway to the lower cave chamber admitted some light into the cave, enough for her to see her way during daytime. During the rains, water cascaded through the crack and down the worn stairs to the bathing pool and nearby cistern, replenishing her supply of fresh water. Now the morning fog rolled heavily into the bay, bringing light and moisture. She listened to the slow drip of water on the stairs, sniffed the moist air to smell the sea, then threw back the covers.

When she left the cave an hour later, the Daystar had climbed well above Peak Willenden, burning away the morning mist, which still clung in patches to the bay. She hid her boat in its crevice on the beach, then glanced around carefully. The cove was empty of visitors, even the errant boys who sometimes came exploring the high rocks for seaweed and shells. Above her beach, the trees on the bluff top and the sea slope beyond moved gently in the morning air, their leaves dancing in the sunlight. The wind blew cool and fresh from the ocean. She took off her hat and shook loose her hair, letting the sunlight beat upon her face, delighting in the brisk wind. The world sparkled with light and life. On such a morning all things seemed possible.

Since Brierley's earliest memories, her mother had warned her against her true nature and had practiced what she taught by refusing all parts of her shari'a self. She would not hear the thoughts of others, not even Brierley's. She would not try to heal, disclaiming any skill in the art, even that of a mother's in tending her child's hurts. Jocater hated the strange senses that colored each day in ways others could not see, and tried to teach her daughter the same hatred, urging her daughter to wall up her shari'a self to be forgotten and despised, as Jocater herself had despised and forgotten. Fearful of discovery, her mother avoided friendships with the other women, and forbade Brierley to play with the other children of the town, lest her child seem strange to them and they guess what she was and so bring down the end. And Brierley had obeyed Jocater for a time, frightened by her mother's earnestness.

As a child, she had watched the other children at their play, yearning to join in, and one day, when she was nine years old, she had suddenly found herself friends with a blacksmith's son named Jared. How that had happened, she didn't know, but suddenly Jared was there before her, smiling and teasing, and daring her to race him on the beach. For several sun-drenched afternoons, they had hunted seashells and assaulted any shell-star unlucky enough to crawl across their path, and had built a fort in the rocks, where Jared defended her against the dragons who attacked their castle, and Brierley had helped him fight with her own stick-sword. He told her jokes and made her laugh, and deliberately fell down over his own feet so that she would laugh again, and she had run to him, afraid he was hurt, and saw him laughing up at her, promising her he was all right. And she had loved him.

Jocater finally heard of it, and solemnly forbade her to see Jared again. Sadly Brierley had obeyed. But she could not tell Jared so, could not say the words to make him go away, and so had stood before him mute, tears filling her eyes, as he looked first baffled, then hurt by her refusal to talk to him, then very angry, and he had run off. Twice more he had tried to talk to her, and each time she had been struck mute, unable to speak such words to him, and so had hurt him as thoroughly as if she had spoken the harsh words Jocater insisted. In the years since, she had seen Jared from time to time in the town, and had heard that he was now a soldier in Revil's guard, and doing well. But she had never told him why.

It was on a day such as this a few years later, she remembered, looking again around the peaceful cove, a day like this that she had changed her mind about what she was. There had been no great event moving the choice, no desperate peril that demanded action: only the quiet of the day, when even the sea rocks seemed spirit-filled and the suns had struck down from the sky, touching all with a shimmering light. Life had called to her that day, the life bound into the gift. She had never regretted the choice—but, to spare her mother anxiety, she had not told Jocater.

She picked up her staff and slung her cloth bag on her shoulder, then climbed the path up the sea bluff to the coast road. To the south lay the track to Natheby and Amelin, the fishing towns governed by Earl Melfallan's cousin and vassal, Count Revil; to the north, a well-traveled road led to Port Tiol and Yarvannet Castle. At the top of the bluff, she turned north and walked along the road, breathing deeply of the morning sea air. In a nearby pine grove, a sea lark caroled its welcome to the day. She walked along easily, watching the trees move on each side of the road, happy with the day.

She had walked nearly a mile when a voice hailed loudly from behind her. She turned. A stocky, bluff-faced man seated on a wagon tipped his wide felt hat to her, his white teeth gleaming in the shadows of the road.

"Mistress Brierley!" he called. "A good morning to you!" His stout wife nodded shyly from the wagon seat beside him, and two small boys popped up their heads in the back, their dark eyes alight with mischief.

Brierley smiled up at the man as he tugged his mule to a halt beside her. "And a good morning to you, Master Harmon," she replied. "More vegetables for the earl?"

"Ah, no, not today. Fish!" He reached behind him and took a gleaming mackerel from a sack and waved it about. "Count Revil's steward took my new onions for part of yesterday's catch. Isn't this a fine fish?"

She stepped closer to inspect the fish, then solemnly agreed on its quality. The oldest boy sniggered and she glanced at him; both boys promptly ducked behind the sacks, giggling. Harmon turned and gave a measured swat on the nearest behind.

"Hey, there, lads," he bellowed. "Give respect to the mistress. She brought you into the world, young Egal, and don't you forget it!" He turned back and beamed proudly at his wife. "And another to come in the spring!"

Brierley smiled. "Congratulations, Harmon. That is good news."

"Ah, yes, my wife is a jewel, a fine mother and help to me, aren't you, Clara?" His wife ducked her eyes and flushed, a pleased smile on her broad face. "We'll want you for the midwifery again, Mistress Bri, if you will."

"Of course."

"Good, good. Are you going into the town? Want a ride?"

Brierley looked over the well-laden wagon and the two hefty occupants of the wagon seat. "I hardly think you have room, Harmon, but I'll be glad to walk beside you."

"Ocean, no, my boys can walk. They've younger legs than

you or me." The boys promptly wailed a unisoned protest, but Harmon chased them out and made a place for Brierley among the heavy sacks. She leaned gingerly on a sack, and the ripe stench of sun-warmed fish swirled past her nose.

"Comfortable?" Harmon bellowed genially.

"Yes, thank you," Brierley lied.

Harmon chucked the reins at his mule, and the small cart lurched into motion. "Haven't seen you about lately," he called over his shoulder, "not that you're easy to notice with the way you slip about. Are you up on your news?" Without waiting for an answer, Harmon waved his hand expansively. "Master Cormley had another prize foal out of that black mare of his. The creature had scarcely dropped to the ground when five bidders came swanning around the birthing stable, slavering to beat all over a mere animal. Was a sight, believe me."

Harmon and Cormley, Brierley remembered, had a years-long rivalry over their stock lines, with neither impressed by the other's.

Harmon waved his hand again. "Count Revil's having a festival next week, celebrating something or other. Biggest wheat crop in five years? Most shell-stars caught ever? I forget, myself. Then a big to-do by a northerner captain about witches loose in the port. Usual stuff."

Brierley hid a smile. Harmon Jacoby would watch the skies fall down, eyes mildly agog, then get back to his business of minding crops, wife, and sons. "Witches?" she asked casually.

"Who pays attention to northerners?" Harmon shook himself irritably. "Them and their fancy ways, snooting at decent folk. Everyone knows—who has any sense, mind you—that the High Lords stamped out that evil long ago. Destroyed half the land and the sea besides and themselves, too, the tales say, but they did it. But there they go, half of Natheby, running and screaming in circles, looking for a witch!"

"Did they find one?" Brierley asked.

"Aren't any witches, girl, not now." Harmon snorted and hunched his shoulders over the reins.

Brierley hesitated. It was too bright a morning to disturb Harmon with such probing. Harmon believed more of his beloved tales than he pretended, but the local commonfolk had no better weather vane. Harmon heard everything in time and sifted it through his jocular commonsense humor, his dislike for prance and outlandish finery, and his love for his land, his wife and sons, and his good lord.

Would that life were that simple, she thought, but guessed it might be for Harmon. Let it be, Brierley, she told herself, for Harmon's sake.

Harmon noticed her silence and turned to wink at her. "Don't you worry yourself, Brierley. I'll wager that captain had a fine laugh afterward. If you ask me, he knows too much of Duke Tejar's prancing finery and arrogant ways."

"Not too loud, Harmon," Brierley reproved. "You can lose your head talking that way about Melfallan's own lord."

"And who's here save you and my boys and my Clara? And you a slip of a girl no one would notice in the shade?" He waggled his finger at her. "You should eat more, Bri. Skin and bones you are, and too pale for a sea-shine lass." His face lit with a sudden idea. "Hey now, I'll give you one of my fish to fatten you!"

She laughed and waved him away. "You and your fish!"

"Fine fish!" he shouted and snapped the reins smartly. "Get up, mule. We haven't got all day!"

The cart jounced down the cobbled road that wound along the seashore bluff toward the port. When the boys began to puff, Clara took pity on the youngest, barely three years old, and lifted him to her ample lap to cuddle him. His brother clambered back into the wagon as it stopped and sat a precarious perch atop the sacks, his face aglow at the shifting, scary ride as the cart again lurched forward.

"Mind you hold on, Evan!" Harmon bellowed.

"I will, Papa!" the boy shrieked, his voice high with excitement. Brierley smiled, amused, and prudently took hold of Evan's small belt to steady him.

At the next long rise, the road passed the northern headland's broad foot and turned downward in an easy grade toward the harbor. They passed a mule train hauling logs, then met a brightly dressed party of lords and ladies riding leisurely up the slope. A lean-limbed forester followed them, balancing a pair of hooded falcons on hand and saddle horn. Harmon waved at them all and received a stern answering nod from the forester. The others, the noble folk, ignored the farmer's genial greeting, content with their own graceful conversations and soft laughter.

Brierley watched the several women ride by, each accompanied by an attentive suitor and aflutter with scarves and high fashion, and wondered if they were happy. Unwillingly, she caught a flash of worry from one, fatuous vanity from another, a stab of despair from a third. She turned her face away. Sometimes, after a healing and a night's sanctuary in her cave, her witch-sense dulled for a time, giving her unaccustomed peace out in the world: she wanted to keep it a while longer, if she could. As Harmon does with witch's rumors, she thought. She smiled to herself, understanding him very well, then smiled more broadly at the irony that each could be a grief to the other, his exuberant emotions, her witchly shadowy dangerous self.

"Get up, mule!" Harmon shouted, and snapped the reins smartly on the mule's hindquarters. Through the narrow scrabble of trees on the bluff edge, Brierley could see sunlight shimmering on the wide sea below. "Get up, mule! We haven't got all day!" The mule put new effort into its stride, and stepped along briskly. As they rounded the last curve of the descending road, Harmon pointed ahead. "Look there, Evan," he said. "Port Tiol and our earl's own castle!"

"I see it, Papa!" Evan cried.

Beneath them, Yarvannet's capital and principal fishing town spread itself around the curve of a wide bay, with a neat assembly of dock storage and piers, cobbled streets, low-standing stables, and clapboard houses. Several ships bobbed in the calm waters near the central wharf, their mast pennons flapping in the sharp sea breeze. To the left, ranked beneath the lee slope of the headland, stood the stone mansions of Yarvannet's nobility, each with a private stable and armory, a narrow wooden stair descending precipitously to the beach, and a pier with small watercraft. The white stone and painted wood of Tiol's many houses shone in the sunlight, brilliant color against the gray-green waters of the bay.

Above the town, the headland grew rocky and hard, rising into the massive stony outcrop that served as foundation for Melfallan's lofty castle. Its pinnacles and towers rose five hundred feet above the sea, sheer cliff on three sides, a narrow and easily defended bridge on the fourth. She saw a host of tiny figures traveling to and fro along the crest road and bridge into Yarvannet Castle. Far above the travelers' heads, metal glinted on the castle heights as Earl Melfallan's soldiers kept their never-ending watch against pirates and any other disorder that might disturb the earl's lands.

As Yarvannet's earl, Melfallan enforced the laws of road and sea, kept the peace, and occupied himself in other lordly affairs of which Brierley had only vague understanding. She usually avoided Tiol whenever possible, managing that task enough to have never actually seen Melfallan in the flesh—and thus preventing him from seeing her, the more relevant point for a prudent witch. But Harmon thought Melfallan a promising young earl, she reminded herself, well-trained by old Earl Audric in his duties—not as winning as the sunny Count Revil, true, but none had Harmon's higher regard than Natheby's good count.

Harmon clucked sharply to his mule and the wagon lurched forward again. Brierley hastily grabbed the wagon side, then helped Evan regain his seat aboard the fish-soft sacks. As they descended to portside, Harmon hailed all who passed him on the road, a jolly man exuberant with the morning and his load of fish. He drove straight to the fishmonger's store by the central wharf, and there dickered with the sour-faced and freckled proprietor. Harmon's sons promptly vanished into the crowd of passersby like darting bream into seaweed.

Clara called after them, then sighed and clasped her hands placidly on her swelling abdomen. "I expect they'll be back," she said resignedly.

"I expect so." Brierley touched Clara's arm. "Another son, perhaps?" she asked.

"A daughter, surely," Clara promptly declared, her eyes twinkling. "I'd like peace of mind for the first few years and the worry after. Girls are like that, never boys. I should know." She sighed feelingly, then cocked her head. "And you,

Bri, have you a young gentleman yet? You're of a woman's age now. Seventeen, is it?"

"Nineteen next month. And no." Brierley looked away. "Not yet. Besides, one needs a dowry and a father to ask after such things. I have neither."

"I had heard your stepfather's property went to that other relative of his when he died." Clara's head wagged disapprovingly. "Odd that he'd not provide for you, you orphaned and all."

"I wasn't of his blood." Brierley shrugged. "The wealth belonged to the family, and I had no rightful claim on it."

"Nonsense," Clara said briskly. "But, that aside, Harmon'll speak for you, as much as we owe you for your kindness. Now, don't protest. I've often wondered how you keep yourself, but you seem to manage well enough. But too thin and pale, Harmon's right on that." Clara's friendly eyes inspected her from hat to shoes, assessing the possibilities. Brierley shifted to her other foot, uncomfortable under the good woman's scrutiny. "Now, I know a fisherman's son in Amelin that might do, a quiet good-looking boy, quick with a net and lines—"

"Clara," Brierley said desperately.

"Hmmm?"

"Is that Egal down there?" She pointed at random far down the wharf to where several children played among bales of hemp. Three seemed the right size. Clara turned obligingly and squinted.

"Likely so, but Evan will watch out for him. He always does. Oh, you're going?"

"I must. Thank you for the ride."

"Any time, on any occasion," Clara answered, her smile slightly forced. *(Have I offended her?)* Clara's thought dropped neatly into Brierley's mind, followed by a rush of anxiety and shame, asking such personal questions of the young midwife that Harmon so admired. Then confusion, hiding the eyes to examine her clasped hands. (*I hope not. I so like her.*)

"May I come visit you soon?" Brierley asked. "When I have more time?" She had often sensed Clara's loneliness on their isolated farm, a quiet existence with its comforts but too often brightened only by Harmon's trips into town and Brierley's own rare visits. "I would like to very much."

Clara looked up and smiled, her face lighting with shy surprise and pleasure, as always. "Oh, yes. Please do. You are always welcome, Bri."

"Then I shall. Good-bye then . . . for today."

"Good-bye, Mistress Bri."

I preserve the gentle ones of the world. As Brierley walked down the broad seaside wharf, she remembered that passage from the book of Thora Jodann. Thora had not written often or at length, but somehow her words remained vivid in the memory. Hers was an older book of uncertain age, much worn and bent, often quoted. Other witches of the cave had studied deeply into alchemy and the healing arts, filling many volumes with their research; a few had turned in other directions, coveting power for its own sake—from their books came the occasional histories of Yarvannet's political fortunes. Thora had ignored the intellectual arts, forswore any influence over others, and had poured herself out in a brief span of years, then ended abruptly, from one day to the next.

Several writers had called Thora a fool; others had championed her with elaborate argument. A few contended that Thora had seen the Disasters at first hand and had founded the line of shari'a witches in Yarvannet's secret cave, writing the First of All Books. Some of her words implied as much. None could ignore her.

Brierley stopped at the end of the wharf and watched the flow of tradesmen, sailors, fishwives, and boys pass up and down the short staircase to the street. Each swept a brief shadow across the broad planking, a dancing, shifting pattern of tall angular shadows, a blend of swift and slow movements, blurred by the double shadow of the two suns. The wood vibrated slightly with their footsteps, in fascinating rhythm with their passing shadows. And, as always, underlying the pattern lay the ever-moving sound of the sea.

Whom do I preserve? she wondered, as her witch-sense awoke to full strength. She perceived the passersby as a current with many eddies, a light of many variations. She listened, entranced by the patterns of their fellow minds. Whenever she tired, those patterns oppressed and bewildered, driving her to the sanctuary of her cave, but now—

Whom? That skew-faced tailor, mind-twisting and hating? That fatuous wife, plotting her revenge on her neighbor? That steward, who has robbed his master? Allemanii or not, these were the only people she had known, these gentle—and not so gentle—people of Yarvannet's sea and wharfside. But the High Lords who had destroyed the shari'a long ago slept in uneasy graves, and these folk were not at fault. She stepped forward and descended the stair, joining the current of townspeople abroad on their business.

Whom do I preserve? All.

She made her way through the town, then ascended the streets until she reached the turning onto the road that bridged the crest of the highland and connected Yarvannet Castle to the port town it defended. On the crest road, the character of the townspeople changed: the clothes turned to finer cloth, more intricate stitchery, velvets instead of homespun; the horses bore ornaments of gold in their bridles instead of bright ribbons; and minds held different worries, different assumptions. She stepped to the grassy edge of the road to make way for another party of young noblefolk, then stepped aside again as a company of soldiers strode by, the sun glinting on their sword belts and spears.

A supply wagon rumbled past her toward the castle, laden with stores, its driver hunched comfortably over the reins. The boy's dark eyes flicked with casual interest over all who passed, as he thought of his stomach grumbling for a noon meal, the understeward's promise of sword-training next spring, a servant girl's smile the previous evening. *(I wonder if she . . . or was she smiling at Maxter? The twit—he gets all the pretty girls.)* Brierley followed in the boy's dusty wake, taking advantage of his wagon's bow wave through the stream of horsemen and people flowing outward from the castle.

In the sky above, the Daystar had passed its zenith and now cast shadows at opposite angle on the castle walls ahead, strong dusky gray to the muted blue of the Companion. The suns warmed the sea below, and crosscurrents of air swirled, plucking at hat brims and ribbons and blowing lustily over the headland, interrupted briefly by flurries of water-rich scent from the sea. On either side of the crest road, sea grass rippled in broad patterns of purple and silver, and a fine dust rose from the roadbed, swirling upward and away over the castle towers.

At the final rise to the castle bridge, she sat down on a stone to catch her breath, and admired the white granite of the massive gate wall, her head cocked beneath her broad-brimmed hat, her staff grasped firmly in her slender hands. At this distance, barely three hundred yards from the castle gates, she could hear the vast murmur of the many minds within Earl Melfallan's stony fortress, a restless shifting of thoughts and emotions at the edge of her perception, but there nonetheless, as changeable a rhythm as the surf and the stir of the breeze and the sea larks piping high above her head.

More soldiers stamped back and forth on the crest road, carters hied to their mules, and another party of gentlefolk rode by, bright with ribbons and gold. With each person passed a flash of emotion, a fragment of thought, and, in a deeper sense, the sum of each personality, quickly past. Brierley tipped her hat brim forward, shading her face from the sunlight, and studied her pale hands and their grip on her staff.

When I am old, she thought peaceably, I will sit like this in the suns' light and listen as I do now, drowsing now and then, foolish in my old age and the mock of children when they pass. Get up, old woman! they'll cry. Stir yourself about! Stop sleeping! And when I blink at them sleepily, doddery in my oldness, the children will point at me and laugh, their voices high and piping. They will run away and skip and jump, bright youth on the morning.

When I am old—

I preserve, she thought with sudden fierceness, and tightened her slender fingers on her staff.

Her mother had refused the gift, and had thus denied her essential self as shari'a and witch. Perhaps others of the shari'a did the same, if others still existed anywhere, and so hid away from the High Lords' cruel justice. Brierley breathed deeply of the brisk wind and smiled. On a day like today she had chosen differently. On a day like today, *this day*, she chose again—to heal, to practice her witch's craft.

Content, she waited, knowing the Calling impended, and soon.

2

Earl Melfallan Courtray sat at his worktable in his tower eyrie, gazing distractedly out the open window. The tall glazed panes stood open, admitting the brisk sea air and the brilliant sunlight of the morning. The murmur of a voice rose from a courtyard far below, counterpointed by the steady tramp of the nearest guard on the castle battlements, and, as always, the distant whisper of waves in Tiol's wide harbor. Yarvannet was a coastland holding, dependent on its sea trade and fishing, and the ocean dominated most of its affairs. Though not particularly a religious man, Melfallan found that dependence fitting: Mother Ocean had guided Allemanii fortunes since the Founding, and he considered Her constant presence a safeguard for his lands. No guarantee, true, but still a comfort.

But Ocean had not saved Earl Audric from a hard death, and that omission tormented him still. His grandfather had died the previous spring of a mysterious cause, and Melfallan suspected poison, but had no proof. The castle healer agreed it likely was poison, but without proof of the herb or oil or especially a specific name and the opportunity, the suspicion had not led far. Old men were prone to sudden strikes of ill health either in the head or bowels, and persons of all ages could die of the hag's breath any winter, although this had not been plague. His grandfather had been a mortal man like every other, whatever his qualities as earl, and so was as vulnerable to such maladies as Melfallan would be if he reached similar years. The official report had thus concluded a sudden intestinal malady, one that had killed quickly with great pain, and made no accusation.

In his private thoughts, Melfallan supplemented the report by mentally accusing any one of several, a few among his own Yarvannet lords. Whoever had slipped the poison into Earl Audric's bowl or glass, the likely origin of that act lay in Darhel, Duke Tejar's capital. Whether Tejar had ordered the poisoning or now merely took advantage of it, Duke Tejar would not mourn the death of Earl Audric. Tejar had hated Audric viciously, as he hated most of his father's principal lords, and now chose new friends among Ingal's minor nobility, men whose fortunes depended solely on his favor. That choosing had attracted a new type of lord into Darhel's court, the schemer and sycophant and grasper. Melfallan's grandfather had lectured Tejar on his poor choices, which had not endeared the earl to his duke. Audric said what he thought, and challenged the world to make him act differently—to the day of his death, the world had never managed to change him.

I miss you, Grandfather. How I miss you. Melfallan felt the familiar pall of grief descend on him. Although six months had now passed since Audric's death, his grief remained sharp, keen-pointed, a constant presence in the back of his mind. At any moment Melfallan expected to hear his grandfather's step on the stone stair, the rasp of his voice, his bark of laughter—but all that haunted Yarvannet Castle was the hollowness of his absence. Yarvannet had lost its earl, and a new earl had stepped into his place. Of all things, Melfallan resented that the most, that the world merely went on, pausing briefly to note a man departed, then turning back to its own affairs.

His grandfather had been the suns and sky to Melfallan. His parents had died of plague when Melfallan was a young boy, and, stripped of both father and mother, the boy Melfallan had turned desperately to his grandfather, the earl. Audric had stood like a tall ever-oak in his life ever since, never defeated, never afraid, a tumultuous noise storming through the castle when he chose, a mild rise of the eyebrow when he chose, a hearty laugh or angry bellow booming through the hall when he chose. His grandfather had defied everyone to change him in the slightest degree and never lost that challenge: how, then, could his grandfather die? How could it be that a coward's sly malice, a slipping of poison, had destroyed such a grand old man, stripping him out of Melfallan's life in a mere hand-span of days? How could Mother Ocean allow such an evil?

Melfallan idly tapped his writing pen on the wooden surface of the table, then sighed. However long he thought on it, he never found an answer. Likely he wasted time in the effort, time he owed to other, more pressing matters. Likely there was no answer, save a caution to himself to watch for similar plots against himself. But in a deep corner of himself, in the corner that had cherished his grandfather as the one certainty in his life, Melfallan wished himself wherever his grandfather had gone. When he was six years old and had lost his parents, Audric had been there. Now Audric was lost and all Melfallan had was himself—and did not always like what he found.

He was twenty-four, too young to be earl. The politics of the High Lords were devious at best, and likely other lords already plotted his death, with Yarvannet for the taking if they succeeded. Melfallan cursed himself for his moping all these months, desperately worried for Yarvannet that he was not the earl Audric had been, and worried he could never be. The worry solved nothing, of course, yet he could not make himself stop his mopery. Such hesitation at a crucial time could be fatal, and he knew it, yet still he wasted his customary morning hours in his solitary tower retreat on wishing for things he could not have, thinking on problems he could not solve. No, Melfallan was not his grandfather: he'd spent the six months since his accession proving it every day.

Stop this, he told himself for the hundredth time. Stop it.

Earl Audric had been old Duke Selwyn's most trusted friend, but both men were dead now, and Selwyn's son, Tejar, had other favorites. Aware of Tejar's enmity, Audric had prudently married his daughter, Rowena, into the duke's own southern county of Airlie, and had later betrothed Melfallan to Lady Saray, the Earl of Mionn's youngest daughter. The marital alliances south and east of Duke Tejar's principal lands had bought the Courtrays some security during Audric's lifetime, but they would not buy it forever. Fortunes could turn too easily against any noble house, brought by plague riding the winter wind or a wife's failure to bear a living child.

Melfallan's mother had died early in childbed, a victim with Melfallan's newborn sister of that year's plague. Three years later, the winter plague had struck again, carrying off Melfallan's father and uncle and too many other folk. Strong men had sickened from one day to the next, then died before the next morning. Their wives and children took sick as well, sometimes lingering for days—or not, dying as quickly as their men. In terror, many Yarvannet folk had fled inland to caves high in the coastal mountains or had boarded themselves up in their houses, threatening any visitor with pitchfork and sword. A pall had lain over Tiol and the southern towns, with empty ships flapping their sails at the piers, animals untended in their stalls, the streets emptied of folk.

It was said the shari'a witches had made the plague, and had then loosed it into the world in their malice and spite. In the Great Plague three centuries before, when the hag's breath had first struck the winter after Rahorsum's attack on Witchmere, a quarter of the Allemanii people had died in a span of mere months, emptying entire hamlets, piling corpses in the streets and fields to rot untended, murdering whole familes, including the duke and his only legitimate heir. In time, the hag's breath lost part of its deadly force and killed less each winter, and then it did not come every year, but every other year, and then every third year, although it always returned in time, and even now it still killed many that it struck.

He still remembered the silence of that horrible winter in his boyhood, an aching empty silence that lay over the towns and hillsides, the sound of looming death, in which nothing moved, nothing at all. He sometimes dreamed of it, and woke sweated in his bed, and worried that he dreamed not of the past, but a future that still impended. A duke's malice he could counter, if he was clever and ruthless in his politics, but plague struck as it willed. The hag's breath, the Allemanii called it, and feared each winter for its coming.

He stood up and restlessly paced the room. The chain mail under his tunic chimed softly with each step, a familiar sound when he moved. After Audric's death, Melfallan's advisors had urged him to wear the light armor as a prudence, lest the plot that killed Audric include Melfallan's own assassination. In the months since, he'd grown used to the weight of the metal, to the faint bell chime of its links, but had felt no more safe from treachery by the caution. His food was tasted in advance by condemned prisoners in the dungeon, his chambers inspected daily for poisonous insects or serpents that might be placed there by a malicious hand. Guards stood watch at every doorway he might pass, and Melfallan's castellan, Sir Micay, checked constantly for subversion in the castle troops. His justiciar watched the vassal lords in Melfallan's court, his ear to every doorjamb to pick up gossip, his hawk's eye watching every shift of expression, every quiet conversation, that might threaten his earl. It took only one knife thrust, one slip of poison, to end an earl, and both men were determined not to fail their trust again.

And so Melfallan now examined every person near him, mistrusted every corner and dish, and expected treachery at any turn. Until the guilty were known, even the most trusted had to be suspect. Trust had now become a matter of degrees, with the highest trust given to Sir Micay and his justiciar, to his wife Saray, and a few others, but never total trust, not even to Saray—in the Allemanii's long history of tumultuous wars and politics, noble wives had on occasion murdered their husbands, for hatred or money or sexual passion or even personal rule. A chance of birth had given Melfallan an earldom: that he had never consented to the price was irrelevant. His chance of birth was as inexorable as the plague, and as unwinnable.

So why do you complain? he asked himself sourly. What does it gain you? He stopped in front of the open window and blinked in the warmth of the sunlight, the air sifting over his face with a delicious coolness. Ocean preserve him, at least he had told no others about his maunderings. They would think him weak, probably a coward as well, and that invited treachery. Even the most devoted of servants might turn on an incompetent lord, if only to preserve their own lives and fortunes when a noble house fell. Certainly the other High Lords, once they sensed that weakness, would build new possibilities. A High Lord's rule belonged to the strong and ruthless.

Duke Tejar wanted Melfallan dead, as dead as Audric, and only bided his time. Melfallan knew that fact with the same certainty as his own need for breath. If Melfallan died without a body heir, Tejar could then deliver Yarvannet to one of his kept northerner lordlings, a lordling to be as disposable as Tejar pleased. How would Tejar attack Yarvannet? By open war? There were no signs of that as yet, and Yarvannet's armies equaled Tejar's own. No, Tejar had too great a chance of losing, at least right now, but there was always the future. The longer Melfallan survived, the more war between Ingal and Yarvannet became inevitable. But not yet. By more devious plot? Through what means and what trusted retainer? And how should Melfallan manipulate his other alliances to frustrate the duke's intention? At stake was Melfallan's own life, and all else that Melfallan owned and loved.

Well, you're earl now, Melfallan thought sourly. You can't change that. Perhaps, you idiot, you ought to accept it, and start deciding something.

Indeed.

He took another tour of his small eyrie, scowling at the books and ledgers on the shelves, the detailed maps on the opposing wall of Yarvannet and the wider Allemanii lands, the long worktable, the few chairs. For two hours every morning, borrowing Audric's own practice as earl, Melfallan had insisted on solitude in this tower room. "Plotting time," Audric had told Melfallan with a predatory smile, and had vanished into this same tower room every morning, except when Audric rode the lands to visit his vassals or led field training for his army or traveled to Darhel to see Duke Selwyn. Melfallan had always wondered what his grandfather did in his private room each day, what he thought and planned there, and why he always insisted on being alone. Melfallan hadn't yet discovered those answers, but stubbornly kept trying.

He heard the soft chime of the castle bells, announcing the new hour, and felt candidly relieved. Another morning's self-torture had ended: now he could forget himself in action and events, at least for the remainder of this day. Saray planned a entertainment for this evening at dinner, he remembered; his portmaster would give Melfallan his weekly report this morning. And perhaps he might go hawking this afternoon, a chance to do something physical, outside the castle. His spirits lifted at the thought. With a motive not too far from escape, he raised the door latch and exited the room.

"My earl, I must protest!"

Melfallan recoiled in midstride, startled by the sudden shout in his face. His hand fell automatically to his dagger hilt, but it was not attack, not yet. Lord Landreth of Farlost stood outside Melfallan's study, hands on his fleshy hips, his sour face filled with indignation. The stocky marsh lord, resplendent in a cloth-of-gold surcoat, glittering chains on his breast, his legs covered by elegant hose and boots, firmly blocked Melfallan's descent, but seemed determined only to nag his earl.

Melfallan menaced him with a scowl and relaxed slightly, the alarm jangling his nerves. His people often lay in wait outside this door each morning, impatient for their earl's emergence into the day, and so accosted him regularly when he appeared. It was an assassin's opportunity, too, one not yet taken. It was his own fault not to expect it, after all the times others had waited for him.

Still, of all such persons, Lord Landreth usually made himself the most unwelcome. Close in age to Melfallan, Landreth was heir to Farlost, one of Melfallan's two principal counties, and his father had sent him some years ago to Tiol to be a courtier in the earl's court. In that role, Landreth constantly presumed a trust Melfallan did not extend to him, and, worse, assumed a friendship that had never existed. Behind Landreth's deference and constant attendance, his protests and gadfly advice, his constant meddling in every decision, Melfallan suspected Landreth and his sour-minded father of ambition to be Yarvannet's next earl. They had the local bloodline: Landreth's father had chosen the right side in Earl Pullen's revolt, and so had kept his lands when Selwyn gave Yarvannet to Audric. All they needed was Tejar's favor, and both count and son were highest on Melfallan's mental list of suspects for Audric's death. Unfortunately, Melfallan could not prove it—yet—and so had to tolerate the son to avoid offending the father, however much he'd rather be rid of both of them.

"Not now, Landreth," he said irritably. He sidestepped around Landreth's glittering magnificence, and descended the stairs to the landing below. Landreth promptly followed him, stomping down the stair.

"We cannot ignore Captain Bartol!" Landreth declared with agitation, feigned or otherwise. "He's been sent by Duke Tejar himself!"

Lord Landreth maintained a constant visible awe for Duke Tejar, as if Tejar preserved all existence by merely breathing each day. To Landreth's constant protestation, no lord had greater wisdom in judgment, nor wonder in battle, nor wealth in person. Had Landreth been female, his passion for Tejar would no doubt have cast him at the duke's feet, no matter who watched, to offer all, right there on the spot. Landreth's constant topic of Wonderful Tejar grated on Melfallan, as Landreth no doubt intended, for it bore an implicit commentary on Melfallan as the lesser man.

"*We*?" Melfallan asked ironically, and kept walking, making Landreth hurry to keep up. The stocky lord had already started to puff. "You're not earl yet, Landreth—and won't be, I promise you. I fully intend to keep my present rank."

"Your grace," Landreth cried, "you misjudge me!" He became a picture of wounded trust. "I am a loyal lord to Yarvannet. My father—"

"—was the only Yarvannet lord not to join in Earl Pullen's rebellion," Melfallan finished for him. "And so kept his lands when my grandfather crushed the revolt, unlike all the others. Yes, I know, Landreth. I know all about your family's loyalty." Melfallan glanced out a broad window of the upper hall as he passed by, checking the angle of the suns' light. Portmaster Ennis was always early, and seemed oblivious that his diligence thus made his earl always late.

"I think—" Landreth began in another whine.

Melfallan's patience vanished on that instant, and he turned abruptly on his heel, quickly enough that Landreth nearly ran him down. "Enough!" Melfallan shouted. "I'll see him when I choose!"

Landreth's mouth sagged open in shock at Melfallan's tone, so intemperate to the situation, so unseemly toward a loyal lord's effort to be helpful. Melfallan bit back another hot retort, knowing that Landreth deliberately provoked him with this playacting, as he already had with his nags.

"As you will, your grace," Landreth answered, soft-voiced, wounded, deferent.

"I do will it," Melfallan snapped. He spun on his heel again and stalked onward, fuming, and Landreth mercifully did not follow.

"Perhaps later, my earl," Landreth called after him solicitously, "when you are less troubled in mind."

Melfallan nearly halted in midstep at *that*, but forced himself to keep going, though it ground his teeth to do it.

I could lock Landreth up in my dungeon, he reminded himself furiously. I could tie him up with a hundred feet of rope, and dangle him from the castle walls. I could dump him in the harbor and ruin his pretty clothes. I could do all those things, and Landreth would still be Count Sadon's son and heir. Duke Tejar would love it, when he got the legal appeal.

Melfallan scowled at a chambermaid who peered wide-eyed around a doorjamb and sent her scurrying, then stalked past the soldier at the hallway corner, mentally daring him to twitch an eyebrow. The man, obedient and true and loyal to his earl, saluted smartly but showed nothing more, as if earls shouted rudely at lords every day. Good man.

He turned the corner of the hallway and had a quick glimpse of the sea through a window, shining and flashing in the suns' light, then rattled down a stone staircase, completing his descent to the broad platform of the castle's upper floors. Though he was late to his meeting with Portmaster Ennis, he slowed his pace as he entered the upper cloister hall, watching the sea and the fine morning through the passing windows.

One lead-paned window stood open, freshening the hall air with scents of the sea. Melfallan stopped in front of it and sniffed appreciatively, the slight breeze through the window ruffling his blond hair. Tiol Harbor lay below, the water shimmering in the suns' daylight, with ships at the wharves and the townspeople bustling on their business. His Courtray forebears had been formerly the counts of Tyndale in the north, a county of river plains and low hills. Melfallan had been born and raised in seaside Yarvannet, and counted himself blessed for it. But the shore could bring its own perils.

Five years ago, in the first year of their marriage, the winter plague had struck again at Yarvannet, nearly killing Saray, heavily pregnant with their first child, a son she quickly miscarried. Since then, to their mutual dismay, Saray had miscarried two other pregnancies, and then had been slow to conceive the fourth time. Now Saray was pregnant again, and Melfallan knew much depended on a successful birth, and that the child be son, not daughter. By Allemanii law, succession by a daughter or his cousin Revil required the duke's approval, an approval Tejar would surely deny.

A son for Yarvannet, he thought yearningly. A son. The problem never really left his thoughts, but lingered in the back of his mind each day, coloring every decision, bending every hope. His lack of a son encouraged Count Sadon's secret ambitions, as well as the similar ambitions of others in Duke Tejar's northern court. It troubled Melfallan's advisors, though they had the grace not to mention it to Melfallan too often. Without a son, all was put in doubt, whatever Melfallan's other qualities as earl.

A son to anchor the Courtray holding in Yarvannet, he thought, looking out over the harbor he loved. A son to make Saray happy.

Theirs was a political marriage, arranged by others, not by themselves. He had liked Saray when they married, attracted by her prettiness and shy manners, but he had not loved her. As had Saray, he had expected love to grow after the wedding, as it often did in such marriages, but had found himself baffled by his wife's docility. Mionn, the more ancient earldom of the various lands, had a conservative court, and its ladies were trained to keep their place. Saray's mother had trained Saray well. *Too* well, Melfallan thought.

And so Saray avoided unseemly passions, even in their marriage bed, and likewise ignored unpleasant situations by pretending they were otherwise. She took little interest in the politics and trade which often consumed her husband's attention. The governance of Yarvannet she left wholly to Melfallan, as she deemed proper for a gentle lady, and occupied herself only with managing their immediate household, the friendship of her waiting-ladies, and the gentle feminine arts. When he tried to discuss matters outside that sphere, Saray smiled sweetly and listened, but contributed nothing.

His aunt Rowena, the dowager countess of Airlie, did not adopt such lady's rules: widowed for several years, she ruled her county as regent for her ten-year-old son, the young Count Axel, and ruled it decisively, contending often with Duke Tejar and any other lord who thought women unsuited for rule. Saray professed that she admired Rowena, a fondness Rowena returned, but Melfallan knew Saray little understood his formidable aunt.

Does she understand me, he wondered, even a little? Sometimes he felt as if he talked to her through a vague curtain that muffled his words, removing all sense.

In the third year of his marriage, after another son had miscarried, Melfallan had strayed into an affair with a pretty maidservant, and might have fathered the daughter born some months later. Bronwyn was popular with the castle men and easy with her favors: there had been other lovers beside Melfallan at the critical time. Later, she had married a baker in the town, and now seemed happy with him. Melfallan sometimes visited Bronwyn and her dark-haired little girl at the baker's shop, checking that all was well with both, but saw too little resemblance in the child's face to take the matter much further.

Perhaps Saray suspected that affair and its possible outcome: if so, his lapse was one of the unpleasant things Saray chose never to discuss. After Bronwyn, Melfallan had been tempted now and then by another pretty face, a lilting voice, a sweetness of person, but the conquests had been too easy to satisfy him, and now he no longer tried. No maidservant would say no to a lord, as most young noblemen discovered early in life and sometimes abused. Melfallan had the good sense not to seduce Yarvannet's noble wives and daughters, but did not count himself much credit for it.

Sadly, Melfallan knew that Saray would publicly accept his affairs if she were ever forced to acknowledge them. In Mionn, a husband's wandering eye was often a high lady's lot, and a high lady endured such embarrassments with dignity and silence. And so Saray would not protest or weep, threaten or demand: she would yield, as she always yielded, and consider it her duty to let her husband betray her. Melfallan sometimes wished that Saray would throw a lamp at him and call him the names he deserved, but knew the hope was useless. It wasn't Saray's fault. And so he allowed Saray her silence on the matter, the pretending it had never happened, if Saray even knew. Did she know?

A son for Yarvannet, he thought yearningly. A son for Saray, that she might be happy despite her husband.

The passing shadow of a seabird distracted him, and he suddenly remembered Ennis, waiting patiently on the battlements. With a snort of dismay, Melfallan set off again, making for the wide doorway at the cloister's end that led to the castle's upper walls.

Another soldier saluted as he passed the doorway, spear thumping smartly against his chest. Melfallan nodded in acknowledgment, his eyes flicking over the man's alert posture and neat dress. He could rely on Sir Micay to police the castle's soldiers: all were well trained and duty-conscious, an asset to the earl. It was one less worry for Melfallan: at least Yarvannet was well guarded, if not exactly war-ready. The Tyndale veterans who had helped Audric defeat Pullen were now long since retired or dead, and the younger men trained in peacetime were not yet their equal. Given Duke Tejar's open enmity, first to Audric and now to Melfallan, Yarvannet's army was a strength Melfallan would need in the future.

He entered the open air of the battlements, a broad walkway thirty feet wide that ran the full length of the upper walls.

Several yards ahead, his portmaster stood looking down at the harbor. Master Ennis turned as he heard Melfallan's footsteps, then bowed in his rough manner, awkward and embarrassed by his own attempt at courtliness. Too long a simple fisherman before Earl Audric appointed the capable man as Tiol's portmaster, Ennis had few polished arts and wanted none—but, for his earl's sake, he still tried.

"Good morning, Ennis."

"Your grace." Ennis tried another awkward bow, his badge of office thumping on his barrel chest. Melfallan waved him off impatiently, as he always did, and got an answering grin from Ennis, a startling flash of white teeth in the older man's weather-beaten face. "I have been practicing my bows," Ennis announced haughtily, looking suspiciously like Melfallan's pompous chief butler. The two men did not get along, nor had they tried to, a fact both freely admitted. "A proper lord would appreciate my efforts."

Melfallan clapped Ennis on his shoulder. "Oh, I do, Ennis. But it's no use. You're as likely to manage a proper bow as me to learn patience for ladies' talk about their stitchery."

"Stitchery is a goodly art," Ennis allowed.

"So are courtly bows," Melfallan agreed as solemnly. "But that doesn't mean we have to inflict them on each other. True?"

"True, your grace." Ennis chuckled comfortably, and they both turned automatically to study the ships in the harbor. Melfallan counted a half-dozen fishing boats in port, as well as the smaller craft that beetled up and down the wharfside. The others that usually harbored in Tiol were out at sea on this fine sunny day, fishing the shallow banks just off the point. One of the ships still in the harbor fluttered the duke's golden banner at its masthead, reminding Melfallan of the spy in Melfallan's own port, the spy Landreth now nagged him to meet.

I'll deal with Bartol later, he thought irritably. Landreth will see to that.

The two suns now bracketed the zenith, casting double shadows on the white stone of the castle, and the wharfside activity below moved briskly. To the far right, his folk went up and down the headland road, raising puffs of dust quickly caught up by the wind. He saw the bright flashing of spears as a company of soldiers set out on patrol, and a steady row of wagons bringing supplies to the castle. He looked beyond the town and headland to the low hills surrounding Tiol's small bay, each patterned with the irregular green squares of fields heavy with grain, then to the coastal mountains rising behind them, deeply shadowed with forest green.

A son, to keep all this.

According to the accounts of the Founding, the Allemanii had once lived in a land like Yarvannet far to the west, where another seacoast had been warm and fertile with life. They had shared the western coastlands with other peoples like themselves, and had often warred with their neighbors, as much for the sport as any need. Between their joyous battles, the Allemanii had fished and hunted, and ordered themselves peaceably under High Lords of their choosing. But then a blight had struck the western coastline, bringing an algae bloom that smothered all life out of the sea. The Allemanii's most violent neighbor to the south, its people starving and half-mad with fear about the dying sea, had suddenly attacked the Allemanii villages in the night, killing and looting for food. The Allemanii survivors had fled the attack into the safety of their longships, saving what they could. Then, led by two brothers among their High Lords, the Allemanii had sailed bravely out into the open ocean, in search of a new land far from the death and wars behind them.

For a thousand miles they had sailed, following a rim of islands that fringed the ocean's northern border, but found only frozen wastelands and icy uninhabitable shores. The ocean teemed with fish, giving life and new hope, and on occasion the longships stopped for a year or two on a frozen island for repairs and a testing of the land as a home, only to sail onward, still searching. What had his ancestors felt when Briding's green shore first appeared on the eastern horizon? Had it been what he felt when he looked out at Yarvannet? Or more?

"The ocean catch is up, with good hauls," Ennis began, his tone faintly reproving, and abruptly jarred Melfallan from his thoughts. He glanced at Ennis and grinned at his portmaster's careful expression. The practical Ennis had little patience with his earl's daze-minded staring, but would drown before saying so.

"Your pardon, Ennis. I'm awake."

"I should hope so, your grace," Ennis replied with a sniff. "As I said, the ocean catch is up, and the sturgeon run is starting in the Sarandon and the Ewry, with the gomphreys coming upriver behind them. The rivermen are hauling good catches there, too."

"How many gomphreys?" Melfallan asked. The great sea snakes, usually benign toward men and their ships, sometimes attacked riverboats during the frenzy of their annual hunt for a favorite prey.

"Two so far, both in the Sarandon River, one sixty feet long, the other well over a hundred. The bigger one upended a barge to dump the wheat and then ate all the sturgeon who swam over to eat the wheat it dumped. Got quite a haul of its own, nearly forty sturgeon for lunch, nicely seasoned with grain, and all it had to do was open wide. And you still argue those beasties aren't intelligent?"

"I never said they weren't intelligent," Melfallan retorted mildly. "I just say it's not proven."

Ennis grunted, unimpressed. "Same thing." He fumbled inside his leather vest and brought out a much-folded packet of papers from an inner pocket. "I brought you my written reports, as usual. A good season so far, your grace."

"Let's hope it continues, Master Ennis," Melfallan replied as formally.

"Expect it will, Ocean helping."

Melfallan took the papers and glanced through them, then paused to wonder what Ennis thought about Bartol. The northern ship had lain at dock in Yarvannet for three days, long enough for Ennis to gather some news. Melfallan valued his portmaster's judgment, for Ennis had a seaman's clear eye and generally little fear in speaking frankly. Frankness was a quality not unknown among his advisors, and Melfallan valued it when he found it. "How long has Captain Bartol been in port?" he asked, raising the subject.

"Arrived this morning," Ennis replied immediately, as if he were waiting for the question, as he probably was. "Went to Natheby first, I heard." Together they studied Bartol's ship far below. The pennant snapped in the fresh breeze, and sailors scurried on the deck. A tall figure emerged on the deck, glinting with the splash of gold at throat and belt. The captain himself, no doubt, out to sniff the breeze. "Elegant ship, I'd say," Ennis drawled, "one of the duke's best. Lines all coiled neatly, paint freshened up. Sailors all neat in their shirts and ducks. Doubt he's fished at all on his trip down the coast, to stay that neat."

"What's he fishing, if not fish?" Melfallan asked.

"You, my earl. What else?" Ennis squinted at him. "He's another spy, of course, sent down by Duke Tejar to sniff about and bedevil you. He's been all over Natheby, looking into this and that, asked a meeting with Count Revil, who refused it, of course, sending him first to you. Paying too much for supplies, buying ale for any man in sight, making himself noticed. Started a ruckus on the Natheby docks, claiming he saw a shari'a witch."

"A *what*?" Melfallan's head jerked around.

Ennis shrugged. "A hag, your grace, a witch right out of legend. She was standing right there on the Natheby dock, Bartol said. Tried to bewitch him with her foul arts, he said, too. Had the Natheby folk running up and down for a while, shrieking, until they got some sense back. Was a sight, I'm told, while it went on."

Melfallan scowled. He hadn't heard this bit of news, and wondered why Landreth had omitted it. "The shari'a no longer exist, Ennis—if they ever did."

"Lots of folk think they did, your grace, and your own history books confirm it, or so I've heard. But you want *proof*, I suppose," he added, twigging his earl.

Melfallan had inherited Audric's long argument with Ennis about gomphreys along with the rest of his earldom, and he cheerfully defended Audric's side of the debate every time Ennis brought it up. "I'd sooner admit gomphreys think than witches walk among us," he said. He puzzled for a moment. "Why would Bartol start such a rumor? For what purpose?"

"Maybe he saw a witch," Ennis suggested, then sniffed at the sea wind. "Breeze is changing," he added absently.

"Oh, I doubt that, Ennis. You can't be serious."

"Well, maybe he did," Ennis said vigorously. "Maybe he saw a witch, right here in Yarvannet." He paused for effect. "Imagine what Duke Tejar could do with that." He eyed Melfallan carefully, and let him think about it.

Melfallan could imagine quite well. A High Lord had the responsibility of enforcing the shari'a laws, and the mere fact of a shari'a witch within Melfallan's borders showed a serious lapse, a failure that might be exploited. Of all his imaginings of Tejar's probable plots, Melfallan had not thought about the shari'a. But what High Lord had burned a witch in recent memory? Many years ago Countess Rowena had sheltered a woman some had thought a witch, but Rowena had her own reasons to hate the duke and ultimately nothing had been proven but the girl's dementia. Still—

"Ah," he said.

"Yes, ah." Ennis twitched his eyebrows fiercely. "This Bartol is a dangerous man, your grace. He's not another silly lordling sent down the coast in a pretty ship to plague you with his silly pretensions. He's got cunning. This matter of stirring up Natheby with witch rumors—it's not right, using our commonfolk to make Tejar's mischief."

"Have you met him?"

"Not yet—and I'd rather not, if you'll allow me. Let Lord Landreth wine and dine him. They're a finely matched pair." Ennis fully shared Melfallan's opinion about Landreth and showed no fear in saying so, though he usually confined the saying to his earl's own ears. A tactful man, his Ennis. "Put your gomphreys in one basket, I say."

"A basket for gomphreys," Melfallan drawled, amused by the image, "would be a sight in itself." The juvenile gomphreys who ventured into the rivers to hunt sturgeon averaged a hundred feet. Sailors' tales of gomphreys sighted at sea sometimes claimed five times that length.

"But a basket worth the making, I'd hazard," Ennis said, and grinned back. "If only a gomphrey basket could solve a problem that easily."

"True. Did anybody else see this hag of Bartol's?"

"Not that I heard, but I'd not want some unfortunate Natheby girl to get accused of it. It's easy to accuse and not so easy to undo it later, if you get my meaning. Even if it's nonsense, people remember and her life's not the same afterward." He shook his head.

"Witches loose in Natheby," Melfallan muttered in disgust. "That's the last thing I need."

"The last thing anybody needs," Ennis agreed.

Melfallan looked at his portmaster curiously. "Do you believe in the shari'a, Ennis?" he asked.

"Never seen one, your grace," Ennis answered gruffly. "I have seen a gomphrey. Believe in those." He shot a quick glance at Melfallan, then looked slightly abashed at his flippancy. "But I suppose you're wanting an honest answer," he said. Ennis thought a moment, frowning. "I don't know if I do or not. There's the histories, but they say such unlikely things about them. Odd things, strange powers, evils beyond counting. They say the shari'a made the hag's breath, as if a mortal folk could have Daughter Sea's divine power to close lives. And there's your lord's laws that are just as unlikely, condemning the shari'a for daring to be alive, laws allowing torture of an accused witch when torture is banned for all other crimes, however heinous, laws still there on the books." Ennis shook his head slowly. "I can't honestly say, your grace, and that's the truth. It doesn't make sense to me. If the shari'a witches ever existed, they're gone now, vanished away after our longships came over the sea and took these lands."

"Legends," Melfallan muttered. "Legends come to life."

"Gomphreys can think," Ennis retorted, "whatever you say, young earl. And you might have a witch hiding in Natheby, real witch or no. She doesn't have to be shari'a for Tejar to use her. Remember the trouble your aunt had about her young woman in Airlie, and how that got used against her, and still is. I'd think about the implications, begging my presumption to say so." He smiled grimly. "It's my observation, your grace, that High Lords can get into a habit of thinking the world should bend to their wishes, whatever the wish and whatever the reasons otherwise. I warned your grandfather of that from time to time when he needed it, and he took it well. I'd be loath to see my new earl acquire the same lordly disease."

"I haven't yet, Ennis?" Melfallan asked with a smile.

"Not so far as I've seen," Ennis answered lightly. "But bearing on your question, I don't know if I believe in shari'a, at least in these days and times. Maybe when I meet one, I can say then. But it's a good fishing season, Earl Melfallan, that I *can* say. I hope your fishing is as useful, though your fish walk on two legs, that being a lordly task I'll leave to you." He paused and grimaced. "You'll have to meet Bartol, I suppose."

"Yes, I will. I can't ignore Tejar's spy. It wouldn't be polite."

Ennis chuckled and shook his head.

For the next half-hour Ennis watched the port activity while Melfallan reviewed his written reports, answering the several questions Melfallan had on the details, and then they parted, Ennis back to his office at dockside, and Melfallan to the next business of the day. He expected Landreth to be hovering, and so he was.

"My earl, I must protest!" Landreth barred his path, his sallow face filled with solicitous anxiety. His fat hands fluttered. "You must meet Captain Bartol!"

Melfallan repressed a weary sigh, and promised to keep his temper this time—well, longer, at least. Practice, he told himself. Practice.

Brierley sat on the headland for nearly an hour, watching the patterns of mind and wind and sea, as she waited patiently for the inner impulse of the Calling into the Now. In her early years of conscious practice of the gift, she had sometimes imagined a Calling or had confused her own willed thoughts with those of others. The witch-sense could not be forced and, for a time of some months in her second year of witching, had deserted her completely. She had waited the first days in quiet panic, searching through her books for answers, some hope, but the writers who had shared the experience had been as perplexed and lost. A few had never regained the gift and eventually left the cave in despair, their journal fallen silent after the last anguished, baffled, grieving entry.

As the days had become weeks that second year, she had almost turned back to a normal life, with other hopes, other needs, and told herself she would be happier but knew otherwise. Then, for reasons her books could not tell her, her witch-sense had returned, and ever since had never fully flickered into another darkness—though it might again, of course. She had not known why she had lost it, or why she regained it: the mystery kept her wary of depending too much.

Each shari'a's gift obeyed its own rules, it seemed, and varied enough for each individual to defeat any clear prescription or technique. When walking abroad, she usually sensed the minds of persons within her line of sight, but her awareness could extend beyond corners and walls when she willed it. On the other hand, the walls of her sea cave blocked her perceptions, even of the fishermen who sailed along the nearby sea stones, fishing for shell-stars and rockfish. Why?

Usually her own gift was receptive, a passive perception of thought and emotion in others, but was not limited to perception. If she willed it, she could bend other minds slightly, cloud a perception, divert and distract. She usually avoided the influencing of other minds, for it was a part of the gift with which she felt uncomfortable. She preferred to listen, not control, but knew that other shari'a had chosen differently, and perhaps thus incurred the hatred that fueled the High Lords' laws. Only on rare occasions, as with Captain Bartol, did Brierley distract another's attention from herself, usually to allow herself the chance to escape a difficulty. But clouding minds bore its special perils, for it could be sometimes detected by an Allemanii.

She did not know the manner and means by which she healed: she knew only a few rules learned from experience. When she attempted a more difficult healing, her witch-sense ebbed for a time afterward, as if the gift drew itself inward while she healed herself. At times, she could shield herself from her perceptions, turning away from thoughts and emotions not her own. At other times, she felt buffeted by the sea of mental voices, near drowning in them, and fled to her cave for relief. It was an endless play, watching herself, and slowly by trial and error she had learned to blend her healer's craft with hidden witchery. Even so, the gift was not always obedient, another part of its fascination, the same and yet not the same, endlessly patterned on itself, Mother Ocean's precious gift to young Brierley Mefell, whatever the High Lords' contrary opinions.

We all find our peace as we can. Thora's words again. *The gift is as it is, and blessed are we to possess it.*

Brierley dreamed often of Thora Jodann, giving her a face and a voice in her dreams as convincing as real life, as if she dreamed of someone she knew personally, had met. In her dreams, she and Thora had conversations and shared a dream-place—a library, a boat, a coast road. It was all fancy and nonsense, of course—Thora had died centuries ago—but still the dreams brought their own comfort.

I *preserve*, Thora had written, and had tended the same folk of Yarvannet's shore as Brierley now did. Thora preserved a people who had invaded shari'a lands from the sea, eventually to take and conquer, not share peaceably, and had then killed what they chose to hate. But the Allemanii commoner-folk like Harmon and Clara, the farmers and seamen who made up Brierley's world, had not wrought the Disasters, only descended from those who had, and Thora had made a similar distinction between Allemanii noblefolk and commoner in her own time, a choice contested by some occupants of the cave, accepted by others. Some shari'a of the cave had argued for subversion and struggle against the conquerors: one witch, suborning her way into Yarvannet Castle as a valued healer and counselor, had poisoned Yarvannet's earl with a gut-strike oil, and later gloated in her journal about the agony of her victim's death. That witch had disappeared shortly afterward, and Brierley suspected her destroyer was not the Allemanii but the Beast itself. Any gift could be perverted, and the Beast was the special penalty of the shari'a healers.

That old war was not her own, and had never been. Her

choice was simply to heal or not heal, not to preserve an ancient struggle the shari'a had long ago lost. The losing was not by Brierley's making, nor by the making of Harmon or Clara or even Earl Melfallan himself. What kind of victory would it be to empty the land of Allemanii, as the Allemanii had emptied the land of the shari'a? All that resulted would be an empty land, ghost-ridden and desolate. Her people, even defeated and scattered, deserved a better memorial.

Or so Thora's champions had argued in their journals, as Brierley had argued herself. Still, she sometimes felt uneasy with Thora's answer, as if it were incomplete. Could conquest and the fire ever be truly forgiven? Did Brierley, by her healing of the distant children of the conquerors, betray the memory of her own people? Did the hate-filled woman who had poisoned an earl have the better truth? And if Brierley ever faced capture and the pyre, would she choose that other truth, abandoning every sure principle of her healer's life?

I don't know, she thought, disturbed by the possibility. I wish I did. I also hope I never find out, she added fervently. Pray Ocean I never do.

She waited in the sun and wind, watching the traffic on the bridge road, as the patterns swirled around her, combining, dispersing, recombining, an endless play of the waves in the surf. A gull swept by overhead, wheeling, dipping, effortlessly sailing the wind, then dropped from sight behind the grasses and stone of the slope. She rose and picked up her bag, then crossed the bridge into the castle.

At the tall castle gate, a soldier stood guard, his alert eyes inspecting all who walked under the wide portcullis. As she walked across the bridge toward him, Brierley positioned herself behind a stocky baker laden with a mountain of bread loaves. The man stumped toward the gate, sweating heavily from the effort of his unwieldy burden.

"Hey, there, Artis," the guard teased. "Where's your bread wagon?"

"Broke an axle, you son of a sea drake," the man puffed. "Leave me be."

"Look like a jolly partridge nest you do," the guard said. "Do bakers lay their loaves, I wonder?" As the baker maneuvered sidewise to glare around his mound of loaves, Brierley slipped past them both through the gate.

"Stuff them up your arse," Artis growled to the guard.

"Ah, I'd rather eat them," the guard said. He patted his stomach meaningfully and then called to a servant boy. "Here, boy, help Artis with his load."

Brierley crossed the neat flagstones of the inner gate into a small square courtyard crowded by the people passing to and fro, then turned right into a descending tunnel. Her footsteps echoed from the surrounding stone, and the sound vanished as she emerged into the stableyard beyond.

The afternoon light cast long conflicting shadows onto the tall stone walls enclosing the yard, and the pleasant but redolent smell of horses filled the air. Small thatched sheds clung to the walls, each with a rack of harness, bucket, and grain sacks before the wide door. Several lanky boys attentively groomed the fine-limbed horses standing in the stone square, supervised by the watchful eye of a grizzled and wizened underhostler. Brierley moved behind a haywagon near the opposite wall, and watched them from the shadows.

A young man dressed in riding leathers strode into the stableyard from an inner castle door, inspected the work of his groom, and saddled his horse, shrugging aside the boy's help. He mounted and clattered briskly past Brierley into the tunnel, preoccupied with his errand for the castle steward. The pattern of the courtyard settled again, made of the boys' long brush strokes, the horses' restless nods and pretend bites at each other as they stamped, and the underhostler's officious stride to and fro.

A pack of children suddenly ran shrieking into the stableyard, startling two of the horses. They reared, fighting the restraining ropes held by the grooms, then danced sidewise, shaking their heads. The underhostler shouted angrily at the children and chased them out of the stableyard, answered by their high-pitched laughter and jeers.

"Damnable whelps!" he shouted after them in fury.

The pattern settled yet again. Brierley shifted her weight to her other foot and leaned on her staff, waiting patiently. The matching pattern of her future selves grew closer, and began to merge into the scene before her. A few minutes later, she heard the tread of more booted feet in the inner passageway, and two men emerged into the yard, each dressed in nobleman's finery.

The taller man, lean and blond, was dressed in a fine green doublet and black hose, with both longsword and dagger at his belt, the edge of a mail shirt glinting at the hem of his tunic. On his breast gleamed an intricately crafted necklace of rubies and gold, the price of Amelin's largest fishing boat confined in that small circlet. His blond hair was bound by a leather band inset with jewels, and framed a squarish face with a strong nose, firm straight lips, and restless eyes. She noticed the eyes particularly: they flicked restlessly, noting, calculating, constantly gathering information for that eager mind.

His companion, stockier and of shorter stature, was dressed in soft gray and glittering cloth-of-gold but seemed the lesser man: his face looked petulant and sour, his mouth bracketed by the deep lines of a habitual sneer. As he walked, he impatiently slapped his riding gloves against his bulky thigh. "Your grace," he growled, "I still think you should reconsider."

"I've heard what you think," the nobleman in green replied, "but I have better things to do today than meet with another lordling Tejar sends my way."

"He's more than a lordling," the other protested. "He is an experienced sea captain with much news from the north. I really think—"

"I've heard what you think." The man in green smiled mockingly. "Lord Landreth, you are always my voice of caution. Sometimes I think you'd have me watch behind me for fear my shadow might actually be there."

"I am your liegeman," Landreth said pompously, obviously displeased by the raillery, "and it is my duty to advise—"

The other man sighed. "Oh, all right. Bring him to the castle. I'll see him."

"In an hour?" Landreth asked eagerly.

"Yes, an hour." He thumped Landreth's arm gently with his fist. "But there's a price—you leave me alone for the rest of today. No more importuning for me to meet your other friends."

"He's not my friend, your grace—"

"All day," the man in green said, his tone suddenly sharp. "See to it." Landreth flushed at the open reproof.

The underhostler turned at the sound of their voices and saw the man in green, then bowed low. "Earl Melfallan!" he cried. Every groom in the yard promptly copied his bow.

Brierley gasped and shrank back farther into the shadows of the haywagon. She looked frantically to each side for a better hiding place, then suddenly felt her future selves merge and cross into the Now, and knew the Calling involved these two men. Not in front of the earl! she thought frantically. Not him! She waited, biting her lip, and watched helplessly as the Calling took shape before her.

Lord Landreth stomped ahead of Melfallan and grabbed the reins of a bay stallion from a groom. "What's this?" he shouted angrily at the hostler, his fury at the earl spilling out at an easier target. "You allow this idiot to handle my horse?"

"But my Lord Landreth—" The hostler groveled abjectly. "Of course the boys—my lord—"

The groom, a light-haired, thin boy no older than twelve, cowered backward from Landreth's anger, his eyes wide with alarm and confusion. Before any could intervene, Landreth swung a fist at the boy, connecting too hard with the boy's midsection. The boy's breath exploded outward and he staggered back a pace, then fell heavily on the flagstones. Brierley shuddered with the impact of the blow, felt the rupture of spleen and bowel, then the smack of elbow bone on granite. A heartbeat, another, and pain arched through the boy's body, drawing the knees upward. She cried out with the boy, her cry masked by his ragged scream.

Melfallan seized Landreth and roughly dragged him back. Landreth was shouting hoarsely at the screaming boy as he struggled against Melfallan's grip, then furiously shrugged off Melfallan's hold. "Leave me be," Landreth said. "I said, leave me be. It's nothing." Brierley left her hiding place and walked forward.

"Nothing?" Melfallan asked incredulously. "You've killed the lad!"

"He's not that hurt," Landreth protested. "Does a boy good to be beaten when he's wrong—" His voice died uneasily as Melfallan stared at him; then his gaze shifted as Brierley knelt beside the suffering boy. She laid her palm on the boy's forehead, willing him into unconsciousness, then carefully straightened his thin body as it relaxed.

"Who the Hells are you?" Landreth demanded. She sensed the roiling fury within this man, a complex of baffled ambition and hopes, laced by a cruelty that enjoyed hurting. She heard also in Melfallan's shocked surprise that Landreth usually better hid his darker impulses in his earl's company.

She opened her cloth bag. "A healer, lord," she said meekly, cautious of Landreth's anger. "This boy is hurt."

Landreth took a menacing step toward her, his emotion ugly, but stopped as Melfallan caught at his arm again. Like a shift of color across the sea wave of Landreth's evil, Brierley sensed Melfallan's anger at the cruel assault on the boy, as Melfallan hated all such cruelties. *A decent man,* she thought, surprised: she had not thought any of the nobility much worth admiring.

"As you will," Landreth muttered without grace. Melfallan scowled at him, then gestured at the underhostler.

"Send for Marina to help, man," he ordered, then bent forward to peer under Brierley's hat brim. "What's your name, girl?" She promptly tipped her hat farther, denying him the view.

"A young healer from the south, my lord," she replied vaguely. She found her packet of bandages in her bag and turned from him, then pointed at a nearby stable. "Could you have the grooms carry him in there? He'll be more comfortable."

"Surely. Do it, lads. Carefully now!"

Four of the grooms leaped to his command and lifted the unconscious boy, then carried him to the stable. They laid him on the straw just inside the stable door, and Brierley knelt beside him, setting aside her staff. She laid the bandages on the straw, then brought forth several vials and a packet of sleep-weed from her bag.

"Water," she told one of the boys. He grabbed a bucket from the harness rack and raced for the stone cistern. The other boys whispered nervously to each other, glancing back at Landreth as he argued with Earl Melfallan in the bright sunlight outside the stable. Brierley saw Landreth mount his horse and clatter toward the gateway; Earl Melfallan hesitated, then walked toward the stable. She bit her lip.

Mother Ocean.

Daughter Sea—

"Well," she said aloud, "there's no help for it."

"Mistress—" a brown-haired boy quavered in response. "Will he die?" The group of boys shuffled their feet and waited for her answer, their half-dozen pairs of anxious eyes—blue, brown, hazel—focused on her intently. This young groom—*Gramil, is it?*—was much loved.

"He won't die," she said firmly to all of them. "Move back now, so I can practice my craft."

She heard Melfallan's booted footsteps approach, then put his presence out of her mind. Taking a bandage strip, she lifted Gramil by the shoulders and wound the linen several times around his body, pacing her breath to her motions as she concentrated. *I preserve the gentle ones of the world . . . Beast, I deny you this boy.*

Round and round she laid the bandage. When the other groom returned with water, she added herbs to the bucket and laved water on the bandages, smoothing them into a fine plaster. As her hands again moved repeatedly over the bandages, her shari'a senses probed the injuries, touching deep into the ruptured and bleeding flesh. She yielded herself to the gift, and felt the first answering twinges within her own body.

Live! she called silently, insistently, and felt a faint and uncomprehending response from the injured boy. *Live!* she urged again. *For you are loved, so very loved, Gramil.* The boy moaned softly and turned his head blindly toward her, eyes still closed, the pale lashes feathered on his cheeks. She bent more closely over him and drew forth his pain into her own body, mending flesh, defeating death. Like a swimmer fighting a deep undertow, Gramil responded to her.

(Who . . . ?)

It was enough. *Sleep now,* she answered him gently. She withdrew from him, wary of the sympathetic bond between their bodies that pulled at her: if she yielded too far, she could inflict real wounds on her own flesh. She caressed Gramil's face and eased him into forgetful sleep, then arranged his body more comfortably on the soft straw. As she finished, a wash of fatigue swept over her, bringing with it the oppressive weight of surrounding minds.

"Is he badly hurt?" Melfallan's voice jangled in her ears.

She looked up. Yarvannet's young earl stood framed in the stable doorway, his figure backlit by the brilliant sunlight in the square. He had seen everything but did not comprehend. His restless eyes took in her face *(. . . young. I don't remember seeing her before),* then glanced aside at the sleeping groom. "Is he badly hurt?" he repeated impatiently.

She looked down at her hands, concealing her face with her hat brim. "Not badly hurt, my lord," she answered. "Only bruised and sore. He will recover in time. Your healer will know what to do."

Melfallan sighed audibly. "Good, very good." His relief was obvious, as much for the boy's sake as an awkward problem avoided. Even a groom had some protection against murder, and too many had witnessed Lord Landreth's blow. Melfallan scowled, forgetting himself a moment, then remembered the crowd of people around him and controlled his expression. "Where is Marina?" he asked, turning toward the others. "I sent for her."

"The 'ostler went, your grace," a boy piped.

"Ah, yes. Stay with him, girl, until Marina comes," he said to Brierley, and his tone made it an order. He fumbled at his belt pouch and brought out a coin, then offered it to her. "For your good help today."

"Thank you, my lord."

Melfallan hesitated and thought to say more *(odd somehow, that healing . . . how pale she is),* then turned abruptly and walked toward the gate tunnel.

Brierley's shoulders sagged a moment, but she stirred herself to pack her medicines and gather up her staff. Her fatigue dragged at her, slowing muscles, blurring mind. She hadn't much time. "Stay with him," she told the boys. "Give him a drink of the herb water if he wakes."

"But the earl said you should stay," an older boy protested.

"Yes, I know."

She rose and swept past him into the gate tunnel, then slowed, cautious of overtaking Earl Melfallan, who had gone in this same direction. As she emerged into the gate square, she saw the guard salute smartly as Melfallan walked toward him. She moved to the far side of a wagon lumbering outward and walked beside it, concealed from his view.

"Lord Landreth will be returning with Captain Bartol," Melfallan said, then raised his voice as the wagon rumbled loudly past. "Tell them to come directly to the Great Hall."

"Yes, your grace," the guard replied.

Brierley tightened her fingers painfully on her staff. *Your grace,* Landreth had said, *I think you should reconsider.*

Oh, all right, Landreth. I'll see him.

And what tales would Bartol tell? A new offer of trade? A confidential message from his duke, carried by a trusted relative? Perhaps. Or a wild tale of witches loose in Natheby?

She trudged across the bridge beside the wagon, guessing too well why Bartol might seek this urgent audience with Yarvannet's earl. A fear struck deep is not easily dislodged. Sear the man! she thought with a wash of dismay. And Earl Melfallan had seen her face, would remember the healing. He had seen how hard Landreth had struck the boy, would guess such a blow would do more than mere bruises.

Would he remember too well?

The Daystar had sunk far in the west and now spread a flattened orb upon the distant ocean horizon, its fading ruddy light shading the Companion's twilight to faint lavenders. As she walked slowly along the crest road, the sea wind whipped her skirts against her legs and snatched rudely at her hat brim, chilling her into a deeper exhaustion. Far below, among the broken rocks of the headland shore, the sea called restlessly, promising the Beast. Already it moved through deep waters beyond the shore, approaching the shallows.

Would he remember?

M*y child,* Brierley wrote, *you might take interest in Saranen's writings: look for the tall blue book on the fourth shelf. Saranen has several studies about the substance of material things beyond herb-craft, especially the character of stone. I think many of the raw jewels in the storeroom are by her finding.*

Saranen also wondered about the ether above the wind and clouds, where the stars dwell. She found a reference in an older text—now too fragile for you or I to read—about shari'a who sailed the stars in ships of fantastic design. It sounds more like a heroic legend to me, but so much was lost during the Disasters: how can we now tell a legend from something once true, however unlikely or mysterious? And if we decide prudently, calling it legend, do we give up the stars?

Remember, my child, that you and I are legend now, and that an evil legend of the High Lords' choosing. No shari'a has openly practiced the craft since the Disasters, lest the High Lords descend again with their flame and destruction. Perhaps the starships had a similar truth before men lost even their legend: perhaps in time men will forget us, too. Does a false legend have a greater fragility—or greater strength if it suits men's fears? Or does our legend have a partial truth that makes it invincible?

I wonder how one might begin building a ship to sail the stars—

More practically, I wonder how one battles a legend, especially one's own. Yesterday a man rock-fishing along the beach told me that Yarvannet is abuzz with rumors about Bartol's witch, and the tale has grown with the telling, especially since Bartol had his private meeting with Earl Melfallan. Now I am a black hag who used the Evil Breath to steal Bartol's soul, narrowly averted by Bartol's quick action with an amulet (when I saw that stone last, it was his trade badge). I suspect Bartol of multiple designs, if indeed he even believes his own tale. Half the port vies to do business with his ship, and he has dined with Lord Landreth every night of this past week.

Have a care, Captain: Landreth is prone to bend his tools during use.

Yes, I would wish for a starship—with Bartol aboard, never to return. And maybe I'd conjure that black hag of his, too, and put her aboard for a chase of a few thousand stars. One should be wary of legends that might choose to be true.

She put down her pen and stretched her shoulders, then rearranged the wide sleeves of her pale satin gown, admiring the play of light on the ancient fabric. A heavy chain girdle encircled her waist and dropped golden links to the floor, where jeweled sandals hid under the embroidered hem of her gown. The costume was altogether lovely, and made Brierley feel like a fine lady, highborn and proud, so whispering was its satin, so rich its shine.

The gown had belonged to her predecessor in the cave, Marlenda Josay. It had been one of Marlenda's most prized possessions, a beloved memento of her girlhood days at Yarvannet's court. As a daughter of Yarvannet's minor nobility, Marlenda had walked easily in noble halls, not told until she had grown into young womanhood that she had been adopted and was not the natural daughter of the woman she thought her mother. Not wholly conscious of her witch-gift, Marlenda had believed the Beast only an occasional nightmare, and thought her flickering witch-sense mere fancy. Perhaps that ignorance had protected her from exposure as shari'a, that and her adoring parents and the affections of her numerous and well-connected family.

All that had changed in Marlenda's sixteenth year. Marlenda's father had supported the previous earl of Yarvannet, Earl Pullen, in his rebellion against Duke Selwyn. That loyalty had earned him, like Pullen's other supporters, a quick disgrace and ruin and death. In terror of Audric's soldiers, Marlenda had fled her father's house and had found the safety of the cave. She had concealed herself in the cave for years, living a lonely life of hiding and fear. Rarely had she ventured onto the shore, for fear of the new earl's soldiers, and had finally caught a mortal sickness from the chill air. It had been her bones Brierley had found later, the sad pitiful remains of a girl's life ended by her father's ambition.

Brierley rearranged her sleeves again, sad for the young noble girl who had so loved this gown. In the thirty years since Pullen's rebellion, Yarvannet had prospered under the Courtrays, their northern blood soon forgotten as memories and resentment dimmed. Earl Audric had earned respect from Yarvannet's people with wise if stern rule, and few remembered Marlenda's father, if any did. Most had even forgotten Pullen. And of Marlenda nothing remained except a slim book on Brierley's shelf and a pile of bones long since buried.

Marlenda had danced in this dress. Brierley lifted her arms to spread the sleeves like gull wings, then rose and danced lightly across the stone floor, her arms curved around an imaginary partner. Perhaps Marlenda had danced thus with the young lord of her current affections. According to her journal, there had been many such young lords in Marlenda's short life as nobly favored daughter, and Brierley had no cause to doubt her claim.

Nobly favored: I wonder how it feels, Brierley mused. She lifted her chin, affecting a noble lady's pride, and posed, her gown a whisper of beauty on her tall and slim body, her neck and arms glittering with jewels. Ah, he sees me, she thought, and glanced quickly toward the bookcase and then away. I will ignore him, she decided, and thus build his ardor for me. Grandly, she dragged her gown's flowing train in imagined procession with the other high lords and ladies. They entered an imaginary banquet hall to the sound of trumpets and a chamberlain's exultant praise. *Here she is!* the chamberlain cried as Brierley appeared in the doorway. The waiting crowd sighed as one, their mouths rounded with pleasure as Brierley came into view, glittering and proud. *Here she is!* the chamberlain shouted again, and waved his plumed hat. *Brierley Mefell, Lady of . . . what?* Well, no matter. Brierley nodded courteously to left and right, a high lady who still deigned to notice mere persons, odd as that was. The assembled nobility admired her with openmouthed awe and—

Brierley's foot caught hard on a crack in the cave's stone floor, then tangled in her skirt hem. She sawed like a windmill for balance and nearly fell, then caught herself with one hand on the table. It knocked her journal to the floor and jostled the ink, but she held fast to the table edge until she was sure of her balance. She laughed softly as she rearranged her feet inside her skirt hem.

Ah, Marlenda, no ladying for me, she thought. I haven't your art in it, sweet friend—but I love your dress, too.

She picked up the journal from the floor, and dabbed at the splash of ink with a rag. Then, bunching her satin skirts in her hands, she bounded up the narrow staircase near Everlight's corridor, the skirt train a whispering silkiness on the stone treads. The winding stairwell emerged in a crevice between two massive stones atop the island, each a perch for wind-sculpted trees. Eighty feet below the cleft, the sea waves surged against the hard foundation of her island.

She leaned back against one of the door stones and faced the broad expanse of the open ocean, and watched the dawn light spread across the sea from the Daystar's rising behind her. A few faint stars still gleamed above the western horizon, not yet banished by the dawn. In the far distance a fishing trawler winked over the horizon as it sailed to the offshore banks on this fine morning. Closer in, a school of fish suddenly broke the surface of the water, splashing a sparkle of spray as they leaped and plunged. The sea's voice comforted, promising life and all manner of good things.

Mother Ocean,
Daughter Sea,

Waves unending,
Life to me.

Mother Ocean she was called, revered by the Allemanii as their mother and protectress. As Mother, the infinite Ocean gave birth to all life on sea and land, and cherished that life in all its forms. As Daughter, Ocean brought each life to a close, and returned every creature to the Mother for rebirth. Life given, life renewed: it was the great rhythm of all existence, and one the Allemanii saw encompassed in the flowing and unending movements of the sea. In her books, Brierley had read of the shari'a belief in spirit-dragons of air and fire, forest and sea, but Jocater had determined that Brierley would live a normal life, and so had taught her daughter the Allemanii religion. Brierley was content with it. She sniffed the sea wind and let it blow her gown and hair into billows, then lifted her chin, suddenly impatient with her confinement.

"Enough," she told the waves. "A week of hiding is enough for any caution, and I'm tired of dune-skulking to hear rumors." She spread her skirt in a graceful arc from jeweled toes to slender fingers, then bowed grandly to the broad sea horizon. "But I will, dear Mother Ocean, go south, not north. Yes, indeed."

She lingered to watch the sky turn from muted blue-grays to broad streamers of pink and gold, and relished the coolness of the wind-borne spray. A sea lark spun and dipped over the waves, catching its morning meal; the morning light flashed off its iridescent wings, a living beacon to the Daystar. As the lark vanished into the distant mist, Brierley sensed a new Calling later that afternoon—prudently south in Amelin—and smiled. Twice in the past week she had resisted Callings northward and rued her enforced isolation, but now, rumors or no, she would be out and about.

She turned and descended the inner stair. She could visit Clara, too, as she had promised, and belled her silken skirts in a quick pirouette on the last stair tread. If she left soon, there should be time before the afternoon Calling.

Brierley wrapped the silken gown in its linen mats and repacked it with the sandals and belt in a narrow box in the storeroom. A few details to neaten in the pantry, a refreshing bath in the bathing pool, a porridge for breakfast, and then, dressed in homespun with her hat and staff, she left the cave.

"South," she told her cockleboat as a freak wave caught the boat and spun it sidewise. She paddled determinedly and turned the boat aright again. Then she lifted her chin, her eyes narrowing at the bluff crest just above the beach. "Hmmm."

She measured the time for the boys to mount the crest and the distance to her usual beach landing, then whipped her boat to the right and raced for the nearest sea rock standing inward toward the beach. As she passed behind the rock, buffeted by the waves crashing against its base, she listened for the halloa behind her—but the boys saw nothing, too intent on their own games to watch for boats in the cove. She heard their shrieks as they tumbled down the hillside, pushing at each other and swinging wild and joyful fists as they rolled.

Once Brierley had feared discovery of her cave by such boys, but the Everlight warded any outsider's approach to her island. The local boys never climbed her sea rock, though she knew they climbed others—nor did Yarvannet's rockfishers come by its base to seek the shell-stars and anemones sheltered in its lee. In the three centuries since the Disasters, no witch had recorded a close approach to the island by any of the local townfolk. An intruder had never surprised the witch there, nor disturbed the journals and its other furnishings, nor plundered the cave of its small cache of jewels and coins. The Everlight permitted only the witch known to it, her journals guessed, and warded away all others who might intrude. How? Brierley wondered. What *was* the Everlight? How did it protect her cave? By what means? Her books hinted but none really knew—another truth, perhaps, lost in the Disasters.

Were there other Everlights by other shores in the High Lords' lands, protecting other lines of witches? If so, would she ever find them? Would an Everlight ward away even a witch it did not know? Or, as she feared, was her Everlight the only such guardian that had survived the Disasters, leaving no hope of other witches anywhere? Who could tell her?

In time, she had decided to trust in the Everlight's security, whatever other questions remained unanswered, but always took great care in her coming and going. She paddled sedately around another sea chimney, then put into shore several hundred yards beyond her own beach. Then, her boat again concealed in another safe place, she walked southward on the beach sands, hunting a path upward. Twenty minutes later, she joined the early-morning traffic of cart and horse, wagon and foot traveler on the coast road, greeting those she knew with a nod and smile, looking with interest at those less familiar. At the crossroad bending southeast to Natheby, the road climbed upward over a wide bluff, needing a whip's urging on mule-quarters for the steep incline, wagon brakes for the descent. Across the bluff top, pines and everwillow overgrew the road, creating a cool tunnel of swaying branches and the flash of bird wings. She shifted her cloth bag to her other shoulder and watched the leafy canopy as she walked, careless of the roughness of the rutted road.

She remembered the first time she had traveled this stretch of coast road years before. The boys had thrown rocks at her that day, and Jared had stood apart from their jeering, watching her with hurt and angry eyes, then had suddenly thrown himself on the nearest boy, punching and shouting. He pushed the much larger boy down into the street and flung himself on him, then disappeared beneath the pile of other boys as they fell on him to punish him for his treachery. Brierley had screamed at the boys who were hurting Jared, and her shout had opened a half-dozen windows in the nearby houses. As the adults spilled into the street, Brierley had turned and run away from the boys, from the adults shouting their questions, from Jared, who needed her. She had run out of Amelin and up this coast road, attracting still more attention from the people there with her wild sobbing and mad flight. A carter had tried to catch her, but she had eluded him, plunging out of sight down the bluff to the beach. The adults had finally summoned Alarson from his shop, and they had hunted for Brierley on the beach for over an hour. She had hidden from them all in a crevice in the stones, curled up tightly, her face hidden against her knees.

She stayed in the crevice long after they gave up their search, huddled in her misery. She had sensed Alarson's fury about Jocater's useless girl taking him away from his work, embarrassing him in front of the town again. She had sensed the angry emotions on the bluff overhead when Alarson had quarreled briefly with Jared's father, who had first blamed Brierley, not the boys, for Jared's broken wrist and bruised eye. Later the father had reconsidered his hasty words, but Alarson had stiffly refused the apology, choosing to blame Brierley and Jocater for the trouble they caused him, and had nursed his resentment for weeks afterward.

I won't go back, she had sobbed to herself, knowing how it would be, as it always was. I won't go back. The soothing murmur of the nearby surf had surrounded her as she cried for herself, and for Jared, whom she had betrayed, and for her mother, whom she had failed again. The murmuring sound of the water echoed hollowly inside the crevice, and the sea air teased her hair with invisible fingers, bringing comfort. And then a voice had spoken her name, as if close to her ear. She jerked up her head and looked around her warily, but saw no one. She listened hard, and thought she heard the voice again, then rose quickly to her feet to look up and down the beach, but there was no one there, not on the sand, not by the rocks, not on the bluff overhead. No one.

For three weeks she had returned repeatedly to the beach to hunt the voice, looking in every crevice, behind every rock. She had waded into the surf and probed the underwater sand and rocks with her fingers, then hunted the bluff overhead and into the forest beside the road, but the voice seemed to fade there. She returned to the beach and thought she heard the voice coming from one of the sea rocks along the shore, then swam to it through the choppy waves of the cove, but found nothing. One by one, she had hunted the line of sea rocks, and in one of the larger sea stones she had found a tunnel in the side facing the sea. From the darkness of the tunnel, the voice had called her, clear and commanding, and recklessly Brierley had thrown herself into the surging water. The surf battered her against the hard stone, bruising her elbow and knee, but at the end of the tunnel, above a rough stone landing and next to a darkened doorway, she had found the Everlight.

How long had she stood entranced as she looked at it, her clothes dripping seawater onto the landing, her hair in clammy wet strings? How long until she finally reached to touch it, and felt for the first time its resonance in her mind? And how long had she stood there, her hand warm on its glowing face, as the Everlight exulted in its welcome to her, and gave its love to her, to her and to only her, to Brierley Mefell, a love without reservation, without shadow of compromise? She never really knew.

In the years since, she had never again heard the voice that had called to her: if the voice had belonged to the Everlight, it never spoke to her afterward. But the Everlight knew her, and welcomed her when she returned to the cave, and sorrowed mildly when she left it, and was a constant presence in her mind whenever she was near the island. Of all the comforts in her life, excepting only Thora's book, she loved the Everlight best, and knew somehow it loved her as much, perhaps even more.

What *is* the Everlight? she wondered, digging the end of her staff into the dirt of the road. Will I ever know?

Will I ever know all I want to know?

She smiled at the trees and the bright flash of a bird in the branches, and thought about that day when her life had changed for the first time, bringing her the cave and its journals, and the understanding and hope she found in them, and then to that one day on the beach when she chose for herself. Since her mother's death, Brierley had practiced her secret craft mainly in Count Revil's southern towns, so much so that the inhabitants of Natheby thought she still lived in Amelin, and those of Amelin that she had moved to Natheby, a vague confusion she encouraged. She had grown up in Amelin, and knew its fisherfolk and farmers well: among them, she felt at ease, and offered freely of her secret gift to their tending. It was not a choice her mother would have willed for her, but Brierley's different choice was long past now, and Jocater dead nearly as long.

Wary of her mother's troubles, Brierley had tried to avoid close friendships, mistrusting her ability to hide her witch-sense if people knew her too well. It was one of Jocater's cautions she had decided was wise, whatever pain it caused. Even so, despite her determinations, she had become good friends with the Jacobys and a very few others, risking that exception to her careful coolness, her sleight-of-hand in meetings, her lonely life. She had other acquaintances scattered among the homesteads and fisheries, and a much larger web of persons who knew her as healer: it seemed enough, or so she chose to believe.

Perhaps I will meet the child who will be heir to my cave, she reminded herself. She smiled, accepting that it might never happen, then thought happily of that meeting. I will teach her all that I am, and never be alone again. Brierley thought about that, too, and wondered how it felt not to be alone. She knew many persons lived alone, even within the bosom of their families: that knowledge brought its comfort and made the waiting easier.

Perhaps someday, she thought, we will meet, she and I.

A carter waved as he passed her, his face stretched in a wide smile. She bowed, returning the smile, and walked onward. Another carter passed, his wagon laden with harvest tools, metal sticks of strange shape and utility, and he, too, waved his hat and smiled, brightening the day with his cheer. In a few weeks, Revil's farm people would begin their harvest of the last fall grains, working the long day from the Daystar's dawning to the Companion's setting, filling the air with their songs and laughter as they reaped the silvery grains of ash barley and golden beads of thyme for their storehouses. In the town, the fishermen and blacksmiths also prepared for winter, stepping up their catches at sea and making urgent repairs for fisher and farmer alike. The restlessness of harvest was abroad on the air, and the folk of Natheby and Amelin moved more quickly, more joyfully. Autumn was her favorite season of the year.

After a walk of nearly an hour, she emerged from the wood at an overlook high above Natheby. The clapboard houses of Count Revil's lesser town clustered along the river, each sheltered by trees and fronted by a narrow dock on the water. Behind the town, the fields made a random pattern of green and brown to the edges of a dusky forest. To the right, mule-drawn barges moved slowly along the estuary canal to the sea docks three miles away, where a few light craft sailed the estuary's silted rills, their white sails glinting bravely in the sunlight. She rested a few minutes in the shade of a broad everwillow, watching the sails bob in the sun, then began the easy descent into the valley.

Harmon's small farm lay a mile beyond Natheby against the forest edge: a small farmhouse, a weathered windmill and barn, the ordered rows of crops and hayfield. She walked up the narrow lane with its neat white rails, then leaned on the gate as Harmon's two dogs yapped a noisy protest inches from her shoes. When she did not retreat, the smaller dog snapped his teeth under the lowest rail; she moved back a step.

"Good dog." The dog growled a vigorous disagreement and snapped again. "Bad dog," she amended severely. "Leave me be."

"Brierley!" Clara appeared in the farmhouse doorway, her stout face alight with pleased surprise. Egal peeked from behind her, his mouth smeared with jam from a slab of bread clutched messily in one hand.

"I said I'd come visit, Clara," Brierley called. "Perhaps you could tell your dogs."

"Nick! Jem! Get back from there!"

The dogs retreated reluctantly, fangs still bared in silent threat. Clara chased them off into the backyard and invited Brierley into the house, then seated her with great ceremony in a wooden chair by the kitchen hearth. Blue linen curtains fluttered at the windows, and large burnished pots hung in neat order on the whitewashed walls; the heavy oak table and chairs gleamed with polish. On the long kitchen counter, a pile of tree carrots and greens lay next to a large yellowish cheese, and Brierley could smell the sweet scent of baking bread.

"Have you eaten?" Clara asked, wiping her hands on her apron.

Brierley smiled. "I had breakfast."

Clara promptly took a fat loaf of bread from a shelf and cut a thick slice, then spread it with currant jam. "Harmon and Evan are out in the fields," she said. "Egal! Go tell your father that Mistress Brierley is here." Clara caught the boy near the kitchen door, took his bread for safe keeping, and wiped the jam from his face. Then she bent and kissed him. "There! You're presentable now." Egal raced out of the house, shrieking his message before he scarcely passed the doorsill. "What a noise!" Clara exclaimed and seated herself in a chair at the table. "Boys!"

"Girls are better," Brierley agreed, and they laughed softly together. Brierley bit into the crusty bread, relishing the taste, then dabbed jam off her nose. Perhaps someday I will have a house like this, she thought, looking around her with pleasure. Perhaps. "You keep a fine house, Clara," she said, putting her thought into words, knowing that it would please Clara.

"Thank you," Clara said shyly, then bustled again to the counter for teacups and a bowl of currants. "It is so good to see you again." She reseated herself and took a currant for herself. Here in the familiar surroundings of her kitchen, Clara felt more at ease, able to forget her usual painful awareness of herself. Housewifery and motherhood suited Clara, talents even Clara had to admit. Brierley smiled again, liking this gentle and contented woman, and felt pleased that she had followed her impulse to visit today. For caution's sake and her midwife's work elsewhere, she did not come often to the Jacoby farm, allowing long weeks of absence between each visit. She suddenly decided that would change. Marlenda hid from the world, she thought, and suffered for it. I have hidden too much, I think.

They chatted about the children and Clara's new stitchery-work, which Brierley admired as Clara brought it out, then discussed mutual acquaintances in town. Brierley relaxed into the pleasant gossip, then accepted another piece of Clara's excellent bread. After a half-hour, a stamping of heavy boots on the porch announced Harmon's approach. His two sons blew into the house, bumping and poking each other as they giggled, followed by the red-faced and sweaty farmer.

"Mistress Bri!" he bellowed, his face split wide by a grin. "Come to dinner, have you? Welcome, welcome!" Harmon hung his broad hat on a peg and started across the parlor floor in his muddy boots, then checked himself at Clara's prompt cluck of warning. "Oops!" Harmon retreated and removed his boots, then took a vain swipe with a stockinged foot at the muddy splotches. "Boys! Get back here and take off those muddy shoes!"

"Too late, Harmon," Clara said, exasperated. "And I washed that floor only this morning."

"Sorry, wife," Harmon said meekly, then tried to tread lightly as he came into the kitchen, as if softer steps might somehow spare the floor. "What's for dinner?" He bent to buss Clara's cheek and turned to smile at Brierley.

"You go clean up and you'll find out," Clara declared.

Harmon sighed. "A husband's life is a hard one," he ventured.

"Not as much as a wife's," Clara retorted, "especially with a husband like you, Harmon." She scowled past her husband at her dirty floor, then scowled a ferocious warning at her boys. Egal giggled and ducked behind Brierley's chair.

"Hoo-boy, are we in trouble!" Harmon exclaimed. "Come on, boys: let's clean up and then we'll make amends to your mother." He kissed Clara again and stamped out of the kitchen.

"Boys, young and old!" Clara said and laughed. "Ocean save us."

She fetched a mop from the cupboard and repaired the damage, then returned to her cooking. Brierley watched Clara as she worked, listening to the murmur of voices in the other room as Harmon supervised his sons in a splashy and exuberant washing-up. Perhaps I will have a house like this someday, she thought again. Perhaps even sons, to splash and giggle with their father. It was likely a vain hope: her mother had tried and failed to make such a home. But perhaps—

Thora Jodann had always sought out the commonfolk for her healing, she remembered, and had avoided the noble families until the rumor of her healer's skills had brought the inevitable summons to the earl. Thora had conceded reluctantly, out of prudence, but still gave most of herself to the commoners, persisting in her chosen craft. When the earl of that time demanded she attend him as a castle servant, healing only the highborn, she had refused, then hid herself in her cave for two years as the earl's soldiers sought her throughout Yarvannet. It was a dangerous time for Thora, perhaps the underpinning of the growing weariness that led to her death. She had written most of her journal during those two lonely years, as if she could preserve her heart on paper as her world unraveled. *I serve those who have only the air to breathe, the simplest things of the world,* she had declared defiantly.

Must there be such a choice? Brierley wondered, watching Clara as she bustled from counter to stove. I would choose you, Clara, but must there be a choice, one or the other, commoner or nobleman, that one and not those? *Love is the reason,* Thora had written. *Love answers. Seek the fire of love, the breath of life, my daughters. See all that lives around you, in forest or sea, and rejoice! The Four bless us with joy in our living, that we may prosper: love answers the joy, and makes all living worthwhile, whatever its costs. Fire and storm, forest and sea: the Four Spirits of the world will never abandon you, my beloved daughters, if you love.*

Great words, Brierley thought admiringly, but can love truly bind what so naturally divides? Can a shari'a witch be herself and yet be like the other folk? After all our centuries of hatred and death? Likely not, she knew, but here in Clara's house and her friend's good company—Brierley sometimes thought it possible. She looked around the comfortable kitchen, then watched Clara vigorously stir her pot on the stove. Perhaps someday I shall have such a pot, such a stove, Brierley thought happily. Perhaps two can be one, if one tries hard enough—if one *loves* hard enough, as Thora loved.

Harmon strode into the room, dressed in fresh clothes and cleaner than he had been. He shooed the boys into their small chairs at the table, then courteously rearranged Brierley's own chair to face the repast. Clara brought the meal to the table and smiled benignly as all loaded their plates with the steaming food. After dinner had continued to dessert of fresh-baked currant pie, Harmon scooted back his chair and stretched out his legs in contentment, his pie plate balanced on his ample stomach.

"Glad to see you eat well, Brierley," he said. "You're too skinny."

"Hush, Harmon," Clara reproved.

"Well, it's true." He leaned over and pinched Brierley's arm meaningfully. "Look at that, Clara: barely a thin muscle and hardly any flesh at all. Need to fatten you up, Bri."

"For what?" Brierley asked in mock alarm, rolling her eyes at small Egal. The boys giggled.

"For your husband, of course." Harmon winked at her, then smiled as his wife fluttered her hands in dismay. "Hush yourself, wife. This is serious business."

"I don't want a husband," Brierley said firmly. Harmon pretended shock.

"Now that's a poor attitude. Why not?"

"I'm too busy."

"Well, un-busy yourself. I want to stand up for your first-born and pronounce him, then look for a good apprenticeship to get him started. Hmmm." Harmon's brows contracted as he thought. "Old Marseth needs a boy in his smithy, now that his grandson got married and went off to Tiol."

Brierley laughed. "Harmon, he's not even born yet!"

"That's my point. You've got to get started on this, young mistress. How else can I get things arranged?"

Brierley wrinkled her nose at him. "You're a treasure, Master Harmon. I'm quite content, thank you."

Harmon grumbled, making a show of a crestfallen expression, then obeyed his wife's determined pinch. "All right, all right—for now." He glanced at his wife, saw her narrowed eyes, and made the right decision. He held out his plate for more pie. "Be a dear, Clara."

"You've already had two slices, Harmon."

"I'm in a mind for three," he cajoled good-humoredly. "Good pie, wife." As she cut him another piece of pie, Clara raised an inquiring eyebrow at Brierley.

"One is enough, thank you," Brierley said.

Harmon took a huge bite and munched, then waved his fork as he swallowed. "Speaking of babes, I hear Lady Saray is nearing her time. Have you been called to the midwifing, Bri?"

"Me?" Brierley asked in surprise. "Oh, not me. I'm not known to the highborn. Besides, Earl Melfallan has his own midwife in the castle. Soon, you say?" She had heard of the latest pregnancy of Melfallan's lady wife, after the cruel disappointments of earlier years—had it been that many months?

Harmon nodded. "And Melfallan's heir in her womb at last, Ocean willing. A noble lady, I've heard, gentle and kind to the needy, for all she's northern-born. It's a relief she's finally carrying a child nearly to term, I tell you, and to be safely delivered well before winter, too." He shook his head ruefully. "Hard on a noble lady to have such failures, and on Yarvannet, too: I don't fancy Landreth as Natheby's lord." He feigned a shudder.

"Landreth?" Brierley asked in surprise, remembering that sour-faced cruel lord. "I thought Count Revil was Melfallan's heir."

"Oh, he is, but he has just the two girls, at least so far, and Duke Tejar has to agree before a cousin or an heiress takes Yarvannet." He snorted. "Small chance of that, the way *he* feels about the Courtrays, and about Earl Melfallan in particular."

"Why?" Brierley asked curiously. Perhaps she should have paid more attention to lordly affairs. "What did Earl Melfallan do to him?"

"Nothing! It's quite another reason. Don't you know that story?" Brierley shook her head, to Harmon's obvious delight. "Well, now," he said with relish, "Tejar was Duke Selwyn's third son and not liked much by the Ingal folk, not even by his father. A snivelly sneaking lad, often sickly, and always in trouble of one kind or another. Then the plague took the oldest two, and so we got stuck with Tejar when Duke Selwyn passed on. Duke Tejar's good at hating, from what I've heard, especially at hating whomever his father liked, the way that goes. And Selwyn liked Earl Audric and favored Melfallan as a boy when they visited his court, and Tejar hated Melfallan for it. That's where it started, and it's gotten worse since. A nasty man, our Duke Tejar. Where'd you learn your history, young miss?"

"Be polite, Harmon," Brierley retorted. "I pay attention to what I think is important."

"Hmmph!" Harmon pretended shock again. "Important? Aren't earls and dukes important? I think so."

"Harmon," Clara warned, her hands fluttering.

"Ah, wife, I'm not being harsh to her. She knows that. Look at her smile at me, mocking me and my gossip about my betters." He winked at them both. "But you still come around to hear me talk, don't you, Mistress Bri?"

"That I do, Harmon."

"I like the lords I have," Harmon said firmly. "Don't want them changed. Not now, not ever." He shrugged expansively. "Not that Lord Landreth spends much time in his marshes, I'm noting. He likes it more in Yarvannet Castle, where he can watch things with those marsh-rat eyes of his." Clara looked up from pouring milk for Egal and frowned at her husband's language. "Now, I don't blame Lord Landreth for wanting a change," Harmon rolled on, "but not at *my* expense, if you get my meaning." He winked again at Brierley. "Are you coming to the festival next week, Bri?"

"*Another* festival?"

Harmon smiled broadly, a man content with his world. "Count Revil understands the right of things. Melfallan is a good lord, too, it seems, but he's got the high-and-mighty to worry about, like keeping Duke Tejar away and safely north where he belongs. Captain Bartol's been all over the place with that witch story of his." Harmon scowled, then snorted. "Northerners! Life's too short for such plagues."

"Hush, Harmon," Clara reproved again. "You and your talk'll be the grief of us."

"I say what I see," Harmon said to her. "Nothing wrong with that."

"You *see* too much. So hush." Clara rolled her eyes at Brierley.

"Yes, wife." Harmon lifted his shoulders resignedly and let them fall, then caught hastily at his plate as it slipped. "Oops."

"Give us a story, Papa!" Evan pleaded. "Won't you? Please?" Egal nodded vigorously in agreement, then darted a cautious glance at his mother.

"A tale! You want a tale, my boys? Hmm, hmm." Harmon took a huge bite of pie, then chewed slowly as he thought. Brierley accepted a mug of hot tea from Clara and settled back in her chair. Harmon had a gift in tale-telling, and she watched the farmer's broad face with nearly as much interest as his sons did.

"A tale, then," Harmon said, his eyes twinkling at his small sons. "Now long ago, my lads, before your grandfather's time and even *his* grandfather's time, a very long time ago, back when Duke Rahorsum ruled in Ingal, in a capital near the mountains named Iverway, not Darhel like today, but a grander town up the river. His castle had eight pinnacles and eight bridges over a deep moat, with eight roads for the wagons and horses and soldiers and traders who came and went from Iverway."

"Now deep in the mountains nearby, the shari'a witch-women had made a secret place named Witchmere, a place of dark caverns and flickering lamps, an evil place men avoided. There they cast their evil spells to prey on the people, making cattle ill with foot rot or head bloat, spreading disease and madness in the ports and the river towns and the farms, and stealing children such as you, young Egal, or you, my Evan, for their secret cult. It was a desperate time when the shari'a still had power in Witchmere." He shook his head sadly.

"They stole *children*?" Egal asked, his eyes round. "What happened to them?"

"No one knows," Harmon said gravely.

Brierley quietly set her mug on the table, then looked down to watch her fingers twist unhappily in her lap. In her books, from the witches' perspective, Duke Rahorsum had titles beyond High Lord, names as evil as the tales Harmon told of the witches. She glanced at Harmon's sons, wondering. Did we steal children? Why?

Harmon cleared his throat, pleased with his boys' awed reaction. "Now, as I said, the shari'a had created disease throughout the land, even reaching out their evil hands to Duke Rahorsum's own son and heir, striking him with twitching and mumblings, taking his mind into their dark mists.

Rahorsum grieved mightily, then rose up from his lord's seat and summoned the other High Lords to his council. For eight days and eight days more, the High Lords consulted." Harmon paused dramatically, then stretched the moment with another bite into his pie.

"And what did they do?" Evan prompted.

"Do? They raised an army and marched into the mountains, found Witchmere after a long and dangerous search, then slew the witches right and left, forward and backward. Oh, it was a great battle against their magic, a battle with great cost. Some soldiers ignited like a torch and died horribly. Others strangled, as if drowning in the air. Others found their swords turned upon themselves, as if bewitched, for indeed they were. Horses neighed in fright and trampled the foot soldiers all around them, then fled through the caverns until they fell into sinkholes and crevices, taking their riders with them. Some of the witches took on their catling form, with their long fangs and cat-slitted eyes, and threw themselves on the soldiers, slashing with their talons, and shrieking their demon curses. The army battled for a night and a day, until Duke Rahorsum himself fought his way to the chief witches, those old crones with no teeth and boils on their faces and long lanky hair, and cut out their evil hearts." Harmon sighed. "And so the High Lords ended Witchmere and its evil, and the land was clean again."

"Did they find the children?" Egal asked, his small face troubled.

Harmon blinked, caught back a moment. "A few, lad," he reassured his smaller son, "all of them well and hearty—but only a few. No one knows, even now, what happened to the others." He waggled his finger warningly.

"Are there any witches left?" Evan asked, his expression far away as he imagined himself as Duke Rahorsum glittering on horseback. Brierley looked away. It still continues, she thought, a tradition as solid as my own, this matter of hating witch-kind. Why?

"None," Harmon said firmly. "He got them all."

Evan looked disappointed. "But what if he didn't? What if they're hiding somewhere?"

"Now, don't you worry about that, Evan."

"But what if they *are*?" Evan demanded.

"They aren't, and that's enough of the tale, boys. Here, take my plate to the sink and help your mother a bit. Oh, you're leaving, Bri?"

Brierley made herself smile as she gathered up her bag and staff. "I have a place to go before the sun sets." It happened to be true, and gave a convincing tone to her excuses. "Thank you for the good meal, Clara."

"I was hoping you'd stay longer," Clara said, clearly disappointed.

Brierley smiled warmly at the farm woman. "Maybe next time."

"Come back again!" Harmon said exuberantly as she retreated toward the door. "Sooner! And stay longer!"

"I shall. Good-bye." She knew her haste was awkward, but felt too uncomfortable to find the grace to do better.

As she passed through the Jacobys' yard gate, she frowned at herself. I should have stayed longer, she thought. It meant too much to Clara. How can old tales hurt me? Even so, she continued walking down the lane toward Natheby, her staff digging small depressions in the dirt of the road.

Is it a wish-dream that I belong to them, that they belong to me? She sighed and abruptly tired of her double life. What did we do, truly do, so long ago, we witches, to earn such hatred? Did we truly steal their children? And why?

The questions nagged at her as she regained the track toward Amelin. A passing carter nodded at her genially, and a boy waved as his tiny flock of sheep tumbled across the road toward home. Would they nod and wave if they knew? she wondered. What hatred would I see in faces, what accusations, what dangers from a panicked mob—if they knew?

When she had hid among the Natheby wharf piers the week before, she had felt only irritated with Bartol for his hue and cry. Standing in the wharf shadows on the sea sludge, she thought even sourer wishes on the man when she felt the cold mud sink into her skirt hem and shoes. But not fear, not then. Natheby and Amelin were home, the inhabitants well known, loved.

Love, Thora had urged. *Love answers.*

Would even Harmon turn on me, if he knew?

When Brierley crossed the crest and looked down into Amelin harbor, she found the reason for Harmon's choice of tale today in a bit of news missing from his gossip. Fluttering at the dock, side by side, lay Bartol's northern ship and a larger sloop flying Earl Melfallan's banner. A crowd of distant figures clustered on the dock, many bright with fine fabrics and gold as Count Revil welcomed his kinsman and lord. Brierley stopped short in the road, aghast, then moved hastily aside as a whip cracked behind her in warning.

"Watch out, mistress!" the wagon driver shouted as he yanked on the brake and reins.

"I shall! Excuse me, sir."

"Quite all right," the other mumbled as he rolled past, tipping his broad-brimmed hat. She nodded distractedly in response, then stepped off the road to decide what to do.

Do I hide forever, because of that northerner and his tales? Why are they *here*? She hesitated a moment longer, her breath coming more quickly, then set her jaw. I have a healing to do. And I am not evil. Stubbornly, she walked down the slope toward Amelin and the Calling that awaited on the other side of town. To get there, she must pass the docks. Well, she would do it quietly.

As Brierley walked into the outskirts of Revil's greater town, she sensed the excitement abroad on the air, a quickening of interest and a matching slower pace to errands and chores as the focus of all gossip turned toward the noble party near the ships. Brierley paused in the eave shadow of a wharfside inn, watching the lords across the intervening bales and handcarts on the pier, her face further shadowed by her broad hat. None of the passersby noticed her, not even the innkeeper who found excuse to stand on his doorsill several paces to her left, wiping his hands on his broad apron as he craned his head to see.

In the center of the group on the wharf, Earl Melfallan stood next to Lady Saray as he talked to Revil, with Lord Landreth and Captain Bartol behind him. Count Revil was dressed in a plumed hat and fine blue brocade, neatly cut to his slim figure. As Brierley watched, the count gestured expansively, his short beard waggling as he made some jest. When Melfallan smiled, Revil added to his joke, continuing some droll tale until he could scarcely talk with his own chortling. She heard a short bark of laughter from Melfallan, as much at Revil's manner as at the joke. Beside them, Lord Landreth and Captain Bartol scowled mightily, two chickpeas in a seedpod, indeed. Brierley rose on her toes, trying to catch what the nobles were saying to each other—and why Landreth scowled so fiercely.

"What's the joke?" a fat cook asked the innkeeper.

"Something about witches—I think. Here, boy," the innkeeper said, gesturing at one of the kitchen boys in the inn doorway, "go a little closer and listen for me." As the boy sidled off around a stack of bales, the innkeeper craned his neck, trying to stretch his own ears.

"Witches are funny?" the cook squeaked, her hands fluttering to her face in alarm. The man shrugged a fleshy shoulder and harrumphed.

"When they're a northerner making mischief, they do. That's Captain Bartol from Duke Tejar's court, the one who led Natheby on a merry chase last week." The innkeeper spat into the street. "Northerners. Count Revil is right to laugh at him. Faugh!"

On the dock, Revil clapped a hand on Melfallan's shoulder, adding some further jest. Melfallan shook his head, a smile on his face, then glanced at his wife. Lady Saray, far advanced in her pregnancy, could not hide her discomfort well, not after all this time in the hot noontime sun. Like the faint touch of a vagrant breeze, Brierley caught the edge of Saray's strain, as legs trembled uncontrollably beneath the heavy skirts and sweat prickled unpleasantly on nape and scalp. Saray's wealth of red-gold hair and richly colored bodice only made her ashen complexion the more apparent, for all that she was fair as fine linen.

Belatedly, Melfallan noticed his wife's discomfort and immediately took her arm to lead her off the wharf. The other dignitaries followed, nodding and chatting to each other. Brierley shrank backward into the shadows, then prudently retreated around the inn corner into the alleyside. Best time to go, Brierley told herself as she hurried down the alley. Pick up your feet.

As she splashed through the puddles in the muddy alley, she heard the voices behind her grow louder, then echo briefly as the party passed the mouth of the alley. She stepped quickly to the inn wall and pressed her back against its smooth planks, removing movement from the alley that might catch attention. Too late, she learned an instant later.

"Hey!" She heard the shout and recognized Bartol's voice. She pushed off from the wall and walked onward, wanting to run wildly, madly, but kept her pace sedate, unhurried. Ahead, the alley stretched another twenty paces before its turn behind the inn. "Hey, woman!" Bartol shouted hoarsely.

Brierley heard heavy booted steps behind her, and dared a glance back. Two of Bartol's sailors pursued her at a half-run, their hands on sword hilts, their expressions fierce. Behind them, the party of dignitaries, most with confused expressions, stood in a group at the mouth of the alley, staring at her. Bartol's finger jabbed toward Brierley as he mouthed something to Melfallan, and she saw him then seize Melfallan's arm in his urgency. Brierley reached the corner and slipped around it. To her relief, a doorway stood open just ahead.

"Wait, woman!" one of the sailors yelled behind her in the alley. "Stop!"

Brierley turned smoothly into the open kitchen door, and walked among the ranks of shelves, pots, and cutlery to the wide hearth room within. A carcass turned over the open fire, tended by a cook's mate, while two girls scrubbed busily at dishes in the washing trough. The boy at the fire turned and looked at her, surprised.

"Can you tell me if Merchant Sorson is guesting at the inn?" she asked him. Behind her, the sailors pounded past the kitchen door in a full run. "I am a healer and his wife needs a potion." She raised her cloth bag slightly. "I thought the front entry too grand for such an inquiry."

"You know our innkeeper then?" the boy piped, rolling his

eyes roguishly. "He'd agree with that, him and his airs about his worthless inn!"

"Rason!" one of the girls hissed over her shoulder, her arms plunged into soapy water. "Watch your mouth!" The girl looked anxiously at the inner door.

"So?" Rason retorted. "Is he here? He's too busy watching the gentry. Through there, mistress," he added, tipping his chin toward the inner doorway. "Take the right stair, two doors left, and you'll find the housekeeper's desk. She can tell you what room."

"Thank you." In the lane outside, Brierley heard the approaching stamp of booted feet as Bartol's sailors retraced their steps, hunting.

Still moving unhurriedly, Brierley walked through the kitchen, climbed the stairs, spotted the opposite stairway down, and scooted past the vacant housekeeper's desk. As she reached the stair bottom, she reluctantly propped her staff in a curtained alcove, biting her lip at its probable loss, then took off her hat and shoved it and her bag under her skirt. Harmon thought her overdue on pregnancy, did he?

Calmly, both hands lightly supporting her abdomen as pregnant women often did, she descended the stair, swayed through the common room and a nearby gallery lined with chairs, and walked out the front door. Fifty feet away, just visible through the crowd, Bartol was still looking down the alley, with Lord Landreth and another sailor at his side to help with the looking, but Melfallan and his lady were now walking away, Count Revil and the others in their wake. Graciously, sedately, Brierley nodded at the preoccupied innkeeper, who scarcely spared her an irritable glance, then turned in the opposite direction. She walked onward, not hurrying, and proceeded on up the wharfside, calmly, gravidly.

At the edge of town, she stopped and stepped behind a bush to retrieve her hat and bag, then sat down disgruntedly on a fence railing. *Blast that man!* Bartol had passed beyond inconvenience—and apparently had too good a memory for faces or a hat or whatever he'd spied. Then she smiled despite herself, and covered her face with her hands, hiding the smile. A great joke, one she wished she could share with Harmon and Clara if only she dared—only now the Calling impended, within this hour, and she had taken the wrong way out of town.

Perhaps the lords have gone inside the inn, she hoped. Or to Revil's mansion up the slope, above the neat rows of fishermen's cottages. Whatever the noble party's course, both inn and mansion stood along the main street through town, cross-streeted with the wharf, and detours would consume time. The Calling grew more distinct as the future melded into the near present: a forester's only daughter, burning with fever from an infected wound. A dangerous fever, possibly fatal—

She rose and stepped onto the road, then bent her hat into sections to fit into her bag, a necessary prudence. First my staff, she thought irritably, and now my hat: what else will Bartol take today? Maybe she *would* do something about Bartol, though she hadn't an idea what.

Brierley walked uneventfully back through the town, her eyes and witch-sense alert. As always, the patterns of mind and suns' shadow shifted lazily as she walked, in ever-present rhythm to the distant roar of the surf. Melfallan's party had indeed moved on, she saw, the wharfside crowd dispersing back to chores or following to gawk more. She sighed to herself and followed the Calling like a traveler bent upon a distant lantern across the sea dunes, her senses focusing as her present self melded to one of a dozen possible futures.

She stopped outside the gate of a tiny cottage, one of a row of four abutting a narrow lane. The whitewashed wall boards showed recent care, the porch a thorough sweeping, and a neat row of bright-hued flowers lined the graveled path leading from the gate. Brierley opened the gate and walked up the path.

Her knock brought a bustling of movement inside the house, then the stamp of feet to the door.

"Good afternoon," Brierley said to the middle-aged woman who answered the door. *Her mother*. The woman eyed her suspiciously. Beyond the parlor, in a small bedroom, Brierley sensed the young girl's fevered pain, a heat and restlessness that nothing seemed to ease. An injured foot throbbed, for all the binding of a cool poultice. "I am Brierley Mefell, a healer," she told the woman. "I heard in town that your daughter is ill. May I help?"

"Mefell? Yes, I've heard of you, mistress." The woman hesitated. "Young, aren't you?"

"Yes, I am." Brierley smiled confidently and gained a reluctant nod in answer, accepting.

"Well, come in then, if you will." The woman swung the door full open and moved aside. "This way. I hope you can do something. I've had old Marcom come to see her foot, but his poultice doesn't help the wound. She stepped on a broken shell last week, down at the beach, a bad cut. Now she's burning up with fever." The mother's voice rose in anguish. "She's her father's favorite, you see: he's gone to Yarvannet to seek the castle's healer, for what good that asking might do." She snorted her opinion of that useless quest.

"What is her name?" Brierley asked as the mother opened the bedroom door.

"Yanna. I am Marta." Marta looked distractedly through the doorway, her fear for the child written plainly on her face, unguarded now. Brierley touched her arm.

"Bring me hot water and fresh cloths, please. I will see what I can do." Brierley walked into the bedroom and bent over Yanna's bed. Vivid blue eyes, hazed with fever, flew open at her touch and eyed her confusedly. Yanna was a pretty child, with a wide mouth and yellow hair, a sprinkling of freckles across her nose. "Hello, Yanna."

"Hello. Who are you?"

Brierley sat down on the edge of the bed. "A healer. I heard you've been sick."

"I still *am* sick," the girl corrected, with all the scorn of youth for the aged.

Brierley laid her palm on Yanna's forehead and felt an answering twinge in her own foot, a brief flash of heat spreading upward. The present merged fully with the future, engaging the Beast. Brierley checked the child's pulse, then wrapped her fingers around the child's wrist, squeezing gently. Already the power flowed through her fingers, lending strength. At times, with certain souls, Brierley found an immediate empathy at the outset of her healing, with no need for searching. She and this girl must share much. She smiled down at the child.

"That's true," she said equably. "But you will be better—only next time watch where you're walking."

Yanna rolled her eyes. "So everybody tells me—over and over."

"I'll only tell you once. Is that a trade?"

"All right."

Marta bustled in, her arms laden with cloths and a pan of water. Brierley rose and joined her at the washstand against the wall, then brought out herbs from her bag to mix with the steaming water. She considered the herbs in her bag, thinking more of the mother to explain the healing nearly completed, then selected a small vial of impressive shape. She added a few drops from it into the water. "I have found that sheep's oil is good for fever. We will bind the foot with new cloths and let the medicine help fight the infection."

"I hope it works," Marta said, not really believing.

"We shall see." Brierley turned back to the bed and winked at Yanna. "Won't we?"

"Are you sure you're a healer?" the girl asked pertly. "You surely don't act like one."

"Why?"

"You're supposed to pull at your chin." Yanna demonstrated, lowering her eyebrows and sticking out her lips. She scowled ferociously. "Then you give me awful-tasting stuff and poke at my stomach, then whisper with Mother in the corner."

"Really? Do healers do that?"

"The ones I've seen do."

Brierley lowered her brows and pulled at her chin. "How's that?" Yanna giggled.

"Yanna!" Marta said reprovingly.

"Oh, I don't mind," Brierley said. "Perhaps in a few years, when I'm full of myself about my art, I might." She smiled at Marta and teased gently. "There's an advantage to youth." Marta harrumphed, not sure she like being teased, not at all. Then Marta looked at her daughter's laughing face, and Brierley sensed an easing of the mother's fear, a new web strand to the power flowing toward the child.

Healing extends in many directions. Thora had written. *Remember those who worry in the room's shadows.*

"Will you help me with the foot, Marta? You'll need to change the compress again in the morning, and I'd like to show you how."

"All right." Marta glanced distractedly at her daughter a second time. "She does look better."

"Thank you." Brierley smiled. "Now this is what you must do," she began, speaking confidently.

As she cleaned Yanna's foot and rebound it, she explained each step to Marta, again at one with her Calling. Yanna bore the changing well, her eyes fixed on Brierley's face. When that was done, Marta insisted on serving Brierley a cup of cool milk in her small parlor, then excused herself after a few minutes to carry a cup and a small cake into Yanna's bedroom.

"She *does* look better," Marta announced when she returned, and sounded slightly startled. She eyed Brierley with some wonder. "Does that come from being young, too?"

She meant to joke, and Brierley felt Marta's abrupt discomfort with her own brusque comment. Marta was often brusque, she sensed, meaning well but speaking too quickly and regretting afterward. Brierley smiled and extended her hand.

"I wasn't offended, Marta." Marta took Brierley's hand in her own, a warm and pleasant touch of Marta's callused fingers. "I *am* young. Ask Yanna; she'll tell you."

"That she will—that and all the sun tales you can imagine."

"I believe it," Brierley declared. "She has that look." Brierley chuckled as Marta sighed feelingly. "Sun tales brighten the world, I'm thinking, and you agree, though you pretend you don't."

"Her father doesn't like them," Marta murmured, looking distressed. "I can't encourage her, not with him disapproving—" Her hand tightened on Brierley's. "She'll really be well?"

"I believe that firmly," Brierley said. "I could come back in a day or two, just to make sure."

"I would like that, mistress, very much," Marta said gratefully. "Bless you."

"Then I shall."

4

As soon as their party reached Revil's mansion in the town, Melfallan guided Saray to the nearest room and to a chair, then helped her to sit. She smiled up at him gratefully, sweat beaded on her forehead, as pale as snowy linen, and he silently cursed his inattention. She had insisted on coming to Amelin, bent on her duties as his noble wife: on some issues, Melfallan usually lost their argument, especially those when Saray's concept of her role of wife stood at the core. She had a point, he supposed, but not at the baby's risk.

"I've quite all right, Melfallan," Saray said, and gently pushed away his hand. "You needn't worry."

"No, you're not all right," he argued. Her delicate jaw set stubbornly in response, and he looked at her in frustration. In Saray's mind, noble ladies scarcely noticed they were pregnant, that being an indelicate issue outside polite company. Melfallan thought the attitude was absurd and had told her so, but Saray had not budged an inch. "I'm not going to argue with you," he said warningly, and struggled to keep his voice soft. Saray hated it when he shouted, especially at her, and he could wound her feelings for days if he did. "You *will* see the healer, Saray, when she comes." He looked behind him anxiously at the doorway, and Revil nodded as he entered the room.

"I've sent for Kaisa," his cousin assured him. With brisk

efficiency, Revil gestured one of his soldiers into each corner of the room, then his steward to stand at the doorway. Several other retainers in their party crowded the mansion entryway, but Revil ordered them away. Bartol and Landreth still chased the witch in town, Bartol's sailors with them. For the moment, the Courtrays had some needed privacy.

Revil looked sternly at Melfallan's lady. "Don't be foolish now, Saray. I agree with him. And we've been through this before." Sometimes Revil could talk more sense in Melfallan's wife than her husband could, but Saray's eyes still flashed stubbornly.

"I—" she began.

"No," Melfallan pleaded, forestalling her. "My love, please. You worry me when you resist like this."

Saray's expression abruptly changed, becoming sweet again. Somehow Melfallan had stumbled on the right words. By Mionn standards, a noble wife created peace in the home for her husband's ease, yielding to his needs always, and never, never caused him worry. Melfallan could practically hear Lady Mionn reciting the dictum: Ocean knew he'd heard Saray repeat it often enough to her ladies when she didn't know he was listening. Saray pushed back her heavy reddish hair and smiled up at him. "I don't want you to worry, Melfallan," she said softly.

"Then—"

"All right," she conceded. Melfallan straightened and sighed. Saray tried not to worry him, yet her very efforts to spare him created frustration just as severe. It was the pattern of their marriage, one he could not understand. Still, as always, he made himself smile at her, and bent to lightly caress her face.

"You do worry me, but only a little," he said, tempering his protest into a half-lie for her sake. "Please, Saray, be more cautious. You're so near your time."

Saray ignored the comment on her pregnancy, as always, and tipped her head at him. Her smile teased. "Isn't it nice when battles are so easily won?" she asked drolly, as if her adamant resistance were only a little joke, a little thing that had hardly endangered their child.

"When the battles have a point," he muttered, and dared to scowl at her. She *must* take care of herself and the baby instead of this constant dance for what she thought was his favor. She must. Saray giggled at his scowl and hid her mouth behind her hand, her eyes dancing in laughter. Ocean's blessing, he thought in distraction, Saray was lovely when she laughed. To Melfallan's relief, already she looked less ill, and a few moments later Revil's healer bustled into the room. With a soft sigh of ladylike embarrassment, Saray allowed herself to be conducted away.

Revil poured wine at the side table and handed Melfallan a glass, then raised an eyebrow. Melfallan sighed.

"You never have this trouble," he complained.

"My lady's Amelin-bred," Revil said, "not from Mionn. My dear cousin, that is the *only* difference." He raised his glass in salute.

Melfallan and Revil had grown up together in Yarvannet Castle, both fostered by Earl Audric after plague had taken their fathers, and were as close as brothers. On a list of men to trust, Revil's name had scarcely a shadow: if Melfallan could not trust Revil, trusting wasn't worth the effort—nor was life worth the living, for that matter. Revil had no ambition for the earldom, none at all: he had seen too much of the earl's burdens. Melfallan often envied Revil his contentment with his life, his open joy with its favors, as if the suns always shown brightly for Revil, as if all manner of folk were his personal treasures, each one a jewel to admire without loss.

He shrugged at his cousin and Revil waggled his eyebrows back. They both knew Saray all too well, even if Revil was better at managing her, Ocean knew why. "Women," Revil ventured.

"My lady wife," Melfallan corrected. "Not all women, but mostly her mother, Ocean sink her, who taught Saray all those stupid rules."

"Now, now, Melfallan, I've heard Lady Mionn is a most genteel woman."

"Drown genteel," Melfallan growled. "And drown Mionn."

He swallowed half the wine in his glass and glowered at his cousin.

"Not so loud," Revil advised humorously, nodding at the soldiers in the room. "I remind you that Mionn is our principal ally. We mustn't be drowning right and left, dear earl: we might need Mionn." Revil saluted him courteously with his wineglass. "To your good health, my earl, and your lady's, and the heir she carries."

"And to you and yours, cousin," Melfallan answered, meaning it.

Revil raised an eyebrow. "Shall we undrown Lady Mionn, at least until the good captain is safely gone from Yarvannet?"

"As you wish, cousin," Melfallan said. "But I still say my mother-in-law deserves to be drowned. And if your soldiers and steward think I mean it, their lack of brains is more threat to Yarvannet than any tale carried to northern ears." Two of the soldiers flashed an answering grin, but Revil's steward only wrung his hands, looking anxious. Well, the man always wrung his hands and looked anxious, Melfallan remembered, a habit that would drive Melfallan to distraction. It had little effect on the more comfortable Revil, but Melfallan often wondered why Revil kept the overnervous man in his station. He started to pace.

A heavy stomping of feet and a murmur of voices announced the arrival of Captain Bartol and his party, and quickly extinguished whatever other advice Revil might have given. Melfallan regretted that loss: sometimes his affable cousin could see more clearly than himself, especially dealing with the problems of people, especially a wife. More than once, Revil had helped Saray and Melfallan through a domestic crisis, an argument blown up out of nothing that bent feelings and divided them, and Melfallan had yet to repay those favors.

Put that aside, he told himself quickly, as Captain Bartol strode through the doorway. Not now. Lord Landreth followed in Bartol's wake, his scowl unpleasant. Both bowed low to Melfallan, with a subtle mockery in the depth of the bows impossible to challenge, then gave a precisely identical bow to Revil, its equal deference thereby insulting Melfallan again. They had exquisite grace in bowing, Melfallan thought sourly, and responded with a nod. Why do I feel like hanging them both?

"We couldn't find her, your grace," Bartol said, with an obvious chagrin. Melfallan had no doubt the emotion was genuine. A bird in the glove satisfied far more than a bird loose on the wind, especially with a duke's plots at stake. Bartol sighed and dramatically gestured a blessing over his trade badge. "She must have used a spell to escape. Thank Ocean I have my amulet's protection."

Melfallan narrowed his eyes and did not reply. Surely Bartol did not believe in such charms; surely he worked more of his duke's mischief in such idiot talk. The captain stared back coolly, a slight smile on his lips, and Melfallan caught a ghost of contempt that flickered in Bartol's eyes.

So.

Melfallan glanced at Landreth, then lifted an eyebrow. "No mind," he said with studied unconcern. "Revil sets a good table, lords. I'll think you'll find it quite up to Darhel standards, Captain. And Lord Landreth, will you join us as well? I think Revil favors one of your father's wines." He turned affably to Count Revil. "Don't you, cousin?"

"Of the proper vintage," Revil said loftily, catching exactly the right pose and arrogant timbre. Revil hadn't a pompous bone in his body, but could play the part at the slightest cue. Landreth's expression flickered in surprise, quickly suppressed. Landreth thought Revil a pleasant but silly count, as did many of Tejar's sycophant lords, but Revil sometimes twigged him neatly.

"Actually, your grace," Bartol said, "I must return to my ship. Who knows what evil that woman might bring on my men, now that she knows I've seen her?" Bartol even took his kerchief from his pocket and dabbed his brow. Landreth's face quickly adopted the same anxiety, and the two turned to each other and traded a meaningful glance. Games.

"I doubt she has any menace," Melfallan said casually. "The shari'a are children's tales, Captain, and of little importance."

"I feel concern that your grace thinks so," Bartol protested.

"Alertness is crucial. The shari'a can appear anywhere, anytime, to work their treacheries." Melfallan enjoyed the irony in Bartol's remark. Mefallan did not need some dim-witted girl for his worries; he had only to look to his lords. He watched the captain and Landreth trade another look, this one of feigned concern.

"If you say so," Melfallan said, waving his hand. He took another swallow of his wine and made himself sway slightly, as if the earl of Yarvannet were already in his cups at this ridiculous hour of the morning, no doubt tippling below decks as they had sailed to Amelin, and was now three glasses to Revil's one in the short half-hour Bartol had been chasing his witch. Melfallan watched Bartol's eyes narrow thoughtfully, and knew he'd seen Melfallan's sway, as Melfallan fully intended: another tidbit for the duke. Bear it away, spy, Melfallan thought and smiled broadly. "Well, too bad you must leave," he said, waving his hand. "A captain must look to his ship first." It was a dismissal and Melfallan accepted their bows. "Until tomorrow or perhaps the day after, Captain. Perhaps you might call at the castle both days. I may have time for you in one of the afternoons."

Bartol hesitated, waiting for a better commitment, which Melfallan happily withheld. Finally, when the moment had stretched a bit too long, the captain turned and stalked out of the room, Landreth following in his wake like a rowboat tied to a ship's stern. Melfallan waited until he heard the slam of the outer door.

"A pretty play," Revil said, and sipped at his wine. "You're a nice drunk, Melfallan."

"I try."

"I'm surprised Landreth makes his new connection so obvious."

"He knows I've seen his games before and did nothing about them. Why should I change?" Melfallan glanced at the soldiers, and Revil dismissed them along with his steward, then shut the door to give them privacy. Melfallan paced the room. "What is Bartol up to with this witch business, Revil? Ennis thinks mischief-making for Tejar's sake, with Landreth helping him."

"I'd trust any opinion of Master Ennis," Revil avowed. "And I don't like his choosing one of my folk to harass. Not at all."

"Do you know this woman, the one the sailors chased?"

"Yes. Her name is Brierley Mefell. She's a healer, spoken well of, not old, barely more than a girl, actually. Kaisa could tell you more, after she's done tending Saray. I suppose you'll need to stay the night, Melfallan? You'll be welcome."

Melfallan sighed. "It would be prudent. Saray's not due for another month, but— Why *won't* she listen to reason? I don't even know how I lose the arguments."

Revil grinned. "A husband's common fate, Melfallan. Solange wins most of ours, and I never know quite how, either." He shrugged, then watched Melfallan pace for several moments. "I think you worry too much, cousin, about too many things. I wish you didn't."

"I appreciate the concern, but how do you stop the wind from blowing? Worrying is an earl's lot." Melfallan shrugged as if it didn't matter, but Revil knew him too well. His cousin held out the wine bottle, offering, and refilled Melfallan's glass.

"I wish I could help you more," Revil said quietly. "I understand the burden, Melfallan, and I worry for you."

"You do help. Just be yourself, Revil. Don't change."

"Too much has changed, I agree. I miss Grandfather, too. He was a father to both of us, and I thought he'd live forever. Any progress on who did it?"

"None. Likely the proof's long vanished. We may never know." They shared a bleak look. "I hate watching my back, suspecting every trusted servant who's served the family for years, wondering if every noise in the corridor is the dagger that's finally come for me. I know who I *think* it was, but I can't prove it was Farlost. I'd like to rid us of both Sadon and Landreth, but we haven't the proof. And even then Tejar might overrule me and force me to keep Sadon as count, and Ocean knows what would happen then. War, I expect. If it *was* Sadon, of course."

Revil snorted. "Sadon's a fool if he thinks Tejar will give him Yarvannet. Tejar has half a dozen lordlings for the gifting, men who will rule as Tejar pleases. And Tejar hates the Courtrays, always has. We need to watch our backs with this duke, especially you, Melfallan. Solange had a letter from her sister in Airlie, and apparently our aunt has adopted greater prudence. Rowena hasn't been to Darhel for months. Even the Earl of Mionn is finding excuses to stay home from the autumn court."

"That can't last," Melfallan said in dismay. "Someone will have to make a move."

"Maybe someone has—by crying witch in *my* port." Revil scowled fiercely. "I won't let him hurt one of my people," he burst out. "Never! I'm good friends with the earl, and I expect him to back me up." He glared at Melfallan, daring him to say otherwise.

"There aren't any witches, cousin," Melfallan temporized. "It's only a legend."

Revil shook his head. "That's not the issue. I don't care if the shari'a are silly legend or horrible reality. I won't have Mistress Mefell hurt by that—that *toady* of a captain. I won't!"

Revil turned away abruptly. Melfallan watched him splash more wine in his glass, and guessed he and his cousin might end up drunk this night, the way the afternoon was going. He sighed and ran his fingers through his blond hair. Revil was a fine and canny count, devoted to his fisherfolk, and received their devotion in turn. His cousin's passion did not surprise him, but Revil had no right to demand a particular verdict, and they both knew it.

"Revil—" he began.

"I'm sorry," Revil muttered, not looking at him. "I don't mean to pressure you, but can't you see that it's wrong? She's a *healer*, a young woman of fine reputation. She can't be shari'a, but how does she prove she's not? Let me call Kaisa. She'll tell you. She'll—"

Melfallan gripped Revil's arm. "It's not necessary. I believe you, Revil. We'll keep her safe. I promise."

Revil stared at him. "Just like that? You take my word and act on it?"

"A person's conduct speaks for itself, as you say. A healer

earns her respect through her healing, and if Kaisa speaks well of her, enough to convince you, that's enough for me, as her lord and yours. I have to trust somebody, Revil." He made a face, realizing he'd revealed more than he intended.

Revil pressed Melfallan's hand with his own. "Tejar gets along without that trouble of trusting, Melfallan, and you would be wiser to follow his example, or so some would say. But in trusting me, I swear it will never be misplaced. You are my earl, and that will never change, whatever happens." He saluted Melfallan solemnly with his wineglass, and then drained the wine in a long swallow. "I also know a shari'a accusation is not that simple. The shari'a laws cannot be ignored."

"It's simple enough for you. You simply defend your folk."

Revil gave him a roguish smile. "I don't have to make the decision. I *do* know the difference." He shrugged another apology. "Again, I'm sorry to push at you. I won't hold you to your promise, as much as I value it: I spoke rashly. But for her sake, I beg you to consider mercy." He picked up the wine bottle with a flourish and then changed the subject, to Melfallan's relief. "I think that was my fourth glass—at least I think so, which means it must be time for dinner."

"Nothing wrong with getting drunk," Melfallan said casually. His cousin knew how to drink happily, hilariously, and never minded the heavy head afterward, cheerful as always even in his cups. Melfallan suddenly longed for a long and raucous drunken evening with Revil, with idiot jokes and laughter and bawdy songs, and then its comfortable oblivion afterward. Here, away from Tiol and surrounded by Revil's soldiers, it would be safe enough. And Saray was resting and wouldn't be downstairs to disapprove. "Nothing at all wrong," he declared firmly.

"Really?" Revil blinked, and then spread a delighted grin over his face. "I will take you up on that, my earl. It's been a while since I saw you drunk. I always thought it a treat. You get this delusion you can sing."

"You'll pay for that taunt, you cur." Melfallan put on the pose Revil had played a few minutes before, and it won him another wide grin, only half of it from the wine.

"After you?" Revil bowed with a flourish toward the door, and his low bow was a perfect mimicry of Bartol's. Melfallan gave a short bark of laughter, then laughed again for the joy of it. "I look forward to your singing, your grace," Revil added, his grin as broad as a ship's beam, "more than you know."

"After you, good count. And it's 'your grace and wonder' now, not just 'your grace.' " Melfallan paused. "Better, 'your *superb* grace and wonder.' Yes, I like that."

"Ah! And when did this change happen?"

"Just now." Melfallan airily waved his hand. "Earls can do things whenever they want. Hadn't you heard?"

"No—really?" Revil asked. They looked at each other with mock solemnity.

"I'm sure it's so," Melfallan said.

"Except sing," Revil corrected him cheerfully. "That, Melfallan, you cannot do, even as earl. As you'll prove tonight, no doubt, but I am prepared for even that." He laughed and threw an arm around Melfallan's shoulder, and they left the room together.

That evening Brierley rested in her cave, watching the sea from the door stones until sunset, and then researched the cave's journals to refresh her knowledge about infection. The following morning, as the Daystar light slanted over the stairs, she continued her study.

Most of Brierley's Callings involved trauma—a fall, a scalding, a knife wound: fever rarely called to her. Why? she wondered. The local herbwomen had a dozen medicines for fever and infection, all quickly palliative except for the winter plague. That malady had no stable remedies: an herb that worked one season might have no effect the next. Why? And why was she never called to plague? According to their writings, none of the cave witches were called to such healings—and all had been immune to the plague. Why? Perhaps her witch-sense, however it chose the Callings, avoided the pernicious effect of infection on her own body. Perhaps. But other cave witches had healed fever often. Brierley made a face. *Why?*

Am I the only one who wonders this much? Why do these questions bother me but never bothered them, at least not so much? She understood so little of her gift, and her books often seemed as confused.

What was a Calling? How did she know where to go, when to go? How could she sense the future? Why did her witch sense fade sometimes and not other times? Why could she sometimes hear minds a half-mile away, and other times barely a few paces? Why?

Just when she thought she had divined a general rule, her shari'a senses abruptly went elsewise, doing what they pleased, who cares for you? It was maddening.

Why were witches always women? Why no men? Not one of her books mentioned a male witch, though it seemed the gift could descend through father as well as mother. One of the cave witches had surmised her grandmother was shari'a, based on clues from her own experience of the gift, and so must have passed the witch-sense to her granddaughter through her son. But the gift still appeared only in daughters, when it descended at all, and never in sons. Why? And the gift did not always occur in the same degree. Marlenda could scarcely recognize her shari'a self, so weakly did it flicker, yet the witch-sense had dominated Brierley's waking life from her earliest memories. Why? And Allemanii blood did not weaken the gift: all of the cave witches had some Allemanii blood, as Brierley likely did herself. Why *not*?

Some of her books' discussions about the specifics of the gift made little more sense, although Brierley had tried a few of the meditations, a chant or two, even a few of the more impressive spell-throwings. Her books talked about potions and magicks and marvelous events, often detailing the oddest procedures, but will as she might, her spell for shifting a stone had not shifted as much as a sand grain, and a spell for stormwinds had not raised even a draft in her cave. No stone-shifter or storm-speller was she, apparently, but even the discussions about healing often mismatched her own experience. Several of her books mentioned the mysterious Callings and there was mention of the Beast in its many forms, but little else matched. Putting words to the gift had troubled every witch in the cave, and only a few had persisted in the attempt.

Half of witchery is asking questions and having no answers, she thought. I wish I knew who had the answers, for it surely isn't me. Perhaps my heir will do better. She smiled at the thought of her future apprentice. On occasion a witch and her successor had overlapped, living together in the cave for a time, sharing their lives. Mother Ocean did not answer all prayers, but did answer some. That hope of her apprentice was her dearest, enough that each new face brought a catch of the heart, an anxious moment of hoping, so far disappointed—until the next time.

In the cave journals, she found a connection to other shari'a women who had possessed the gift and wondered about it, who had lived a secret life as she did, who healed despite the risk. But the journals were not the women who had written them, not in the sense of true living, a voice that could speak, a face that could smile, a hand that could touch. They could not look out at the day and see what Brierley saw, nor listen and hear what Brierley heard. They could not answer when she spoke to them, and said no more, no less, than the exact words on their pages.

If they were living, they would not deny the shari'a as her mother had denied them: Jocater's silence had been adamant and unbending, the choice of her determined will, and of all things Brierley mourned her mother's silence the most. It had divided them, and made Brierley a disappointment to Jocater, not a joy. Jocater's choosing had erased all chance that Brierley might be a comfort to her, that she might delight in her daughter, and share with her the nature they had in common. If Mother Ocean blessed Brierley with a witch-daughter to cherish, she would lavish on her everything Jocater had withheld, and in that, atone for Jocater's denial of Brierley and herself. Whatever her mother had removed from the world's goodness by her choosing, Brierley would refill, and thus bring peace to her mother's memory.

Perhaps someday, if Ocean allows— She sighed, knowing it might never happen.

She tipped back her chair and idly pushed off a shoe, then dropped the other on the floor beside it. She yawned and leaned back further, then wrinkled her nose. The sea wind was rising, bringing rain to the coast. She listened for a few moments to the comforting music of moving air. Why did rain come more often in autumn? she wondered. Who decided such matters of rain and wind? Mother Ocean? How, dear Mother, and by what technique? No one seemed quite sure.

Someday, perhaps, she thought wistfully, I will know all things.

Perhaps. She made a rude noise at herself for the silly wishing.

She thumped her chair back to its upright position, and took another book from her stack, then paused and listened to her body. The few times she dealt with serious fever, she usually struggled overlong against the Beast and felt weak for days afterward. Today after Yanna's healing, she felt a deep lassitude, as if something within her had been gravely depleted, though the feeling steadily eased as the day wore on. Perhaps her talent bent to one direction over another, making her awkward with fever. Perhaps. After judicious considering, she decided she felt a little light-headed. Was that a slight tremor of the limbs? An extra warmth to her face? She laid her palm on her forehead. It felt cool and smooth.

More likely, she decided with a snort, such symptoms had more to do with skipping breakfast. She looked at the stair and saw the light slanting at the angle of late afternoon. And lunch, too: where has the time gone? She closed the book firmly and restacked it atop the others. Eat now, she told herself sternly, before you forget again.

She rummaged in the pantry and found cheese and the last of the hard roll bought a week ago in Natheby, then dipped a mug of clear water from the ledge pool near the stair. Meal in hand, she sat down at her table and retrieved her book from the stack. It was an old volume, well worn and apparently recopied before the original volume disintegrated. Thora's journal had been recopied four times, according to the superscript. How long had Lorena's stood on the shelf until long handling made it fragile?

She thumbed the pages, then consulted the index. Sheep's oil: Lorena would have a fit about that choice! Lorena had had little patience with incompetents: her forceful opinions of other healers of her time sometimes blistered the page. In Yanna's case, sheep's oil had been an inspiration of the moment, compounded of Marta's own ignorance of such matters and the impressive curves of that particular flask, but hardly credible to a healer. From such a casual misstep could come her undoing, to be sorely regretted afterward. She skimmed the pages as she ate, reviewing Lorena's herb-craft.

My child, she read, *be aware that infection is an invasion of the body. Kill the infection and the body will heal: indeed, the body itself fights the infection with natural defenses. Thus, the development of pus, and thus the reddening of the skin from activity of the blood. Many herbs contain substances which poison the infective cause and sometimes the body, so you must choose judiciously. Of such herbs, too little may be ineffective, too much dangerous. In such cases, proper dosage is the key to recovery.*

Brierley frowned. She sometimes wondered if Lorena ever used witch-sense, so preoccupied was her journal with herbs and technique. She never mentioned the sympathetic flush and dull ache of responsive pain that Brierley herself experienced. Perhaps Lorena did not feel them—or chose to ignore them. Still, the Everlight had called to Lorena, too, summoning her to the cave. The able herbwoman had acknowledged as much, though she understood the cave's guardian not at all, and seemed not to wonder much about it. Perhaps the Everlight had sensed something beyond witch-sense in that capable woman.

"Everfern, Iverway moss, dark sea lichen, the roots of blue-grass—" Brierley recited the curative herbs from Lorena's list, ticking them off her fingers, then hunted vainly in her head for the rest of the list. She looked in the book, then recited again.

"—Yarvan greenstalk, new buds of everwillow, the bark of carmilla." She counted her fingers. "That's seven. What are they again, Brierley?"

She ran through the list, getting six. Again to the book.

"Carmilla, carmilla. And again, you lack-brain!" After two more tries, she remembered all seven and sighed, wondering how long the list would stay in her head. She was never very good with lists. "Why?" she asked aloud. Her lips quirked with amused annoyance. After every answer came another question, until her head could spin.

She had no problem discussing the healing art with other healers: their knowledge lay in their minds as they talked, giving her the necessary clues. All she needed to employ were knowing nods, a few pertinent questions, and steady deference. The ignorant were her bane—and their tales borne away to other ears that knew better.

One slip and I may be undone. Have I already slipped? She felt a chill of foreboding. Restlessly, she stood up and paced the cave, wrapping her arms tighter in her shawl.

Will they hunt me, when they know?

The doubt haunted her into her dreams that night, and took her to a familiar place she had dreamed before. She found herself again in a graystoned cavern lit by blazing torches. Heavy and richly carved furniture stood against three of the walls: glass-doored bookcases, tall cabinets, two carved chairs, and a wide couch upholstered in a deep velvety green. Beyond a wide doorway on the fourth wall stretched a tiled corridor, deeply shadowed. On the stone floor of the chamber, mica veins flashed in the dark granite as the torch flames moved, like a winking of diamondlike sparks against a night sea. Above her, she saw only a clinging darkness where the ceiling receded high above the torchlight.

What is this place? her dream-self wondered, and turned slowly around, looking at every part of the chamber. *I have been here before—have I?*

Carved into the walls between the tall shelves of books were four murals of rich color, each depicting one of the revered spirit-dragons of the shari'a. In one tall panel to the left, a golden dragon screamed into the wind as it rode the storms of spring, lightning shivering in its claws. In another, enclosed by the dark stone of an underground cavern, a hot-eyed dragon glowed ember-red, a priceless jewel clutched in its claws. In a third, the forest dragon with shadowed emerald scales sifted like dark smoke through the canopy of a tree, its eyes depthless, and finally, nearest the doorway, an azure sea dragon with silver fins curled on a dark sea stone, a healer's simple cup in its talons.

She stepped toward the sea dragon, and became suddenly aware of the heavy rich fabric of her skirt, the smooth touch of silk in the shawl around her shoulders. Her sandals, delicate golden thongs, tapped a slow tread on the smooth tiles. She stopped and looked down at them, as if her feet, too, belonged to someone else. She raised her hand to the velvet hood that covered her hair, and noticed the band of aquamarines bound in gold that circled her wrist: the gems caught the torchlight, gleaming as brilliantly as the sea dragon's eyes. Where am I? she wondered. She looked around confusedly, then fingered the rich velvet of her skirt.

Who am I?

"Brierley."

She whirled, startled by the sound of a voice behind her. A shadowed woman stood in the outer hallway, her slender figure a darker shadow against the darkness beyond, her face concealed.

Brierley gasped. "Who are you?"

"Thora, of course." Thora Jodann stepped forward into the light and smiled gently, then tipped her head to the side, her earrings dancing with the movement. "My child, how can you not know me?"

Thora walked forward into the chamber, emerging fully from the shadows. Tall and slender, she was as richly dressed in velvet and gold as Brierley herself, with gold links winking at wrist and throat, a rich border of silver thread on sleeves and skirt hem. The rich dress suited her, for she bore herself proudly, her walk elegant and restrained. Thora stopped a few paces away, her eyes fixed on Brierley's face. Then she smiled, her face lighting with pleasure and joy.

"My child," she said, her voice a caress. She lifted her hand in solemn greeting. "I was the first among the last," she said, her voice resonating throughout the room, "the slender chance of a last desperate hope after all other hopes had fled." She studied Brierley for a long moment, looking her up and down from hood to sandals. "Harmon is right," she decided. "You *are* too thin."

"I eat quite enough, thank you," Brierley said with dignity.

"Indeed!" Thora shrugged. "I had the same stubbornness, my child, and I suspect it did me about as much good. Have courage, Brierley. As long as there is but one, yet one who still believes, more can follow. Remember that."

"Believes? Believes in what?"

"In the life of the Calling, of course. In that life will come the dawning of the new day for the shari'a, all of us, in the purpose of what we are." Thora spread her hands. "Can you not see it? Do you not know? Can you not see the reasons?"

Brierley shook her head in confusion. "You talk in riddles again." Whenever her dreams brought her to this library, Thora's words rarely rose above the obscure—yet a meaning tantalized in her words, needing only a single clue, a talisman, for full understanding. But what clue? What talisman?

Thora sighed and looked away, as frustrated as Brierley. "Only because you will not understand the truth, Brierley. Only because you will not see." She gestured at the library around them. "This is Witchmere, my child, our ancient capital. Although our people preferred their homes in our forests and hills, our scholars and leaders came to these caverns to consult together, and to study the nature of the real and be guided by the Four, and thus made us great." She looked around the chamber. "I remember this library," she said softly. "I remember these halls when they blazed with light and movement. I remember my girlhood before the Disasters, when Duke Rahorsum did not hate us, not yet."

"Why did he hate us, Thora?" Brierley asked. "Were we truly evil? Did we steal children?"

"Why does a fabric unravel?" Thora replied. "Why does a single falling stone turn into a cascade?" Thora slowly paced the chamber and stopped in front of the mosaic of the sea dragon, then looked up at the panel, her face bereft. "How could the Four forsake the shari'a and allow the Disasters?

We share an interest in answers, dear one, but to some questions there is no answer, none."

She turned to face Brierley again. "Why did Rahorsum hate us, you ask? He was not a bad duke, not in the beginning. There were shari'a who resented the Allemanii's invasion, although their seafolk kept to the rivers and shoresides, leaving us the hills we preferred. These were our lands from times long forgotten, and those shari'a did not wish to share them with anyone, whatever the Allemanii's need and the lack of cost to us. It began there. It began with us."

Thora shrugged. "A small fault, our avarice for our lands, to which the Allemanii contributed their own faults. One stone led to another, and anger to anger, and outrage to outrage, and then the witches struck at Rahorsum's only son and tried to control the duke's mind, unbalancing him with both." She paced the room again, her sandals muffled on the stone. "Or so I believe. I was not present in Witchmere when it happened, but I knew those among our scholars capable of such acts. And I knew the witch who made the plague." She looked at Brierley in despair. "No, my beloved, we did not steal children, but we did acts equal in their evil, we shari'a of Witchmere, and caused the Four to deny us. Rahorsum was perhaps only Their instrument."

"Then we *were* evil," Brierley said, appalled.

"No, my child. Only afraid. We were not warriors, not as the Allemanii were, and not many, as they quickly became. Did our fear merit out obliteration? I think not. And we were not wholly in the fault. The Allemanii, too, chose to do evil." She spread her hands sadly. "Does such evil close a door forever? Is there no rising from such an ending as we have suffered? Can a witch's belief, although a belief almost shattered beyond repair, mend what is broken—if she believes enough to change the world? Can you not see it, my daughter?"

"See what?" Brierley asked. "Believe in what?" She shivered as the cool air abruptly sighed through the room, plucking invisible fingers. "I don't know what you mean. *Help* me to see."

Thora stamped her sandaled foot impatiently. "What do

you think I'm *trying* to do, you dunce? Why can't you understand me?"

Brierley crossed her arms. "Why don't you talk better sense?" They glared mildly at each other.

Thora shook her head in frustration, then sighed. " 'Why' is a problem word for both of us, I think," she said, and tipped up the corners of her mouth. "Do you think we'd be better off without it?" she teased, her earbobs bouncing. "I do often. In fact—"

Thora tensed and looked behind her at the shadows in the outer hallway. In the silence beyond, a shuffling began, and a dripping of seawater as if limbs coiled and recoiled, hunting through the tunnels.

"Remember!" Thora said urgently, and moved swiftly through the doorway. "Do not forget!" Thora vanished into the shadows, and was swallowed up by the darkness, one instant to the next.

"Thora!" Brierley called after her. "Wait!" Recklessly, she plunged after her friend through the doorway and felt the floor slide oddly beneath her feet—then dissolve, tumbling her downward into blankness. "No!" she cried, as the Beast's roar shattered the air around her. "No! Thora, wait!"

In the void, the Beast seized her with its stinking coils, and crushed her breath from her body, roaring in its triumph. *Little shari'a, you are mine. Mine! Mine! Mine!* Brierley shrieked as the Beast tore off her limbs and ripped open her body with its daggered claw, spilling her steaming intestines. It plucked out her eyes, and smacked its mouth on her extracted brain, and her mouth opened in wordless agony—

Brierley woke with a start, her heart pounding a frantic rhythm in her ears. She lay still in her bed for several moments, not yet quite sure what was dream and what was not. In the Everlight's corridor, the water slapped at the stone with the choppier rhythm of a distant storm, and she heard the splash of a fish. Comfortable sounds, as familiar as the Daystar's dawn light reflecting into the stairway from the cracks above the stair. The sea air sighed through the cave, real enough as it caressed her face with cool fingers. A dream, surely. She gave a shuddering sigh and turned on her side, then pulled the bedclothes closer.

Believe in what? she wondered sleepily. And why did she dream of Thora now? She felt a new chill of foreboding, too vague for any direction of its threat. One could fall prey to the fancy of dreams, thinking nonsense had meaning. She rubbed her nose slowly. Believe in what, Thora? The answer eluded her.

I should stay in my cave today, she thought. If I were prudent, I would: you'll take one too many chances, Brierley, and end it all in stupidity. Restlessly, she threw off the covers and rose to light the lamp on the table, then sat down in her chair.

If I were prudent—

I preserve the gentle ones of the world. Infection could turn again on the body, she worried, seizing a child with new fever if not tended properly. With a wound, Brierley always knew when she could safely leave, having little doubt of the full healing, but she felt awkward with fever and had too little experience with its healing. Had she done enough for Yanna? She wasn't certain.

I should go see, she thought, arguing with her better judgment. And I did promise Marta.

She rose and paced the stone floor, knowing the danger of that temptation, especially with her witch-sense still dulled by the recent healing. Recently her risk of exposure had come far too close with Bartol's chasing on the wharf, and then the castle healing, then this latest narrow escape through the inn kitchen. She had made herself too obvious.

Although she kept to herself and kept few close friends, her face was still known in Revil's small towns, first as Alarson's stepdaughter, then through her recent years as young midwife to the local commonfolk. In time, her luck could run out, a disaster perhaps set in motion by an odd chance of a northerner captain's glancing in the wrong direction at the wrong time—and she had made a host of other odd chances the past few days. She sat down and drummed her fingers irritably on her table. I should stay home.

It wouldn't take very long, she thought wistfully. I could

be there and back here in only a few hours. She looked around at the familiar furnishings of her cave. Only a few hours, if I hurry. She got up determinedly and dressed, her fingers flying with the button loops and the flash of her shawl around her shoulders, then left the cave and paddled into the first faint blue glow of the Companion's dawning.

~

She reached the outskirts of Amelin after a brisk walk, then took a roundabout way through several fields to reach the edge of town near Yanna's house. A few townspeople were already about on their business, a few nodding greeting to her as she walked inward into the town. As she expected, her witch-sense flickered fitfully, still dulled by Yanna's healing. Fever always took more out of her, took longer for recovery: another reason to turn back, she thought, and nearly did. She was nearly blind today, blind and deaf—and likely a fool. Twice she stopped short in the street and hesitated, then each time continued onward. Fool! But if the fever had returned—

She passed other early-morning risers and raised no apparent alarm, then allowed herself a cautious relief. Finally she turned up one street, then hurried to the next, Yanna's street. The short lane was deserted, with no one in the yards, not even children. She walked along the dusty dirt of the street by the street-edge fences of several houses, glancing cautiously ahead and once back, then reached the gate she sought. As her hand reached for the latch, the house door crashed open and a soldier in Melfallan's blue and gray livery rushed out toward her, his sword drawn. She gasped and whirled to run, then saw another soldier, this one Revil's, rush from behind the opposite house, then a third man in forester's green jump from behind a tall fence beside the next. She froze, wary of an easy sword thrust for a wrong move, so fiercely did they run toward her.

She put her hand on a picket in the fence to steady herself, then lifted her chin. The Yarvannet guardsman reached her first and seized her arm hard, jerking her around toward him. "Don't you move," he growled. He was a narrow-faced young man, with black lanky hair and sunken eyes. His fingers dug into her flesh, hurting her.

"I won't!" she cried.

He raised his sword blade warningly in emphasis, then vaulted lightly over the gate into the street, dragging her with him. Beyond him, Brierley saw Marta standing in the house's door, hands raised to her white face.

"Is Yanna well, Marta?" Brierley called. "I came to see, as I told you I would."

"Quiet, woman!" the soldier ordered, giving Brierley another hard shake. His two companions, the Amelin soldier and the forester, encircled her, boxing her against the fence, each with sword drawn and expressions just as fierce. With an effort, Brierley shook off the first soldier's grasp and faced them all proudly, as Thora had stood proudly in her dream, and lifted her chin.

"I will go with you," she said, glaring at the soldier who had seized her. "I will not resist. You have no need for shouts, curses, or violence." She rubbed her bruised arm and grimaced, then called again to Marta on the porch. "Is she well, Marta?"

"She is well, young healer!" Marta called back. "She is very well. Thank you." The forester threw Marta a black look, his hand clenching convulsively on his short sword. (*. . . she never listens to me.*) His anguished thought dropped into Brierley's mind. (*. . . and now look what's happened.*) The man was filled with fear for Yanna, of the witch's taint taken by a child through a wife's sweet folly. Yanna's father, Brierley realized. At her husband's fierce glare, Marta fled back into the house, the door slamming fast behind her.

"No talking!" the Yarvannet soldier ordered imperiously and flourished his sword yet again in Brierley's face.

Brierley scowled at him impatiently, sensing the cruelty in this youth, the liking for sharp metal and boasting threats. He scowled back at her, now more angry than fearful, and ready for anything as he waved his sword. Brierley pushed the blade aside, irritated by his noisy bravado, then looked at the other two men who stood around her. "Three to arrest a simple midwife?" she said dryly. "I'm flattered."

The sword point leveled at her nose, nearly touching it. "I won't warn you again, mistress. No talking." Brierley shrugged and waited, staring at him. The three men looked at each other uncertainly.

"Maybe we should search her for amulets," muttered the forester. He looked at Brierley nervously, then quickly looked away, unable to meet her eyes. He *is* afraid of me, she realized sadly. He thinks I really am a witch, one of those evil hags in the legend. He protects his daughter in this. Well, she thought bleakly, there is honor in that.

She looked beyond the man at the houses, the neat-kept yards, the edge of distant forest along the rooftops. And yet—all these years among them, healing them, caring for them, and he so easily believes such evil of me.

"Amulets?" Revil's man asked, obviously confused. He was a muscular young man, too stocky for comfort in his body mail and tight green tunic, and he looked familiar to Brierley. With a start, she suddenly recognized Jared, and saw him smile as she blinked at him in surprise. "Hullo, Brierley," he said softly, pleased that she knew him. "What's going on?"

"Lord Bartol said his amulet held her off," the forester said. He gestured at Brierley. "Maybe she uses them, too, to work her—" He stopped as Jared stared at him. "Well, it's possible," he said stubbornly.

"Amulets?" Jared scoffed, then laughed aloud. Brierley rolled her eyes drolly and Jared saw it. He put on a hasty scowl, belatedly remembering his soldier's duty. "The earl has questions, Mistress Mefell," he said sternly. "And Count Revil wants to see you, too. You healed that groom boy in Yarvannet last week, didn't you?" Brierley crossed her arms and said nothing, earning herself a frown a bit more genuine. "They say you don't go to Tiol often. Why is that?" Brierley clamped her lips tighter. "Oh, Ocean's waves," Jared said, exasperated, "you can talk if you want. Are you really a witch like Captain Bartol says?"

"You expect me to admit it if I am?" she asked incredulously.

"Well, uh, I suppose not." Jared shrugged, then laughed

shortly. "But Earl Melfallan wants to see you, and the count said to bring you, so we must."

"Are you asking her *permission*?" demanded the Yarvannet soldier. "What kind of arrest is this?"

"One deserving of the healing she has given Amelin and Natheby," Jared retorted. "This isn't your town, Shay, it's hers and mine—and we aren't as high and mighty here as you Tiol sorts about commoner rights." He shot a glance at the forester, who had the grace to look abashed. "She's only been accused, and that by a northerner, a duke's man who has no proper business accusing our folk in Yarvannet. Nothing's been proven. Besides, I know Brierley. She's no witch."

"And maybe she's turned your mind with her shari'a arts," Shay accused. "That's what Captain Bartol said she tried to do to him—but a highborn lord isn't as easily seduced as you, it seems." He gestured with his blade. "Stand aside, Jared," he ordered.

"I'm in charge here," Jared protested. "Count Revil said—"

"Not anymore, you're not, not when she's obviously turned your will against common sense. Stand aside!" The man stepped forward and jerked Brierley off balance, then shoved his face close to hers. "I'm not as easy to turn, witch. And you'll be sorrier than you know if you try. And *my* orders to you are to shut up." He pushed her ahead of him on down the street, then shoved her again as she staggered, making her drop her herb bag. As she bent to pick it up, Shay kicked the bag out of reach. "Leave that alone," he ordered. Biting her lip, Brierley obeyed.

Shay marched her down the lane, Jared and the forester following hastily after them, then hurried her through the town toward the wharf. They walked quickly enough to attract attention from the people they passed. A few followed, but Shay ignored the questions they called to him—and thereby drew more along until over a dozen townfolk followed their party, hurrying to keep up with the pace that Shay set.

"What's the matter?" she heard someone say behind her. "Isn't that the young midwife, Alarson's stepdaughter?"

"Yes, it is. What's the matter? Is she being arrested? Hey, there, soldiers! Wait up! *Jared*! What's going on here?"

Shay seized Brierley's arm and pulled her sharply left into the street that fronted the wharf. A small single-masted ship bobbed at the central piers, ready for sailing, Melfallan's pennant at its masthead. Their footsteps rang hollowly as they walked onto the wharf timbers, still followed by the townfolk who called their questions. At the ship's side, Shay whirled and faced the crowd. "Get back to your business!" he shouted. "This doesn't concern you!"

"What has she done?" a man in baker's dress shouted back angrily. "You can't just haul her off like that. How are we to know if this is proper? What goes on here?"

Several others in the crowd added their own angry voices and one shook his fist, though likely most hardly knew Brierley by more than face or name: Bartol had stirred up more than he thought in Revil's quiet towns, both bywaters accustomed to their genial lord and impatient with more arrogant nobility, especially the duke's troublemakers. Four men in front stepped onto the wharf and advanced down the planks, their faces determined, for all they were unarmed against soldiers. Several others followed after them.

Shay drew his sword and laid its point against Brierley's throat, then stared down into her face. "I know it's you doing this," he said with menace. "You've drawn the crowd along with us—to make them riot? I'll slice your throat before you get your rescue, witch." His face contorted and Brierley shrank from him as the sword point actually pricked her throat.

"I'm not doing anything!" she protested. "I'm not!"

"Get hold of yourself, Shay!" Jared knocked Shay's blade aside with his hand, then shoved Brierley backward out of sword range. Shay lunged after her and the two men grappled.

Brierley retreated quickly to the edge of the wharf. She looked to either side, tempted to run, then gasped as Shay wrenched Jared off balance, throwing him down hard on the wharf. As Shay raised his sword, the crowd hastened forward, a growl rising from a dozen throats. Shay hesitated, perhaps not knowing himself what he intended, his eyes wild as the crowd came at him, pounding down the wharf. Quickly,

Brierley stepped forward and seized hard on Shay's wrist, then forced down his arm with an effort.

"This stops," she said levelly. "This stops now. You will not harm my folk."

She twisted his wrist hard and winced with his pain, then heard the clang of the blade on the wharf. She released the Yarvannet man and stepped back, then calmly turned and walked the remaining few yards to the ship. She turned again to face the crowd.

"I have been summoned by Earl Melfallan," she called to them. "I will go to Tiol." She spread her hands, pleading with them. "Go home now. It's all right."

The Amelin folk hesitated uneasily, but a few at the back turned and walked off the wharf, followed by others who cast several backward glances at the ship, each muttering to his neighbor. When she saw all were truly leaving, Brierley stepped into the ship, nodded shortly to the wide-eyed pilot and his ship's mate, and sat down on a seat plank by the railing.

Fool, she thought ruefully. You could have run. But where? She bowed her head. Fool. But at least it had its drama, here at the end of things.

She heard the thud of bootsteps on the wharf alongside, then felt the ship move as Shay, then Jared, clambered aboard. The forester hung back, hesitating, then turned and hurried after the crowd. "Cast off," Jared called to the pilot. "We sail to Tiol!"

"You aren't coming," Shay protested. "Count Revil said—"

"If the count were here," Jared retorted angrily, "he'd agree. I'm making sure she makes it to Yarvannet Castle, the crazy way you're acting, Shay. Shoving her around, putting a sword to her throat, *killing* her in front of everyone? Have you lost your senses?" As Shay opened his mouth, Jared took a warning step toward him. "Shut up and put it away, or Ocean help me, I'll deck you for good!" Shay flushed and hesitated, then stomped away toward the front of the ship.

As the ship's pilot cast off his lines and took his station at the tiller, Jared sat down by Brierley and glowered at Shay.

The ship's mate shook out the sail and the small ship drifted away from the wharf, then heeled slightly as the rudder bit into the water, turning the ship into the wind. They gathered speed, bobbed up and down on a large swell, then steadied on course out of Amelin's harbor.

"Don't push it too much," Brierley murmured to Jared, too low for the others to hear. "You'll be tainted by what has seized on me."

"You wouldn't let me defend you when we were children," he answered gruffly, "but I'll defend you now, Brierley, whether you like it or not. Oh, don't look so worried. I can take care of myself." Jared crossed his arms and relaxed against the rail, his feet braced on the planking against the sway of the ship as he kept his eyes on Shay.

"Don't, I beg you."

He glanced sharply at her, and she bowed her head, hiding her face with her hat brim, saying nothing more. Silently, she and Jared sat together by the railing as the small ship steered out of Amelin harbor, heading north toward the distant headland. Twice Shay started back toward them, then retreated hastily when Jared got to his feet each time, his hand on his sword hilt in warning. Finally Shay gave it up and sat glumly on a coil of hemp in the bow, watching the ship move gracefully through the water.

As they rounded the headland, Brierley watched a sea lark dip and spin above the masthead, then plunge into the water ahead of the ship, catching a fish. The lark rose, a tiny sliver of silver in its talons, and spun away toward the high cliff, flashing bright wings in the sunlight. The Daystar's light glinted off the sea, braiding itself into a delicate pattern of foam and flashing water, a heaving watery carpet that stretched to the wide horizon. The world seems so alive today, she thought distractedly, bright silver and cool blues, alive.

Mother Ocean,
Daughter Sea,
Life unending,
Life to me. . . .

Brierley folded her hands and bowed her hat brim low.

Fool.

A half-hour later, the ship sailed into Tiol Harbor and anchored at the wharfside beneath the lee slope and its array of noblemen's houses. A sergeant with grizzled hair and hard blue eyes stood waiting on the wharf with a half-dozen soldiers in the earl's blue and gray livery, and took custody of Brierley as she stepped off the ship onto the planking. "She's expected," the sergeant growled, glancing sourly at Brierley. He dismissed both Shay and Jared with a curt nod, waving them away. "You're dismissed, both of you."

Shay took himself off without a glance backward, but Jared stubbornly followed Brierley and the guards toward the winding cliffside stair at the end of the dock. When Jared began to climb the steps after them, the sergeant turned irritably and again gestured Jared toward the ship, his manner giving no quarter. "You're dismissed, I said."

"I was sent by Count Revil," Jared protested. "I have to report to the count—and to Earl Melfallan, too!" Jared lacked the guile to bring off the lie well, and the sergeant scowled fiercely at the earnest young man.

"So report to the portmaster," the sergeant growled. "Master Ennis will send on your report to the lords if he thinks it worthy." The sergeant's tone placed no value whatsoever in Jared's reports or opinions or any other aspect of Jared's person, and obviously assumed Ennis would think the same.

"Is Count Revil here at Tiol?" Jared asked desperately.

"He is." His finger stabbed at Brierley. "Because of *her*, as you can well guess."

"Then I must report directly to Count Revil. It is my duty." Jared glared at the sergeant, daring him to say otherwise. When the sergeant hesitated, Jared stamped up the stairsteps to face the castle sergeant squarely, feet set apart and his hand on his sword hilt. "I have my duty, Sergeant, as binding as yours."

The sergeant harrumphed, then gave it up with a shrug. "Come along, then," he said condescendingly. "Hardly be me to deny a man his *duty*." He barked a laugh and turned away.

Jared gave Brierley a triumphant look, then hesitated as she frowned another warning. Why wouldn't he listen? Whyever Jared chose to champion her, she couldn't fathom—or perhaps she could. Perhaps he had forgiven her long ago without her knowing, and so mended what she had broken. Jared set his jaw defiantly again, stubborn about her cautions, and she smiled at him, and saw his eyes light in response. "Well, there then," he said with a satisfied nod. He gestured grandly to the sergeant with his hand, motioning for the sergeant and his soldiers to proceed up the stairs, as if Jared had the authority for such ordering.

The sergeant gave him a sour look, but let it be. "Move on, men!" he barked.

With Jared following closely behind, Brierley walked up the stair with the soldiers, surrounded on each side by the wink of chain mail, clanking swords, and blank expressions she could not read, her witch-sense still as muted as all this morning. Had it deserted her again? Strange that Yanna's healing might be the last she would know of it, of the gift that made all the world alive for her. Her heart thumped with fear: was this the end, brought down on her by kindness to a child?

At the top of the stair, the Yarvannet soldiers reached the castle road she had walked some days before and tramped onward, their sergeant parting the flow of traffic with imperious gestures. Folk stopped and stared, then talked worriedly among themselves. Who is she? they asked each other. What has she done? The sergeant ignored them loftily.

Yes, oh, yes, Brierley thought. What have I done? She struggled to remain calm.

They marched her across the bridge and past the gate guard and down another descending tunnel to a latticed gate. The sergeant then dismissed half his soldiers back to the wharf and brought out an iron key, then worked it in the gate lock. The gate swung open with a metal groan, and he curtly motioned Brierley into the courtyard beyond.

"Wait here!" he told Jared and the remaining soldiers, then grasped Brierley's arm and pulled her roughly after him through the gate.

"Hey!" Jared called, but the sergeant slammed the gate in his face, then dared him with a look to push his wishes any further. "Wait here, I said!"

Brierley and the sergeant walked past another gate and down a stairway, then turned left and left again to a metal door with a grille and another key plate and a single torch lamp to the side. The air was damp and cold, with a scent of salt in the unseen draft. As the door swung open, the sergeant shoved Brierley into the small room beyond. "And *you* wait here."

The door crashed shut. She heard the sergeant's bootsteps recede up the corridor, leaving her alone in the semidarkness.

She stood still and waited for her eyes to adjust to the gloom, then picked out the faint shadows of the straw flooring, the cracked stone of the cell walls. Water dripped somewhere nearby, and there was a smell of mold. She reached out her hand and touched the short bars of the door grille, then felt her way around the four walls, measuring the size of the room. On the third wall, her knee bumped against a low cot and she fingered the thin mattress on top of it, then finished her circuit of the room, ending again at the door. Cautiously, she looked out the grille into the corridor, but saw no one.

Through the stone of the cell floor, she sensed the faint vibration of waves on rock as the sea beat against the castle's foundation. A dungeon, then. Well, she'd known Yarvannet Castle had a dungeon, and likely had several dungeons of differing degree. A prisoner's fault was ranked by how deeply the earl buried him in stone. Perhaps one might have hope, a slight hope but a hope, if one's dungeon cell had the courtesy of a lamp's light outside and a breath of the clean sea air from a few floors above. She curled her fingers around one of the grille's bars and leaned against the door, its metal cool against her cheek.

This isn't quite what I expected, she thought, tempted by that tentative hope of light and air—for all it was foolish to hope anything. Her books had filled her with a dread of the mob that tore a witch apart when they knew what she was, of the hue and cry when lords hunted a witch through the forest, the dogs baying wildly, the horses screaming, ending a woman's life with a lance-thrust through the heart. Once she was known, her books said, a witch died violently, so great was the fear that drove the folk, so great the fury of the High Lords. The Natheby wharfside crowd had panicked merely because Bartol cried *A witch among you!* She had believed her books, although not enough to be prudent, not enough to be safe. But where were the hounds? Where was the mob?

Instead she had been calmly marched off to Melfallan's dungeon, defended by the crowd she had always dreaded, even championed by one of the soldiers sent to seize her. The world spins, she thought. She pressed her cheek against the metal door and closed her eyes, listening to her own slow breaths, the beating of her heart.

Believe, Thora had said.

Believe? Can I believe, right to the end? Or will they wait until I lose myself and cry out that I don't believe, not anymore, then kill me? She walked to the cot to sit down, then covered her face with her hands.

This part I did expect: I expected to be this afraid, when it came.

5

Brierley waited through slow hours, cut off from the daylight and the two suns' slow movement across the zenith to their setting, from the cool touch of the wind, the ever-present sounds of the forest and sea she had known all her life. Toward evening, or so she guessed it was, a guard brought her water and a bowl of stew, shoving the jug and plate through the door and leaving in a stamp of boots and jingling keys. She ate slowly, then lay down on the cot, trying to think of nothing whatsoever.

She was half-asleep when they came for her. She started up as the door crashed open and lifted herself to one elbow, blinking dazedly against the flare of the lantern and the shadowed forms beyond the door. She saw three guards in Melfallan's blue-and-silver livery, each in helmets and gauntlets, long broadswords on their belts, the harsh shine of mail on foot and breast and head. "Come, mistress," one ordered harshly, raising the lantern higher to see her face. "Earl Melfallan will see you now."

Brierley rose quietly and shook out the wrinkles from her skirt, then walked through the cell door. The three guards stepped back a pace, their eyes glittering from the eyeholes of their helmets, then positioned themselves to either side of her and behind. She walked slowly up the corridor, not allowing them to hurry her in her fatigue, and sensed their impatience—and dread—as her witch-sense flickered suddenly.

(. . . *she looks harmless enough*) came a random thought. She sighed and watched the stone flagging approach her feet in their steady measure, her shoes moving back and forth beneath her skirt hem. At the end of the hall, she lifted her skirts slightly and climbed the winding staircase upward to the left, the guards following.

"That way," a guard growled as she turned the wrong way at the upper landing. Obediently, she turned in the indicated direction and continued her long walk, her eyes still bent on the floor. The guards said nothing more to her. Torchlight threw stark shadows at measured intervals, counted by the flagstones that stretched before her, another long series of steps, another hallway. Measure and measure, with each breath, each thought, each beat of her heart.

At the top of another stair and another turning, the guards brought her into a large brightly lit hall ablaze with torches and richly-colored tapestries on the walls. On a long dais along the far wall sat an array of four lords, Earl Melfallan with Count Revil at his right, Landreth and Captain Bartol on his left. She saw Bartol whisper something to Lord Landreth, and Landreth slowly nod his head. A flicker then, of Landreth's dark mind, of Bartol's quick and eager ambition, as quickly gone.

Other impressions flashed at her, too quick to catch any true sense, then vanished, a few from the lords at the dais, others from the several noble ladies who sat in a railed gallery on the right side. Lesser noblemen and high castle stewards stood near the walls, talking casually in low voices behind their hands.

Captain Bartol bent again and whispered in Landreth's ear, making much of his connection to that sour lord in front of Melfallan's court. On that day in Natheby, she remembered, Bartol had bragged to Brierley of his noble blood, trying to impress her with his bastard connection to Tejar's house, the duke's confidence in him, the duke's favor: his noble birthright might gain Bartol a role here as judge as well as witness, though it seemed hardly fair to herself.

Fair? Could she expect justice here?

In the gallery, Lady Saray and her several ladies sat on

cushioned chairs, bright in their intricate dresses and jewels, fluttering their fans as they talked to each other. Saray, ungainly in her pregnancy but gay in her smile, nodded as another lady bent to say something to her. Saray fluttered her golden fan and nodded at another pleasantry, her pale face serene. Why not? Brierley thought with sudden bitterness. It's not every day one can have such an entertainment, such a fascinating social affair, as the sight of a witch. She felt a stab of anger at Saray, of dull-ached envy and even dislike for this sweet-faced earl's wife. Their eyes met for a moment across the room, and Brierley looked away.

On the other side of the room, a broad staircase led downward to a large banquet hall where servants were busy laying out a meal, their steps quick and light on the lower flagstones. And after the condemning, dinner, where the entertainment could be discussed brilliantly with many a jest and wry joke, as the young ladies flirted coyly with their courtiers, and the dowagers watched benignly as they sipped their soup with silver spoons. Brierley felt her stomach churn with sour acid. A nobleman's life, indeed, she thought, looking at the rich appointments of the hall, the beautiful ladies in the gallery, and the magnificently dressed lords on the dais. A life Marlenda had loved, and had bitterly lost.

I serve those who have only the air to breathe, the simplest things of the world, Thora had cried. What had Thora known of lords to make that division of herself, denying the Allemanii gentry her healing? What noble hauteur, what admiration of themselves, what casual cruelties? Among the nobility, Landreth was not alone in his dark-minded intents: a commoner maid alone on the road wisely fled from any group of dashing noble gentlemen cantering toward her. The laws gave protection to commoner women from rape and other assaults, but the lords enforced the laws. Any maid's protection proved slender if the lords willed it so. Earl Audric had ruled justly, and his grandson, too, in his short months as earl, she had heard. But what had Thora known in her day?

Perhaps this, exactly this, she thought, watching the nobility watch her.

One of the guards took her arm firmly and led her toward

a chair set midway before the panel of lords. As she walked forward, she felt the prick of silent interest as Melfallan's court inspected her—some bemused, others skeptical, a few fearful in their superstition, all confident of their rank and authority, an Allemanii lord's perception of the world that little could dent. Her witch-sense flickered, bringing many impressions. Only Captain Bartol truly dreaded her person—and behind that fear, she sensed another fear. He thinks we're alike! He wonders if he's a witch, too! She nearly stopped short to stare at him, but managed only a slight hesitation in her walk before making that sure betrayal. The captain's eyes flicked toward her, then uncomfortably away. Again he bent toward Landreth, whispering.

As the guard seated her in the chair and bowed low to the lords, then retreated to the doorway, Brierley looked askance at Bartol, wondering. I would know the Blood, I'm sure of it, she thought, although she admitted that particular skill was still untested in any stranger. But I'd expect shari'a marks in the mind that would be known instantly, as my mother had, as I have. She looked down at her shoes, hiding her face behind her hat brim, her thoughts in a turmoil.

Had Bartol met a shari'a in the north, enough to frighten him of a witch's touch? When? Where? In Duke Tejar's capital, Darhel? Did Jocater come from Darhel, so many years ago? Her mother had come from the north, and Darhel lay north. A longing as keen as a sharp pain wrenched at her vitals, to sail to Darhel and search throughout the city, looking for one other witch's touch, one who would welcome her, not fear her. The touch of only one other shari'a—she would ask nothing more than that.

"Brierley Mefell," Melfallan said. A whisper sighed through the room from the assembly, and all grew still.

Brierley took a deep breath and raised her head to look at him. He sat proudly in his gilded chair, his tunic richly embroidered and finespun, a silver circlet binding his blond hair. In the torchlight, he seemed older than his true years, weighted down by his High Lord's dignity. What did he feel to see her brought before him? Dismay, she realized. But why? At the sight of Melfallan's troubled face, her dread eased a little with a small stab of hope.

He had recognized her as she sat down, and now questions warred in his mind, laced by his surprise and dismay to see her, two emotions he struggled to hide from the hostile lords seated at his left. More imported here than the simple ordeal of a witch, she sensed: Melfallan saw danger to himself and Yarvannet in this meeting for reasons she did not understand, although the direction seemed to lie in the duke's malice. Why? Why should my fate threaten Yarvannet? Why threaten *him*?

Yet, to his compliment, she realized, his concern was mostly for her, Brierley Mefell, a young commoner girl of his cousin's lands, as if that simple fact were enough reason for any care, all effort. How can that be? she wondered, amazed. He hardly knows me. Are lords truly like this? Her witch-sense flickered like a guttering flame, tossing light into far shadows, then waning almost to extinction: she tried to concentrate on Yarvannet's earl, ignoring the distractions of her overtired mind.

"I am Brierley Mefell," she said softly, lifting her chin.

Landreth scowled and lifted a finger. "You will speak only to answer questions," he growled, and twitched his eyebrows. "Nothing else. We'll have no impassioned women's speeches here."

She felt herself bridle at the arrogance of Landreth's look, the pride and indifference for all beneath his rank, and would have liked to give him cause to doubt such certitude. Brierley clenched her teeth, forcing away that most imprudent reaction. She might have prepared herself better, she realized, by associating more with noble folk. It is easier to abide what is expected.

Melfallan's eyes flicked back to her and saw more, perhaps, than she wished, and knew it for certain when Melfallan spoke. "This is a place of *my* justice," he announced firmly. "And any judgment in Yarvannet shall be a just judgment. Mistress Mefell will be permitted to speak in her defense, as is her right as commoner in my lands." Count Revil nodded a vigorous agreement, and shot an angry look at Landreth.

Landreth flushed at the public reproof, but chose to lean back casually in his chair, then nod an indifferent concession. "As you say, my lord earl. It has always been so."

"Maybe not always," Melfallan said wryly, "but it will be here tonight. You are accused, Brierley Mefell, of shari'a witchery by Captain Bartol. How do you answer?"

"Witchery, my lord?" she hedged, knowing that the battle for life began in that simplest of questions. "What does Captain Bartol mean by that?"

"You *know* what I mean, witch!" Bartol shouted furiously, half-rising from his chair.

"Sit down, Captain!" Melfallan said sharply, and waited until Bartol complied. Then he continued, his voice smooth and even, carefully controlled. "The accused has asked you to clarify your charge. This *is* the woman you have accused?"

"Yes!" Bartol looked at Brierley with open distaste.

"Then state what you mean," Melfallan ordered inexorably. Bartol crossed his arms, his chin set outward in careful defiance. "In the proper court, I shall," he declared.

"As I have explained to you, Captain," Melfallan said tightly, "this *is* the proper court. I am earl of Yarvannet and this young woman lives in my lands. She has her commoner right to ask justice of her own lord, not yours. Our laws protect the accused, not the accuser."

"Duke Tejar is *your* lord also, Earl Melfallan," Bartol shot back in open challenge, "both your lord and hers. The justice lies with *him* to decide any matter of witchery. Only the duke can judge a witch. That is the law."

"That is *not* the law," Melfallan shot back. "My justiciar and I have reviewed the texts, and Sir James agrees with me. Any High Lord may judge a witch, if she is found within his lands."

"The duke will agree with me," Bartol said proudly. "There are other precedents."

"Indeed?" Melfallan asked with sarcasm. "When did you research the issue? Do you carry a law library aboard your ship?"

"I speak only what everyone knows," Bartol retorted. "The duke deals with witches, not the lesser lords." He sniffed with contempt. Lord Landreth hid a smirk and toyed with the golden fringe on his sleeve.

Why is my undoing a benefit to Landreth? Brierley wondered, sensing again the connection between Melfallan's two opponents. And why opponents? Landreth's ambition she could understand, but why did Captain Bartol contend with Yarvannet's earl? By the duke's order? By Landreth's prodding? Bartol had dined many times with Landreth, the rockfisher had said, and perhaps they shared a temperament, a common ambition. But for what? An earl's circlet? Is that why Bartol now speaks so contemptuously to Melfallan, rudely enough to drop the mouths of half the audience? Did Bartol think himself invulnerable? *That* highly favored by the duke? She looked askance at Bartol, wishing her witch-sense could pluck deeper knowledge from his devious mind.

"It is the law," Captain Bartol repeated smugly.

Melfallan's scowl had deepened. "In Yarvannet, Captain, I am all the lord that is necessary for my own court. This young woman is here in *my* court now, as is her legal right. I don't believe this young girl is a witch. There are no shari'a: Duke Rahorsum killed them all centuries ago."

"That is for Duke Tejar to decide," Bartol declared.

Melfallan smiled thinly, then leaned back in his chair. "Let the duke first decide if he even wishes to hear the matter. He may not. A duke is busy with many pressing affairs." He shrugged casually and glanced at his wife in the gallery. "In any event, until my lady wife comes to childbed, I cannot travel to Darhel—and all of mine have the right to be defended by their lord, even in the duke's court, as I shall defend Brierley Mefell." A low murmur of surprise slipped around the room, and Bartol's face froze in open astonishment.

Count Revil smiled benignly at Brierley from the dais. "As shall I," he declared in his high tenor, and nodded vigorously enough to make his hat plume waggle. "I opposed this arrest from the start, and I've already had delegations from my Amelin and Natheby folk, protesting on her sake." He lifted his chin and glared at Captain Bartol. "As her count, I will defend her even if others don't, and I don't believe she's a witch, either. There are no witches." Revil gave Bartol another look of active dislike. "And if that costs me a few shiploads of Darhel wares, Captain," he added loftily, "bear them away." Revil waved his hand airily.

Landreth's eyes shifted from Melfallan to Revil, but he carefully hid his fury behind a bland face. Behind his mask, Landreth was raging, cursing Melfallan, whom he despised, hating the small smattering of applause that had followed Revil's defense. (*. . . and you, too, Revil, when it's time*). Landreth had not expected this defense of me, Brierley thought, surprised herself by Revil's intervention. Or am I a pawn even for Amelin's pleasant count? Where are the arrogant lords I expected? Why do they speak up for me, a commoner midwife of no account? The High Lords did not defend shari'a: they burn them. My books say so. And the Amelin folk have protested to Revil? For my sake?

She straightened in her chair, her eyes intent on Earl Melfallan's face. He gazed back at her solemnly, without hostility, without disdain. Melfallan liked his commoner folk, often more than he liked the nobility: that, too, stood in her favor, for he was inclined to like her as well. To her surprise, she realized that most of the highborn folk in the room wished her well, although thoughts were pricked with noble pride and a self-conscious regard of rank.

The vainest of the noblemen thought her not pretty enough for interest and looked elsewhere, but none truly believed her a witch. Witch? Ridiculous. Several of the ladies seated near Saray disdained her homespun dress, her simple hat, her small person, a disdain Brierley could bear easily, she decided. Among them all, only Bartol looked at her with open hatred, for Landreth hid his feelings with the playacting he had perfected to hide his cruelty. She watched as Bartol again nudged Landreth and whispered low.

"Until we can petition the duke, then," Melfallan said. He sat back, lounging in his chair, and flicked his eyes over the room. "Until then, I release Mistress Mefell on my parole, upon her word not to leave Yarvannet until I have heard officially from Darhel. Do I have your word, mistress?"

"Yes, my lord," Brierley said quietly. Her heart began pounding in her chest. He would set her free?

"Then go peaceably, Mistress Mefell." Melfallan dismissed her with a casual wave of his hand. "My justiciar, Sir James, will summon you when you are needed again."

Brierley rose and swayed uncertainly on her feet, then blinked as the many emotions loose in the room swept through her like a high-beach wave, gently coursing up the sands to expire like a rime of vanishing foam. Free? As she hesitated, Melfallan nodded at her calmly, then leaned to talk behind his hand to Count Revil. Brierley turned toward the doorway to the stair and took a step, but no guard reached to seize her. She took another, then glanced back at Melfallan. The surge of voices rose in the room, a pleasant murmur, and several of the ladies had stood.

Free!

A hushed shiver of whispers followed her as she walked toward the doorway. At the archway, a guard stepped forward from the shadows of the hall and grasped her elbow firmly. "Wait," he muttered, his eyes very hard behind his metal visor.

"But Earl Melfallan has bid me go," she said, protesting, pulling vainly at his grip.

"You will still wait." He drew her aside into the shadows of the archway and stood with her, his fingers digging into the flesh of her arm. Landreth's man, she realized, for all he wore Melfallan's livery. She sighed and bowed her head, a dull throb of panic beating in her breast.

I could slip his hold and run, she thought. I know the way out of the castle: it lies in his mind and now in mine. I could escape. But a slender trust in Melfallan held her, that through him she might still escape full discovery and the hue and cry that would follow. Flight would only confirm her guilt, and she would not throw away Melfallan's parole so easily.

I cannot run. Not yet.

The noble folk talked and laughed among themselves as they slowly left the room, descending the long stairway to the banquet hall. Brierley lifted her head as Lady Saray passed by her, and was caught up by the eddy of sweet temper and patience that the lady carried with her. She watched as Melfallan's lady followed her husband and other lords and ladies across the room, walking gracefully on the stone floor with a swishing of long skirts. Saray reached the staircase to the next room, with Lord Landreth closely behind her. As Saray's foot swung forward to descend the first step downward, Brierley gasped as Landreth trod deliberately on the skirt fabric of her train.

Saray cried out in surprise as she lost her balance and began to fall. Landreth made no attempt to catch her, none, and no other lord or lady was near enough to catch as Saray fell forward, landing hard on the stone risers and tumbling helplessly downward. Saray's scream cut through the air, ending abruptly as her head struck stone hard. The pain exploded through Brierley's own skull, and she knew instantly the injury was mortal. *No!* Recklessly, Brierley wrenched away from Landreth's soldier and ran forward.

At the base of the stairs, Saray lay crumpled in a heap of satin and fine linen. The noble folk rushed back toward her, Earl Melfallan in the lead. He knelt beside his wife, his hand hesitating as he stared wide-eyed at the spreading pool of blood beneath Saray's head. A low moan of shock burst from his mouth, and he looked wildly around at everyone, unable to believe.

Brierley descended the stairs in a rush, then knelt beside Saray. Gently, she turned Saray on her side, probing the skull wound with her fingers. Already the injury had slowed Saray's breathing, depressing her body functions nearer the cold stillness of death. In the distance, the Beast uncoiled and came at them with great speed, its many tentacles flailing, its single eye blazing with an unholy triumph.

"No!" Brierley shrieked at the Beast, unmindful of the noble folk that surrounded her, of Earl Melfallan beside her. "You shall not have her, Beast! I do not permit!"

She threw up her head, defying the Beast, and it hesitated, its malevolence beating upon her. It hesitated, but it did not retreat. She had a little time still, but too many distractions in this crowd. The Beast was too near.

Brierley took a ragged breath and turned to Melfallan, who

was staring wide-eyed at her outburst. "Take her to her chamber," Brierley commanded, her voice ringing through the hall. "I will not permit her death."

Numbly, Melfallan gestured to the guards and together they bore Saray up the stairs. Brierley followed them across the audience chamber to an outside corridor and a stairway leading upward. A burst of surprised talk broke out behind her, and many of the court followed Melfallan and his stricken lady.

I serve—Brierley thought in despair as she hurried behind the guards and their burden, knowing that she might have thrown away herself in this madness. What was Lady Saray to her? What did it matter that she die and her child with her? At the price of Brierley's life? Who set such balances of lives, one for the other? The Beast uncoiled its limbs and moved closer, and grimly she shook away all thought of herself.

You shall not have her, she told the Beast fiercely, hating its foul touch as she had always hated it. At whatever cost, I will not let you have her. Balance lives as you will, wreak your fortunes. You shall not have her!

The soldiers carried Lady Saray into a finely appointed chamber high in the eastern tower, then laid her gently on the wide curtained bed. Two of Saray's ladies hovered anxiously outside the bedchamber, whispering urgently to each other. As Brierley moved toward them, they retreated hastily, fear on their faces. With a few brisk steps, Brierley pursued them to the doorway and saw them hesitate again, looking back. "I am not what the legends say. If you love your lady, help me."

The elder, a tall and dignified woman in her middle years, clasped her hands in front of her lacy bodice and steeled herself. "What shall we do?" Her companion gave a breathless squeak of dismay and received a sharp jab from an elbow. "Mistress?" the older woman prompted.

"Have you helped a midwife?"

"Yes."

"Then bring what you have brought to your midwife for other births. She is too close to term for such a fall." The older woman plucked at her companion's sleeve and bustled her off down the corridor. In the distance, Brierley could hear a stamping of boots on the stairway as some of the nobles arrived in the tower hallway, Melfallan for certain, others with him. She turned to one of the guards who had carried Saray and pointed at him. He promptly recoiled in fear. "Ocean abounding, man!" she said in exasperation. "Where is your sense? How can you serve our lord and lack a brain?"

He stiffened and glared. "I have a brain, thank you."

"Then use it and find the castle's midwife." She spread her hands. "Please, sir—for your lady's sake." After a moment, he nodded, his dark eyes glittering behind his visor.

"And me?" the other asked.

"Stand guard outside, if you please, until Earl Melfallan comes." Then, as the one guard hurried away and the other took station in the anteroom, Brierley turned and approached the bed to tend Saray. Gently she straightened Saray's body and bent over her, her fingers probing the bloody head wound. Through her direct contact with Saray, flesh to flesh, she felt the first convulsive birth shudder and slipped her hand to Saray's abdomen, testing the age of the fetus. It was too soon, a month too early, but such a child could live if its breath were assisted. It was a patterning she had taught to the family in other early births. Was there any damage to the child itself from Saray's hard fall? She probed deeper, and felt the Beast's attention on the infant boy as well.

Neither, she swore to herself fiercely. With gentle fingers, she loosened Saray's upper garment and moved Saray's limbs to a still more comfortable position, then returned her hands to the skull fracture. The depression lay low on the skull over the life centers: she concentrated, patterning her own breathing to Saray as support. *Saray, my lady,* she called, but received no response, nothing in the darkness of Saray's profound unconsciousness. She probed gently, finding the edges of the fractured bone, then traced the tear in the scalp that bled steadily onto the pillow, staining it bright red. Saray could not afford much blood loss with the birth impending; the laceration should be stitched. Distractedly, Brierley looked toward the door. Where was the midwife?

She heard a stamping of feet and then the rising murmur of voices raised in argument in the anteroom, a noise she heard only as a crashing of heavy surf on the rocks, without meaning. She shook her head angrily, trying to push away her distraction. The emotions outside the chamber beat at her, clamoring: Landreth was there, arguing with Melfallan, his purposes twisted—and Bartol and too many others, all contending. As Saray's two ladies approached them in the hallway, hurrying with their arms filled with cloths and a steaming jug of water, Captain Bartol abruptly stopped them, and another argument joined the loud contention.

"Earl Melfallan!" Brierley cried out. Melfallan's tall figure stepped into view in the doorway. "Remove your lords, I beg you."

Melfallan looked in anguish at his wife, then glanced around as voices clamored at him again from behind, demanding, pushing, high with alarm and confusion. As he looked back again, hesitating, he saw the child move visibly beneath Saray's clothing and his eyes filled with panic.

Brierley shoved herself away from the bed and swept into the anteroom outside the chamber, then glared at the nobles assembled there, not sparing Bartol or Landreth. Behind her, Saray's life flickered again, stalked by the Beast as it moved beneath deep waves.

"I am the last!" she shouted passionately at the angry faces, defying them all. "The last sure flame! And neither you nor you nor *you*," she said, her finger jabbing especially at Bartol, "shall stop me from saving her! Get out! You can kill her with your arguing as surely as her fall on stone. *Out*!"

"The healer asks," Melfallan said loudly. "Do it!" He gestured angrily, waving the lords backward.

"My earl!" Landreth protested. "Surely you can't—"

"Out!" Melfallan cut him off with a chopping gesture of his hand, his eyes hard. "I saw a boy with a ruptured bowel healed before my eyes: I know how hard your blow landed, Landreth. Yet it was nothing afterward, nothing at all, which was a wonder." He turned to Brierley and seized her hand. "Save my lady, mistress," he pleaded, without care for his pride in front of the others. "Hang the cost!"

"Cost?" Brierley looked up into his anguished eyes, then laid her other hand gently on his chest, quieting him. "There is no cost, gentle lord, not to you, not to her. Give trust that none shall be harmed. I promise it."

He looked down into her face for a long moment, then visibly relaxed. "What do you need, mistress?"

"What the two ladies bear—and your midwife."

"You shall have them. Where is Marina?" he shouted, turning toward the corridor.

"My earl!" Lord Landreth protested in a loud voice.

"Get out!" Brierley shouted, whirling toward him. "Or I shall bespell you all, don't think I won't!" As one, every noble person took a step backward in dismay. At another time, it might have amused her, but not now. Brierley threw up her hands in total exasperation. "You idiot lords—"

Then, in the near distance, Brierley heard the Beast begin his roar of triumph as he swept onto the beach. She plunged back into the bedchamber, her hands reaching for Saray. Death came *now* in this healing, not conveniently later in her cave, but *now*, betraying everything with nothing left to conceal. Desperately, Brierley bent over the injured woman, her hands moving restlessly from head to shoulder to belly. *Saray!*

In the darkness of Saray's mind, she heard a slight stirring, the vaguest of movements as Saray sensed the death that came only breaths away. Brierley seized on that acknowledgment and supported it, like a breath stirring a candle to a brighter flame.

Saray, she crooned in her mind, calling deeply into the swirling mists of Saray's darkness. *My gentle lady: hear me!*

(*Who?*) Saray's thought stirred vaguely and felt the pain, recoiled from its harsh beat.

Meet the pain, for the sake of your life, for your child.

(*Who?*) The thought shuddered and blew itself away to fragments, taking Brierley with her into Saray's darkness, to a distant beach where the Beast sought their lives.

On that beach, Brierley crouched on the cold sand with Saray in her arms. A breeze heavy with the smell of sea grass and fish blew strongly into their faces, icy cold in its touch. Before them, the ocean's waves moved sluggishly, dull gray in color to match a leaden sky. One by one, the waves surged and spent themselves on the sand, shirring as they splashed to a wide fan of thin foam racing upward toward them. Brierley lay Saray gently on the sand and stood upright, facing the sea, the cold wind whipping at her clothing. In a convulsive movement, she stripped off her hat and let it fly on the wind.

"You shall not take her!" she cried in defiance, her words torn away by the air. "I do not permit!"

Beyond the breakers, a massive shape stirred its own great wave, moving parallel to the beach, its pallid flesh tinted gray and green by the concealing water. The Beast dove deeper, vanishing from sight, then raised itself again, its malevolent eye watching her from a fathom deep. Slowly, it fluttered its long appendages and rose still further until it rested just beneath the watery surface. It suspended, floating effortlessly. Its low growl shuddered through the water.

"I do not permit!" Brierley shouted, challenging the Beast. She lifted her hand and crafted a sword from the wind, its bright metal gleaming, sharp and true, its silver hilt fitted perfectly to her hand. "I shall kill you, Beast!" She brandished the sword defiantly, making it hiss through the air. "I shall kill you, Death!"

A low rumbling of laughter shook the waves. Lazily, the Beast turned on its side and swam a few yards to the side, sporting in the water. Then, abruptly, it swerved and surged above the water, rushing onto the beach toward them. Brierley stepped over Saray and stumbled toward the Beast, her sword raised high.

"Yaaaaaa!" she screamed as it met her in the shallows, reaching with its limbs. She swung her sword and sliced off one of the coiling tentacles, then swung again and missed, panting. It shifted quickly, nearly surrounded her, but she slipped aside again, striking downward at its noxious flesh.

The Beast surged forward, reaching yet again, his stench belching a poisonous cloud that burned Brierley's body and stole away her breath. She swung again, striking at the Beast, but missed, then nearly fell as a tentacle coiled around her ankle and seized hard. She wrenched herself free in an instant, knowing her own death could lay in that awful touch, then danced out of range, retreating toward Saray. The Beast heaved its body forward onto the beach, following relentlessly.

"Never!" Brierley shouted, whirling her sword. The Beast roared its fury and she met it again, slashing furiously, driving it backward into the waves. Again, it surged onto the beach, forcing her to retreat even closer to Saray; again, she fought it backward, her arms growing leaden with fatigue. She felt hot pain in her chest as the cold sea air tore at her lungs, a gripping convulsion in her bowel as Saray's body twisted in another birth pang. Panting, Brierley stumbled awkwardly over the sand, pursuing the Beast as it retreated back into the water.

The Beast toyed with her, laughing, trying to entice her into deeper water where water could hide a snaking tentacle or a wave's weight could stagger her and tear the blade from her hand. She refused its enticing and waited higher on the beach, the dying waves pulling sand from beneath her shoes and plucking at her skirt hem. As the Beast moved sidewise, she followed, her sword ready; it flipped into a quick turn and swam several yards in the other direction: she followed again. It swam with a burst of speed a dozen yards up the beach and came ashore, trying to outflank her in its effort to reach Saray: she ran forward, cutting off its advance, and drove it back into the sea.

The Beast roared in frustrated rage, slyly tempting her to assume her victory, to be snatched away in those few seconds of inattention. She refused the error and it roared again, then feinted left, then right. It retreated to deeper water, watching her, then rushed forward, then retreated yet again, taunting her.

"I will fight you," she told it, her voice rising strongly above the sound of wave and wind. "Take this sword and I'll make another; take that sword, and a third will come to me from the air. You shall not have her or the child! I do not permit!"

The Beast floated into the deeper waves, its pallid body changing shape as it sank downward. Then, abruptly, it was gone.

Brierley scanned the water anxiously, her sword raised,

then retreated several steps toward Saray before she lowered her blade, wary of the Beast's treachery. She waited, breathing heavily of the painful air, but the Beast did not return. Had she won? Her head throbbed with jagged lightnings, and her arms seemed weighted with heavy nets. Despite her willing otherwise, she sagged to her knees. Her sword fell from useless fingers. Slowly she collapsed full-length beside Saray, the wet gritty sand cold against her cheek, and two unmoving figures lay on the sullen beach. The waves surged uneasily at their fingertips, wetting them with airy foam.

A dark mist swirled around her, and she found herself again in Saray's upper chamber again, leaning weakly on the carved wooden footing of the bed. Several people stood in the room, for what reason she didn't know at first: she looked around herself dazedly, catching flashes of alarm and fear, of herself, for Saray, for the child now being born. A dark-haired midwife of middle years bent over Saray, calling her encouragements as she repositioned Saray's legs and arranged a concealing blanket. The woman bustled to the side to check a steaming basin and white cloths, then came back again with the basin, her actions panicked and too quick, as they both knew better.

Brierley stepped forward and took the basin from the midwife's hands before she dropped it, then set it on the side table. The woman shied backward from her, her plain face filled with apprehension. Was this Marina? Brierley sensed a stolid courage in her, a midwife's courage that met every crisis with calm and strength. Brierley hadn't a clue how she'd behaved in front of these folk when she battled the Beast, but the woman's expression gave some suggestion, that and the sudden tension of the watchers when Brierley moved. One of Saray's other ladies came quickly forward, as if to forestall her. Brierley shook her head at her, then spoke directly to the midwife.

"You have helped many children into the world," she said. "There is no need for hurry; the child will come when it comes," she added, reciting from a text known to them both. The midwife stared at her a moment, then nodded with a quick jerk of her chin. "Marina?" Brierley asked. The woman nodded again. "I have heard well of you."

"And I of you, Brierley Mefell." Marina drew herself up straighter and shook herself slightly. "Above all, a midwife must be calm," she recited from a text Brierley also knew. "Lady Saray's contractions are narrowing quickly."

"First births are sometimes precipitate," Brierley answered, quoting the same text.

They smiled at each other in mutual recognition, and Marina relaxed still further, despite the noblefolk who stared at the both of them from the anteroom. Brierley nodded and turned back to the bed and there met Saray's open eyes, then saw the lady's smile. She bent forward, having to steady herself on the mattress with one hand as she swayed off balance.

"I don't have much left to give, my lady," she said. "You have most of the work now but, then, it's always so in childbirth." Saray's smile widened and she raised her hand and laid it on Brierley's cheek, caressing her lightly. A fine sheen of sweat covered her forehead, the strain obvious in her face—but it was only strain of childbirth. Of the head wound, Brierley sensed nothing left.

"Thank you, mistress," Saray whispered. "I am indebted."

How much had Saray sensed of the beach and her struggle against the Beast? Brierley couldn't tell, but felt the woman's acceptance, even love—and her intense joy as another labor pain seized at her body. Saray pressed her hands against her abdomen, threw back her head, the contraction rippling through her belly. "Arrrr—" she cried, then bit back her scream. She smiled with ecstatic joy, her lips skinned back, her teeth clenched with the pain.

"Ride the wave, my lady," Marina crooned. "Ride through it. Your baby is coming."

With her witch-sense, Brierley probed again for any lingering effect of the head injury and found nothing, as if it had never been. In that same touch, Brierley felt the whole of Saray's quiet life, her love for her lord, the emotional gulf between herself and Melfallan that Saray could not understand, the stillbirths that had brought grief after grief and seemed the easiest blame for Melfallan's distance. "Your baby is coming," Brierley promised gently. "He is being born now."

"Help me, mistress," Saray panted, her eyes fixed on Brierley. Her face contorted again as another contraction seized her. "Help me."

"I will try." Brierley leaned on the carved wood of the bedstead. With a sigh, Brierley bowed her head and rested a little, exquisitely aware of Saray's person and pain, sharing with her the childbirth as if she brought her own child into the world. When Marina lifted the child and slapped its buttocks, it did not cry, and a wave of horror swept through the watchers in the hall.

Saray covered her face with her hands. "No, no! Not again!" she cried out in anguish. "My lord! Melfallan! I'm sorry!"

In the far distance beyond the beach, Brierley heard the Beast's baffled roar, too distant to threaten Saray or her son. "He is alive, Saray!" she insisted. "Not dead!" Saray moaned, not believing, and turned her face into the pillow.

Brierley lifted her hands. "Give him to me, Marina," she ordered. Without hesitation, Marina came to her and gave her the child swaddled in his birthing blanket.

Live, dear son, Brierley urged. She smiled down at the baby, and felt the child move in her arms, kicking gently at the blanket. *Live.* As Brierley looked down at the tiny face, the room faded and re-formed on the distant beach, a beach she knew well, a beach now without dangers. Crooning a soft lullaby, Brierley began to pace the cold sand of that distant beach, Melfallan's son cradled in her arms. *Live, my own.* Dimly, aloft on the cold wind, she heard the infant's first weak cry, distant but clear, then Lady Saray's shriek of joy. The baby kicked vigorously against Brierley's hand, and she laughed in triumph.

Mother Ocean,
Daughter Sea,
In this life of beginnings,
Begin with me.

Brierley paced up and down the bedchamber floor, singing to the boy, and guarded his first breaths, and infused her own strength into him. *I preserve*, she thought in fierce exaltation. *I preserve*. Her witch-sense flickered with future images of this boy, this son, as a stout-legged toddler, as a lean-limbed boy running on the beach, as a young man striding clear-eyed across his father's castle courtyard. Like Gramil, this boy would be much loved.

Believe! Thora had bid her. *Believe!*

Yes, love answers, dear friend. I know it now. And I love you, baby boy.

The baby quieted and soon fell asleep in her arms, and still Brierley paced slowly up and down, crooning her soft lullaby to the sleeping child. She was vaguely aware when Marina briskly ordered the watchers out of the doorway, was conscious that Saray's eyes followed her constantly as she walked. She walked until her feet dragged and her arms grew heavy with the small weight she guarded, walked until Marina gently intervened and took the child away.

The night beyond Saray's windows was full black, the bedchamber lit by a single lamp. Brierley was alone with Marina and Saray, and a deep quiet lay all about them. "Mistress," Marina said, "you must rest now." Brierley looked at Marina stupidly, not comprehending. "Now," Marina said firmly. "I insist." She guided Brierley to a chair and made her sit. "Your task is done, dear Brierley, and you will follow *my* orders now."

"Will I?" Brierley asked vaguely.

"Absolutely. I insist upon it." Marina bent and Brierley felt the press of her lips on her hair. "Now."

With a sigh, Brierley yielded and laid her head on her arm, too exhausted for thinking, and welcomed the darkness that swept down upon her.

6

Melfallan waited in the antechamber to Saray's room. He looked up as he heard footsteps approach the bedchamber door, wondering if his long vigil had finally ended. One of Saray's ladies opened the door, with towels folded neatly over one arm. She curtsied quickly to him and passed through the anteroom, hurrying away on another errand. The door closed and, with a sigh, Melfallan returned to his waiting.

He had sent the other lords away, although Revil and Landreth had protested vigorously, each for their separate reasons. Melfallan chose to wait alone, watching for a glimpse of the inner room whenever someone came in or out. Each time the door had opened and closed, he had seen Brierley walking with the baby in her arms, singing to the child of Mother Ocean and sea larks, of life and stars and the sea's endless voice. Even when the door closed, he still heard the murmuring of her song, light and sweet. Its sound profoundly comforted him, easing troubles, bringing hope. She wove a spell with her voice, a spell of peace and triumph, and of new life. He sat and listened, moved beyond words by the beauty of her spelling, if spell it was.

He sank backward onto the comfortable couch in Saray's anteroom, content to wait. He had needed time to think, now that he knew his son and Saray were safe. Thanks to a young woman, pale and slender, who had battled Death before his eyes and the amazed eyes of a dozen others of his court. A young woman Captain Bartol claimed to be evil. A young woman to whom Melfallan knew Saray and his son owed their lives. He was convinced of it.

He listened to her sweet voice murmuring beyond the door, then closed his eyes wearily. What in the Hells do I do now? he asked himself.

He and Sir James, his justiciar, had scoured the castle library before Brierley's summons to the Great Hall, but found little of substance about the shari'a. The Yarvannet earls had not burned a witch for nearly two hundred years. The earl of that time had tried to provide some fairness in the trial, for the girl was clearly insane. She had mumbled incoherently at the trial, then suffered a palsy fit in her cell and lain unconscious for days, awaking blank-eyed and mute, unable to move one arm. In her ramblings, however, she had claimed responsibility for several recent deaths, including a drowning miles out at sea, and the townspeople had believed it. The plague had struck hard the previous winter, killing nearly a hundred folk in Amelin, and two children had disappeared shortly afterward, almost certainly taken by shire wolves, but the witch was blamed. A farmer's entire stock had mysteriously died, and the girl had been seen wandering near his fields. A merchant died of a heart stoppage, and the girl had pointed her finger at him the week before, or so it was said. In the end, the girl was blamed for every evil that had befallen Yarvannet in two years, and the town clamored for her death. She had no relatives who would claim her, no lord who would speak for her. And so the earl had condemned and burned her. Poor soul.

Most Allemanii scholars dismissed as pure fancy most of the fragmented stories about Witchmere that survived the Great Plague and the civil wars that followed. Much knowledge had been lost in those bitter years, never reclaimed, and the wild tales about the shari'a in the older histories exceeded belief. Control storms? Kill cattle with a wish? Hear a man's inner thoughts? Change to catling form at a wish? Devour *children*? The tales had no sense, only a lingering and sifting malice that could kill the innocent. As those legends might easily kill Brierley Mefell.

If High Lord politics did not kill her first, he realized grimly. Duke Tejar would certainly exploit her as a means to strike at Melfallan. A change of earl in Yarvannet would upset political alliances that had been stable for a generation, but, in that upset, Tejar would find opportunities that Yarvannet's alliances now blocked, opportunities that Tejar might need to insure he died in bed at a ripe old age. The Kobus dukes had always ruled uneasily, with potential rebellion on every side. Both Briding and Airlie had previously fostered ducal houses, and so might rightfully claim the coronet by fact of birth. Both earls had the wealth and armies, assuming sufficient support from other High Lords, to strip the duke of his duke-dom at will, and every duke knew it. It had been done before; it would almost certainly be done again.

Three times since the Founding the ducal coronet had changed noble houses, twice by war, once by murder. Ra-horsum had been the third of the Karlsson dukes, a grandson of Duke Aidan the Founder, but he and his legitimate son had died in the Great Plague. One of Rahorsum's bastards, Bram of Ingal, then claimed the coronet, and the viciousness of his conquest of his own counties, with hundreds of folk executed for imagined crimes, had deservedly earned him the name Bram the Butcher.

Appalled by Bram's slaughter in Ingal, the earls of Mionn and Yarvannet had leagued together and attacked Bram from the south and east. The four years of civil war destroyed what was left of Ingal's trade and dispossessed hundreds of folk, forcing them into banditry to survive, and no road was safe. After Bram was duly caught and executed with grim cere-mony, the earls then chose Count Lutke of Briding as their new duke.

The Lutkes ruled for over a hundred years, until the center of power suddenly shifted east through an earl's treachery. Supported secretly by the Earl of Mionn, the Count of Airlie married a Lutke daughter, then married two sons into the Briding nobility. Then, claiming a need for military exercises, Airlie moved his army into Briding, an excuse no one believed. Trusting that his old friend, the Earl of Mionn, would come to his support, the duke had ridden confidently into battle against his son-in-law, only to have Mionn withhold his soldiers at the critical moment. And so the Lutke house fell, and the Hamelin house began, with Mionn profiting greatly from Hamelin gratitude.

The Hamelins gave the lands six dukes, who ruled peaceably if not particularly well, until Lionel Kobus, the trusted castellan of the last Hamelin duke, murdered the duke in his bed and seized the coronet, then dared the other High Lords to deny his right to it. When the war was over, Lionel was still duke and both earls still kept their circlets, but Tyndale and Lim needed new High Lords, their counts being dead, and their sons with them. Two years later, in an attempt to extinguish the cadet Hamelin house, Lionel invaded Airlie, but failed when the new Count of Tyndale, Lionel's own nephew, changed sides. When everyone had gone home, Lionel had his nephew poisoned, then elevated a gentleman knight of his castle guard, Mourire Courtray, to be the new Count of Tyndale.

Because of that, Melfallan thought gloomily, I'm now an earl. It was all Grandsir's fault.

Count Mourire had marched with Duke Lionel the following spring when the duke attacked Briding, continuing his efforts to eliminate rivals. Lionel's assault came to an abrupt end and a forced hasty retreat when Mionn struck at Ingal from the east. Saray's grandfather, Earl Robert, had tired of the constant warfare since Lionel's accession, with its turmoils and depletion of trade, and so gave the duke an ultimatum. Earl Robert would support Lionel's claim to the coronet if—and only if—Lionel stopped attacking his own counties. Lionel yielded, however ungraciously, and both the duke and Mionn then bullied Yarvannet into agreement. And so there came peace, a peace that had lasted for seventy years—more or less. Lim had rebelled when Selwyn acceded, and Pullen of Yarvannet had marched north ten years later, but the other High Lords had not supported either rebellion and both had failed.

The mainstay of the long peace, Sir James had taught him,

was the alliance between Mionn and Yarvannet, the two earldoms. When the earls acted in concert, the duke's power was restrained, stabilizing both Allemanii politics and the ruling ducal house. When they acted together, the earls could stop a civil war, as they had twice—or start a war they would most probably win. That possibility of war restrained the duke's options, lessening his political threat to the earls, and thereby prompting neither side into war. Did Tejar know that? Probably not, Melfallan decided. Tejar's hostility to Yarvannet had been too marked, so very marked that his intentions had become obvious. Being obvious could be a High Lord's last misstep, and Tejar's lapse about Yarvannet had added to the other High Lords' distrust of him.

Yet if the duke could disrupt the earls' alliance by replacing Yarvannet's earl with his own toady, he could isolate Mionn and then attack Briding and Airlie as he pleased. For a time, that is—Count Parlie had an able army, and Rowena's was almost as good. Both counties could be expected to support each other if one was attacked. With two counties in rebellion, Lim uncertain in its loyalties, and Tyndale inept, Ingal would be convulsed by a war Tejar might not win. Unless Yarvannet's new earl marched north, which would in turn force Mionn to march west, and—

Melfallan grimaced. Not many men could claim that he averted civil war merely by breathing.

Did Tejar have the subtlety to *not* exploit Yarvannet's witch? No, Melfallan decided glumly, not this duke, and expected that Sir James would agree with him. Tejar was too consumed by his resentments, hating because he wished to hate. He would snap at the chance like a gomphrey lunging at its prey.

Then how to counter him? How to marshal Melfallan's alliances and deny the duke his opportunity? Could Melfallan win an acquittal at Brierley's trial? He thought about each of the other High Lords who might sit as Brierley's judges, and measured his choices. Perhaps, if the court included certain lords and not others—perhaps. He felt a small stab of hope.

Am I lord enough to save her? he wondered then, and worried desperately that he was not. With a sigh, he leaned forward and slowly rubbed his face, exhausted by the emotions of the night.

I'd sooner gomphreys think than witches walk among us, he had said carelessly to Ennis a week ago. Was Brierley truly a witch? Melfallan scowled, troubled by his second dilemma. He was a High Lord, charged by the shari'a laws with protecting his people from witch-kind, but he had not believed such women still existed, not now, if they ever had. Yet who could explain what all had witnessed tonight?

Was this truly witchcraft? Did a shari'a witch truly walk in Yarvannet? Oh, blessed land of Yarvannet! And blessed earl, to have such a witch in his land. "Hang the cost," he whispered, then leaned his elbows on his knees and stared at the plush carpet beneath his boots. "Hang it all."

Who *was* this girl? he wondered. How could she have passed by him unremarked? He listened as Brierley paced back and forth, back and forth, protecting his son and Saray and all others with the gentle sound of her voice. If this is witchery, he thought, his heart full, may it rule the world. If this is witchery—

Witchery—

She could have taken his parole and fled Yarvannet, as he had hoped she would do. Once a shari'a accusation was made, he doubted a woman could ever escape its taint, false or not. Ennis had the right of that. Melfallan had thought Bartol's claim was a ruse—well, of course he had. Witches? What nonsense! He grimaced. Easier for him if she had fled; easier for her. In another place, again hidden in obscurity, she could have found a new beginning. And he could have kept his illusions, his comfortable certainties. But no—she had thrown it away, that chance, thrown it away for Saray and his son.

If she were shari'a, she had no reason to love the High Lords. Why had she done it? She had no reason to love the Courtrays, nor care about who had Yarvannet's rule. She could have slipped away and let Saray die. She could have found her safety. He listened to Brierley's voice, murmuring in the inner room, and suspected this young woman thought not at all in those terms. He suspected that her reasons had nothing to do with himself and Yarvannet's fortunes, nor with safety, but wholly with Saray and a healer's duty, when there is need.

And I saw it all when she healed the stableboy, he thought, wondering at his own blindness. I saw it all, and yet didn't see a thing. How deft she was in the indirection, how elusive! He had seen the force of Landreth's blow and had heard the boy's shriek of agony, yet hadn't wondered at mere bruises afterward. And he had let her slip away, merely annoyed that she'd left before he had chance again to talk with her, but no more than that.

He became aware that her singing had stopped, and looked up in alarm. But peace still flowed outward from the room, touching the heart with its balm. All around them, True Night lay deeply on the castle, muffling all sounds and sending its slight chill through the castle hallways. Brierley's peace lay on Yarvannet Castle, and all lay hushed, waiting for the dawn. Melfallan drew in a deep breath, his heart filled with gladness. Sweet mistress, what beauty you weave! he thought, and shivered in reaction. It seemed he could not draw breath deeply enough.

He heard quiet movement within the inner room, and he got to his feet as Marina opened the inner door. The castle midwife held her finger to her lips, then beckoned to him.

"Saray is well?" he asked anxiously. He dared not ask about his son, not yet.

"Fast asleep, my lord."

"And Mistress Mefell?" he asked, too loudly.

She hushed him again, a finger to her lips. "Melfallan, you will be quiet as I command," she said firmly in her low, controlled voice. The finger thumped her breast. "I rule here."

Her smile was impish, and nothing but such raillery could have eased him more—as Marina likely intended. Wasn't there a midwife's instruction about "those who wait in the room corners"? He had heard Marina and Brierley quote such texts at each other, and found recognition in each other through them.

He stepped past Marina into the bedchamber, and his eyes were drawn immediately to the young woman slumped in a chair at the foot of Saray's bed. She slept awkwardly, her face hidden on one arm, long hair tumbled. One shoe had slipped off her foot, and she seemed hardly to breathe at all. And pale, so very pale. Had she paid her life for this healing? he wondered, and felt a new stab of sudden fear. "And Mistress Mefell?" he whispered urgently, nodding at Brierley.

"She sleeps, too," Marina said, folding her hands. She sighed, seeing the question in his face. "I feel there is no danger, my lord. Beyond that, her art is her own. I have never seen the like." Marina shook her head in amazement. "What I would give for such a gift!" she said, clasping her hands together. "Oh, truly! To will another to health, to erase wounds, to sing breath into a dying child! If this is witchery, your grace, Duke Rahorsum robbed us of a great good."

Uncannily, Marina had echoed his own thoughts, a fact he found comforting in its familiarity. Since his boyhood, Marina had bent over his own bedside when he ailed, and seemed to know how best to ease him without asking. She had taken a part in the common mothering by the castle's women of Earl Audric's orphaned grandson and heir. Marina had a healer's clear sight, and the heart to match, and he valued her profoundly.

"Was it witchery?" he asked her, troubled. A High Lord punished witchery with condemnation and fire. He knew the laws, and knew Duke Tejar would demand it of him. He knew just as certainly that he could not comply. To punish for the gift of his son, of Saray's life? Erase such gratitude? Destroy the healer who wrought such wonders? But if he did not condemn, what then? What would happen to the Courtrays and Yarvannet? To Brierley?

"You ask me if it is witchery?" Marina's face clouded with distress. "You ask me to pronounce this great good as evil? I will not. I swear I will not. Saray's head injury was mortal, Melfallan. Her head was shattered by her fall. I saw it myself, yet now—" Marina shook her head again and spread her hands wide. "Now her skull is fully mended, with no sign of any injury. And I cannot say I could have saved the child: it would have been a race between my knife and Saray's death. Death came into this room tonight, hunting both of them. You saw that yourself."

"So did others see," Melfallan said grimly, "and will bear tales elsewhere."

"A High Lord defends the good," Marina threw back, giving him a fierce glare. "Whatever the cost."

Melfallan laid his hand on Marina's cheek, stilling her protest. "Such ferocity, Marina," he said. "Are all healers so adamant in their defense?"

Marina relaxed her glare, and smiled. "All, my lord." She looked at Brierley sleeping in the chair. "You saw it yourself."

"Yes. Yes, I saw." Like the others who had witnessed it, Melfallan had watched Brierley fight an unseen presence with an invisible sword, slashing and feinting, pressing hard, retreating quickly, fighting a fierce swordfight around the bedchamber against an enemy only she could see. She had cried her defiance at a Beast, a Beast that had wanted Saray—and his son.

His son. His eyes shifted to the cradle near the window.

Marina laughed softly and tugged at his arm. "Come see. A fine boy. He looks like you!"

"Does he?" Melfallan let himself be pulled onward, and tried to walk quietly across the carpet, then leaned over the cradle. His son was wrapped to his eyebrows in soft blankets, a tiny swaddled form in the shadows of the crib. Marina reached into the cradle and rearranged the coverings, revealing a tiny face and two tiny clenched fists. "He looks like me?" Melfallan asked dubiously.

"A midwife can tell," Marina assured him, and then she laughed softly at him, as likely she laughed at all new fathers. There was probably, he thought comfortably, a quotable text about that, too.

Tentatively, Melfallan curled a finger under one of the tiny hands, and felt the small perfect fingers tighten in a sure clasp. A wave of love swept through him at the touch. A son! A boy! He had not believed in a live child, not truly, not after the earlier disappointments, not with so much worry attending the birth. "My son," he murmured.

"A son for Yarvannet," Marina whispered proudly.

The baby opened his eyes and yawned widely, then immediately fell asleep again, unimpressed by the wonder of his tiny self, even less by the wonder of his tall father standing by his cribside. "Is he supposed to sleep this much?" Melfallan asked in concern.

"Yes, Melfallan," Marina answered. "He's supposed to sleep this much."

Melfallan gently drew up the blanket and tucked it in snugly around the baby's chin. "Don't sound patient with me, Marina," he said. "Don't laud yourself about as superior midwife, with women knowing everything and men nothing. I won't have it."

"Truth is truth," Marina retorted, and he laughed. "Hush!" she said, shushing him again. "You're too loud."

She pointed urgently at the bed, where Saray slept peacefully, half-turned on her side. His wife's face looked wan and tired, but a smile turned up the corners of her mouth, even in her sleep.

"A son for Saray, too," he said, looking at his wife. Saray had so wanted a child, even more than he. Perhaps our son will make a difference, Melfallan thought, the wish as suddenly keen as a blade. Perhaps their son might build a bridge between them, something more than social convention and their separate worlds, one a lord's high affairs, the other a lady's gentle arts. In this night, all things seemed possible. It was Brierley's gift, that possibility. Hers.

"Melfallan?" Saray murmured sleepily, and he saw her eyes open. He leaned a hand on the mattress and bent over her. "You will not punish her," Saray said.

"It's not as easy as that, Saray," Melfallan replied gently. "The law—"

"—is a bad law." Saray set her jaw and tried to glare at him, as mildly as always for a placid woman. "You won't," Saray repeated more strongly, her eyes glinting.

"I don't want to. Don't worry." He leaned forward and kissed her forehead. "Rest now and be easy. Think about our son."

"You won't punish her," Saray insisted. "You're always wanting me to ask for myself, and now I will." She sighed, and her fingers plucked restlessly at the coverlet. "I know you don't love me as much as I love you, Melfallan. I know that, and I accept it. I am pleased with your affection and the honor you give me. I don't know how I fail you, but I'll keep trying. But do this for me, for the promise of the trying."

"Saray—" Melfallan broke off and looked at her helplessly, not knowing how to respond. It was more than Saray had ever admitted, had ever ventured to say.

Saray's gentle face was determined. "Why deny it? I'm not bitter. Arranged marriages can often be pleasant, as ours is, and I treasure your effort to pretend it's more than it is. If I could be bitter," she added, quirking her mouth, "perhaps I'd be more the woman for you, my fair lord. But, for what we are to each other, all that we have been for five years, I ask mercy for Brierley Mefell." She took his hand and pressed it weakly. "Please."

"I'll try," he said. He raised her hand and held her fingers against his lips. "Honor, my lady."

"Honor to both of us, my lord." Her eyes fluttered shut and she sighed deeply. "And now I will sleep. What a difference, Melfallan, to know our baby is nearby, alive." She smiled gently to herself. "What a wonder!" Her eyes flew open again and she gave him a look of pure joy. Impulsively, he bent and kissed her, and she laughed softly against his mouth.

"Yes, what a difference," he said as he straightened, smiling down at her.

"What will we name him? I hadn't chosen a name," she added candidly, for once admitting her hidden despair about three lost children. Saray hadn't believed in a living child, either, just as he had not, for all their desperate hoping.

"Go to sleep, Saray," Melfallan said gently. "We have *years* to choose a name, if we need it."

Saray smiled obediently and closed her eyes. When she was truly asleep, Melfallan carefully detached his hand from hers. He turned and looked at Brierley sleeping in the chair.

"What are you going to do, your grace?" Marina asked. Her sharp tone held more than the simple question of the next hour. The fierceness was back in Marina's face, as if she doubted him and would defy his choice, as well as she knew him. Would others misjudge him as easily, as Saray had already? Did they really think him capable of answering such a gift with condemnation and death?

He took both Marina's hands in his and drew her away from the bed, and she looked at him doubtfully. "Now we begin a desperate game, Marina," he said. "You know what the law decrees for a witch. And the duke will use this chance: he's only been waiting the opportunity to strike at me. Do you understand the peril?" Marina nodded tentatively, though her gaze was still fierce. What defenders Brierley Mefell gains, Melfallan thought, and rightly so. Melfallan pressed Marina's hands even more tightly. "And so I must be the righteous High Lord, impartial and stern. If I lose that role, she has little chance. The duke will burn her, and then use her against Yarvannet." He paused, then plunged onward. "And so I must put Brierley Mefell back in my dungeon, and then take her to Darhel for trial."

"No, Melfallan!" Marina cried out. Saray jerked in her sleep at her outcry, and Melfallan drew Marina nearly to the door, shushing her with a finger to his lips.

"It's your turn to hush. Listen to me, Marina. If I can win acquittal at that trial, she will be free. It's the only way." Marina struggled against his grip and indignantly pulled her hands free, as if his touch was tainted. "Will you listen?"

"Acquittal?" Marina asked in disbelief. "After *this*?" She waved her hand at all the room.

"Yes, after this. Witchery is foul," he said. "It says so in the laws. And this was not foul, and so therefore is not witchery." He quirked his mouth. "It's all a matter of definition."

Marina snorted. "Duke Tejar won't listen to your definitions, that I can promise you."

Melfallan shrugged. "Likely not, but the other High Lords might, and more than Tejar will sit on that court. The Earl of Mionn has few reasons to love Tejar, and I'm married to his daughter. The Count of Briding has been our secret friend for years, but the duke doesn't know that, and might name him as his court designate. I'll name Rowena as mine, and pocket two votes as certain. All I need is four votes, Marina, just four. Three votes might be challenged, but four would make it certain. She won't be harassed afterward if I can get four. She could live here in peace."

He saw the lingering doubt in Marina's eyes, and took her hands again into his. " 'I preserve,' she said. Preserve what? Witches don't preserve—they destroy. Witches don't heal—they kill. They made the plague, and nearly destroyed us with it. They killed cattle and babies and strong men with their evil wishing. Where in all the legends does it claim the shari'a healed like this? With a mere touch? With an invisible sword that battled Death?"

"The legends have tales just as unlikely," Marina countered.

"But not this. *This* we chose to forget, or else our own healers would have been at risk—even you, Marina. I know your talents at the sickbed. What if I named you witch because of them? You know too much of secret herbish things that I do not. You have too much power over me when I am ill. I choose not to like it at all. I name you witch!"

"Nonsense!" Marina jerked her hands away and glared at him, her eyes flashing with indignation. "I'm not a witch!" she sputtered. "How dare you!"

"Is Brierley?" He pointed at the young woman asleep in the chair. "Is *she* a witch, Marina? Is she what the legends say? Witches don't preserve or heal; they destroy. But Brierley preserves and, sweet Ocean, she heals. Gramil's injury was just as desperate as Saray's: I saw Landreth's blow. I saw the boy's agony. Yet, after a few bandages and her gentle touch, the boy had only bruises. It was a wonder, and I never saw it." He threw up his hands in exasperation. "She eluded me, so very easily. I saw it all with my own eyes, and I didn't see a thing."

"You object to the eluding?" Marina asked in surprise.

"Yes, I do," he said firmly. "I'm her lord. I'm supposed to know everything. People tell me things. It's my right."

Marina chuckled. "She didn't tell you, whatever your right—and she may not. She has no reason to trust a High Lord, Melfallan, not if *her* books have tales about High Lords like ours do about witches."

"Do you think she has books?" Melfallan asked, surprised in turn. "What kind?"

"Now, how would I know that?" Marina asked reasonably.

Melfallan grinned. "Ah, well. Perhaps Mistress Brierley will tell me, when she comes to trust me a little. I've been sitting out here, trying to puzzle out what I must do. I have a goal *there*," he said, pointing to the far wall, "and a problem *here*." He pointed to his feet. "I have to get from here to there, and there's a pit in the middle. And it's her life and perhaps Yarvannet itself at stake." He grimaced. "I can't dance around Tejar's animosity any longer. That is clear, if nothing else is. Not now. I'm certain Bartol sailed for Darhel with the startide."

"A dangerous game, your grace," Marina said slowly. "With much at stake if you lose. You could lose not only Brierley, but all of Yarvannet."

"Do you think Brierley is worth a land?" he asked bluntly.

"I am a healer," Marina answered, with visible distress. "I know the remedy for this ill, the treatment for that injury. I bring children into the world and love them afterward. How can I measure the worth of one person against a whole land?"

"Is she worth it?" he insisted.

"Oh, Melfallan!" Marina exclaimed. "You must discuss this with others. I do not have the wisdom—" She stopped and bowed her head in mute agony. "You choose your counselors poorly," she accused, with tears in her voice.

"Is she?" Melfallan repeated, but Marina was silent. "Then speak to me as a healer, Marina," he said gently. "If a healer were lord, what would be the answer?"

"If a healer were lord?" Marina raised her eyes to his, and he saw her healer's calm strength resettle into her careworn face. "Is a person worth a whole land?" she asked. "Yes, Melfallan. Of course, yes. Any healer will tell you. Any person is worth the whole world. Ask any mother about her child. Ask any healer about her patient at the sickbed." She smiled. "Ask any lord, when he is a proper lord, about any of his folk."

He sighed. "A hard principle to live by. Some would call it impossible."

Marina nodded. "And a hard time to test it, true. But what other choice do you have, after this, this—*wonder* she has made? What lord would you be to choose Tejar's own inclination? I think you're right to protect her, since that is the assurance you're asking from me. Even if she is shari'a, you as her lord are bound to her defense. Even without gratitude for what happened today, and even without Tejar's menace to Yarvannet. And even," she added briskly, "without your foolery of consulting a midwife on such a high matter."

"I like midwives," Melfallan said comfortably. "They have sense."

"Hmmph," Marina said and put her hands on her hip to glare again.

"Well, it's so," he told her. "You shouldn't argue with me."

"Someone must," she said tartly.

He winked at her, and got an amused snort back. "Yet some would—" He turned suddenly to look at Brierley again. "Does she breathe?" he asked with concern, so still she was.

"Yes, she breathes." Marina walked forward, glancing at Saray's bed, where his wife slept soundly, undisturbed by their voices, then laid light fingers on Brierley's throat to feel her pulse. She frowned distractedly. "I think it only an exhausted sleep, though I admit her healing is beyond me." She smiled, bemused. "Perhaps she will discuss her craft with me, when she is recovered. I have wished to meet her."

"I thought you knew all the midwives."

"Oh, not this one, but I've heard of her. She is well respected in the southern towns, though no one knows quite where she lives. I am getting old enough now to think of my successor, and had thought sometimes of sending a message to Mistress Mefell. For an interview, you see. Ah, well." She shrugged mockery at herself. "No need of that now. If you are to be her champion, Melfallan," she added, more soberly, "you must tell her soon that you are. It would be too cruel for her to waken in a cell, not knowing. Who knows what dire tales she believes about the High Lords? And remember that Airlie's witch hanged herself without telling the countess first. Desperate souls will do desperate acts." She looked at him solemnly.

"Hmm," Melfallan said, taken aback. "I hadn't thought of that. I should have. Thank you, Marina. She may take some persuading. I think she might be stubborn."

"Oh, no doubt of that," Marina said briskly. "I will help, if I can. Here, you are swaying from fatigue yourself. Take her off now to the dungeon if you must, and I'll be along shortly to tend her."

Melfallan bent over the chair at the foot of the bed and gathered Brierley into his arms. She hung limply, her head loose against his shoulder, but her flesh was warm, her breaths even and well spaced. Impulsively, he pressed his lips against her hair, and breathed in the sweet scent of her. Was it heather? Or the crisp cleanness of the sea wind? What *was* this girl? He sighed and nearly swayed off his balance, then caught himself with a jerk.

"Catch her shoe, will you, Marina?" He waited as Marina stooped and slipped the vagrant shoe back on Brierley's foot. "And is that her hat? Bring it, will you?" He studied Brierley's slack face against his shoulder. "She looks too pale to me," he said worriedly.

"I think she's always pale," Marina answered, and seemed quite unconcerned. Marina's judgment on matters of healing was better than his, Melfallan reminded himself, and he trusted in that. Without further argument, he carried Brierley out of Saray's bedchamber, his mind as weary as his body, and bore her down to Yarvannet's dungeons.

After a long struggle through desperate dreams, Brierley sensed the movement of someone nearby, and came to herself slowly, feeling utterly drained beyond any strength. She tried to move her hand, and could not, tried to open her eyes, but they would not open. She took a deeper breath and felt close dank air scented with tallow smoke fill her lungs. Another breath, a painful swallow, and a chair scraped beside her as someone bent forward.

"She's waking up, my lords," a woman's voice murmured

near her bedside. A cool cloth touched Brierley's face, caressing it.

"Better she not wake," Landreth's voice said harshly elsewhere in the room. "This is most unwise, your grace."

"As I have heard repeatedly from you since," Melfallan said, his voice rough with answering displeasure. "But Saray is alive and has spoken to me, and our son is born safely. What would you have me do, Landreth? Put a dagger into her heart before she wakes?"

"Captain Bartol says—"

"Bartol has never met the witch he dreads in all his wanderings, and I don't believe in such hags. Mistress Mefell's healing may have been overdramatic, but there was no witchery in it. There *are* no witches."

"But Saray's wound was mortal, my lord!"

"Marina says it wasn't," Melfallan retorted. "Serious, yes, but not mortal. Ask her yourself, Landreth."

"Every healer has her own methods," Marina said smoothly. "Who am I to question the art of another healer?" The cool hand came again, and adjusted the compress on Brierley's forehead. Brierley reached up for Marina's hand, and felt her hand caught by strong fingers, then pressed tightly and given a little shake.

Brierley could not sense Marina's presence beyond the touch. Her witch-sense was blank, guttered out. Vaguely, she remembered dreams of long battle against the Beast, with Thora and a shimmering blue dragon fighting at her side, and then a long darkness, without feeling or movement. A weight dragged on her, removing strength, leaching the will. She shivered with sickness.

"True or not," Landreth said sourly, "Bartol will bear word to Duke Tejar."

"And when the duke's inquiry comes," Melfallan said, "I will reply. And perhaps you are right, Landreth. Perhaps witchery must be considered. But until the duke's summons comes and we need face that issue, Mistress Brierley shall have quiet and all the peace I can allow her—and my gratitude when she wakes and can hear me say so. Go away now and leave us be."

"I wish only to advise you, your grace," Landreth said pompously.

"And I listen to your advice, Lord Landreth," Melfallan replied, "and appreciate it." Brierley doubted either man believed a whit of the other's assurances.

She heard a shuffling of feet, then the opening of a door, a shutting, and the murmur of voices drawing away. Gathering her ragged strength, she opened her eyes onto a small room dimly lit by a lamp in a bracket on the wall. She lay on a narrow cot against the adjoining wall, a warm coverlet drawn up to her waist. Marina sat beside the cot, a basin in her lap for her cooling cloth, and Earl Melfallan stood near the door, looking out through the grille at the hallway.

"Did he take the guard away?" Marina asked in a low voice.

"Yes," Melfallan replied.

Brierley stirred restlessly. "I cannot hear Lady Saray," she murmured in panic.

"Did you say something, mistress?" Marina asked, bending forward. "Is there anything you need?"

"Lady Saray—" Melfallan quickly joined Marina at the cotside.

"—is alive," Marina said, "and the baby born. A son. You are elsewhere in the castle now, but both are well. Is there anything you need?"

"Pattern his breathing—"

Marina curled her fingers around Brierley's wrist, giving her a comforting touch. "Don't worry, mistress: we won't waste the chance you gave him. Be at ease. All is well." Her voice crooned, rich with affection.

"Do you need anything, mistress?" Melfallan echoed anxiously behind her.

Brierley took a ragged breath, but knew some things were beyond even a High Lord's wishing, much less her own. "Nothing, lord." She turned her face to the wall. She could well guess what the lords had seen, and how her own actions had condemned her. Soon the hunt might begin, and then the fire. She would never meet her child, never walk the coast road again, nor read the books in her cave, puzzling over answers. Never.

"I don't believe that, nothing," Melfallan said, his voice jangling in her ears. Marina pressed her wrist again, bringing Brierley back from the darkness that hovered overhead and would engulf her. She wished that darkness now and pulled her hand away. Marina clucked her tongue mildly.

"She is very weak," she told Melfallan.

"Is she is in danger?"

Brierley slipped briefly away into the safe darkness. Dimly, among the billows of darkness, she heard the scrape of the chair, then the low murmur of Marina's voice, and the quick sound of her footsteps receding. The chair scraped again, and another hand took hers, rougher in its touch, with stronger fingers that pressed too hard. Startled, she opened her eyes and looked at Earl Melfallan seated beside her.

"I haven't the faintest idea of what rules might apply," he said hurriedly, "but surely there are rules for such magicks. I saw a warrior's battle enacted before my eyes as you fought—what you fought, I don't know. Was it Death itself? Then Marina told me that Saray's skull fracture was surely fatal, that the child would have died with her before she could cut open her—" He broke off uncomfortably. "Well, before that."

"But Marina just told Lord Landreth—"

"She lied," he said, and winked. Brierley blinked in mild shock. Did a lord wink at a witch? Had the world turned upside down while she was away? "So you were awake then, were you? Are you still awake, mistress?" He shook her wrist lightly. "Or should I wait to spin out my babbling? Do I oppress you?"

She forced herself to smile at him. "You are gracious, Earl Melfallan. I didn't know lords could be so pleasant." She heard a ghostly chuckle elsewhere in the room. Melfallan looked at someone behind her cot head in the far corner, a smile tugging at his mouth.

"Do you hear that, cousin?" he teased, perfectly easy, as if holding the hand of a witch were nothing toward. "Here's one of yours you haven't won over yet, with all your wooing of the commonfolk. I wonder who's right about you, those you've wooed or Mistress Mefell."

"I'll woo as I will, Melfallan," Count Revil retorted, and stepped into Brierley's view. "You have slept too long, mistress, the night around and most of the day. We have been worried."

"Worried?" Brierley asked, astonished. She gaped at the two lords. How long had Melfallan and the count kept watch together by her bed? The air had a definite touch of deep night, dank and chill, when even the Companion had moved to the other side of the world, chilling the land. The night and day around? Had the fight against the Beast lasted that long? She lifted her head and realized with dismay where she was. "I'm in a cell!"

"I have no choice in that," Melfallan said quickly. "Can you understand why? You heard Bartol. Only the duke's court can judge a witch. That's not written in the laws, but it has the weight of tradition, starting with Rahorsum himself. If I insist otherwise and refuse Tejar's demand, which I know will come as surely as the suns will rise tomorrow, Tejar could name it rebellion and bring war to Yarvannet." He grimaced. "Rebellion, too, can be a matter of definition, one Tejar would love to use. I won't give him that easy opening." He tightened his mouth. "Not now. Not ever."

"But if you lose—" she said weakly.

"I'm not going to lose," Melfallan replied firmly. "It's all politics, damn the reality of it, and the truth will be twisted to political ends. That being so, I intend to twist it first." He shrugged. "But I want the truth, too. You could have taken my parole and fled Yarvannet, as I hoped you would—if the witchery were true, that is. You could have escaped me and my High Lord's justice, found a new life of hiding elsewhere. You could have been safe. 'I preserve,' you said. Preserve what? Witches don't preserve—they destroy. Witches don't heal—they kill. But *this* witch preserves and, sweet Ocean, you heal, don't you, Mistress Mefell?"

Brierley closed her eyes and sighed helplessly, and felt Melfallan's hand tighten on hers again.

"It's a narrow game I have to play, mistress. Can you trust

me?" He waited, then spoke again, seeking some assurance she did not understand. "You who have no reason to trust lords, none at all, or so Marina has reminded me." She opened her eyes again, but still said nothing. He studied her face. "Or do you know much of lords at all?" he asked skeptically.

"No."

"I thought not. You've been quite deft in hiding, young mistress, but among the many bits of advice I've had about you, I've heard some news. Marina had heard of you, despite all your hiding, and several of Count Revil's townsmen have already rushed into Yarvannet to make your defense. I am besieged, truly." He paused. "Did you think we would kill you the instant you were found?"

Brierley closed her eyes, unwilling to meet his eyes, and sighed deeply. "I suppose it would do no good to deny I'm a witch," she said. "If there are witches," she added hastily, opening her eyes again. "And I do deny it."

"That came a little too late," Melfallan observed dryly.

"I still deny it."

Melfallan shrugged. "As you will. It'll help, I think."

She stared at him again, and rued the loss of her witch-sense to know his meaning. High Lords did not defend a hapless witch: they harried and condemned. Rahorsum had killed hundreds in his butchery, and every shari'a found alive since had joined the others at the stake, or so her books told her. Did Melfallan's gratitude for a live child extend that far—and would it last? It was hard to trust, when her books described only cruelty and implacable justice, but Melfallan seemed clearly friendly, and Revil looked kindly at her, too. She moved restlessly on the cot mattress.

"They'll say I shifted your mind," she warned them.

"Nonsense!" Revil declared. "Bartol's stories." He flipped his hand, dismissing them with contempt.

Brierley quirked her mouth. "Earlier, I'll hazard, neither of you believed in witches. Yet here we are." She gave Melfallan a level look. "If I am a witch, that is."

"If you are," Melfallan agreed affably.

"They'll say it, anyway, and don't be so dismissive of the

legends, my lord. It is legends you'll have to battle, not the truth in the suns' light."

"Let me trust my own judgments, mistress," Melfallan replied. "As you trust yours, to my gracious benefit." His hand tightened on hers. "Thank you for Saray's life. Had I thanked you yet? If not, I do."

"It is my craft," she answered unwarily, and instantly regretted her words. How easily he lulled her into incaution, how easily she trusted too much. She drew away from him, and tried to hide her dismay. Had she lost all prudence? Was this how the end began, with easy flattery and a lord's affable words?

"We will talk again, when you are better. Rest now." Melfallan started to rise to his feet.

"Lord Landreth stepped on her skirt train," Brierley said. "I think it was deliberate."

Melfallan's rising stopped abruptly, followed by a long look shared with Count Revil. "Indeed," Melfallan said slowly. "Does he want it all?" His voice was sharp, demanding what she knew and could know. In that sharpness, Brierley saw clearly the perils of a witch who counseled lords—and guessed how Witchmere might have partly brought about its own doom in the doing. A pit gaped beneath her feet, a danger that would breed new dangers upon dangers, and change what she was.

She sighed deeply, and met his eyes reluctantly. "I don't know much more. I know he is cruel and hides it from you, and that he didn't care if the groom died. I have heard from the commonfolk he has sat at many dinners with Bartol, who is also dangerous to you. But I know nothing of lords, nothing. Don't ask me for more." She covered her face with her arm. "Don't."

She started in surprise as Melfallan gently took her hand again, then watched incredulously as he raised her hand to his lips and held it there, as if she were a highborn lady due compliments. Shocked, she snatched her hand away from him, then grimaced in dismay at the unthinking discourtesy she had done him. But Melfallan chuckled, and she found the strength to glare. "I think you haven't had your hand kissed often," he teased.

"Of course not; I'm not highborn," she replied crossly, and so unwittingly handed him another discourtesy. "Ocean save me from lords," she said in despair. Revil chuckled, and Melfallan laughed out loud, quite unoffended.

She stared again, and that, too, amused them both, but not unkindly. She belatedly shut her mouth and wished she had more strength for keeping her dignity. If Melfallan's hair had turned green, she could not have been more surprised. Were these truly lords? They seemed so.

"I am relieved," Melfallan said dryly, "that you already seem more yourself. Marina tells me you are probably stubborn. It seems you are. Do keep that prayer to yourself, mistress, when among other lords. Most of us think lords are an essential part of being."

"You should not defend me, Earl Melfallan, if that is your intent. It is too dangerous."

"I will defend you nonetheless," he answered firmly. "It is not your choosing, mistress: it is mine." He bowed, and he and Revil left her cell, shutting the door behind them. She heard a guard's footsteps tramp toward the door after they left, then the clanking and small grunt of his settling on guard. After a time, Marina returned with a tray, and sat beside her cot and wheedled her to eat.

She tried to feed herself, but her hand trembled with the effort, spilling soup on her bodice. Marina clucked her tongue mildly and dabbed with a cloth, then patiently fed Brierley, spoon by spoon.

"I shall require you, Brierley," she said as she dipped again into the bowl, "to tell me your medical needs. I have assumed an exhausted sleep, but worried it might be worse, and that some part of it threatened you through my ignorance. Those doubts are not risks I'll take with you. You must advise me." She gave Brierley a stern look.

"I am undone," Brierley muttered helplessly.

"Did Earl Melfallan not persuade you? I thought not, but he is a trusty lord, Brierley Mefell, and no enemy to you." She put down her spoon into the bowl and caressed Brierley's face, a mother's touch. Brierley's eyes filled with tears at the kindness. "There, now, what have I said?" Marina asked briskly. "I think you are overtired and tears come far too easily. But it is often so, when we are tired. Do not worry." She patted Brierley's shoulder, and picked up the spoon again.

"You don't hate me, Marina?" Brierley asked plaintively. How could she not hate, when she was there at the birthing, had seen everything?

Marina paused in her spooning and gave Brierley a sharp look. "My child, I think you are worth all the world," she answered simply, "and I have told Earl Melfallan so. Here. Eat a little more, and then sleep again. All will be better in the morning."

It was a comfort Brierley herself had offered to those she healed, that a new day began all things anew. She smiled at the incongruity, the healer being healed, and Marina smiled with her, understanding quite well.

7

Later that night, near the dawn, she had another visitor. As she lay dozing on her cot, she heard booted footsteps approaching her cell. The keys jangled and the door swung open; the bulky shadow of Lord Landreth filled the doorway. He was dressed in an unflattering doublet and hose, pale gray and piped in black, with a small jeweled dagger in his belt. It was not a costume he would wear in noble society, but perhaps he wished himself unnoticed this dawn. A young man in castle livery, little older than a page, stood behind him, shifting uncomfortably from foot to foot. He held the cell-block keys in his hand.

"My lord Landreth," the boy said with a quaver, "Earl Melfallan had ordered no visitors. You heard the dungeon guard tell you that."

"And as I told him," Landreth said, "the earl told *me* to interview this woman without delay. I want no interruptions. Shut the door and lock it, then watch the stairs. Allow no one down here, on my orders."

"But, my lord—"

"Obey me, you fool!"

The boy grimaced and swung shut the door with a thud. There was another jangling of keys as he locked the door, then the patter of his boots as he left.

Without preamble, Landreth took three quick strides and tore away Brierley's coverlet, then upended her onto the floor with a rough yank at her cot. She gasped with shock at she landed hard on stone.

"Stand up when I enter the room," Landreth barked. "You insolent wretch!"

He yanked her to her feet and spun her against the wall. She caught herself on the stones and clung there, her head spinning.

"What do you want, Landreth?" she demanded, trying to control her shaking knees. She had strength barely enough to stand, and feared her weakness. Landreth's mind was shuttered against her gift, her witch-sense still in oblivion. She could not tell his purpose, and that lack frightened her. He smirked.

"It's *Lord* Landreth to you, girl. Say it. *Lord*."

With a quick stride, Landreth reached her and boxed her escape with his hands against the wall, then slowly leaned into her, pressing against her with his full length. "Lord," he whispered and nuzzled her ear, his wet tongue exploring its folds. "Say it, mistress," he crooned softly. "*Lord* Landreth." His tongue flicked again and she shuddered violently. If he meant to intimidate her, the tactic was well chosen.

"Get away from me!" She shoved at his chest hard.

Landreth gave a low bark of laughter and released her. "Now that we've met as man and woman," he said with a leer, "you will answer me as your lord."

"You're no lord of mine," she declared. "I look to Count Revil, and to Revil's own lord the earl, not you. I know what you are, Landreth. So does Earl Melfallan. You made a mistake when you struck that groom."

"Nonsense. I'm Melfallan's trusted advisor and friend, and that groom was nothing and still is. Ask the earl yourself. And it's *Lord* Landreth, mistress. How often must I repeat that? I see I'll have to teach you courtesy, and perhaps other things." He leered again.

Brierley sidled several steps away from him, and then stopped when he smiled in triumph at her fear. With a sweet smile, Brierley sidled back again to her original place against the wall, and saw him scowl.

He leaned against the cell door and crossed his arms.

"You're in a pretty fix, aren't you?" he said. "All those dramatics to get the earl's attention, but what did it get you?" He gestured at the stone walls of the cell. "This. What was your aim in that fine display? A post in Melfallan's castle, riches, maybe even a noble title? I admire your initiative in taking your chance when you saw it, mistress. Yes, I'll say that honestly." He gave her a mocking bow. "I admire you. Very creative, to take an old fright tale and spin a fortune. But, sadly, you misjudged. A High Lord must take shari'a claims seriously when the duke's own man is the accuser." He smiled tightly. "But I could help you, if you're willing. I have Melfallan's ear—and Captain Bartol's, too. You might be surprised who is the greater man."

"Your delusions are fascinating," she said. "And I don't need your help."

"Don't you? Bartol had accused you of witchery, and that's a charge hard to answer when you're a woman. You played right into his hand, for which he thanks you heartily, mistress. He's gone off to tell the duke, sailed yesterday on the evening tide. And what will Melfallan do when Tejar demands an answer? You think he'll protect you? He can't, even if he had the spine to try. But I could help you—for a price." He smiled laviciously, and Brierley marveled that he seemed to think his invitation had any attraction whatsoever.

"You can keep your price," she said coldly. "Earl Melfallan will not listen to you—and he has no reason to love the duke. Nor to love *you*, Lord Landreth, not after what happened on the stair."

"Ah. What stair?" Landreth asked with a mocking smile.

Brierley said nothing. After a moment, Landreth straightened and lost his arrogant pose, glaring at her. "What did you see?" he demanded.

"Ah," Brierley said. "You make quick connections. That shows a nimble mind."

"Answer my question!"

"What did I see? I saw the lords and ladies. I saw your guard who blocked my way. I saw the floor and the tapestries and the walls. I saw the servants and your dinner. What was I supposed to see?" She waved her hand. "Both Melfallan's lady and his son are well, I hear. A son for Yarvannet, a son. Rejoice, *Lord* Landreth, Melfallan has a son, a son to take Yarvannet." She leaned forward slightly. "Have I mentioned that Melfallan has a son? For he does have one now, you foul and misfavored man. Yes, I saw you step on her skirts to make her fall, and I've told Melfallan I did. He knows. He knows all about you."

Landreth clenched his fists, then forced himself to relax again. "Melfallan doesn't know everything," he said contemptuously.

"I told him about *that*, too," she said promptly, although she hadn't a clue what he meant. "I told him all about it," she declared boldly.

Landreth looked stunned. "How did you know about Audric?"

Audric? Brierley still hadn't a clue, but she wanted no resumption of ear-licking. The longer she stalled him, the more chance someone might come. Let him worry—let him worry very badly, whatever it was he had done. She lifted her chin and smiled.

"How do you think?" she taunted, making a lilting boast of it—and suddenly saw her danger.

"You sea-bitch!" Landreth shouted in fury, and lunged at her. Brierley gasped in surprise and sprang aside, but he intercepted her easily, then lifted her as she kicked and struck at him. One flailing hand landed solidly on his nose, bloodying it, and Landreth cursed. Grunting with the effort, he forced her arms behind her back and threw her to the floor, then pinned her with his body. Brierley shrieked.

"I'll kill you, shari'a witch," Landreth cried. "You hell-spawned soul thief—how could you know? Is Bartol right about you? It's *true*? Ocean curse you!" He fumbled for his belt knife, his face a mask of rage—and twisted fear. The Beast roared in Brierley's ears, deafening her to all but her own high shrieks, impossibly high. "Shut up!" Landreth growled and cuffed her hard. The blow maddened her.

With an animal snarl, her strength surged and she broke his grip, then threw him off and staggered to her feet. She struck out at him wildly as he lunged for her, and the knife went skittering into the corner. That same instant, the cell door boomed open, and two guards rushed into the chamber, swords in hand. Brierley darted between them and ran into the hallway, where she crashed full-tilt into Melfallan.

She knocked him smartly off his feet and they fell hard together. For a moment Brierley sprawled on top of him, but then she was up again, still possessed by the panic of her flight. Melfallan caught one arm and by sheer force she dragged him to his feet, then staggered as he wrapped his arms around her waist, holding her back. She fought him wildly.

"No!" he cried. "Sweet mistress, stop! It's over now. You're safe!"

Other hands helped him, but she fought them all, powered by the madness of her flight. "Let me go!" she cried.

"Only if you won't run," Melfallan said roughly in her ear, and tightened his arms as she still struggled against him. "It's over now, mistress. You're safe, safe."

She understood him then and sagged, her breath coming in great gusts. The world tipped and spun, and suddenly her legs would not hold her up. Melfallan's hands supported her gently as she sank to the floor. With a moan, she clung to his legs for support.

In the cell doorway, Brierley saw Landreth pinioned between the two guards, blood streaming from his nose. Melfallan pointed at him. "Arrest him, guards," he said, his voice tight with fury. "Arrest Lord Landreth for attempted rape."

Landreth's face flushed with disbelief. "For *what*?" he asked. He sputtered incoherently and struggled hard against the soldier's grip. "She attacked *me*!"

Given the content of their talk, Brierley supposed, he might think that. A quick-witted man, Lord Landreth.

"Attacked you with what?" Melfallan retorted. "Her shoe? Her fright shows the truth; she was half-mad with it. She wasn't willing, Landreth. And that makes it rape."

"You can't arrest me!" Landreth sputtered. "I'm the heir to Farlost."

"And I'm earl of Yarvannet!" Melfallan retorted. "And, yes, I dare!"

Landreth's eyes shifted and he glared at the boy standing behind Melfallan, the same young page who had earlier let him into Brierley's cell. "You damnable cur. Went running to the earl, did you? I'll teach you better later."

"No, you won't," Melfallan said coldly. "Lock him up, guards."

The guards dragged Landreth into the hallway and bore him away. Landreth fought them halfway down the hall, cursing and threatening, then desisted into an angry mutter. As the three went up the stair, Brierley bowed her head and sighed, then covered her face with her hands.

"Ocean damn him," Melfallan muttered. He knelt down beside her. "Are you hurt? Did he harm you?" She shook her head mutely, but could not look at him. Her heart still pounded like a hammer, filling her ears with the sound. She took a shuddering breath and heard Melfallan shift uneasily in response.

Beside them, the page shuffled his feet. "He is a cruel master, my lord," he said hesitantly. "He's had many women brought to his chamber, though not as many lately after Earl Audric died. With her, I thought it best—"

"*Many* women?" Melfallan demanded. "In *my* castle?

The boy drew in a sharp breath, and began babbling in fright. "I'm only his servant, lord. I have to do what he says, don't I? He threatens them and they never complain, my lord. Then he gives them presents. They like those. Some even come back willingly. They're only servant girls—" He broke off abruptly at another of Melfallan's angry exclamations, and shuffled his feet more frantically. "I wasn't supposed to tell you," the boy cried in terrified protest. "He'll whip me. He'll strip my back."

"No, boy," Melfallan assured him hastily before the lad bolted in sheer fright. "Don't worry about Landreth's whipping. You're in my service, remember, and you'll have another lord to serve now. Go find the chief steward and tell him what's happened here, then go back to bed."

"Yes, your grace." The boy gulped and hurried away.

"Only servant girls," Melfallan muttered. "Sweet Ocean's breath!" He spoke to the remaining guard, who had watched all with sobered eyes. "Go find Count Revil and bring him to me. And my justiciar. Immediately!"

"Your grace!" The soldier thumped his fist to his chest and left in haste.

Melfallan raised Brierley gently to her knees. He smoothed back her hair, as if no other task existed in all the world. "What kind of lord you must think me, Brierley! I promise you my protection and this happens." He swore softly to himself. "No reason to trust me, Marina said. She was right, as she always is."

"It wasn't your fault," Brierley objected. "You didn't know he would move so soon."

"Of course it was my fault," Melfallan answered roughly, ignoring her protest. "How clever I am! How very clever!" He hammered his fist on his thigh, hard enough to bruise. Brierley caught the hand and held it.

"Nothing happened, lord. I was frightened but I'm all right now. I would have escaped."

"You think so?" he asked gruffly.

"I was nearly to the door when you arrived." She smiled. "Do not underestimate a witch."

He harrumphed. "So you admit that now?"

"Only to you and my other champions, of whom there might be several, it seems."

"You think too much of me if you count me as your champion," he growled. "I should have expected Landreth to do something." He ground his teeth in new anger at himself, unfairly, she thought. Melfallan set a standard for himself that few men could meet.

She took a deep breath and smoothed back her hair to better neatness, then took another breath and straightened her skirt. It gave them both time to find better composure. "I don't expect lords to be perfect, Earl Melfallan."

Melfallan snorted. "Meaning you don't expect much of lords at all, I suppose."

"Well, there is that," she said. She tried another smile, but he was still too angry at himself. A noise of approaching steps, many men by its sound, echoed in the stairwell at the end of the corridor and distracted him. Brierley tugged at his arm to get his attention. "Landreth has done something else, but I don't know what," she whispered urgently.

Melfallan's head swiveled around to her. "What did you say?"

"I accused him of making Lady Saray fall, and he asked if you knew about Audric, too. *Earl* Audric, your grandfather? Can you guess what he meant?" His hand came crushingly down on hers, and she winced. "You're hurting my hand. Please."

His grip loosened immediately and then, to her astonishment, he pulled her hand to his lips and kissed it passionately. His eyes flashed with an emotion she could not read, excitement perhaps, or perhaps relief. Rage? But over what? *What* about Earl Audric? She managed not to snatch her hand away, and thus not repeat her earlier blunder, not that he'd been offended before—

"You are a gracious witch," Melfallan said fervently, then laughed at her confused expression, reading more there than she liked. "In fact—"

He was given no time to say more. Another clatter preceded a rush of several more soldiers into the corridor, followed by a tall gray-haired man dressed in midnight blue. Melfallan let his breath gust and rose to his feet.

"I am quite all right," Brierley said, as he held out his hand to help her.

"You are kind to say so, but I don't believe you."

As she stood, her faithless knees buckled beneath her. Melfallan gave a muttered oath, then lifted her into his arms with a swoosh of Brierley's skirts and carried her into the cell. He set her down on the cot as if she were made of spun crystal. "Call Marina—quickly!"

She blinked, and Melfallan was gone, and Marina leaned instead over her cot, her careworn face filled with indignation.

"Did he dare?" Marina burst out, and Brierley shut her eyes against the gentle midwife's agitation. "Is the rumor true? He came here to—" Marina could not say the rest, and sputtered angrily.

"Rumors move fast," Brierley said, her voice a bare whisper. "And increase in the travel. Yes, I am all right." She reached out for Marina's hand, but the cell tipped and spun unpleasantly as the last of her strength deserted her. She struggled weakly against the blackness that hovered, and realized to her dismay she was about to faint again. "But I'm not a noble lady," Brierley murmured in protest. Noble ladies fainted with ease, Marlenda had said, to make their noble gentlemen rush to their side, fluttering and anxious. But where is my gentleman?

Here she is, Brierley Mefell! the chamberlain cried, waving his plumed hat. And all the glittering people in the room turned in awe to see her—

"What, child?"

And before their amazed eyes, magnificent as always, Lady Brierley fainted, drawing five *dozen* gentlemen to her side, fluttering.

"Are people like lamps, Marina, with only so much fuel to burn? I wonder sometimes. My oil has run out."

Marina clucked her tongue briskly, and her hands became gentler. "You aren't making sense, Brierley, but no mind to that. People are lamps, if you wish them to be. Lie back and rest."

"Nothing makes sense, Marina. And I wish—too many things— Oh, look! The chamberlain is waving his hat again!" Brierley sighed happily, and let the darkness take her.

She dreamed of her beach and her cockleboat, floating by Yarvannet's shore. In the sky above, the Companion gleamed as a brilliant jewel, tingeing sea and sky with a dozen shades of blue and silver. It was the twilight of autumn, when only the Companion illuminated the evenings, a time of harvest songs and preparation for the dark winter. The little boat coasted easily on the swell, dipping and soaring with gentle motion. Brierley dipped her hand in the water, relishing its coolness, then looked at the young woman seated in the other end of the boat.

Like Brierley, she wore homespun and a broad-brimmed hat, but her hair was red-gold, her skin alabaster white. Gone were the fine dress and jewels of the library, the imperious air of command, the tension of danger. Thora gazed placidly toward the headland, her face smooth and calm. She turned her head and smiled at Brierley, her gray eyes tinted with the shifting blues of the twilight.

"How can you possibly," Brierley asked, "be in my boat?"

"What is memory but a waking dream?" Thora answered elliptically, and dipped her slender hand into the sea. "You have dreamed of me often, Brierley, as did I of you and other daughters when I was still living." She glanced aside at Brierley and smiled. "Which applies, I wonder? Do I dream of you, my future daughter, or do you dream of me, your ancestor? Perhaps we dream of each other. Does it matter who is the dreamer? Only the Everlight knows, I think."

"Or I dream of myself," Brierley retorted, "imagining me in two persons, and all else is nonsense."

"That, too," Thora agreed amiably. "Dreams can be many things."

"Or you're a ghost." Brierley eyed her warily, but the young shade seemed harmless enough, sitting there in the end of Brierley's boat.

"Am I?" Thora looked amused.

"Don't you know?"

Thora shook water off her fingers and laughed. "Should I? Perhaps I'm the Everlight, a guider of dreams. Or perhaps I am the blue-scaled dragon of the Four, the shari'a spirit who has watched over you all your life, Brierley, and called to you that shimmering day on the beach, called you to living. Perhaps you dream of that spirit in new form. Me." She tapped her finger on her breast. "Does it matter?"

"Well, yes. It does matter." Brierley frowned at her.

"Then perhaps I am all those things, memory and ghost and dragon and Everlight. Perhaps you are also many things. All is possible in dreams."

Brierley wrinkled her nose. "Perhaps." Thora chuckled deep in her throat, and then sniffed the wind. They drifted for a time, comfortable with the silence between them, as the headland slowly passed by. "Was the Everlight yours,

Thora?" Brierley asked. "Did you bring it out of the Disasters?"

"Yes, it was mine. It was old even then, and did not speak often to me, its mistress. Now it cannot speak at all: it is too old. Even the Everlights grow old, although it takes centuries." She looked out over the waves, her face sad. "My Everlight brings us together in dreams, you and I, but its voice is lost to us forever." She sighed. "For a long time, it was my only true friend. I miss its voice."

She looked back at Brierley, and her look sharpened. "Do not mourn for what is lost, my child. Look to the future and what it can hold. It is the only way we shari'a will survive. And you must survive, Brierley Mefell. There are very few of us left in these ending days, so precious few. But from a single beginning, a lone survivor, the gifted could grow again, if you have the will, if you find the strength to endure what is to come."

"How can I endure?" Brierley asked in despair. "I am exposed as a witch, and the outcome is set. Duke Tejar will condemn me."

Thora waved away her protest. "There are others of the Blood in these lands. Look for them. And seek out Witchmere in the High Pass above Ingal, in our ancient caverns where the Power once ruled. Its entrances are hidden, but you can find them. Its perils are great, so be wary. But the knowledge lies there for the renewal, if you can win the way." She leaned forward, her face intent. "Seize the hope, my daughter. We are a lamp guttering to darkness, and you must be the renewing spark."

"I am a simple midwife," Brierley protested. "How can I do such grand things?"

Thora laughed. "I was a simple midwife, too, and wanted nothing else but that, as do you. But some called me great. Some called me other names, and for all my willing, I could not stop the Disasters." She waggled her finger at Brierley. "But I built again after I fled Witchmere, there in our isolated cave, among the honest folk of Amelin and Natheby. I could not last for long, not in those times, but I founded a new beginning. You are my legacy, my dear child. You are the living flame of my heart, the love that answers. And I have waited for you, Brierley Mefell, my true daughter, my sea-born daughter favored by the Four." She sighed deeply. "Now you will be taken away from me for a time, into a place of peril far from me. It will be lonely, my child, so very lonely, while I wait for your return." A shadow crossed her face.

"You, within the Everlight?" Brierley asked. "You? And now within my dreams? I'm not sure you're real, Thora." She paused and frowned. "But then is the Beast real? It seems real when it comes."

"It *is* real, but of a different reality, as am I in your dreams, as are the Four in this plane of existence. A different manner of being, but living nonetheless. Our gift draws from the Four and shares their nature, but even at our height of power, the shari'a never really understood our gift, not as we should have understood it. Had we truly understood, the Allemanii might not have destroyed us. Perhaps, in our new beginning, we will be wiser."

"Perhaps," Brierley replied dubiously.

"Stubborn, as always," Thora said. "So be the skeptic for a time. I can wait. I have outwaited many."

"As have I," Brierley rejoined, lifting her chin to pose.

"We will outwait them all." Thora smiled back, then sniffed the wind again, her face happy. "A fine day, my child. Let us sail a while longer, you and I."

"Yes, I would like that. I think you're most likely nonsense, Thora of My Dreams, but it is a fine day, indeed."

"I am a dream-friend, dear one, comforting when I come but still only a dream. I died long ago, in a different time, a different world that is forgotten. Most of me has passed beyond this reality, but a fragment remains in the memory of the Everlight who loved me, and that fragment can be sent to you in dreams. There! I have told you what I am." She spread her hands expressively. "I am ghost and memory, hope and guide. I am the Everlight."

Brierley eyed her skeptically. "The Everlight watches over my cave, and I have not heard of it traveling abroad. How can it reach me here in Melfallan's castle? And it has never spoken to me, not once."

"Not in words, true. It no longer uses words, as I told you. There are other means." She pointed to herself and smiled. "Before the Disasters, we shari'a commanded devices of metal and glass and stone over which any voice could leap the leagues. Other devices were themselves gifted and patrolled Witchmere, our fierce guardians few enemies ever bested. The Four taught their adepts many things, and all shari'a benefited from their craftings. One such witchly device was the Everlight, as scholar, teacher, and friend."

"Like you?" Brierley asked with a smile. "As scholar, teacher, friend?"

"Is not any mother a scholar, a teacher, and a friend?" Thora looked at her solemnly, her gray eyes clear and tender. "My daughter, is it not so?"

"I already had a mother," Brierley said uncomfortably, and shook her head. "I don't need another."

"Don't you? Your mother denied herself and all her kin—and denied you, child, when she destroyed herself. Your mother had so great a fear of our gift that she abandoned your twin sister in Darhel's kitchens, saving only you—" Brierley raised her head with a jerk. Thora spread her fingers and sighed, then shook her head slowly. "Yes, a sister. I have not told you all these years, for fear I would wound your heart and send you on a useless quest. But now you must go to Darhel, and might find your sister there. I don't know her fate, for Jocater herself did not know, and my knowing does not reach to Darhel."

"Why did Mother leave her behind?" Brierley asked, anguished. "Why?"

"A good reason, if not the best. Jocater could not easily hide both infants on her journey, and secrecy was necessary. Her milk was not strong, and she could not feed you both as you needed. One of you might cry from hunger during a crisis, and so expose her to danger and then death, as her cousin had recently died in Airlie, as others have died. And so she fled Darhel with only one of her daughters, and when she resolved to leave, she chose the one who did not cry."

"Because of only that?" Brierley asked, appalled.

"Yes, dear child, because at that moment your sister cried

and you did not. Your mother spent the rest of her life trying to forget how she had chosen between her daughters, and how she had fled, and she buried her gift with it." Thora dipped her hand into the water and swirled it slowly. "But Jocater did better than she knew. She saved the quiet one. The one with strength. The one who endures."

"Perhaps," Brierley said, unconvinced.

Thora laughed and splashed water at her. "My point, little skeptic, is not to persuade you of certain witchly artifacts or your mother's history, but to encourage you to hope. There are other guides outside of dreams, if you look for them. You are not alone among the Allemanii, whatever your fears otherwise. Melfallan can be trusted, however ensnared he feels by his earl's rank. Harmon and Clara and others who know you best will not abandon you, witch or not. And young Jared will be fierce in his protection. No outcome is set."

"Truly?" Brierley asked, and yearned to be persuaded.

"Wait, my child," Thora said, and folded her hands comfortably in her lap. "You will see."

~

Fifteen days after Lady Saray's healing, Brierley's witch-sense awoke fully after its prolonged lapse. She welcomed its return with relief. Had her witch-sense not been dulled, she would not have misjudged and discovered Landreth's other secret. Knowing that danger, she could have screamed earlier, bringing the guard. She might even taken Landreth's dagger and threatened him with it, though that success was less certain. She knew nothing about daggers. She could have done many things, but sadly had not. To be without the gift made her blind; she relied on it more than she knew.

As the days had passed, time had dragged slowly in her prison cell, broken chiefly by the bringing of meals by the guard and the windings of her own thoughts. Marina came often, bringing a sharing of their common craft and the castle gossip, the latter she suspected at Melfallan's instruction. Publicly, Melfallan had announced that close contact with Brierley might prove dangerous, if Mistress Mefell was truly witch, and so much of the time Brierley was left alone, to rest and heal and sleep. Melfallan himself kept prudently away, and had forbidden Saray to visit her also, angering that gentle lady. Lord Landreth he kept locked up, and the rumors about that unpopular lord swirled through the castle folk, growing larger in each telling.

Sir James, Melfallan's justiciar, had begun an investigation into the servant boy's tale of other rape, and already a kitchen girl had come forward to accuse him. Not all women could be shari'a, after all, and the kitchen maid had been but thirteen. Knowing Melfallan's certain verdict if Melfallan sat as his judge, Landreth had appealed directly to the duke's justice, apparently his right as noblefolk. And so, to complete the play, Lord Landreth would be transported by the same ship as Brierley and tried also in Duke Tejar's court.

Brierley sighed and put her hands behind her head. What a turning on an ear, she thought, what a shifting of the tide! Lord Landreth had been a noble-born boy raised to think himself above other men, as noble boys often were taught, indulged by flattery from his father's courtiers, his cruelties overlooked or excused. He now faced years of prison or banishment, robbed of fortune, land, and reputation. Marina said Melfallan would hang Landreth if he had the choosing, but expected Duke Tejar would spare his life—if only because Earl Melfallan wished otherwise. Hearing Marina's gossip of Melfallan's affairs opened up an entirely new world for Brierley, one of noble politics and risk, subtlety and malice, and she better appreciated what risks Melfallan took to defend her.

But it might be advantage, too, she knew. Melfallan had not known about Landreth's role in the old earl's death, and there might be other knowledge she could pluck from other minds for his use. And create still a greater danger? What would the other lords do if they realized Melfallan employed a shari'a witch? Her books had hinted that such counsel might have started the trouble with the High Lords, for a counselor's role led to greater power. It was a slippery path, that line of choosing—and too easy to take.

Marina had not explained Melfallan's reasons for promptly yielding to the duke's summons, but that summons had duly come by return ship the day before, waved aloft with triumph by Captain Bartol. After meeting with Earl Melfallan, Bartol had hurried to Landreth's chambers with his anxious news and found the rooms empty, the bed stripped of its mattress, the shelves of their rich possessions. When he learned the reason, Bartol had scurried back to his ship with even greater speed and sailed on the startide. More news for the duke, to arrive before Melfallan. *Aboard a ship for a thousand stars,* Brierley thought irritably. She waved her hands idly in front of her face, mocking a spell. *I conjure a hag, and a starry ship for them both.* Would it were so easy.

A witch could not help but be a lordly affair, it seemed, fraught with peril for both shari'a and lord. Her books had made it sound otherwise, with the witch always condemned by the lord, and she wondered where the truth lay. Lordly affairs, she thought irritably. I do not wish to be a lordly affair. She conjured with her hands again. *A ship for Duke Tejar, too.*

On this fifteenth day, she lay comfortably on her cot under a warm blanket, listening to the sea's distant murmur. The week before, after Harmon and his wife had finally won an interview to accost Count Revil, Melfallan had moved her to another cell high under the gate, just beneath the cobbled roadway that led into the castle. She listened as the horses overhead stamped their hooves and wagons rumbled busily, remembering that other day when she had ventured willingly into Yarvannet Castle. It all began then that day, she thought, but was it an ending—or a beginning?

Above her head, the thoughts and emotions of the castle moved in a bewildering randomness, too complicated for her to understand any one mind with clarity. Her efforts to find Saray among the many voices were frustrated, but Marina had assured her that all was still well with lady and child. Melfallan's son grew steadily, cosseted by Saray's ladies and his wet nurse, and Saray had quickly recovered her strength. Sometimes, when Brierley had lain on her dungeon cot, she had also sought out Earl Melfallan among the many mental voices that suffused the castle, but he, too, flickered among the sea waves of her witch-sense, briefly there, then gone.

She heard a clanking in the corridor outside her cell and sat up. Bootsteps tramped up to her door and the door was unlocked with a great jangling of the keys, then swung open. The guard who stood there was an older man dressed in Melfallan's livery, a longsword dangling from his belt, and an officer's pip on his cap. A sergeant, perhaps. She knew little of the soldiers' insignia. In his hand dangled metal cuffs.

She eyed the manacles with dismay. "I must wear *those*?" she asked sharply.

"Earl Melfallan has ordered it," he answered gruffly. "Come along, mistress. The earl's ship sails in an hour. It is time."

He stepped closer and lifted the chains. With a sigh she presented her wrists and suffered him to fasten them with the cuffs. The chains clanked as she lowered her arms.

His weathered face held sympathy, which surprised her, though he grimaced as he saw her expression. "Earl Melfallan has his relatives; so do I, including one Jared who knows you. He told us many things while he haunted the guard quarters, refusing to go home as he should." He eyed her grimly. "You already gather your champions, and I've been wondering how."

She half-turned from him and sighed. "And they say I subverted Jared's will? On a single boat ride?"

"Some do," the sergeant acknowledged with a shrug, "and some don't. It's called an argument. All Yarvannet is abuzz about you, mistress. Did you know about that? Commoners have poured into the city from Revil's towns, waving their arms wildly and presenting their petitions to the earl and count both. All the marketplace can talk about is you and your healing of Lady Saray. No one can escape it." He looked at her, bemused. "Did you know, Brierley Mefell, how admired you are?"

Then he remembered the deathly peril of her presence and tightened his hand on his sword hilt. His glare was fierce.

She sighed again, wondering what purpose he had in telling her such things. "I don't appreciate your gloating," she said sourly, giving it the worst color. "Take me to the ship and leave me be."

"How do you know about the ship?" the sergeant asked sharply, forgetting he had told her but the minute before.

"You are a fool, sir." She took her hat from the end of her cot and put it on, her chains clanking with the movement, then walked around him into the corridor. With a snort, the man followed, close on her heels.

They climbed the stairs and emerged into the bright sunshine of the empty square above. After the next tunnel through an interior wall, a phalanx of guards in Melfallan's livery surrounded them on all sides, concealing her from view. They marched her outward through the gate, across the bridge, and along the ridge road toward the stair that led down the bluffside to the town, the traffic of the ridge road eddying around them.

To her irritation, she sensed that the guard to her right and the one just ahead feared her with a dread that clouded their minds with a sinking fear, driven to this escort only by duty and outright threats from the sergeant. She heard one testing his will anxiously every few seconds. What gossip had been said about her in the towns? What foul lies to make this young man dread her? Suddenly she felt a rage sweep through her, her own cleansing rage, not the emotions of these others. Melfallan might send his secret assurances through Marina and pursue some lordly plan in bending so easily to the duke, but *she* was the unfortunate who walked in chains.

It isn't right, she raged to herself. It's not just. I have done them no harm.

Firmly she planted her foot on the dusty path and stamped the other beside it, stopping so abruptly that the guard behind her, lost in his worried thoughts, nearly ran her down. The other soldiers paced onward and left her behind, then whirled, putting their hands on their sword hilts and double-marching back to surround her again.

"Kill me now," she told them defiantly. "I'm not minded to play your game of shuttles and hawk, not when I am the shuttle and the hawks are far too many." She clanked her chains in emphasis.

"Move on, mistress!" the sergeant ordered, his eyes glinting.

"No. I refuse."

Every soldier to a man turned, bewildered, and shot his glance at their sergeant. In other circumstances, she might have enjoyed the effect. The sergeant took a menacing step toward her, very aware of his men's watching eyes. She braced herself to be carried in a fine shrieking display onto Melfallan's ship at the wharf below. She lifted her chin defiantly. Let them carry her shrieking.

To her surprise, the sergeant instead looked her over from hat to shoes. "Plucky little thing, aren't you?" he asked. "What if I said 'please'?"

"It would do you no good, none at all." She looked away from him, pretending indifference to irk him. "Would you walk so pleasantly in my circumstances?"

He snorted. "I've heard from the talk that you have steel inside you, Mistress Brierley, and that's to be expected, you being a healer and all. It's the 'all' that's the problem with Earl Melfallan, but the 'healer' is the problem with me. I was raised to honor healers, and from all I've heard recently, that honor is fully yours." He gave her a stiff bow, surprising her again—and his men even more. "I'll not humiliate you with force," he continued mildly, when he was done with his bowing. "That's for others to do who care less for our gentle lady and her new babe, or for the champions of degenerates like Lord Landreth." He looked around at his guards and sniffed. "Stand easy, men. I expect we'll be found by somebody shortly." He shifted his shoulders comfortably and settled himself to wait.

"But, Sir Micay," one of the soldiers protested, "we'll attract the attention of the crowd." He looked around nervously at the ridge road just above them, busy with its wagon traffic. At this point immediately above the stair, the bluffside concealed them from the docks and town below, and a slight ridge hid them from the road above. The town's folk could not see them, not yet, and the soldier genuinely feared what might happen when they did. What in Ocean's grace had been happening in the town? she wondered.

"I expect it might." Sir Micay's eyes did not leave Brierley's face and she looked back warily.

"You are Sir Micay?" she asked uncertainly. "The earl's castellan?"

"I am," he growled. "What of it?"

"Since when does the castellan conduct a prisoner?"

"When my earl orders it, young woman, simple as that." Sir Micay gave her a wintry smile. "I follow orders. Why won't you?"

"Sir—" one of the soldiers ventured again.

"Stand easy, I said!" Sir Micay barked.

The others were nervous now, and Brierley truly wondered what had filled the town these past two weeks. Had the townspeople truly threatened riot? Against an earl as popular as Melfallan? And Harmon likely in the forefront, she guessed, and felt a new prick of worry for her stalwart friend. Harmon had the guile and bluster to stir a crowd, and stir it well.

"But what if they riot?" one of the guards asked plaintively.

"Oh, she won't get far," Sir Micay said, unperturbed. "The town's evenly divided."

"*She* didn't know that," the young soldier accused, "and that's why she's made you do this!" His mouth flapped in amazement as he heard his own words. "She's witched you, sir!" he cried, aghast.

Brierley stamped her foot, then stalked right through the ring of guards, moving so abruptly that she caught them all by surprise, even Sir Micay. She was a half-dozen yards away before they broke out of their startlement and ran to catch up. She whirled as the first nearly reached her. She glared at him, and he shrank back with stark fear in his face.

"Damned be all of you!" she shouted at them. "All my life I have given to you in gentleness—and you do this to me!" She raised her chained hands and saw the soldier sidle back in alarm, terrified of some spell. It broke her anger like an eggshell shattering on a kitchen stone. Hot tears filled her eyes and she covered her face with her chained hands, trying with all her strength not to sob a first time. She wouldn't give them the satisfaction, none of them.

There was a short silence and much clearing of throats among the men. Finally Sir Micay stepped forward and touched her sleeve. "Shall we go, Mistress Bri?" he asked softly. "For there is no stopping this now. I have my orders, and he said be gentle and so I will be. We can stand here awhile, if you wish. No rush." She looked up into his weathered face, and saw the kindness there, and the decency. Of all of them, he was not truly afraid of her.

She sighed. What use to run? In their fear, the soldiers might slip Sir Micay's control and murder her on the stair. Her earlier arrest had almost stirred riot in Amelin. If the pursuit reached the wharves, the soldiers might turn their swords on the crowd, as Shay almost had. That possibility lay stark in Sir Micay's mind, as it had in Melfallan's when he met with Sir Micay an hour before. But still Sir Micay waited patiently, giving her time. She looked up at the daytime sky, where the Daystar and Companion shone in their brilliance, and listened to the murmuring of the sea far below. The wind stirred the sea grasses bordering the path, whispering among the blades.

"Let us walk on, Sir Micay," she said. "I thank you for your courtesy."

"It is no burden, mistress."

The guards formed their phalanx around her again and she moved with them, marching down to the quay and the ship that waited there, her despair a cold stone in her breast. The kindness hurts even more than the fear, she realized sadly. It mocks my hopes.

Their party passed so quickly over the wharves that no one had time to gather, and the soldiers waved back those few who noticed them and stepped forward. At the dock, the ship's crew watched her from their stations at prow and stern: of the noblefolk, she saw none. Brierley looked once more at the sky and sea from the ship's deck, then allowed Sir Micay to lead her down a companionway to a small compartment built against the lower hull. With a clanking of his key, he took off her manacles and glanced briefly around the small compartment, checking its orderliness, then hung the cuffs on a peg near the door as he left. Brierley sat down tiredly on the narrow bed and buried her face in her hands. A short time later, a soldier knocked and brought in a basket filled with

Clara's gifts—a warm blanket, extra clothes, a packet of sweets.

"Thank you," Brierley said, and caressed the handle of the basket. Dear friend. With Clara's basket on her lap, Brierley listened to the slow waves slapping against the hull, together beating a constant and changing rhythm that held no sense.

A half-hour later, as she sat on the narrow bunk, she heard a second prison party approach the ship. An open grille in the ceiling of her compartment brought light and air. Through it, she heard the growing tramp of the soldiers' marching, first booming dully on the wharf, then changing tone as they marched up the wooden gangway into the ship. A moment later, the sound thundered on the deck immediately overhead, and stopped with a sharp command from Sir Micay.

"You and you, take him below," the castellan ordered.

She heard Landreth curse foully at Sir Micay, and then heard the brisk sounds of a struggle that skittered across the deck and continued down the ladderway. One of the soldiers slammed Landreth into the corridor wall next to Brierley's cell, making the wood shudder, and she stiffened in alarm.

"You cur's offal," Landreth swore and was promptly smashed into the wall again. "I'll get you," he promised.

"Shut up," one soldier said furiously.

"Curse as you will, lord," said the other, his voice heavy with contempt. "At least there'll be no more young maids hurt by you. Four now, isn't it? I'll hazard Sir James will find the others, too. There won't be much left of you if you ever come back to Yarvannet. The earl will see to that. And if he won't, others will. Move!"

The shoved Landreth into a nearby compartment and slammed the door on him. Landreth cursed them foully as they left, then subsided into a furious mutter. His mind boiled with rage. (*How dare they? For what? A little fun with a commoner girl? Being attacked by that sly witch?*) Landreth vividly cursed Melfallan and Brierley, and then cursed the page, who stood in peril of his life if Landreth ever got his hands on him. (*They'll all pay for this*), Landreth vowed to himself. (*They'll pay.*) Brierley flinched as Landreth's fists thundered on the wooden timbers of his cell.

Beneath the fury Brierley sensed a prick of fear that no one would pay except Landreth, that the world had turned upside down and might crush him like a seashell beached on the sand. For years his father had encouraged his hatred of the Courtrays, teaching Landreth his own cold malice and pride. After Audric died from the marsh potion sent from Farlost, removing that canny threat, Count Sadon had told Landreth to watch and wait and take his chance if he found it. In a young earl's inexperience might lie an advantage, his father had counseled him, if the duke could be manipulated, if fortune favored Sadon. First Sadon as earl of Yarvannet, his father had promised, then Landreth after. Duke Tejar had promised. And Landreth had believed in the certainty of it, and had trusted his father's guidance.

Brierley sighed. I don't want to know this, she thought wearily. I don't want a reason for what he has done. Easier that he be merely evil and twisted, not a misled boy who grew into a cruel man. But men's reasons often lay in such a tangle, neither wholly fair nor foul.

And Count Sadon is as much a traitor as his son. Does Melfallan know that? Do I tell him, as I told him about Landreth? Where is the line in using the gift—and letting me be used by others, especially by a High Lord?

After a time, she heard more footsteps on the wharfside, and listened as the noblefolk boarded the ship. The ship's captain came forward and greeted Earl Melfallan, and received a pleasant greeting back from the earl and Lady Saray. To her surprise, among the murmur of the several folk who also boarded she heard Harmon's voice. A most persistent friend, she thought, and felt cheered. How had Harmon ever wheedled the lords to include himself in Melfallan's party? Well, he could and would, she thought. When given a goal, Harmon sometimes little bothered himself with opening the barn door before walking into the barn. It was all a matter of will, he would say.

She listened to the murmuring voices overhead, catching a word now and then, but little of its sense. The many minds sifted through her witch-sense, too blended in the crowd to bring much more. Twice she heard Melfallan's voice rise above the murmur; then all was subsumed into the shouts and thumpings of the ship's crew as the captain gave the order to set sail. The ship swayed as it was poled off the wharf, rose choppily as it moved into the swell, then settled into graceful movement across the waters of the harbor.

Will I ever see Yarvannet again? Brierley wondered, and felt her heart beat faster. Will I ever see my cave? With a sigh, she hid her face in her pillow.

That next hour Melfallan's ship began its journey up the coast, beginning with a tedious long night and a long morning for Brierley. The ship rose and fell on the waves in easy motion, with a noisy splashing of waves along the hull and a faint singing of the wind in the rigging. She did not remember her mother's voyage southward, and had never sailed aboard a full-masted ship in all her years since. With a steady current northward near the shore, and an answering southward current some miles outward, ships traveled easily along the coast in all seasons except winter. It would not take long to bear her to Darhel.

Her guard did not allow her on deck and Brierley was forced to listen to the gossip of Saray's ladies through the overhead grating that brought her air and the sound of the sea. They perched on the coaming above her head and chattered like brainless birds for hours on end, and not even Brierley's pillow could keep all of it out. Brierley seemed forgotten, so idly and cheerfully did they talk to each other, as if on a holiday.

On that morning, Brierley listened unwillingly to a lady-maid named Margot talk to another named Natalie about a young lord Natalie fancied, a fine figure of a man with his slim legs and sweet smile, for all he was married to the butler's daughter. "Will you now?" Margot giggled at Natalie. "Has he that much of a roving eye?"

"I'll find out," Natalie said archly. "Wait until you see the gown I've made myself for the duke's court: I'll turn his head." She giggled. "There he is, by the other railing. Isn't he fine-looking?"

Brierley ground her teeth. Both young women were silly and vain, casually cruel in their opinions, and selfishly absorbed in themselves and little else. Both despised their mistress, Lady Saray, sniggling at Saray's clothes and meek behavior, contemptuous of her sweet disposition and favors. Both aspired to a high lady's rank of their own, and thought themselves better than Saray in deserving such fortune: after all, they whispered to each other, a High Lord did marry a lady-maid from time to time, for all that scandal.

"A nicely filled doublet doesn't always mean skill in bed," Margot warned, her voice sharp with jealousy. (*Much luck Natalie will have, with those freckles*), Margot thought, her spite laced with a slipping envy, knowing herself too squat and large-handed to compete with the prettier women like Natalie, freckles or not.

"I don't care," Natalie said blithely. "A man can learn."

At that very moment, a key scraped in Brierley's compartment door, and Earl Melfallan stepped into her small compartment, then pulled the door shut behind him. Brierley caught a glimpse of a soldier stationed by her door as he entered.

"Mind you keep your plans from Lady Saray's knowing," Margot said above their heads. Melfallan looked up at the grille, his eyes widening. "She doesn't like scandal."

"What scandal? Have I *ever* had a scandal?" Natalie laughed. "All a girl needs is sense."

"Which you haven't got, Natalie," Margot retorted. "If Lady Saray ever catches you flipping your skirts—"

"She won't," Natalie said with contempt. "She's too stupid."

Melfallan jerked straight in his outrage, and slammed his head on the overhead timbers hard enough to make stars. Brierley's own vision shifted oddly for a few dazed moments. Melfallan groaned and bent over in agony, clutching at his head.

Natalie's voice chattered onward, oblivious. "Why Earl Melfallan ever chose her—"

"Hush, Natalie! You have no prudence at all!"

"—*her* is beyond me."

"Will you *hush*?"

"Why should I?"

Brierley could stand no more. She sprang up on her cot and thundered her fist on her wooden ceiling, getting a most satisfying boom from the timbers. "*I'd* hush!" she shouted at the top of her lungs, and boomed her hand again. "I'd hush and take it away, you stupid girl!" With a mutual gasp, the voices above stopped, and quick steps hurried away up the ship's deck. Brierley laughed at the grille overhead, then turned around to Melfallan. "Good morning, Earl Melfallan. Are you all right?"

"Hells keep it," Melfallan swore. He fingered his scalp gingerly and winced, then straightened, wary of the low ceiling. She stepped down to the wooden floor. "Sailors are too short," Melfallan growled, "and Saray's ladies too glib. You seem blessed with confidences, mistress. As I remember, that railing's been a popular spot for Saray's ladies all morning. Has it been all in that vein?" His eyes glinted with anger.

"Not all, not even most. Natalie is the worst, my lord, being stupid and no danger to your lady wife." The ship swayed over a large wave, and Brierley sat down abruptly on the sea cot. Keeping what she could of her dignity, she folded her hands on her knee. As the ship surged again, Melfallan himself stepped off balance but caught himself with a hand on the overhead timbers. "Here, lord," she offered, "you sit and I'll stand."

"No," he answered with a quick smile. "I'm minded to take you up into the sunshine for a while. Would you like that?"

"On deck?" she asked, surprised.

"That's where the sunshine is, the last I looked."

"What happened to 'contact is dangerous, should she be witch'?"

Melfallan grimaced. "So Marina told you about that. Good. I hope she told you the rest. If not, I'll fill in the gaps as we sail. We must still be circumspect, but most of the folk aboard are friends—or at least not enemies." He opened the compartment door behind him and stepped out into the corridor, and then waited for her to follow. "If you will, mistress." He held out his hand.

She hesitated, then picked up her hat and joined him in the corridor, glancing nervously at the guard. The guard's head swiveled hard left as Landreth suddenly hammered on the nearby door. Landreth shouted some curse, his words muffled by the wooden planking. "Is that still going on?" Melfallan asked the guard.

"I think he heard your voice, my lord," the guard replied. "He's been quiet, mostly, since he was brought aboard." Indifferent to Landreth's shouts, the guard looked again at Brierley, his expression cool, his eyes steady. "She should be wearing manacles, your grace," he suggested with deference.

"No. Not today." Melfallan took Brierley's hand in his and led her toward the ladderway.

A minute later, Brierley stepped into dazzling sunlight and the crisp sea breeze, and she was immediately noticed as a dozen heads turned toward them. She was not used to such attention, especially from folk not hers, these lords and ladies with their comforts, their prides, their assumptions of ease from birth. The sailors, less impressed by a perilous witch, went about their business of coiling lines and tending the sails. At the stern, the ship's captain stood at the tiller, balancing easily on strong legs as the ship swooped and rose. At least not enemies, Melfallan had said, and she sensed curiosity, some disdain, some indifference, but not great fear.

Above her head, the white canvas of the ship billowed and snapped in the fresh wind. All about the ship, the sea surged with unending movement, lifting and falling in massive swells, deep green, gray, a splash of brilliant blue and silver. The land was only a smudge on the horizon, pale grays and greens. Suddenly a huge fish leaped from the nearby swells, a fish as long as Brierley was tall, its golden fins flashing in the sunlight. It fell back into the depths with a great splash, then leaped again, playing as it raced the ship. She drew in a quick breath of surprise.

"A star dolphin," Melfallan said, grinning. "Have you ever seen one?"

"I've heard of them. How lovely he is!"

"It's racing the ship. They often do—and usually win their race. Maybe we'll even see a gomphrey. The Ewry River mouth isn't far ahead, and the gomphreys are hunting sturgeon right now."

"A sea snake?" She stared at him. "A real gomphrey?"

"Well, they live in the sea." He gestured widely all around them at the waves, pointing out the obvious. "At least the real gomphreys do," he added. "Is there an unreal variety?"

"There's no reason to tease me, lord," she reproved mildly. "I've never been abroad at sea. How could I have seen such wonders?"

Melfallan motioned toward the ship railing and she walked beside him across the wooden deck, then leaned on the banister, the wind fresh in her face. The star dolphin leaped again and smiled at her from midair, then splashed downward into the cool water, plunging deep.

(*Fun!*) he exulted.

Oh, yes, Brierley answered in delight. She hadn't known any of the sea creatures could talk. *And you are fastest, you lovely thing.*

(*I am fastest*), the star dolphin agreed. To show off, he put on a fresh burst of speed, carrying him far ahead of the ship, where he dove and splashed across the surface, weaving a pattern of foam.

Earl Melfallan perched a hip on the wooden banister beside her and lifted his face to the wind, breathing deeply. "I think Mother Ocean meant me to be a fisherman, not an earl," he said. "Comes with the seafaring blood. I always think that when I'm on a ship out here—and then change my mind when my feet are solid on land again. What do you think?"

The star dolphin now plunged and scattered a school of panicked herring, which he chased in delight. Then a deep booming growl came shuddering through the water, and he turned aside, putting distance between himself and the gomphrey now hunting the seafloor below. (*Good-bye!*) he caroled, and faded into the sea.

"Good-bye," Brierley said, and felt a pang at his leaving.

"Pardon?" Melfallan asked in confusion.

"Perhaps everyone is a fisherman," Brierley said quickly, turning to him, then smiled to herself that he would miss nearly all her meaning.

"Perhaps so," Melfallan said uncertainly, but his gaze sharpened the next instant. "What's the smile for?" he demanded.

She did not reply. Instead, she took off her hat and shook her hair loose in the wind. All around them, the sea murmured in Her quiet unending voice, speaking of life, of movement, of the reasons for being. She sighed and closed her eyes, letting the scent of the sea envelop her. The wind tugged at her and dashed her hair into whipping tendrils.

"Better?" Earl Melfallan asked, his voice low.

"Yes. Yes, it is."

She lifted her hands and let the wind push against them, cool and fresh. A flock of sea larks spun overhead, catching the suns' light on their iridescent wings. *Have hope for the future. No outcome is set.* She laughed.

"I'd say you're a fisherman, too," Melfallan observed, pleased.

"No, not really. A sea lark, perhaps, if you would be fanciful. Your lords and ladies are watching you."

"I know. I'm making a statement, a show of sorts. Like Natalie, I'm not always discreet. You'll understand when you know me better."

"Hmm," she said noncommittally.

"I hope you will want to." He stretched casually, loosening joints, then returned to his lounging by the rail. "Right now I'm making myself a small wager: Who will join us first—Master Harmon or Lady Saray? This morning I informed them both that I must now interview you from time to time on this voyage and so must risk your dire presence, Mistress Mefell, but they should continue to stay away. I don't expect either to listen."

Brierley saw Harmon tramping the wooden decking toward them, Clara beaming happily in his wake. "Here comes the answer to your wager, lord," Brierley said, amused. Melfallan turned and saw the couple approaching. He shook his head slightly and frowned at them. Harmon stopped in his tracks, as if he suddenly remembered, as indeed he had.

"Oh, I forgot," he blurted. "I'm not supposed to talk to her."

"As I explained, Master Harmon," Melfallan said patiently. "It's important for your testimony as her witnesses."

"Oh." Harmon brightened. "Then I'll talk to Clara, I will." He promptly turned to his wife. "I think she looks very fine, wife, and I hope she's warm enough. But she's too pale."

"Brierley is always pale, Harmon," Clara replied placidly, "but I think she looks rested." Melfallan crossed his arms across his chest, his mouth twitching. Brierley sighed softly, just loud enough for him to hear, and made it even harder for Melfallan to keep his composure.

Harmon continued onward in his bellowing voice, quite oblivious of everything but his purpose. "I wonder if she needs anything," he said. The whole ship could hear him, without a doubt. "Certainly we've stocked up, just in case. Does she have that blanket we gave her? I think not, knowing those castle guards. And some nourishing food. And the letters we collected from the Amelin and Natheby folk. She needs something to cheer her while she's alone. In fact, I'd say an entire big basket could be filled with—"

"All right, good master!" Melfallan said, raising his hands. "Bring your big basket to the guard. He'll pass it through."

"Good, good." Harmon eyed Melfallan a moment. "Can't we say one word to her, my lord?" he asked plaintively. "I don't understand your rule exactly, but you're the earl, after all. Still—"

"Harmon, hush!" Clara said, touching his arm.

"What did I say?" Harmon protested, looking injured. "It's a fact, it is, that he's the earl. Why is pointing that out—"

It was too much to bear. Brierley stepped past Melfallan and threw her arms around Clara, then was enveloped in Harmon's embrace an instant later. She laughed up at the farmer's broad face. "Harmon, you do know better than to tempt your lord. Whatever are you doing here?"

Harmon snorted. "What a question! Did you hear her,

Clara? I can't believe my ears: truly, I can't. Well, young woman, Cormley is watching my fields and stock, and we gave the boys to my sister: she always likes their visits and lets them run wild, which they like, too. A little holiday for the boys, and a journey for us. Of *course* we're here," he added emphatically, then glanced at Melfallan. "Lords are good in their own way, with respect to you, young earl, but you need friends to watch out for you. And who is best for that but me and my Clara?"

"Friends," Clara said shyly and smiled, then lowered her eyes to her clasped hands.

Brierley embraced Clara again and kissed her cheek, then nudged both Clara and Harmon both toward the far railing. "Go along now, good friends," she said. "You should listen to the earl and his cautions."

"You're all right, Bri?" Harmon asked dubiously, and looked her up and down.

"I am fine. Rich, even." She smiled at both of them.

"Hmmph," Harmon snorted with high skepticism. "I doubt that. You rich? Hmmph."

"Hush, Harmon!" Clara said, though it did no more use than ever. Clara's eyes met Brierley's, and suddenly they laughed together, there on the ship deck, hands clasped, in the view of all. Let them look, Brierley thought fiercely. Let them see.

"Rich," Brierley repeated, and knew that Clara understood her perfectly.

Harmon gave her another quick hug. "We'll work on the earl," he confided into her ear. "I'm sure he'll come around." Then Harmon stamped away down the deck, and Clara looked back at Brierley as she followed, her plain face lit by a smile.

Brierley returned to the railing beside Melfallan and leaned on it with a sigh, then looked out at the broad ocean. Above her head, another sea lark sailed the wind, a flashing shape against a brilliant sky. She watched it dip and soar, then turned to face him, aware he was watching her.

"Rich," she said, as if she challenged Melfallan to contest it.

"That I can see," he replied comfortably. "I thought of that when I let the Jacobys board with us. He and Clara will be a comfort to you during the voyage. Also, a second ship is sailing today from Tiol with Count Revil and others from Amelin and Natheby, all your champions, Brierley, as well as Sir James and the four girls who will testify against Landreth. It will be a large delegation."

"Unfairly weighted by you, it seems."

"Unfairly?" He smiled lazily, then shrugged. "Fairness doesn't count. Ask Duke Tejar if you meet him. I have no choice about going to Darhel, but I do have the choosing in how we go—and more choosing after we get there. Did Marina explain that part of it? I see by your expression that she didn't." He studied her face a moment, then smiled as she chose to put on her hat. "Don't tip the brim. It's too easy a dodge."

"But effective."

"Oh, yes, you eluded me quite neatly in the stableyard. You've eluded me for years. 'A shadow in the shade,' Master Harmon calls you. In fact—" He turned his head and his expression changed. "Ah, but here comes the other half of my wager. Excuse me, mistress."

He walked forward to meet Lady Saray, who was then emerging from the stairwell at the other end of the ship. Saray walked unsteadily on the heaving deck, and caught Melfallan's hand quickly as he reached her. He guided her to the railing, and she caught a hand on that, too, then set a direct course for Brierley, one hand on the railing and the other determinedly on her husband. Melfallan came along without protest, although he looked bemused. They were followed by two of Saray's ladies.

Saray seemed unbothered by the lively sea motion, save for her balance, despite her newness from her encouchment. Another fisherman, perhaps, Brierley thought with approval, as the two walked toward her along the rail. It was easy to like Saray, without worry of the price. This lady would never do willing harm to anyone, especially those she loved, and her loyalty, once given, was unyielding. In Melfallan's mind, however, Brierley glimpsed a different image of his wife, weaker, less admirable, far less valued.

He does not understand her, she realized, sensing the long-held pattern between them. Saray had made herself into two women, one the pleasant and frivolous exterior, the other the inner steel. It was a necessity taught to her in girlhood, that a woman could not be herself, but must be what others wished her to be. She glimpsed the reasons in Saray's assumptions of her woman's life, of a wife's role in a noble house, a daughter's unimportance in a father's regard, a mother too stern and unloving, friends too untrustworthy, a marriage made for political reasons and not love, although love had followed for Saray.

But Melfallan was not attracted to weak women, a concept quite beyond Saray's assumptions of her upbringing. Thinking a woman's weakness a certain means to devoted love, Saray had made herself weak for Melfallan, unaware of the passion it had stifled unborn. And the more he retreated from her, the more she made herself weak, trying to woo him. Her repeated failures only stiffened her resolve, and so she had perfected her outer self, and driven Melfallan further away. Brierley sighed softly and looked down. Sometimes the knowing was not welcome.

"How good to see Mistress Brierley in the sunlight," Saray said when they were a few paces away, and glared mildly at her husband. "I *will* talk to her, Melfallan."

"I agree about the sunlight," he said cheerfully. "I'm the one who brought her up on deck. And have I said no?"

"This morning you said no, as you've said every morning the past two weeks."

"Well, I'm not saying no now."

Intent on her purpose, Saray did not really hear him. "This is ridiculous," Saray declared firmly, beginning a speech she had practiced in private all morning. "Nothing has been proven, and we owe a great debt to Mistress Mefell. She is not dangerous. She—"

"Saray," Melfallan interrupted gently. "I'm not saying no."

"Oh." Saray looked at him uncertainly. "You're not?"

Melfallan made a small show of considering, arms crossed on his chest, his lips pursed. He was well aware of all the eyes and ears around them, including Saray's two agog ladies, but then did his wife a lovely kindness, publicly yielding to her as if only Saray had power to persuade him in such a desperate matter. "I've thought it over again, and I think you're right. I am too cautious. I see no harm in occasional visits, if you wish them."

Saray's eyes widened in pleasure and surprise, and when she turned to Brierley, her smile was triumphant. "Good morning, mistress."

"My lady," Brierley answered, and curtsied to her.

Saray looked her over and frowned delicately. "That dress is wrinkled, mistress, as if you'd slept in it. Haven't you any others?" An expression sharp as a wound crossed Melfallan's face, and he turned away.

Brierley blinked in surprise, abruptly aware of the gulf between this pleasant high lady and herself. In Saray's world, women lived comfortably, and never, never, slept in dayclothes. Another quick image, of silken nightclothes and comfortable feather beds, a luxury so taken for granted it was no longer noticed. She flushed slightly, embarrassed about her clothes despite her better judgment. Did Saray think prisoners had a choice of wardrobe? "I wasn't allowed to bring much else."

"Indeed?" Saray asked and looked indignant. "Well, I'll find something suitable." Saray beckoned to one of her ladies, a young woman with pretty curls and a freckled face. "Natalie," she called in her light voice.

Brierley sighed and looked down at her shoes, feeling a fish out of water, a lark out of the air, a midwife wren among these noble peahens. Lady Saray meant well, but Brierley felt the gulf nonetheless: whatever had bonded between them during the healing was slipping away, rearranged by Saray's firm understanding of her world and how she wanted it. For gratitude and maybe other reasons, Saray, too, was "making a statement." Brierley would be dressed in proper clothes and made presentable, and otherwise ordered into what was proper.

You think so, my lady? Brierley thought stubbornly.

The girl Natalie came swaying over, and raked Brierley with a look Brierley sensed more than saw, half apprehension, half contempt. Such easy contempt, Brierley thought sourly, when the world is easy. "Yes, my lady?" Natalie said in a lilting voice.

"Please take Mistress Brierley below and find her some decent clothes."

"*Her*, my lady?" Natalie asked acidly, too stupid to temper her contempt even before her lady and lord.

"I would rather not," Brierley intervened softly. "Not from Natalie's hands," she added, and saw bafflement sweep across Natalie's face. "But your offer is much appreciated, Lady Saray."

A faint line appeared between Saray's eyebrows. "But I insist," she said firmly, as she always spoke to wayward lady-maids, as Saray's mother had always spoken. Her tone ranked Brierley neatly, and further widened the gulf.

In Saray's ordered feminine world, other women had only three classes: the nobly born, the lady-maid, and the castle servant. Brierley was not nobly born, and thus could not possibly be considered a near-equal. In her gratitude to Brierley, however, Saray could not think Brierley a mere servant, midwife though she was. That left only lady-maid, like Natalie, Saray having no place in her lady's world for any category of witch, and Saray felt pleased with her own flattery. It was not a role that Brierley wanted.

She took a step away and curtsied to Melfallan, then to Lady Saray. "If you will excuse me, my lord, my lady," she said politely. "My parole on deck was only temporary." Before Saray could object, Brierley turned and headed for the stairwell, then descended rapidly down the stairs. She shut the door of her narrow compartment behind her and hung her hat on a nail, then sat down on her cot.

Stubborn, Melfallan called me. Well, I am that. And likely I've offended Saray beyond recall. She'll not wheedle me with fine clothes a second time, I'll hazard.

She lay down and laced her fingers on her stomach, then stared at the plank ceiling, wishing herself far away, safe in her sea cave, safe from the noble uses of a wayward witch. She sighed and forgave Saray her assumptions. She had meant well, and had honestly thought her compliments would please.

She fingered Clara's blanket on her cot and looked at the large basket new-sprung in the corner. I value these more, she thought. Does that make me proud? She smiled, then laughed softly. Thora taught me too well, I think. Yes, I am proud.

I don't want to be Saray's lady-maid. I want what I had, my sea cave and the fisherfolk of Yarvannet and my craft. She slowly rubbed her face with her hands, and sighed again. Will I ever have what I want again, I wonder?

Saray did not insist on dressing Brierley as a lady's maid, nor did she seek many interviews, but Earl Melfallan visited her every morning of their voyage. He told her about the northern lords and what he knew of them, where their lands lay, and whom he counted as allies and whom he did not. As a boy, Melfallan had spent several summers at his aunt's court in Airlie, Ingal's southern county, and later a long autumn in Mionn, the eastern earldom, when the two earls and Countess Rowena had courted Saray for him and arranged their marriage. Seeing her interest, he added descriptions of the mountains and lakes in Airlie, the river plain surrounding Darhel, and the high mountains that divided Ingal and Mionn, and she listened, fascinated, imaging the places in her mind. All her life she had lived near three small towns, a single stretch of coast. Melfallan had traveled far more widely, and enjoyed telling her about the lands elsewhere.

She learned that he and Saray had left their infant son behind at Yarvannet in the care of Marina, his wet nurse, and a half-dozen other trusted servants: better that than the perils of a drafty ship and uncertain fevers in a distant port, Melfallan said, though he sounded unconvincing. She suspected his advisors' platitudes in the decision, and Melfallan now regretted that he had given in. His fear for his baby son shadowed his thoughts, although he had ordered a constant guard on the baby's rooms, with only trusted soldiers personally selected by Sir Micay, and had bid Marina to sleep in the suite each night, where she watched over the baby's every yawn and bubble and squirm. Besides, Melfallan tried to reassure himself, the baby was far safer in Yarvannet than in Darhel, where Tejar's servants were everywhere, a truth that brought him some comfort. Brierley did not know how to comfort him further: until Melfallan returned to Yarvannet and resumed his personal vigilance over his new son, he would worry, whatever she said.

He also told her the names of the others who had petitioned him in her favor, and she thought about those good folk when she was alone. Harmon, of course, but Marta, too, and even old Master Cormley and the sour-minded butcher who'd always cut her purchases short on his scale. Jared's father in Amelin had also submitted his petition, quite a long one, and had also written directly to Brierley, entrusting his letter to Harmon, as had others in Amelin and Natheby. Brierley read the letters in the quiet of her cabin, embarrassed by the praise, but warmed and comforted. Good folk, who took a risk in defending her, not only from lords but from the neighbors who would disapprove any championship of foul witchery.

Dear Mistress Mefell, one letter read, *I don't understand this talk of you being a witch, but I'm sure it's not true, and that the duke will be more sensible than some folk here in Natheby. You'd think people would look to getting in the harvest and keep to their own affairs rather than gossip on the wharves. I told my neighbor that, and she didn't like it at all, but I said it and it's true.*

Dear Mistress Mefell, read another in the herder boy's awkward writing, *I think you are a very good person and a blessing to both our towns. My mother told me to write that to cheer you, but I think so, too. I'm saving you a seashell I found on the beach! I think you will like it.*

Marta's letter was anguished. *My husband rarely speaks to any one, so ashamed he is. Only Yanna can brighten him, I cannot.* She lingered over Marta's letter, and finally asked Clara for some paper and a pen.

Dear Marta, she wrote, *it was not his fault, and not yours. Whatever happens in Darhel, you should talk with Clara Jacoby. She can tell you.* She wrote to the others, too, and entrusted the letters to the Jacobys to carry back to Yarvannet when they could.

As they leaned on the ship rail in the day's bright morning, Melfallan also told her about Countess Rowena's witch twenty years before, and how that incident had imperiled Rowena's county. Tejar had pounced on the rumor of a witch in Airlie and had sent his own justiciar to investigate, meddling in Airlie's governance. Rowena, with her husband's approval, had promptly sent the duke's justiciar back to Darhel on horseback, tied up in ropes to his eyebrows. Duke Tejar thundered threats, which Airlie ignored. The crisis had escalated to Tejar's soldiers marching into Airlie when the witch had suddenly died.

"How did she die?" Brierley asked softly.

Melfallan grimaced. "She hanged herself in the forest. Or someone helped her to it, but I think she did it herself, to save my aunt from a foolish defense that risked too much, or so Jonalyn decided." He stirred restlessly. "Don't solve the problem that way, Brierley. Trust me more than Jonalyn trusted my aunt."

"I will try."

Melfallan drew in a long breath and hesitated, then abruptly changed the subject. Talking of trust and the growing friendship between them had become dangerous. Being so often in his company, Brierley was aware of Melfallan's growing attraction to her, not as commoner to be defended, nor as crux to his lordly affair, but as a woman. She sensed the earlier women in Melfallan's life, and the muddle of his unhappiness afterward, and knew he sometimes grew too aware that they sat alone together on her bed, with a shielding door between them and the guard. He no longer kissed her hand in his gallantry and sat himself carefully away from her in her cabin, then took to standing again, and throughout tried desperately not to think about it. She dared not raise the subject herself, not knowing where the discussion might lead, for her own inclinations were not trusty, either.

In her childhood, until she learned the not-listening that shielded her, Brierley had known what passed between her mother and stepfather in the privacy of their bed, and had felt her mother's desire as if it were her own, and had sensed Alarson's answering lust. As a child, the knowing had confused her badly. Later, when the same desires came with her womanhood, she understood better, but had not sought such love for herself, not yet. From her mother's own unhappy life, she knew the gulf between man and witch, a gulf that could not be bridged. And, in truth, no young man she'd met had stirred her heart to tempt the chance—except perhaps Jared, but she had been only nine when she sent him away.

But I am tempted now, she thought unhappily. As Melfallan is tempted, though he barely admits it to himself. It would be madness. Near the end of their sea voyage, Melfallan found better cause to talk to her in the sunlight on deck, and two mornings did not speak to her at all. It seemed easier for both of them, a prudent restraint, an ending before a beginning.

I never expected this, either, she admitted to herself. I envied Clara her home and kitchen, her sons and good husband, but never truly believed such a life suited me. How much less the likelihood of a lord's love, and that lord the young earl himself? Saray is daughter to the earl of Mionn, Melfallan's principal ally against their hostile duke. Saray is mother of his heir, his son to take Yarvannet. And why should such a gentle lady be hurt, merely because she is blinded by her own upbringing? Melfallan has risked that hurt before with his other affairs, but I should not. One of us must be wise, if the other cannot be.

She lay on her bunk in her narrow cell as the days slowly passed, listening to the rush of the sea air and waves as the ship bore them northward, to a fate she could not foresee.

Were any of my dreams possible? she wondered sadly. And of those dreams, if I could choose one to be real, which would it be?

After a week at sea, they sighted the large inlet several miles in width which led upriver to Darhel, Duke Tejar's capital. North of the inlet lay Tyndale, the Courtrays' original holding in the north and now given to another noble family; south lay the county of Briding, a coastland of gentle hills and steep ravines splashing waterfalls onto the beaches. Twice as they sailed northward the ocean current had borne them nearer the Briding coast, enough to see the land in its details, even the wink of sails near Briding's two small ports. Yarvannet she had thought large: as Brierley now looked at this broadest of rivers and the river plains rolling ahead to the horizon, she realized again there was a wider world than she had known.

At the busy port at the river mouth, the captain went ashore and hired a river pilot, then took advantage of the increasing startide of autumn to breast the river current for several miles. Then, with sturdy ropes tied to four teams of mules, Melfallan's ship entered a large tow canal, beginning the slow ascent of more river miles to Darhel.

Brierley took advantage of Melfallan's parole on deck to watch their progress up the river, as did all the noblefolk and commoners on board. The plains gleamed with frost in the mornings, quickly burned off by the Daystar, but built again with rime after the Companion set in the late evening. The river water seemed colder, too, and a different shade of gray-green, with bright red fish swirling in great schools beneath the ship in the canals. A few fishermen dipped their seine nets and caught the tiny bright fish, spilling their crimson cascades into their wicker baskets. Overhead, the sea larks and a larger bird with bright white patches on inky black swirled and spun, plunging daringly to steal a fish from the catch.

Late on the second day, when the ship turned another bend, they saw ahead a wide valley with a white-stoned city winking distantly in the sunlight, seemingly a child's toy with the distance, and the river a broad shining road winding its way across the plain toward it. Brierley watched small boats descend up and down the open river, the bargers waving their caps at the sailing ships in the canal, their wives busily pounding laundry in river water dipped from the side. Like three swans in procession their own ship and two smaller sailing ships were towed patiently upstream, past the bargers on one side, past small farms and docksides on the other, one plodding mule hoof after another.

One of the two ships in their train was Count Revil's light sloop, swifter on wind and current than Melfallan's larger ship, and so had eventually overhauled Melfallan's ship despite departing a day later from Amelin. Brierley could see the count's slim figure on board his ship's deck, bedecked on top with a magnificent plumed hat as always, and thought she recognized Jared among Revil's soldiers lounging at the rail. Certainly one of the young men saw her looking back from her vantage on the high stern and had bowed low. She had dared to wave back, earning herself a scowl from a nearby lady-maid in fine silk. Brierley put up her chin and waved again at Jared.

"I'll tell the earl," the lady-maid hissed in Margot's voice. "You're not supposed to wave at people."

So this was the ill-favored Margot, Brierley thought. "Halloa and away, mistress," she retorted. "I'll wave as I like." She waggled her fingers at Margot, which did not please that pinched-mouth lady.

"Not for long," Margot said with menace. "The duke will see to that."

"Are you now the duke's confidante, too?" Brierley asked. "You rise quickly in station, lady." Margot sniffed and walked away. Brierley decided the encounter was a tie.

She sighed and leaned an elbow on the railing, then smiled as Jared waved again. Now he had two of the other soldiers waving, and their energetic efforts attracted their sergeant's attention. The older man stalked toward the trio and they hastily scattered back to their duty.

I do find my champions, Brierley thought—and my enemies, she added, looking aside at Margot. And with each quite unaccounted, with reason all their own—or lack of it.

She sniffed the air, colder and damper here in the north, and marveled at the jagged mountains rising beyond Darhel. Already, although it was only late autumn, storms gathered repeatedly over the distant peaks, stirred there by air currents and heated rock. She saw a distant shatter of lightning, like golden eels winking in the sun, and watched the dark clouds build into tall palaces, roiling and tumbling against each other. In Yarvannet, sea storms came at night with a rush of wind and rain, building the surf into a roar. Here the sky built cloud cities, winking gold over dark stone.

She looked at the mountains and the gathering storm, and wished herself a seabird to climb the updrafts higher and higher. There the air's delicious coolness could frost the edges of feathers, cooling the blood. She leaned happily on the rail, watching the mountains, and the wind flirted with her hair.

I like rivers, she decided comfortably. On such a day, I could sail on one forever, watching the land flow past.

"Rain in the mountains," Melfallan said behind her, and she turned. He squinted at the distant hills, then sniffed at the air. "And winter coming soon. This river ices badly in winter, right up to Pass." Why the world's suns passed one another in the sky in early spring, no one knew. Nor did scholars know why the weather turned violent when the suns Passed, blowing away the winter with raging eastern storms that outrivaled every winter gale.

"The mountains are very high," she said. "I can see snow already on the peaks."

"With more to come. Every autumn storm dumps its share of snows on those peaks." He pretended a shiver. "No one crosses the mountains in winter." He smiled down at her. "Do you still like your parole?"

"You are very gracious. Yes, I do."

"I can promise only one more day. We reach Darhel tomorrow night."

"I am ready. Thank you."

He opened his mouth as if to say more, adding some comfort and hope beyond what he truly believed, then merely smiled again and turned away.

Near the evening of the third day in the tow canal, the mules brought Melfallan's ship to the Darhel docks, a busy and noisy length of piers and ship berths and low warehouses that stretched a half-mile in breadth beneath Darhel's tall city walls. Beyond a wide bridge and array of rooftops, Brierley could see the soldiers keeping watch high on the battlements of the duke's tall castle in the middle of the city. A stream of well-dressed people, whether commoner or noble, went in and out of the city gates, some visiting the market stalls along the docks, some lingering on the bridge, all raising a clamor with their voices, a constant movement and sparkle. Indeed, enough people walked within her view on this one riverside dock to fill all of Amelin. Brierley frankly gawked at a city ten times as large as Tiol, a town she had thought rather sizable in itself.

The world is larger than you know, she reminded herself. Although the ocean lay miles behind them, the crowd near the docks created its own surf of movement and voices, the dockside crowd making the closer splash of wave to the distant surf roar of the city itself. Ten thousand souls lived within Darhel, Melfallan had said, and made a loud beating of thought and need she instinctively warded away. She braced herself and felt intangible shields rise to protect her mind against that distant clamor, a guarding she recognized and trusted, although never much needed before. In such a city among too many minds, a witch might drown, as easily as a small child lost between one wave and the next.

Was her sister here in Darhel? Or did she live elsewhere in Ingal? Was she dead or alive? If she was here, how would Brierley find her in such a roaring? Brierley tightened her hands on the railing and closed her eyes with the urgency of her wishing. After a few moments, she sighed and relaxed her painful grip, then listened again to the mental roar of Duke Tejar's city, but heard nothing but incomprehensible noise.

She noticed a horseman winding his way through the bustling crowd on the dock, followed by a lady's sedan chair borne by four liveried servants. Brierley gawked again, never having seen the like of a sedan chair, nor heard of them except in Harmon's more far-ranging tales of the High Lords and their accoutrements. The rich red plush of the curtains swayed with the easy motion of the servants' walk, and the suns' light glinted on fine brass.

The horseman, a young lord with red hair, bent to a gap in the curtains, then straightened and touched his heels to his horse, his jewelry glinting in the late-afternoon sunlight, as rich as his clothing. As the sedan chair pursued a leisurely path through the crowd, the man cantered forward, guiding his horse deftly around a wagon, through a crowd of people, rounding the pier and clattering onto the dock to Melfallan's ship. At the ship gantry, he swept off his hat and smiled up at Brierley.

Surely not at me, she thought with alarm, and looked behind her. Standing on the raised deck in the stern were Earl Melfallan and his lady, arm in arm, and indeed it was they the man greeted. "Welcome, Yarvannet!" he called, and bowed low over the saddle horn, his velvet hat tucked to his breast.

"Ho, Robert," Melfallan called back. "And a good day to you as well!"

"Get off that moldering raft," the man shouted, "and come see the countess. She's come down to the dock to meet you."

"This is my best ship," Melfallan retorted. "Watch your words, brother. I'll get offended."

"As I said," Robert said impudently with a wide grin. "Moldering. It must be that southern wind of yours, eating away at wood and wharf. So offend away, good earl. I am undented."

Melfallan and Saray began moving toward the ship gantry, and the man dismounted with a sweep of his cape. He bounded up the gantry ramp, and brushed past Brierley in a swift striding motion, his hands outstretched. Melfallan seized his hands, smiling as broadly.

"Welcome," Robert said again, then swept up Saray in an enthusiastic embrace, enough to lift Saray's slippers quite off the deck. "And you, too, baby sister. How are you faring? You look hearty enough."

Saray laughed and made him put her down. "You are too bold, Robert," she said. "Where are your manners?"

"I left them behind me in Mionn, as always when not under Father's vigilant eye. There's no help for it, Saray. I think you'd be used to it by now."

The sedan chair had now arrived at the ship, too, and Brierley watched with wonder as a fine lady of middle age emerged, tall and proud and dressed all in silver cloth, with a slash of crimson silk at her waist and throat. She stood and looked up at Melfallan with little expression on her face, but Brierley caught a touch of her glad welcome, a breath of thought, quickly gone. Melfallan hastened down the wooden gantry and bent to kiss her hand, then stepped aside as she embraced Saray.

Beside their ship, Count Revil's ship was now also docking, with glad waving of a plumed hat as Revil saw the countess. Revil bounded down a shipside ladder, not waiting for the gantry to be laid, and joined the party on the dock. Then, talking gaily, the noble people moved away. Brierley gripped the railing tightly and swayed a little, overwhelmed by so much finery, such glad welcomes, and the figure of the silver lady.

"Who is the lady?" she asked Natalie and Margot, who stood nearby. Natalie gave her a sour look and turned away; then both followed Saray's other ladies down the planking to the dock, each burdened with a small bag.

Brierley felt a plump hand slip into hers, and she turned her head to smile into Clara's eyes. The stout farmwife bravely struggled against tears, with a fluttering fear in her mind, a fear for her friend. "Do not worry," Brierley said, and patted her hand.

"Don't be silly," Clara replied. "Of course I will. But Harmon says it will come out all right, Brierley. I trust in that. So should you."

"I will," Brierley assured her, not wholly truthful, but Clara seemed comforted.

As Brierley and Clara watched the noblefolk walk away, the ship's cooper appeared from belowdecks with iron bracelets linked by a strong chain, then walked toward Brierley, his face faintly apologetic. Brierley took a step backward.

"I have orders, mistress," the man said.

"From the earl?"

"Yes." The man's eyes were troubled. "You're to be taken over the bridge, too, although not to such pleasant surroundings as the Countess of Airlie's salon. I'm sorry, mistress. I hope it comes well for you, truly."

"Thank you. Ocean bless you, good man." Brierley sighed and lifted her hands and suffered the cooper to snap on the bracelets.

In a few minutes, Brierley's own greeting party arrived in a phalanx of the duke's soldiers, each armed with a sword and lance and stern determination. They made a circle around her and marched her off the ship onto the dock, attracting every eye about. She heard the whispers begin, the stir of interest spreading along the dockside like a breeze rippling a field of wheat.

Brierley shut her mind against it, bent her head, and watched her shoes move back and forth under her skirt hem, each foot lifting the edge on each stride forward, then vanishing as step succeeded step. When will I run? she asked herself in despair. When will I save myself and run as I should? When will I give up this patient stride across wood and stone, with a rhythmic tramping of soldiers all about me?

I could run now. I could dash away. But Brierley walked slowly onward, her chains clanking, her footsteps in rhythm with the guards' steady tramping.

Behind her, another party of the duke's soldiers met Lord Landreth as he emerged from his cell belowdecks. Brierley glanced around and saw his wild-eyed look at the sky and Darhel's docks. There was a brief scuffle, and then Landreth, too, tramped onto Darhel's docks under guard, his head bowed. Baffled fury showed in every tense line of his body, but the days of his imprisonment had already begun their toll. He did not fight much now, only hated, sullen and uncomprehending and dangerous.

Run, Landreth, Brierley wished him with sudden empathy. Run when you can, as I have not.

9

As his party neared the city gate, Melfallan turned his head and saw Brierley leaving the ship in chains. He scowled, knowing his order was necessary but hating it. A gentle lass did not belong in chains; Revil had the right of that. His aunt rapped his arm sharply with her fan, regaining his attention.

"Mind your eyes, nephew," she said. "We are observed on all sides." She nodded at the guards on the city walls and the bustle of the dockside crowd. "Ah, here is Stefan," she said, as a tall young man with flaxen hair hurried forward to join them. "Stefan, you are late. Where have you been?"

"Forgive me, Countess Rowena." Stefan bowed low. "Your errand took longer than I expected."

"An unlikely story," Rowena said, though she smiled fondly at her liegeman. Stefan fell into step with their party, a deferential two paces behind the countess. "Do you remember Stefan, Melfallan? My steward's son?"

"Of course I do. You forget, Aunt, that as boys Stefan and I coursed your Airlie hills. Good day, Stefan."

"Your grace, I remember those hills well," Stefan answered genially, and managed to bow in midstride, a graceful trick Melfallan knew was well beyond his own ability. Stefan had had the practice: Rowena required much of her liegemen, and proper courtly graces stood at the top of her list. Stefan and Melfallan shared an amused glance as both remembered certain special pranks, most of which Melfallan's aunt had somehow never discovered.

From the corner of his eye, he saw Robert frown slightly at Stefan's easy familiarity. However Robert thought he slipped his traces when he left his own court at Mionn, he still carried Mionn's ordering of propriety and rank with him, an expectation that ran even more strictly than in Airlie or Ingal. Melfallan wondered idly if his brother-in-law had any friends among his own servants in Mionn, as Melfallan had with Ennis in Yarvannet, then wondered what Robert would think of a friendship with a commoner midwife. Melfallan counted on Mionn's support in Brierley's ordeal, and Robert had considerable influence with his father.

They walked several more paces, watching the crowd as the crowd watched them, and then Rowena tapped her fan again, this time at Stefan. "Stefan," she said, "stop ogling Saray's ladies. I won't have any of that. What would Christina say?"

"I wasn't ogling," Stefan declared with injured innocence. "I ogle only Christina, the life of my heart, and she knows it."

"A babe in the woods, that dear child." Rowena tsked, waggling her head. "I must disabuse her."

"Countess—" Stefan looked slightly panicked. Rowena sometimes carried through on such mild threats, and was wholly unpredictable whether she would or would not. It was the bane of Stefan's life in her service. Melfallan hid a smile.

But Rowena smiled fondly at Stefan, and relented. "Perhaps I was mistaken. Yes, I'm sure I was, though I will admit the brunette is quite attractive." She turned to Saray. "Where did you acquire her, Saray?"

"You mean Natalie?" Saray asked. "She's Yarvannet-born, Aunt, and related to our justiciar, Sir James. A grandniece, I think. Shall I introduce her?" Saray turned half-around, ready to summon Natalie forward to her side.

"No, my dear. That's quite all right. I merely wanted the name."

Rowena's dismissal was so pointed that Melfallan wondered what his aunt had seen in the few brief minutes there on the dock. He looked at the lady-maids following in their wake, but Natalie looked no different than usual. What had drowned all of Rowena's interest in Natalie, even for an introduction that the young woman would covet? Melfallan grimaced to himself. He had hoped to dump Natalie into his aunt's entourage, and thus rid Saray of her. That seemed an idle chance now, but Rowena might still be wheedled.

Their party walked into the cool shadows of the city gate and emerged into the bright sunshine of the inner plaza. A faint rippling of applause greeted his aunt as she walked with them, and she nodded and smiled at the crowds bustling through the square. The Countess of Airlie was popular in Darhel, both a measure of his aunt's graciousness and the duke's lack of it.

Saray leaned heavily on his arm and gave a small sigh, and Melfallan signaled for the sedan chair that followed in their wake. "Saray is still tired from childbed, Aunt. May we borrow your sedan?"

"Of course! I didn't think, my dears. Saray, you must forgive me." Rowena was immediately solicitous, which made Saray smile. The two women had always been close, with Rowena as the champion of her marriage to Melfallan years ago, and Saray's constant advocate since. "And the baby!" Rowena exclaimed an instant later. She slapped her palm to her forehead. "Great Ocean, how could I forget the baby? When your courier arrived, I babbled for a week in my joy."

Melfallan assisted Saray onto the cushions of the sedan chair and tucked in her skirts, earning himself a happy smile from his wife. He returned the smile, hoping his effort looked genuine.

"We named him Audric," Saray told Rowena proudly. Saray rearranged her skirts neatly around her ankles, and lay back on the cushions with a sigh.

The countess nodded, approving the choice. "My father would have liked that. The world is strangely empty without an Audric. Did you bring the baby with you?" She glanced over the ladies and servants who trailed after them, obviously hunting the nurse and her precious bundle.

Saray shook her head. "I'm sorry, no. We left him in Yarvannet. After waiting so long, I won't hazard him to the cold drafts of a sea voyage." Another smile, happy and sunny.

For a moment, her eyes met and held Melfallan's, briefly reconnecting them in their mutual joy in their son. Perhaps our son can still make the difference, Melfallan thought, and felt suddenly torn by both an old hope and a new dread. He was conscious of the heat rising to his face, and knew too well that the reason was a sea-shine witch, stubborn and pale and valiant. Saray gave him a puzzled glance, sensitive to his moods however she little understood them. He smiled as naturally as he could, and bent forward to kiss her, for all they were in public. He then rejoined his aunt at the head of their party.

Arm in arm, the countess and Melfallan led the others across the square fronting the ducal palace, where they were met by the duke's chief steward. Walking corridor after corridor of the duke's large castle, they followed the steward to the countess's permanent apartments. Saray occupied herself with directing the servants' unpacking as boxes and chests were brought up from the ship, and Revil went off with Count Robert to see Robert's new stallion in the stables.

Rowena chatted with Saray as gowns and jewels were safely stored; then, when courtesy was fully done, the countess signaled to Melfallan to follow her. They settled in the countess's parlor just off her own bedchamber, a pleasant room of books and statuary and flowers, with candles gleaming in the corners. Stefan brought a tray and chased out two lady-maids, then bowed himself out of the room as well. Rowena poured wine in two goblets from a silver pitcher, and then seated herself in the other chair across from Melfallan.

"So," she said, eyeing him.

"So?" Melfallan sipped at his wine.

"Don't be contrary, Melfallan. Your message omitted any mention of your witch, but the duke has covered that lapse quite thoroughly in its absence. He has summoned the High Lords for the trial and condemning of that young woman. It's obvious he expects only one outcome. Who is she?"

Melfallan dodged the question. "I thought condemnation

came *after* trial, not before it," he said. "Are all the Ingal counts here? And Mionn?"

"The Ingal counts, but Earl Giles sent Robert in his place." Her forehead creased in a frown. "The autumn storms struck early in Mionn, it appears, and have flooded two of his port cities. He claimed greater need for his presence there."

"Earl Giles won't be here?" Melfallan stared at her. "I was counting on—"

"I suspected you were. What are you scheming, if anything at all? What possessed you to cooperate by bringing her here, without protest, without a delay? You could have waited months, making excuses." Rowena's voice sharpened in her distress. "Don't you realize the peril you face now? The duke plans to condemn more than your witch: he'll taint you with the same evil and rid you and Saray of Yarvannet. You play right into his hands!"

"Brierley Mefell is not evil," Melfallan said quietly. "And I'm not a fool." He set his jaw. "You haven't thought it through. Am I that stupid in your eyes? And what of Mionn? Would Earl Giles allow his daughter to lose the rank he arranged for her? I can't believe you'd think such a thing of him—or me."

The countess scowled. "Your grandfather was just as stubborn," she said, "and you perhaps take after him too much, Melfallan. Witch trials can be as perilous for lords as they are for the unfortunate women they victimize. I was once as innocent as you and tried to champion a witch. My husband nearly lost Airlie as a result." She put down her glass and rose with a rustling of her skirts, then paced to the window. "And for what?" she said bitterly. "A suicide in the forest, and an enmity with the duke that has simmered for years. If not for Jonalyn, Tejar and I might have pretended mutual liking for decades, and gone to our graves never having admitted how thoroughly we despise each other, how we wish each other evil and loss." She ground her teeth. "I blame Tejar for tormenting my husband with rumors as he lay dying. And I blame Tejar for trying to ruin Airlie afterward."

"He wanted you as wife, as I heard it, both before and after you married Count Ralf."

"When the mountains melt," Rowena declared, "will I be wife to him."

"I think, Aunt, that Tejar got that point."

Rowena tossed her head. "Just so. But then Jonalyn appeared, and ended in Tejar's near-invasion of my county. Witches were peril to Airlie, Melfallan, and are peril to you."

"Jonalyn died for you, to save you."

"Did she?" The countess turned back to the window. "She did it for herself. What woman wishes to burn on a pyre, with the commoners laughing and jeering as the flames crisp her flesh? Does your witch understand what awaits her?"

Melfallan rose, now as agitated as his aunt. "I don't believe that outcome is fixed. The law says—"

"The law," Rowena interrupted, her voice scornful, "bends as the duke wishes. It always has with this duke. The Earl of Mionn knows that and stays away." She ground her teeth. "How could he? Saray is his own daughter. She will suffer with you, and yet Earl Giles does nothing." Rowena paced again, her skirts rustling.

Melfallan swallowed uneasily, not happy with her interpretation. Rowena in a temper sometimes resembled a Pass storm herself, and her passions sometimes undermined her judgment, as perhaps now. "Maybe Mionn's excuse is genuine. Mionn gets the brunt of the eastern sea storms, and winter is only a month away. You know that. Mionn always gets the worst of the storms. And Robert is capable. He has sense."

"Robert is son, not earl." Rowena gestured dismissingly.

Melfallan sat down again. "I don't believe the outcome is fixed," he said stubbornly.

"I think, dear nephew, you are naïve."

"I think, dear aunt," Melfallan retorted, "that you are overreacting. I want to know why. Come, sit down again and drink your wine and tell me." He gestured at her chair and waited patiently as she stopped her pacing, poised by the window. He valued his aunt's opinions, and valued her strength. Rash as she sometimes was, he rarely saw her this agitated.

Rowena smiled suddenly, and shook her head in wonder. "You mature, Melfallan. I haven't seen you enough since you became earl. What comes next? Accusing me of womanly hysteria?"

"You?" Melfallan snorted. "Hysterical? Not a chance. It's not possible."

Rowena clasped her hands in front of her skirts, wringing them. "You are kind to me. I know exactly how I sound, and I rue it. For three weeks I've been waiting for you, spinning myself into a gyre. I see it all happening again, with such loss at the end, such bitter loss, to no purpose but the triumph of undeserving men." She bit her lip and turned toward the window. "I loved Jonalyn very much, you know. You never met her, you were only a small boy then, but Jonalyn had a delicacy of person, a simple grace of being—"

"I know," Melfallan said quietly.

Rowena turned, caught by his tone, and their eyes met. "She is the same, your witch?" she asked softly.

"I've never met anyone like her." Melfallan shook his head in wonderment. "She— she is—stubborn," he finished in frustration. His aunt gave him a look of sympathy.

"So was Jonalyn," she said sadly. "Too much so. Does she admit to the witchery?" As Melfallan hesitated, Rowena's expression changed again, becoming impatient with him. "I am your ally in this, Melfallan, if anyone is. Does she admit it?"

"It depends on what you mean by witchery. The statute defines—" Rowena made a rude noise, and Melfallan glared at her mildly. "You *will* let me finish, Aunt. Is she a witch, as the statute defines it? I don't know. I thought witches were only an old legend, an evil stamped out centuries ago by Duke Rahorsum. All those stories of plague and controlling minds, of improbable witch magic, magnified by the telling since, magnified by the fears and superstition. But whom did Rahorsum destroy? The evil he described in his chronicles, or women like Jonalyn and Brierley? What did we lords do back then? Whose was the evil? Ours or theirs?"

Rowena sighed. "It is not a simple question, I agree."

"Nor a simple outcome for Brierley, whatever your fears. Don't glare at me, Aunt. I need your help, not your despair. What happened twenty years ago is not fixed to happen again, as if we have no choice in our lives." He paused and eyed her. "Do I have your help?"

"I remind you I changed your diapers as an infant," Rowena said, tossing her head.

"I have no doubt of that," Melfallan replied, "though I profess I don't remember it at all."

His aunt snickered, amused, then at last walked to her chair and sat down. She picked up her glass and took a long swallow. "Fear can sap the blood, I agree," she said. "Forgive me mine, my dear. When Jonalyn died, something precious went out of the world, leaving me bereft. My spirit has never recovered from it. All other fears I can conquer, and have conquered, but this fear still unnerves me." She set down her glass and braced her shoulders. "Well, we are bound with what is. You are here, and events now unfold. I want to meet your Brierley."

"You shall."

"It will be a few days before the trial begins. We must use our time deftly among the assembled lords. Stefan can be our messenger as we conspire."

"I agree."

His aunt shook her head and sighed. "You *have* grown. Now I see Audric in you, in your face, in your gestures. I had hoped I would. I find it easy to confuse you with him, a fact I find comforting." Melfallan took her hand and pressed her fingers, then held her hand comfortably. Little else she could have said would have pleased him more, as she likely well knew. "Earl Audric always prevailed against Tejar's plots, to the benefit of our house. Let us hope you have inherited that quality, too."

"With your help, I am sure of it."

Rowena did not look wholly persuaded, but she nodded. "We shall see," she said. And then he told her who had killed Earl Audric, her father, and how he knew.

"Her word against Landreth's," his aunt judged, her eyes glittering dangerously. "She grows even more valuable with that testimony."

"But still her word against his, and hers easily disbelieved as a lie against an accuser. It's not proof enough to charge him with murder, so I'll use the women he abused and his physical attack on Brierley. One girl he raped was thirteen, and she aborted a child afterward—and will have no other children, Marina says. Her eyes stare a great deal."

"Such lusts are not uncommon among lords with the inclination," Rowena said with a sigh. "He learned it from his father, if not the actual lusting, then the liking for the fear. Sadon is an odorous marsh rat with shifty eyes. You should drown him."

"It's the son I'd like to drown, and not just for Audric's poisoning. Rape is never excusable." He had talked to the servant girl, receiving vague replies that sometimes made little sense, and had pitied her.

"Only because you have never been tempted to rape, dear one," Rowena said, surprising him. "There's no greater power over a woman than that intimate threat, and a man can find deep pleasure in the woman's fear, the cries of pain, the release of his lust at the peak." She calmly took a sip of her wine, then set her glass on the side table. "On that relevant point, I look forward to introducing you to Tejar's new justiciar, Gammel Hagan. Meeting him may help you understand men who find rape attractive. There are rumors about Hagan, disturbing ones."

"Tejar has a new justiciar? What happened to the old one?"

She waved a hand. "He retired, I suppose, and the Count of Lim gave Tejar this Hagan, a rather young man with lightless eyes. Watch out for Lim, by the way: he hides too much. And pay attention to Gammel Hagan: he's the man who will interview your Brierley for the duke. Make sure that Sir James is never far away when he does: Hagan doesn't recognize limits."

"You alarm me, Aunt," Melfallan said soberly.

"I mean to."

~

Brierley looked up from her small table and watched a gull wheel past the barred window of her cell. Although surely Duke Tejar had a dungeon, she had been confined in a tower room near the eastern battlements, a pleasant enough room with a breeze through the window, a faded tapestry on the wall, a comfortable enough bed. She had light and air, the shadowed pattern of sunlight that shifted as the suns moved across the sky, and the occasional seabird flying the heights to a nest under an eave, perhaps mistaking the duke's palace for a cliffside rookery.

She had spent the last two days largely alone, visited briefly three times a day by a silent guard with food. Clara and Harmon had not been permitted to see her: this was not an indulgent earl's castle or ship. Here the duke ruled, and Melfallan's prudence deepened under the duke's direct eye. Melfallan even brought a witness or two to his few short visits to her cell, always a duke's man, a steward or a castle soldier, once a minor lord distantly related to the duchess. Brierley met Sir James, Melfallan's justiciar, and had liked him: he would supervise the formal court's inquiry, and she sensed Sir James would insist on rationality and firmly ignore all nonsense. It is a matter of definition, Melfallan had said lightly, and had shared a confident glance with the older man.

She stood and walked restlessly up and down her small room, then leaned on the window casement for a time, craning her neck to see her limited view from her high tower. The fields surrounding Darhel stretched for miles across the valley. She could not see the peaks from this angle, but could see the river descending toward the sea, busy with boat traffic and the tiny white-sailed shape of another ship being towed upriver to Tejar's capital. Had her mother lived here in this wide valley, this white-stoned city? Had she known Jonalyn in Airlie to the south? Was Jonalyn her cousin, as Thora had said? Or had Jocater traveled from over mountains from Mionn's Flinders Lakes or the Eastern Bay's shoreside? From where had she come? And if from another place, were there shari'a still there in hiding? Were shari'a here in Darhel?

She smiled ruefully and leaned her chin on her hand, a little bored after the hours of nothing to do but think. Well, one shari'a in Darhel, surely, she thought, though I am not admitting that aloud anymore. Prudence becomes me; though it seems as useful now as a farmer closing the barn after his flock has fled over field and road in every direction, baaing and jumping and pushing as they tumbled. A farmer could regather his sheep, if he was quick, but some matters were not as easily rebottled.

She heard heavy footsteps outside her door, then the clanking of a key in the lock. She turned as the door opened and saw a heavyset guard, his eyes shadowed by his visor, one burly hand on the hilt of his sword.

"You will come," he said curtly.

"Where, sir?" Brierley picked up her hat and put it on, smoothing her hair back over her shoulders. The guard said nothing, merely glared. He was a different guard from the pleasant gawky man who brought her food, different in more than one sense, obviously, in his rudeness. She shrugged and followed him out of the room, although her heart beat faster.

They descended a short stair to the guard station, where another guard, also a stranger, waited with manacles. This other man she liked even less: he eyed her with an unpleasant leer, ready to hate and hurt. The jailer took the manacles from him and turned back to her.

"Do I have to wear those?" Brierley asked, stepping back out of reach. She had disliked them before when she was taken unawares on the ship, hated the thought now.

"Either willingly," the man said firmly, "or unwillingly. Your choice, mistress, but you will wear them." His companion flashed his teeth in unpleasant amusement, enjoying Brierley's discomfiture. She eyed him warily.

"Why?" she asked impatiently. "I'm not going anywhere. How can I run with a guard on every corner? And where would I run to?"

"My lord duke's orders," the jailer said impatiently. Brierley retreated another step as he came closer, half inclined to flee upward to her small cell, the only safety she'd known in the past few days, illusory as that safety might be.

"But why?" she insisted, glaring at him.

"To stop your spelling, why do you think?" The man's eyes glinted and the man behind him half-drew his sword in warning. "Without your hands, you can't work witchery, I'm told."

"An interesting theory," she retorted.

The jailer waited with a patience that surprised her, though his jaw was set. This large man was unaccustomed to resistance, at least from a woman. (*Stubborn for such a wisp of a girl*), she heard, his thought dropping neatly into her mind. Staunch and determined, this jailer, she sensed further, with a fat wife he adored and a son growing tall. *(I wonder why the lords think her a witch, but that's lords for you, bless them.)* "With your will or without it, you'll wear them," he repeated stubbornly. "The duke's orders, mistress."

He reminded her of Jared, just a little, as Jared might be in two decades, after a soldier's life had worn away hopes. Brierley held out her hands. "For your patience, sir, in the asking."

The jailer hesitated as he eyed her, mildly baffled by her easy surrender, then snorted and clasped the iron bracelets around her wrists. He took a slight tug at the chain, testing the links. "Come along then. You stay here," he said to the other man. "I can conduct her myself."

"I had orders—" the other man began irritably.

"Now you've got *my* orders," the jailer retorted. "Take the watch here for a few minutes. This won't take long. Come along, mistress."

Brierley followed the jailer down another flight of stairs, then across a wide courtyard cool with the mist from a fountain in the center of the square. They entered another corridor and walked down another flight of steps into yet another courtyard, hot with sunlight and as wide as an entire Amelin house. She heard the whisper of bird wings on the cornices that framed an overhead gallery, a hum of bees in a garden. The Daystar's light glanced down onto smooth cobblestone, still cool with the early hour. Brierley lifted her face to the sunlight and smiled, sniffing at the faint scents of the garden.

The jailer glanced back, checking that she followed, then stopped her at the next doorway. "Wait here," he ordered. He opened the wooden door and stepped through. "Naron, I want that watch list," he said gruffly to someone in the room beyond. "No more stalling."

Brierley glanced around the courtyard at the few people who busied themselves there as a murmured protest answered the jailer. A buxom older woman briskly shook a small carpet by the far courtyard door, and another careworn woman walked quickly across the patio, her arms piled with clothing. Two boys raced through, laughing as one chased the other from one doorway to another. The first woman paused and scowled and called after them in reproof. A servants' area, Brierley guessed, maybe by the kitchens.

By the water trough across the square, a small girl only five or six years of age was struggling with a bucket. She was dressed in tattered homespun, none too clean, her bare legs painfully thin, with her small feet tied into rough shoes by fraying strands of hemp. Her black hair curled in tangles down her back to her waist and would comb longer if groomed. Even at this distance, Brierley could see bruises climbing her arms and marring one cheek. A scullery maid's child, probably, learning the hardness of life too early.

A sea lark swooped suddenly into the square from the sky above, piping a golden cascade of notes, distracting the girl. She turned and looked at the bird flashing across the air, then looked down and saw Brierley standing under the gallery. As their eyes met, Brierley felt the shock of recognition, and saw the same knowledge in the girl's startled face.

My child— Without thinking, Brierley took a step toward her, her hands lifting in amazed joy. *I have waited to find you.*

The little girl dropped the bucket from nerveless fingers. Her mouth worked soundlessly, eyes staring at Brierley in the shadow of the walkway. She had paled to starkest white. Brierley stopped abruptly, suddenly aware of herself in this duke's castle with the jailer only steps away. To be so close!

Child— she sent again, all her yearning in her thought. *Oh, my child, I have longed to meet you, all these years.*

The girl's mental answer was an inarticulate cry of anguish, a silent scream. She covered her ears with her hands and bent over convulsively, stamping her feet in a fast staccato panic. Brierley stepped back a step, appalled, as the terrified little girl shook Brierley out of her thoughts, her knowing. *Don't tell! Don't tell!* A loud voice hammered into the child's mind, followed by a crushing wave of the mental voices all around them. A thin cry of anguish burst from the girl's lips, echoed by Brierley's own answering groan.

She has no mental shields! Brierley thought in panic. She is naked here! How has she survived?

On the far side of the patio, the castlewoman stopped beating the carpet and looked at the girl impatiently. "Megan!" she called. "What's the matter with you now? Why have you spilled the bucket? You careless child!"

The woman left her carpet and stomped across the stones, intending only a shaking to get the girl's distracted attention. Megan darted aside with a screech, eluding her, and ran around the stone wellhead. "You vexsome child!" the woman said irritably. "Come back here!" Megan skipped out of reach again.

Brierley turned away, although it wrenched at her, knowing the peril to the child in her open greeting. She felt the girl's frantic confusion reverberate through her mind, and could have run to her, scooped her up, and held her close until the anguish stilled. Brierley felt her body vibrate with the need, but held herself still. Death walked in that need, as surely as the Beast edged her waking dreams.

I love you, my child. Brierley's thought whispered across the courtyard, trying to soothe in the only way she could. The girl responded with a tumbling mix of confusion and disbelief, inchoate thoughts that were tinged by the ragged edge of madness. Megan did not know the source of Brierley's thought, had already forgotten their anguished first meeting. Her dark eyes looked wildly around the small courtyard, but missed Brierley in the shadows. *Pick up the bucket and finish your chores*, Brierley told her firmly. *Gently now.*

Out of the corner of her eye, she saw the girl draw her sleeve across her face, then bend for the bucket and drop it again into the trough. The castlewoman stopped chasing her and put her hands on her hips, glaring at the girl.

"I've spilled all the water, Sara," Megan said aloud, in a high, piping voice.

"That you did," Sara said mildly. She hesitated, then shook her head and stalked back to her carpet. "But there's lots of water left, child. Draw another bucket of it."

"That's not what Emily thinks," the girl answered disdainfully. She waved her tiny hand at the kitchens, and Brierley sensed a quick image of an older woman, head cook in the kitchen, harsh and demanding. "She's angry too much, and hits me. Hard." She rubbed at a bruise at her arm, then looked directly at Brierley in the shadows. "I never do things right," she piped mournfully. "Are you my mother?"

Brierley closed her eyes and swayed slightly.

"Your mother?" Sara asked. "Are you daft, child? Your mother died when you were born, you know that. You're strange again this morning, Megan. Pull yourself together. Give up your nonsense: it makes talk, bad talk you don't need."

"I don't believe it," Megan replied distractedly. "My mother is somewhere. I hear her in my dreams." Then Megan struck a grand pose, hand on a hip, one foot out, apparently copying someone both she and Sara knew. "Mind your business, woman," she lectured Sara severely.

"Mind your mouth, missy," the woman scolded, though she turned her face to hide a smile. She flapped her carpet vigorously for a moment, then continued: "Or I'll make *you* my business, don't you think I won't!" Megan saucily struck another pose. "And don't you mimic Cook Berthe that way," Sara warned, "or you'll get more bruises, child."

"She shouldn't hit me! I didn't do what she said I did!" Megan declared, her voice rising still more. "I didn't! It's not fair!" In her rage, Megan again forgot her strange contact with Brierley, too young to understand it, too angry to think of anything but her grievance. Megan stamped her feet angrily. "It's not *fair*!" she shrieked.

"Megan!" Sara cajoled. "Calm yourself. Get the water, now. Be a good child."

"No!" Megan declared.

The jailer came out through the wooden door and shut it, then tugged smartly at Brierley's sleeve. "Come along, mistress," he said. He glanced at the angry child in the courtyard, then walked onward, uninterested.

Be brave, Megan, Brierley thought soothingly, dropping

her thought into Megan's anger like a smooth salve. *Believe in what you are.*

The new contact distracted Megan, and her mood shifted. *But what am I? Do you know?* The sent thought was clumsy, barely half-formed, and bent in curious ways by Megan's emotions, but quite clear. The Blood spoke clearly in her thought, an unmistakable tug of the witch-sense Brierley remembered only vaguely from her childhood, before Jocater had completely silenced her own gift, denying it forever.

A witch-child in this place, young and undefended, Brierley thought, her own thoughts as tumultuous as Megan's emotions. And too passionate to survive long, not with such defiance. Megan's bruises showed that all too clearly. Brierley followed the jailer along the porticoed walkway, not looking back.

Do you know? the child demanded.

"Draw the water, Megan," Sara ordered briskly. "Draw the water. Don't be so strange, child. That's a good girl." Sara wheedled now, her voice laced with a rough affection. Megan picked up the bucket and hesitated, then turned to the trough at Brierley's reinforced command.

It's not fair, Megan's thought whispered rebelliously.

Wait for me—

Brierley and the jailer passed through the far doorway, and Brierley took care to walk passively, betraying nothing of her inner turmoil. Careful, now, she told herself. Take great care, Brierley.

They descended another level to a wide lane between blocky apartments, each with a balcony onto the square, then a long spiraling staircase to ground level, then another staircase into the bowels of the duke's castle. At the bottom of the stair, the jailer opened a door and ushered her in.

"You stay here."

"Thank you," Brierley replied courteously.

He gave her a sharp look, then left, locking the outer door behind him. Brierley looked around at the bare room with its small table, a single chair, and a bench, tempted to poke into the few cabinets along one wall or to crane her neck to look out a tiny set-glass window in another door that gave a view into the next room. It seemed a storage room or a jailer's waiting room of some sort, by the dungeons perhaps. Dungeons, my lot of late, she thought, and of which I grow tired.

She paced the narrow room, looking at the furnishings there, but did not open the cabinets, and listened for the child far above among the clamor of other minds. She caught an impression of a large kitchen with a roaring fire, a fat cook with a scowl, and a quick blow that spilled the water bucket and brought another blow for the spilling. Brierley winced and paced harder, wishing herself free to rush above and gather the child in her sure grasp, flying away with her from this place like sea larks spiraling away from a cliff. She listened as Megan crept into her small bed off the kitchen, rubbed her new bruises, then comforted herself with a stubby thumb in her mouth. As the child slipped into a doze, Brierley sat down on the bench underneath the window and sighed.

I can do nothing now, Brierley thought in despair. Nothing for her.

She sat unmoving for a half-hour, aware of Megan's slow breaths, the stir of early dreams, of a heart that beat slowly in a small chest. *My child*, she thought yearningly, dizzy with the abrupt discovery of a shari'a-child here in Darhel, and frustrated by the stone that separated them. She listened but did not disturb, wanting for Megan this precious sleep, this small escape from the kitchen's cruelties.

How? Why? She had a hundred questions, if the child could even answer them, and likely could not. Is she related to me? Did her kin know my mother or sister? Where *is* her mother, her kin? Are there others elsewhere? Where are her people—*our* people? Brierley's mind tumbled with questions, and it took all her will to keep her stillness on her bench. She looked down at the manacles on her wrists and rattled them impatiently.

She started at the sound of a key in the lock of the inner door, then looked up as a thin young man walked in, quite tall, and dressed in a black doublet with a silver chain of office hanging on his breast. He gave her a contemptuous look, then made a ceremony of locking the door behind him. Then, with a odd sound of satisfaction, the man opened a drawer and took out book and pen, then sat down in the single chair at the table. Brierley held herself still, watching him alertly.

"You will stand," he told her in a reedy voice.

No easy defiance here, she sensed, no guard to provoke without penalty. This young man was dangerous, far more dangerous than Lord Landreth and Landreth's self-indulgent vices. She sensed the malice in him, the liking of cruelty, with a quick impression of contorted faces sweated with pain, pain this man had ordered willingly and done in secret. Landreth had his twisted reasons for his cruelty: this man did not worry about reasons. She gathered herself and rose to her feet, then clasped her hands on her skirts in front of her, waiting.

"Your name," the man said, his pen poised over a blank page in his book.

"Brierley Mefell of Natheby in Yarvannet," she answered. "And yours?" she added recklessly.

"You will answer questions, not ask them," the man retorted, then slowly wrote down her name.

(*Gammel Hagan, my lord duke's justiciar*), the man gave her unwittingly. Brierley tightened her fingers hard, keeping her face blank to hide any reaction to that knowledge. Careful, careful: now it begins, the danger. As the duke's justiciar, Hagan had no legal right to interview her, not in Sir James's absence. It was part of her commoner rights, Sir James had explained carefully, that any formal criminal inquiry be conducted by Melfallan's justiciar and by no other official. That rule was written into the laws to safeguard each lord's authority over his own people, and usually lay to the accused's advantage. The secrecy of her summons here suggested Melfallan and Sir James did not know of this meeting. Already the duke bent the rules, even the rules that were his own laws.

Now it begins, she thought, the fight for life. For Megan, for me, perhaps for Earl Melfallan, too.

"When did you begin your witchery?" Hagan asked. He raised his cruel eyes and stared.

Brierley blinked, feigning stupidity. "My what?"

"You will give details and instances of the persons you have harmed and what stock you have killed."

Brierley put on a blank look and let her mouth fall open, gaping at him. So women are to be feared, are they, Gammel Hagan? she thought, as her witch-sense awoke fiercely, bringing her the essence of this man. You think a woman wins by guile and sexual pleasure, with loss to a man's soul each time he surrenders to that evil lure? She wins—and should never win. Hagan enjoyed torturing women the most, she sensed, especially in the sadism he employed in how he took them, using rape as a final degradation of his inquiry, and then mounting them again after they were condemned and hours from the grave. He enjoyed Death's near touch, and played with inflicting that touch on his victims, for the power it gave him, for the rabid lust it eased. In the back of Hagan's mind, she sensed a more recent horror while in Tejar's service, when Hagan had sampled dead flesh fresh from the gallows, still warm but cooling and slack.

Her flesh crawled as she sensed those depths in this evil man's mind. And Duke Tejar kept such a creature in his service? Or did the duke even know of Hagan's obscenities—or worse, did he care? I have never met true evil, she thought: and here it is, now before me. She wanted to look wildly around for escape, perhaps that small window, perhaps some way through the oaken door.

"Details," Hagan prompted.

"I don't know what you're talking about," she answered, as calmly as she could. "I am not a witch."

"Does it matter either way?" Hagan said, smiling slightly. "The end is the same. You can believe me in that."

He examined her slowly from head to foot, his eyes lingering on her breasts, then moved his eyes lower, staring so long that she colored despite herself. "Thin," he sniffed. "But what matter?" He waved his hand idly, a silver ring flashing in the dim light of the room.

"I am under the protection of Earl Melfallan," Brierley said coolly. "You had better not."

"Better not what?" Hagan asked snidely. "How could you know my thought? You betray yourself, witch."

"You stare at my body like that," she riposted, "and wonder how I guess?"

"And feel thrilled by my regard?" he asked with a sneer.

"*Your* regard?" she said automatically, and then chided herself for provoking him. Careful. Hagan's eyes narrowed, and he bent then to write industriously in his book.

"The woman Mefell states," he said as he wrote, "she has on twelve occasions cursed a neighbor's cattle, resulting in their death."

"I said no such thing," Brierley exclaimed. Hagan continued writing.

"The woman Mefell states she has on four occasions stolen and murdered an infant." Hagan raised his head. "What did you do with the bodies?"

Brierley tightened her lips and stared at him.

"Come, woman. We'll learn it all, sooner or later. Did you eat them? Or is there some special potency in an infant's body for your poisons? We wish to know, for the knowledge to protect against your kind."

They stared at each other for several moments. Hagan shrugged and resumed writing. "The woman Mefell admits that she had tampered with noble minds, particularly that of Lord Melfallan Courtray, Earl of Yarvannet, by encouraging the earl in plans of betrayal against his rightful lord, Duke Tejar of Ingal."

Ah. We reach the nub, she thought. Hagan had been well instructed.

"Why does Duke Tejar," Brierley asked curiously, "want to take away Earl Melfallan's lands? Will he give them to Count Sadon?" Hagan's head swung up hard and his eyes widened. So: an examiner who does not believe in the evil he discovers, not really. Hagan did not care for the truth, and so could believe in any assertion he chose—but that he might be in danger from a hidden witch, ah, that truth had not occurred to him. "I would think," Brierley continued casually, as if discussing high lordly politics were a common matter for a country midwife, "that Duke Tejar would better give Yarvannet to some northern lord more beholden to him, some sycophant he can replace just as easily. Don't you think so?"

Hagan slammed his book shut and half-rose from his chair, his face stark white as he stared at her. "How—" he blurted.

"Just some gossip I heard on the wharf," Brierley added in a careless tone. She shrugged. "I don't know the truth of it—or really care." She looked away and fiddled with an end of her hair. "One lord is as good as another," she confided, "especially in bed. I prefer fishermen myself: they like it rough and lusty." She looked back at Hagan and smiled slightly. "So do I."

The comment lingered on the air for a moment. Hagan slowly sat down, stared at her, and then absently licked his pale lips. She widened her smile and shifted her hips slightly, drawing his eyes to them. "What do *you* like, good sir?" Brierley murmured, looking back at him boldly. Natalie apparently had her uses, after all, when a witch needed a model.

Hagan gave a bark of laughter and leaned back in his chair. "And have you sampled Earl Melfallan, young woman, among your conquests?"

"Maybe," Brierley said coyly, and toyed again with her hair. "He is a handsome man, and handsome men know their value to women. Have not the ladies told you that yourself?" She flirted outrageously with him, borrowing directly from Natalie's pursuit of her quarry, the steward's son.

"Hmph." Hagan leaned forward and reopened his book. "The woman Mefell admits she has seduced numerous lords with her foul arts."

Brierley nearly edged the brink by claiming *good* arts, thank you, not foul—if she would claim skill in such a thing, it would be admirable skill—but she kept her silence. He thought he knew her now, a woman like all the others he hated. There was safety for her in that, especially when Melfallan's odd defense could be explained so simply. (*The duke will like this news*), Hagan thought. He wrote silently for several more minutes, smiling to himself as he did, now that he understood her. At the end, he turned the book around and offered the pen.

"Sign it."

Brierley folded her hands tightly. "No. I will not sign lies. I am an honest woman and I am not a shari'a witch and I have not done any of those things."

"You will sign it," Hagan insisted, though he liked it better that she refused. Why? What plot had Hagan hatched with his duke against Melfallan? Hagan himself did not care about politics, and thought little on it. Enough that the duke gave his orders, to be amplified and applied as Hagan chose.

Hagan got up and walked around the table, then walked around her in a slow circle. Brierley clamped her lips as his hand drifted up her bodice to her breast, then stood stolidly as Hagan fondled her, poking his hand behind her laces to pinch and squeeze. As he half-bent to catch up her skirts, she stepped backward quickly, out of reach. "I will scream and bring the jailer," she promised.

"There are many screams here," Hagan said, advancing on her.

"But not yet for my case. Where is Sir James? You have no right to inquire of me." Brierley watched him warily, then felt a sharp stab of relief as he hesitated. The duke might carelessly risk that law, but Hagan was not wholly sure of the duke's hasty instructions. He snorted and stamped past her to the outer door, then threw it open and shouted for the jailer. A few minutes later, as if nothing of moment had happened in the room, nothing at all, she was calmly taken back to her tower cell and left there, alone.

Brierley sat down on her bed and raised her hands to her hot cheeks, free to blush now. Fishermen, I said, because they— Rough and lusty? What would Clara say? Oh, my.

And hinting she had enjoyed lords, too. Well, many a town and castle girl did that, she knew, from their own thoughts, maid and lordling alike. She couldn't avoid the thoughts when the witch-sense was upon her, and so knew far too much for a virgin maid, even as a midwife who saw the sometime consequence nine months later.

Must I play that role in front of the other lords? she wondered, and got up restlessly to pace. In front of Earl Melfallan? Her face flushed hot again. What would Melfallan think of what she had hinted? What possessed her to make such a claim? She stamped her foot. Stop this, you fool. He merely frightened you. Don't lose all sense. She walked more slowly, letting the gentle breeze of her movement cool her face.

For life, for Megan. She paced restlessly. The child still

slept, safe in her little cot off the kitchen, untormented by dreams. Brierley looked out the high window at the sea larks flying, and yearned for her freedom. What would I do with freedom? Would I do anything to be free? I think I might.

What will I do, now that I have another life to guard?

16

That evening, with Saray on his arm, Melfallan surveyed Duke Tejar's ducal Great Hall from its broad doorway. At the far end of the huge hall, on a dais beneath the ducal banners emblazoned with silver and gold, the duke's massive wooden chair was empty. Courtiers hovered expectantly nearby, and the hall steadily filled with other noblefolk dressed in fine clothes and jewels. The rise and fall of their soft voices and laughter was a counterpoint to the bright colors of tapestries, flagged stone, and heavy dark wood.

Tejar's father, Duke Selwyn, had built this magnificent hall and, in his younger years before Yarvannet, Earl Audric had stood among the glittering noblefolk in this hall, tall and lanky and intemperate, a soldier more than courtier, bold more than subtle, the young Selwyn's closest friend, later Selwyn's most trusted advisor. Their friendship had begun in boyhood, when the young Count of Tyndale, then only fifteen, had joined other scions from the Ingal counties as the young duke-to-be's court companions. For more than three decades, their friendship had clung fast, tempered by rebellion and war, founded on mutual loyalty and love, as men love. Sometimes Melfallan's grandmother had teased Audric of loving his duke more than herself or even Yarvannet, and the joke had some truth in it. When Duke Selwyn died, Audric had begun a long but steady decline, as if Duke Selwyn had been the prop of his strength, the very reason for his being.

Melfallan glanced around the Great Hall where it had begun, and felt a familiar stab of grief. He keenly missed his grandfather and likely always would, although the passing years would ease the pain of his grief, bringing instead memories more comforting. In Yarvannet he still listened for the familiar bootsteps in the castle corridor, or the sound of his grating cough, or the impatient slap of his hand on leather leggings. In this room, Audric's ghost also walked, the ghost of the younger man, brash and bold and magnificent, a man Melfallan had seen only in the sometime flash of his grandfather's eye, the vigor of an occasional gesture.

He sighed despite himself, and Saray glanced at him in concern. He tightened his arm around hers and gave her a smile. Saray had dressed in blue velvet, her best dress with its golden lace and fine seed-pearl embroidery, and had taken extra time to arrange her hair, to apply her jewels. She looked very beautiful tonight, her face happy with anticipation. Yarvannet's small court could not compare with the magnificence of Darhel, a court she had known well before her marriage, visiting frequently, making young girlfriends among the many daughters of Ingal's nobility whenever she did.

"I know that you miss Darhel," he said. "We've stayed away too long."

"I miss Mionn more," Saray said, shaking her head. "Do you think we could visit Father next summer? It's only a month's sailing, and the weather should be good in the strait. He'll want to see the baby."

"Of course. Whatever you wish, Saray." They shifted to the side as other folk entered behind them, and Melfallan returned to his survey of the room.

To his left, the elderly Count of Tyndale sat half-drowsing in a comfortable chair, his plain-faced daughter by his side. Three young courtiers lounged pointedly in her vicinity, bright and careless and laughing, darting arch looks at the target of their hopes, but Margaret ignored them with disdain. Now twenty-seven, Margaret of Tyndale had refused every suitor that had come courting, preferring the company of her ladies, among whom she had had a series of particular favorites. Those favorites had caused sly-eyed rumors, now old in the telling but likely true.

A distant relative of the Courtrays, Arbus Wallin had acceded to Tyndale when Duke Selwyn had made Audric Yarvannet's new earl. If Margaret did not relent in her aversion to marriage, the Courtrays' former Ingal county would certainly change hands again when the old count died. Senile for some years, Count Arbus was oblivious to the decline of his house, and as vague about his daughter's secret life as he was about all other matters.

Near him stood Toral Graff, the Count of Lim, a middle-aged, light-haired man with deep-sunken eyes. Toral's county occupied the piedmont plains on the northern coast, sharing an eastern border with Mionn. With his county bracketed by Duke Tejar and Earl Giles, and its prosperity dependent on trade with both, Toral maintained a prudent neutrality, neither supporting nor offending either side. Melfallan scarcely knew the taciturn man, for Toral rarely revealed his true thoughts and chose no lordly friends outside of Lim, if indeed he had any.

Duke Tejar might choose Tyndale as his designated judge for Brierley's trial, but Melfallan would object. Count Arbus was senile and obviously unfit, and Melfallan doubted that Tejar would name contrary Margaret as a substitute. Because Melfallan would choose Airlie, Ingal's southern county, that left Lim or Count Parlie of Briding. Whom would Tejar name? If he'll only choose Parlie—much of Melfallan's best outcome for Brierley depended on that particular choice.

Across the room from the duke's chair and the two Ingal counts, Saray's eldest brother, Count Robert, lounged comfortably in a chair, trading jokes with Revil. Flame-haired like Saray, lean-bodied, handsome and tall in gold velvet and a plumed hat, Robert often stood in for his father at Darhel. Melfallan wished that Earl Giles had not chosen this occasion to send his son rather than himself, but Robert had inherited his father's shrewdness—when he could control the temper that came with his fiery hair. Robert spotted them by the door and waved, and he and Saray made a slow progress toward him, greeting several Ingal people they knew.

"Good evening," Robert said as they reached his side, and rose to kiss his sister. He set Saray back a step and looked her over. "And blooming in health, too. Saray, you are stunning tonight."

"You're sweet, Robert. Thank you." Saray colored slightly but looked pleased, as she always did at anyone's open admiration, especially Robert's. Knowing that, Robert never failed in his fulsome compliments, even if he'd seen her only a few hours before. Saray gestured at his gleaming doublet and trousers. "And so are you."

"I thought I'd make a splash." Robert's restless eyes swept the hall, then focused on Melfallan. "We must talk, brother. Revil, will you entertain Saray while I lure Melfallan into a useful corner?"

"With vast pleasure." Revil turned happily to Saray and borrowed a leaf from Robert. "My lady, I am overwhelmed," he declared and bowed magnificently, enough to make Saray giggle. Robert tugged at Melfallan's sleeve and drew him away.

Melfallan looked around vainly for his aunt, but Rowena had not yet appeared in the assembly. She might not, he realized belatedly. Unlike lords, a high lady could claim all kinds of sick excuses, and so lie fainting and pale on her couch all the evening, her brow cooled by a comforting compress, her fluttering ladies in close attendance. It was a temptation Rowena did not often pass by, not while in unwilling attendance at Darhel. The duke could do absolutely nothing about it, either, which was exactly why Rowena did it.

Melfallan sighed regretfully. He could have used her visible support tonight, and wished she had consulted him first.

He and Robert strolled back outside the hall and found a small gallery nearby with a balcony facing west onto the early evening air. A servant waylaid them with a tray of goblets and, wine in hand, they stepped out onto the balcony. The Daystar had just set, spreading its golds and reds into a darkening sky. Melfallan sniffed at the sea wind blowing up the river and thought of Yarvannet.

"So!" Robert said, without preamble. "You're protecting a witch. It seems to run in the family, Melfallan. Rowena nearly lost Airlie over it twenty years ago. Are you mad?"

For three days, he and Robert had not yet talked privately. First had come a series of fêtes and hunting parties, taking them in opposite directions, then long hours of a lords' council on towage laws, with the duke's inconvenient servants always lurking in corners elsewhere. Their mutual frustration added force to Robert's tone.

"Is that your father's opinion?" Melfallan countered irritably. "Or just yours, Robert?"

Robert shrugged. "Neither, to be fair. Mionn supports you, as always, even when you launch yourself in a damn-fool crusade. The whole court is buzzing."

"I don't admit Mistress Mefell is a witch," Melfallan replied, trying to control his temper. "She is a valued midwife and healer, and Saray owes her life to her. I have a live-born child, a son to be heir, solely because of her. Do I just ignore that? Do I forget loyalty to my own folk? For what? Old legends and superstition? Politics?"

"Lower your voice, brother," Robert cautioned, glancing behind them. "We might be overheard." He gestured peace. "Oceans alive, I'm not reproving you, Melfallan.— Well, hello, Parlie. Hiding behind curtains now?" He turned and glared at the middle-aged stocky man standing behind them.

Parlie Lutke, Count of Briding, grimaced unpleasantly, but looked quite unrepentant for his curtain-lurking. "Such rudeness in the young," he reproved in his nasal voice. "May I join your discussion, my lords?"

"No, you may not," Robert said irritably.

Parlie held the southwestern Ingal county that bordered Yarvannet, a pleasant coastland rich with cattle and wheat, and cultivated his reputation of harmless schemer as assiduously as he cultivated his farms. With his tendency to fat, a deliberate inattention to his clothes, and a deceptive look of stupidity in his pop-eyed heavy face, Parlie navigated the perils of Duke Tejar's court in his own way. For two decades, he had been Earl Audric's ears in Darhel, a role few suspected, especially the duke.

"What do you want, Parlie?" Melfallan asked.

Parlie glanced at the fuming Robert. "Why, to express my

support, of course. It's time our beloved duke was taken down a peg, and I congratulate you, Melfallan, on the conundrum you've presented to him." He smirked as Robert's jaw fell open.

"Now, Parlie," Melfallan chided. "This sudden molting of feathers would startle anyone. Briding was Grandfather's good friend, Robert, if behind the scenes."

"And is yours as well, Melfallan," Parlie said quietly.

Melfallan nodded. "I need my friendships, especially yours, old friend. Do you bring news?"

"Only that the duke is about to arrive in the hall," Parlie said briskly, "and both of you had better be present, not lurking on balconies to conspire."

"Conspiring?" Melfallan protested. "Us?"

"Tell that to the duke, young earl. I'm sure he'll believe you." Parlie's tone was a pointed warning. "Appearances grow heavy now, and you must be more cautious, both of you. I haven't the only set of eyes who saw you leave the hall together." He glared at Robert. "Your father taught you better, Robert. Let's keep rashness in its proper place, hmm?"

Robert opened his mouth for a hot retort, but controlled himself, to Parlie's surprised approval. Robert narrowed his eyes shrewdly at Parlie, and Parlie squinted back, as both men reconsidered long-held assumptions. Melfallan took hold of Robert's elbow, then grabbed Parlie's, and steered them both toward the balcony door. They could reconsider later. The three returned to the Great Hall barely in time.

With a flourish of a trumpet, Duke Tejar marched into the hall from the far door, trailed by half a dozen courtiers and the duchess with her own train of servants. Muscular and squat, his leonine head held proudly, the duke nodded distantly once or twice to favored courtiers as he strode across the tiled floor to his chair and sat down. The hum of conversation slipped into a sudden hush, broken only by the swish of Duchess Charlotte's skirts and her small grunt as she sat down beside her husband. For a moment Charlotte pressed her hand to her ribs, struggling to hide a pain, then solemnly composed herself by folding her hands in her lap. Her ladies anxiously clustered themselves behind her chair.

"She is unwell?" Melfallan whispered to Parlie in surprise.

"A wasting disease, though everyone's still pretending." Melfallan grimaced in quiet distress. Duchess Charlotte, burdened by a hard husband, had always carried herself with dignity. While not loved, she was respected. He swallowed hard as he realized the irony of the duchess's illness right now. If Tejar but knew.

Parlie nudged him in the ribs, and Melfallan looked up to see the duke's gaze fixed on him, unpleasant and sour. With what grace he could marshal, Melfallan bowed courteously, acknowledging the duke's attention.

"You have been too long from my court, Yarvannet," Tejar said, his voice rolling through the hall. "I am displeased."

"Sire, forgive me for my absence," Melfallan answered carefully. "The needs of my lands have kept me away."

"Approach me," the duke ordered abruptly.

A tense murmur swept through the hall as Melfallan walked forward. He repressed an impulse to swagger, repressed his feelings about the duke's rude rebuke in public, repressed everything. Now it begins, he thought. At the foot of the dais, he stopped and bowed again, then bowed more sincerely to Duchess Charlotte.

When he was done, the duke waved his hand savagely at the musicians' balcony above the crowd's head. "Play!" he ordered. Startled by the abrupt command, the master musician hesitated. "Play, you fool!" Tejar shouted at him in rage.

The man turned in panic to his musicians and raised his hands. A tinkle of instruments began, somewhat jerkily at first, then rose in a pleasant melody, filling the room, and likewise covering the duke's conversation with Melfallan, whatever the duke intended for it. On the floor below the musicians' balcony, the assembled crowd promptly began another low murmur of conversation, turning to one another with innocuous talk. Melfallan saw Saray wringing her hands anxiously, with Revil's hand on her elbow. Behind them, out of the duke's line of sight, Parlie had planted his foot firmly on Robert's boot.

Melfallan turned back to the duke and narrowed his eyes. "Sire," he murmured. For a long minute, he stared into Tejar's eyes, showing the open challenge absent from his respectful posture, his quiet manners. "I am pleased to be again at Darhel." It was an obvious lie, and they both knew it.

"With a foul witch in your train," Tejar grated.

"No witch," Melfallan countered smoothly. "Sire, you have been misadvised."

Tejar's eyes sparked with a grim satisfaction he did not bother to hide. "We shall see, Earl Melfallan."

"Yes, sire, we shall see." Melfallan looked back levelly.

Tejar raised a forefinger, dismissing him, and Melfallan backed a few steps, bowed, and then walked back to Saray and Revil, conscious that every eye in the room watched him as he did. He nodded at Saray to reassure her, and his wife allowed herself to be drawn away by one of her court friends toward a nearby group of other women. Melfallan then smiled tautly at Robert, and took a place between his brother-in-law and Count Parlie to watch the room and be watched in turn.

At the central dais, Tejar leaned forward to murmur to a nearby courtier. The messenger left quickly, and a few minutes later brought back a thin young man dressed all in black. As the man pushed through the crowd by the door, a few noblefolk cringed away from his touch as if he had a contagion, but the man in black had eyes only for his duke. He bowed deeply when he reached the duke's dais, then leaned forward slightly, every line of his body taut with deference to his lord. Duke Tejar leaned forward and spoke to him briefly in a low voice.

"Who's that?" Melfallan prompted Parlie with a hard nudge in his ribs. "I haven't seen him before."

"Gammel Hagan, the duke's new justiciar," Parlie replied in a whisper. "A commoner from Lim, I've heard, though no one knows much more about him." Parlie grimaced oddly. "Inquiries haven't been encouraged. The Count of Lim employed him for some years, and then gave him to the duke last spring after old Tagel died. He's the duke's great favorite now—and dangerous for it. The duke likes to bring him into the hall to make everybody squirm." He scowled.

At the dais, Hagan bowed low again. Melfallan and Parlie watched as Hagan quickly left the room, looking neither left nor right, and again creating that slight bow wave in the crowd.

"Remember the fear you see, Melfallan," Parlie whispered in his ear. "It has a reason. More than a new favorite's blaze in the sun, for as long as that lasts."

"What reason?" Melfallan looked at him in surprise. "He's only a justiciar. What is there to fear?" Each of the lords employed such officials for the land's criminal assizes, to determine the facts in accused crimes, to summon witnesses to the criminal court, and keep order during trials. Like Yarvannet's Sir James, most served in that capacity all their lives, an essential part of the local lord's justice.

Parlie scowled. "According to rumor, a justiciar who uses torture. The duke hasn't permitted inconvenient inquiries, not against this newest favorite, and I'm not sure even Tejar knows what transpires in Hagan's dungeon."

Melfallan's eyes widened. "But torture is illegal," he blurted, "except for—" He stopped abruptly.

"—except for witches," Parlie finished for him, his expression grim. "I hope your young woman has strength, Melfallan. She'll need it."

"I won't permit it!" Melfallan declared, far too loudly. Eyes promptly swiveled toward him, and he realized his voice might have carried even to the duke. He rounded desperately on Parlie. "You'll return that cargo, Count, and undo your taxes," he shouted, snatching at the first thing that came to mind. "I won't have my ship rotting in your port all winter."

Parlie squinted back, then puffed himself up magnificently. "My taxes," he blared, even louder, "are not your affair, Yarvannet. If you don't like them, keep your ships out of my ports!"

"And keep yours out of mine!" Melfallan shot back.

"My lords, please!" Revil cried in shock, and stepped toward them. "What is this? What ship, Melfallan?"

Parlie scarcely spared him a glance. "Shut up, Revil," he muttered, then poked Melfallan hard in the chest with his finger, the portrait of lordly indignation. "If you don't like my taxes, put it before the duke's commission. The duke has laws for this kind of dispute. I don't need your threats!"

"Fine!" Melfallan shouted. "I'll have the papers filed in the morning!" Both men abruptly turned away from each other, chins lifted, arms crossed on chests.

"Don't overdo it," Parlie muttered behind him, his voice rough with suppressed laughter. Robert, who heard it all, looked back and forth from earl to count as a light belatedly dawned. Melfallan squinted a warning at him, then gestured expansively to Revil, who now practically danced in his distress.

"My good Revil," he said, "can you talk some sense into this count?"

With a sigh of relief, his cousin promptly complied, first taking Parlie's arm and talking to him earnestly, then turning to Melfallan for the same hard chore. Gradually, Parlie and Melfallan allowed themselves to be reconciled. By then, the crowd's attention had long since shifted elsewhere, and even the duke found other interest, first talking to his duchess, then to a favored lord or two.

Rowena still had not appeared in the hall, to Melfallan's regret. She would have enjoyed the byplay in front of the duke, however it arose from Melfallan's stupidity. Still, a public fight might incline the duke to Yarvannet's secret friend. It had been almost a blunder, but might turn to an advantage.

Might, he reminded himself. You idiot.

He shared a relieved glance with Parlie, then navigated across the room to do some cultivating with Tyndale and Lim. Margaret regarded Melfallan disdainfully as he approached, but spoke pleasantly enough. The earl had fallen asleep in his chair, and as they chatted both he and Margaret kindly ignored her father's soft snores.

After a few minutes, Saray joined him at his side, and added her own pleasantries to their talk. A spark of animation entered Margaret's face—Saray was always good with people—and perhaps they lightened Margaret's life for a few moments. Afterward, he exchanged stiff greetings with Toral, and then continued a slow circuit of the hall, greeting the noblefolk group by group, accepting congratulations on every side for their happy birth, chatting of pleasantries. After another hour, Melfallan took his wife away, relieved to have survived the ordeal.

Saray chattered happily as they walked the long corridors to their quarters, and continued her chatter as she undressed in their bedroom. Listening with half an ear, Melfallan made the proper responses, but his thoughts were a muddle as he mentally played and replayed the events of the evening. Robert's anger, Parlie's sly news, the duke's open antagonism displayed for all, this Hagan as a threat to Brierley, Tyndale's aging decline. Where is the advantage? he thought. Where is the key?

He turned, slightly startled, when Saray came up behind him and entwined her arms around his waist. She leaned against him, then smiled up at his face in open invitation. He blinked at her stupidly. Saray was rarely this bold in their bedroom.

"You were very handsome tonight," she said, her voice happy. "It is so good to be at court again."

Melfallan stared at her in dismay, then felt a sudden uncontrollable repugnance for his wife. She had seen nothing of tonight, guessed at nothing. He felt again that he and Saray lived in wholly different worlds, the same yet not the same, her world of dresses and happy balls and lady's gossip, his own of subtle dangers on every side, especially now. Did she even attempt to understand, to see? Was life all shallow pleasantry for her, stripped of passion, life, or need?

"What's the matter?" Saray asked, disconcerted by whatever she saw in his face. With an effort, Melfallan got himself under control, but Saray had already pulled slightly away, shy again as she was so easily shy in her efforts to please him. "It's not too soon."

"Are you sure?" he fumbled, and put his arms around her, making himself respond as he must.

"I'm sure." Confident again, Saray smiled up at him. He kissed her carefully, his emotions in a turmoil, then released her to finish his undressing. The servant came into the chamber to turn down their bed, to press a warm brick into the foot of the covers, and set out a decanter of water on the bedstand. Melfallan dismissed him and put out the candles himself, then went to his wife in their bed.

An hour later, Saray lay beside Melfallan and felt her husband's body slowly relax into a heavy sleep. She folded her hands on her stomach above the bedcovers, and hoped her intentions had succeeded, though it seemed sadly that again they had not. Melfallan had been so worried lately, and tonight was openly insulted by the duke. And to argue with Count Parlie in such a public manner! Saray put her hands to her face, cooling her hot cheeks. Rarely did Melfallan lose his self-control in that way: he must be truly troubled.

What better easement to ignore that trouble than to speak of pleasant things, then join together as husband and wife? Why, then, had he looked so strangely at her when she suggested it? Perhaps I was wrong to quarrel with him about Mistress Brierley, she thought. Perhaps that explains his silences. Whenever Saray had talked to Melfallan since, he had looked uncomfortable and unhappy. Why? Their lovemaking had been too soon, and hurt more than she expected, but she had not shown her pain, giving all to him. Yet even his lovemaking had seemed forced and distant.

She puzzled again over the odd expression in his face when she had first approached him. It was almost as if he disliked her. How could that be? What had she done wrong? What was wrong in offering a lady's loving duty to her husband? What was wrong in offering love that might make another child? Yet again, somehow, she knew she had failed him—and she didn't know why. She bit her lip and felt tears gather in her eyes, but determinedly fought them away. No sniveling, she told herself sternly. You must simply try harder. But how?

Sometimes Saray felt she and Melfallan lived in different worlds, her world of gentleness and dignity, his of government and lordly affairs. Truly, as her mother had taught her, men and women did live in separate worlds, meeting only at the junctures, alien creatures to each other. Why, then, did her heart ache so? What use to cry about a fact of living?

Did he dislike her now? Why? She had given him a son, a son at last. She clasped her hands at her breasts and felt the keen thrill of joy that had grown familiar since Audric's birth. A son! A glorious son! How could Melfallan dislike me? What have I done? Always I have tried to please him.

She looked at her husband's sleeping face, shadowed by the darkness in the room. Gently she lifted a lock of hair lying over his eye and smoothed it back carefully into place, with a touch so gentle, so fleeting, he would never know it. Greatly daring, she laid her palm on his cheek and felt the warmth there, and wished to wake him, to talk to him, to ask—

But he is tired and troubled, she reminded herself. I must remember my duty. Reluctantly she withdrew her hand, and quietly laid herself back down beside him, conscious of the warmth of his body next to hers, of the quiet sound of his breathing. I must try harder, she told herself.

Lady Saray lay long awake that night, staring unseeingly at the shadowed ceiling of their bedroom, as she cudgeled her brain about what to do, what to try next.

Earlier that afternoon Brierley had been left alone, although she heard the occasional boot-tread of the nearby guard outside her door. Preoccupied with her fears for herself, she had lost mental track of Megan. Without Brierley's noticing, the child had awoken from her nap and had vanished into the mental sea of the castle voices. Brierley began hunting for Megan among the shifting thoughts and emotions of the duke's busy castle. It was not an easy task, for Megan was elusive.

Her encounter with the child by the kitchens that morning gave her a physical direction for her search, but she found "steering" her mental perceptions more difficult than she expected. It was not a skill she had ever needed to practice. In Earl Melfallan's towns, the Callings had not needed her assistance to bring witch to her patient, and she'd had no reason to hunt another of the Blood by such questing, since no other of the Blood existed in Yarvannet. And she'd never sought a specific mind among this many others. The duke's castle must hold two thousand souls, all of them busily thinking and feeling and watching the day.

How do I do this? she asked herself, and welcomed the distraction from darker thoughts. Most of her years of witching she had practiced *avoiding* such contact, so that she could husband her strength from the press of minds. It was not a difficult task away from the towns, and her cave had further protections through the Everlight. Her healings depended upon those times of rest, perhaps were possible only because she had them. But where in this busy castle could a witch rest? she asked herself. How did Megan, an untutored witch-child, survive here?

Blood speaks to Blood, her books said, speaking of times when the shari'a women numbered more than a solitary one or two. How do I do this?

She remembered a few passages from her books that might apply. By relaxing into openness, letting Blood call to Blood, perhaps the same startled self-recognition that she and Megan had shared in the courtyard would leap the physical distance between them. And so Brierley profoundly relaxed, directing her focus several hundred yards down and to the right. Megan should be about . . . *there*—

"Awwkk!" she squawked aloud, and scissored convulsively on the bed as several dozen nearby minds crashed fully into her own. They swept through her, rolling her mentally over and over, as a powerful breaking wave might sweep a wading fisherman off his feet. They drowned her, unpeeling layer after layer of her mind, washing over her; grinding at her like seawater on rock. Reflexively, she scrambled away, already half-drowned, and managed to outdistance them up her mental sands. Slowly the voices faded back into their usual dull murmur, falling back into the sea of minds. She figuratively wrung out her drenched skirts.

"Umph," she said, dismayed. How did witches ever talk to each other in such a surf?

She lay back and scowled at the ceiling. Only a few of her books discussed mental speech in any detail, at least those books that were not too old to handle. It had always teased at her that the more fragile volumes, the ones she dared not handle, held her answers, locked away in crumbling pages and brittle bindings. In the books she had read, the writer either assumed such a facility without giving details, or never had occasion to use it, for lack of a fellow living witch, like herself. Most of the cave occupants had been singleton witches, though a few had been blessed to meet their heir in their older years. As Brierley had now, in her younger years. She smiled.

I am a fisherman, she told herself. See my stick and line. She sketched a cast with her hands in the air, and followed the spinning lure as it dropped in the right direction, downward to the left, to the kitchens. Where is Megan? she wished.

She sensed Sara Gooday, again in the courtyard, a good woman, bent by care and hardened by adversity, but with a spark of kindness not even her hard life could erase. Beating carpets again. Brierley narrowed her focus, squinting against the noise, and listened. Sara knew Megan. She was one of the child's occasional protectors.

In the courtyard, Sara straightened her aching back and blew out a breath, winded by her beating at the carpets on the line. (*Well, time's a-wasting*), she thought, impatient with the dull aching in her back that never seemed to ease. (*I'm getting old*), she told herself, a change that did not bother her, merely inconvenienced. Sara squinted at the old carpet with dismay. Would the dust ever beat fully out?

She had a dozen other chores to finish by supper, and she'd not give Head Cook Emily the satisfaction of a snide remark about any chores undone. Sara positioned her beating wand, swung mightily, and delivered a solid blow to the carpet, then sneezed gustily as the dust billowed. With determination, she hammered steadily at the heavy carpet, smiling happily as she imagined its drooping length as sour-faced Emily herself. Yes, indeed. (*Take that, and that, and that, you wrinkled prune.*)

Brierley cast her line.

Where is Megan?

Sara paused in midstroke. She looked around the courtyard with alarm, and saw only the undercook dumping her bucket in the cistern, and the horse boy darting through the small courtyard, bent on some errand. (*Why am I looking for her here?*) she thought, with an embarrassed snort at her own silliness. (*She's down in the kitchen, paring those vegetables, the last I saw her.*)

Sara smiled then, thinking of Megan, then frowned, still thinking of her. Kitchen urchins had a hard life, but Emily's cruelties seemed to focus mostly on that tiny waif. Raised much the same as Megan in the duke's kitchens, and once just as young and mistreated, Sara still didn't approve of bruises on a child, however lowly. Not that anyone asked her opinion, of course. An undercook's opinion had little value to much of anyone except herself.

But Megan was half-crazy most of the time, just like her dim-witted pretty-faced mother, dead now these six years. Whatever man had fathered the child on Megan's mother had killed her, as surely as using a dagger, by sending a girl that young into childbed. Only twelve she'd been when it was done, but Lana had been as pretty as a sea lark with her blond hair and sweet face, with a coltish body fresh in its womanly blooming. The kitchen's midwife had come too late to save the mother, and now Megan was growing up pretty enough to risk repeating the tragedy in a few years. And Megan was as distracted and whimsical as the mother, Sara thought with worry, and would be unable to protect herself against a man's lust when it came as her lot.

Emily should know better than to chastise the child, Sara thought angrily. It wasn't right to pick on a damaged child.

(*I'll find a sweet for her at dinner*), she decided, (*and take it to her when she's in bed. She'll like a bedtime story, too, I'll hazard.*) Then, satisfied with her thought, Sara dealt her carpet another resounding blow.

Brierley cast again with her hands, downward and to the left.

Her mental line struck the stableboy who had passed Sara in the courtyard. Eric FitzRoy paused in the kitchen doorway, his thumbs jauntily in his belt loops, and scanned the room warily. The underhostler had sent him to fetch a tankard of beer, the hostler's self-appointed reward for a hour of hard labor at the forge, reshoeing Lady Alicia's horse. Eric's errand would be the easier without explaining to the head cook, especially a shrieked-tongued, shriveled old hag like Emily.

(*Women!*) he thought, with all the scorn of his long eleven years. (*What's the use of them? Well, besides that*), he amended. Not that Eric was interested quite yet in *that*, and, to be truthful, wasn't sure he'd ever want to be. From the older boys' talk, it seemed a perilous and complicated muddle for a man to involve himself in. Might be best to just not get started. He scanned the kitchen again, then craned his head to spy around the far corner. Not a sign of Emily. (*Good.*) He spotted the tapped beer keg on the far counter and strode across the neatly flagged kitchen floor, his boots resounding hollowly on the stone. (*Besides*), he thought disdainfully, (*who'd want Emily, anyway? She must be almost forty, old as sin itself.*)

Where is Megan? Brierley sent.

Eric nearly stumbled as the thought dropped neatly into his head, and he looked wildly around the kitchen, then spotted the little girl at the big table by the ovens, seated next to Peggy the fat undercook. (*Oh, yeah, there's the brat*), Eric thought. (*Ocean, why is she crying?*) He almost veered toward her to find out—Megan was a spunky little kid, and was hit upon more than he liked—but then he heard Emily's angry voice echoing down the far hallway, coming fast. (*Cripes!*) Eric crossed the rest of the kitchen floor in a single bound, grabbed an empty tankard from the shelf, gushed beer into it, then beat a quick retreat back to the stableyard, the sloshing tankard cradled in his hands as he ran.

Brierley cast with her hands, mimicking her fisherman's hook and line. *Megan, my child*, she called with joy.

Her line cast true and straight, but the moment before contact it abruptly skittered to the side, missing the catch. Megan was too locked in her grief, sobs shaking her shoulders. *It's not fair*, the child mourned to herself, the rage rising, the fear rising, merging with the rush of noise all around her, the noise that never left, the noise that drummed at her, beat at her, pursued her. She retreated from the assault, locking her mind away—but not wholly successfully. With a shock of concern,

Brierley realized the mental noise might be slowly driving Megan mad, as it had likely driven her mother into insanity.

Alarmed, Brierley cast again with her hands, but again the contact tumbled aside, like a hook striking a seaside rock, skittering uselessly. She could hear the child, but Megan could not hear her. Why? Why could Megan lock out Brierley, but not escape the noise of so many minds?

Cripes, Brierley thought irritably, borrowing Eric's useful word. *Megan!*

"Cut up those carrots, like I told you!" Peggy ordered, and pinched Megan cruelly. "And stop that sniveling. What's a pinch for you to cry about?" She raised her hand warningly. "I'll give you better."

"Don't hit!" Megan shrieked, and her terror washed into Brierley's mind. *Don't!* Brierley cried out silently with her, but Peggy was set on her cruelty. "Don't hit me!" Megan shrieked as Peggy boxed her ears.

Peggy grabbed Megan's shoulders and shook her violently. "Stop that noise! Don't you hear Emily coming? Do you want *her* to hear your noise? Cry, cry, cry: that's all you do, you little sniveler!"

"Let go of me!" Megan struggled wildly in Peggy's grasp. "Let go!"

Peggy dropped Megan hard on the bench. "There, then! Take that to cry about!" She raised her hand and hit out at Megan again, but the little girl dodged nimbly off the bench, then scooted on hands and knees under the table. Peggy grabbed for her hair, but missed. A moment later Megan scrambled from underneath the table and bolted out of the kitchen.

"What's all this?" Emily demanded sourly from the opposite door, her arms planted firmly on her hips. Peggy gulped. "It's that Megan again, ma'am. She ran that way." She pointed helpfully at the door.

Brierley listened as Emily hunted for the child in the sleeping quarters and then each of the storerooms, with Peggy's willing help, but Megan had quite disappeared. Brierley smiled grimly as Emily boxed Peggy's ears hard for losing the child, and it was Peggy who fled the kitchen in tears.

To her chagrin, Brierley had lost contact with Megan again. Without other eyes to see her, other ears to hear, Brierley was as blind and deaf as the angry head cook to Megan's elusive whereabouts. After Emily had given up the search, Brierley cast her mental fishing line into other minds, one after another, growing more adept with the practicing, but no one had noticed the child in flight from the kitchen, nor did any discover her current hiding place. Megan had vanished.

I can't search every mind in the castle, Brierley thought, frustrated. Especially when I doubt any of those minds knows where Megan is.

She bit her lip in worry. Battered by her brutal life in the kitchens, Megan was also battered by the sea of mental voices that surrounded her. The noise deafened the child, with no time to learn defenses, no empty beach or forest or cave for escape. She could not hear Brierley. It was not safe here to be that vulnerable.

Who was Megan's mother? Brierley's lost twin sister? Who had cared for her sister after Jocater left her behind? How soon had she been driven into madness? As Megan would surely be, given another year, perhaps two, no more.

How do I find her? Brierley had been raised in a quiet town, with wide stretches of empty beach and forest. From her earliest memories, her mother had taught her defenses, and had somehow shielded her from emotions that bit and hurt. By the time Jocater died, Brierley had learned to protect herself, and had learned more in the years since. Megan had no one.

How do I find her? she thought frantically. Does Megan have any safe place at all? How does witch speak to witch in such a perilous place?

She thought then of Thora, and her claims about the Everlight. Did the Everlight truly speak to Brierley in dreams, as Thora had told her? Could Brierley speak in dreams to Megan as a similar ghost?

If the Everlight is alive, she wondered, is it a witch? Or, rather— She frowned. Witches were people, not things. A witchly device? Thora had said that it was. Could a witch teach such a device some part of the gift?

Or did the device teach the witch?

The sky had darkened outside her window, bringing the early hours of True Night. Was Megan asleep somewhere? It was worth a try—no, a success. I am the Everlight, she thought. Brierley closed her eyes and relaxed bonelessly, willing herself into a drowse until she hovered on the edge of sleep, then willed herself into dreams not her own—if dreams there be.

Mother Ocean,
Daughter Sea,
Where there is will,
Let love be.

Megan whirled, her dark hair flying into a fan, and stared at the strange woman standing near her on the river sands. She lifted herself on her toes, ready to run away, then saw the woman smile gently at her. The slim young woman took off her broad-brimmed hat and shook out her long hair, then looked upriver into the wind, past the reedbeds and the sparkling river that never ended. Here, in Megan's dream world, the twin suns, Daystar and Companion, always shone brightly in an unending day. Night with its terrors never troubled, though her world held other terrors. A seagull drifted overhead, squawking its rough cry.

"It is hot today," the woman said in a soft voice, then looked back at Megan. "Is it always this warm here?"

Megan gave a quick jerky nod and thought to run.

"I like it here." As Megan stared, the woman sank comfortably down onto the sand, then pulled off a shoe and dumped out the sand in it, watching it fall in a golden cascade. "It is very warm." She dumped her other shoe and set them beside her, then folded her hands around her knees and watched the river sparkle in the sunlight. After a while, Megan watched the river, too.

"Do you live near here?" the woman asked. Megan had nearly forgotten the woman and felt startled all over again when she spoke. But the woman did not come closer, did not try to grab and hit.

Megan gave another nod. "Would you like to see?" she asked, and screamed as a thunder-boom shook the water and tore at the sky. *Do not tell! Do not tell! Do not tell!* Megan wailed in fright and covered her ears, then shrank away as the woman was suddenly kneeling beside her, grabbing. "No! No!"

Megan struggled wildly in the woman's grasp, afraid of the hit, then felt a soft touch on her head, the small tugs as slender fingers untangled her long hair in a slow caress. Then, very gently, the woman pushed on Megan's shoulders and set her back a little, until their faces were even, eye to eye. She had gray eyes, nice eyes.

"You can tell me," she said. "We are the same." And then she smiled, so lightly, so happily, that Megan's own lips turned up in response. "My child," the woman said, her voice resonating with a joy Megan could feel, as if another sun bathed her face with warmth and light. "My dear child. How I have longed to meet you."

She slowly caressed Megan's dark hair, then put it into order on Megan's shoulders. She straightened Megan's shirt with a slight tug, and smiled again, bathing Megan with her warmth. Megan lifted her hand and tentatively poked a finger, wondering if she was real, and touched the woman's nose. The woman giggled, and Megan giggled, too. The woman laughed, and Megan threw back her head and laughed, too.

The woman rose to her feet and held out her hand to Megan. "You have a home here?" she asked. "I have a home, too, by the sea in a cave. Can I see your home, Megan?"

Megan hesitated, not sure, then nodded.

She took the young woman to the small castle by the river, with its three floors and façade of white stone, with the blue latticing on the many windows. A dozen large steps led up to the ironbound wooden door. As the woman followed Megan up the short flight of stairs, with Megan two steps in the lead, Megan looked back at her, suddenly fearful again. Above the woman's head, jagged colors began to sheet across the sky in crimson and green and yellow, the danger colors, the colors of getting hit. She trembled.

Brierley stopped abruptly and folded her hands in front of her, looking up at Megan. "I will not force you, my child," she said. "I can be patient."

Megan raised her hand to the door latch and heard the thunder growl behind them as all the world flashed red. *Don't tell! Don't tell!* She gasped and pushed at the latch and darted inside, then slammed the door behind her, her heart pounding frantically. But the shadows of the entryway did not move; the thunder did not get in.

She waited a time, her hands pressed flat against the door as she panted, but the shadows stayed in place, reassuring her. Nothing moved. Nothing reached out from the walls to grab and hurt. To one side, books gleamed in a library of dark wood and brass; to the other, a kitchen was filled with delicious food bubbling on the stove. Megan sniffed at the good smells. All was safe. Finally Megan opened the door a tiny crack and looked out, but the woman was not there.

Megan opened the door wider, dismayed, and put her head cautiously around the doorjamb, looking right, then left. She saw the river and the reeds, the bright sky with its suns, the soaring gulls, all as it should be. Dim colors of green and gray shifted across the blue and silver sky, but not the danger colors. She threw open the door and stepped out on the top stair.

Gone. She was gone.

Megan sat down lumpily on the top stair and buried her face against her knees, trying not to cry. Why should she cry? Alone was safe. Alone was always safe. When you're alone, you don't tell. When you're alone, you don't get hit.

"Megan—"

Megan jerked up her head and saw the woman standing in front of her again at the bottom of the steps. Slowly the woman raised her hand and held it out. "Let's walk along the river," she said. "You can show me your castle another time—if you want to."

Megan shook her head emphatically. "No! I can't!" Thunder rumbled in the distance, moving closer. Megan shuddered.

The woman lowered her hand and listened with her, her chin uplifted. The thunder did not come closer. When it did not, the woman turned to look at the river and lifted her face to smell the wind. "It is warm here."

And she was gone again, as if she'd never been.

Megan stared at the space where the woman had stood. After a time, she got to her feet and walked down to the space, and felt with her hands through the empty air for the lingering warmth.

"Are you my mother?" she whispered to the sky and reeds and river. Above her head, a gull dashed through the air, beating strong wings against the wind. "Are you?"

"I could be," a voice said behind her. Megan gasped and turned, and the woman was there again. Megan blinked and took a step backward, ready to run, but the woman did not scowl and raise her fists, did not darken with anger. Instead, she smiled, her hair moving lightly in the wind. She looked around at the river and the bright sky, then turned to look up the tall façade of Megan's castle. "This is a good place, a safe place. I like it here. I am glad you are safe somewhere."

"I like it, too," Megan said, greatly daring.

"Child, I will not hit you. Do not be afraid of that." The woman lifted her hands and held them out. "My name is Brierley, and I love you."

"Are you a ghost?" Megan asked in wonderment. The woman laughed merrily.

"I hope so. Dream well, sweet Megan." And she put on her hat and smiled at the river, then walked away along the sand. Her figure vanished into the shimmering light that danced on the water.

Megan watched her go, and thought to call her back, but waited too late. Then, with a sigh, she climbed the steps of her castle and went in.

11

Near midnight, Duke Tejar Kobus sat fuming in his private chamber, waiting for his torturer's arrival. As he waited, he occupied himself with the various papers that littered his desk, nearly all trade reports and memoranda from servants who sought more to impress than inform him. He scowled as he read the reports, wondering if any man of sense still existed among his rivermasters. From time to time as he worked, he glanced irritably at his chamber door, thinking he heard Hagan's booted footsteps, but Hagan did not come. Whatever his other gifts as Tejar's justiciar, Hagan had quickly learned arrogance from the fear he inspired, an arrogance he sometimes dared to flaunt even at his duke. That choice could be Hagan's fatal mistake: Tejar did not tolerate insolence from his tools, not now, not when he was duke.

In his youth, Tejar had been the despised third son of a popular duke, a boy short and fat, weak-eyed and plain, awkward in courtly manners. His two older brothers had been tall and handsome, carefree and easy with all manner of folk, admired by the court gentry, cheered by the commoners. With their every success at hawking or swordplay, his brothers had drawn an unwitting contrast with Tejar, pointing him out as mean and plain, awkward and despised. How he had hated them! And then, in Tejar's sixteenth year, Daughter Sea had suddenly killed both brothers with winter plague, making Tejar sole heir and eventually duke. None called him mean and despised now, at least not to his face. Yet—

Heads turned when Melfallan Courtray entered any room, and eyes lighted to see him. With his beautiful wife on his arm, his dashing brother-in-law and jaunty cousin at his side, Melfallan flashed and sparkled at court, eclipsing his duke. Even when Tejar had showed open disfavor toward Melfallan, his courtiers had still bowed and smiled to Melfallan and his wife as they toured the room afterward. Tejar had watched them do it, his stomach churning sourly.

Tejar hated Melfallan for his youth, his ease, his unconsciously proud bearing. Tejar had once had been young himself, however ungraced, but that youth had gone, leaving him with wrinkles on his body and face, a stoop to his back, a necessity to peer with weak eyes. Oh, he had the bulk of a muscled body and had kept up his sword skills. He had authority people feared, and two sons he had properly cowed, a wife who kept her place and unfaultingly supported him. His thoughts strayed a moment with regret for his doomed duchess, then moved on.

He had hated Earl Audric, too, and now exulted that the old man was dead. His hatred for Audric was far older, and riper by the years he had devoted to it. He had hated Audric for the respect given him by the other High Lords, and had hated him even more for the titles and gifts and affection Duke Selwyn gave Audric before all the court, while Tejar, Selwyn's own son and heir, stood to the side, ignored and despised. He made no apology for his hatreds: a duke had little reason to love his earls. A count could be threatened, outmaneuvered, or cowed, but the earls had wealth and the armies equal to his own. Tactics that quickly overcame a count were useless against the earls, and, worse, if the two earls chose to combine against the duke, they could strip a duke of his coronet and give it to whomever they pleased. It had been done before; it would certainly be done again.

Not *my* coronet, he swore violently to himself. I'll kill them both first.

Tejar got up to pace his chamber, twisting his hands behind his back. He knew his lords lacked affection for him, knew they were restive under his rule. He cared not—they need only obey, not love him. But he also knew that each change of ducal house had begun with a single gambit by an ambitious High Lord, each time with the complicity of the earls. The earls had made a Lutke duke, and later a Hamelin. Duke Lionel had seized the coronet with his sword, but had kept it only because the earls agreed. It was intolerable.

Earl Audric had been content with his earldom, but did his grandson want more? To be duke? And did Earl Giles support that intent? With a son, and Melfallan now had a son, Ocean curse him, Melfallan might be tempted.

Why had Melfallan yielded so promptly to Tejar's summons to Darhel? That choice baffled Tejar still, and fueled new suspicions. Melfallan had every reason to delay, were he prudent, but had not. Was Melfallan stupid? Or more sly than Tejar knew? This shari'a could be a ploy, a means to trap Tejar into a fatal mistake. But what mistake? And what ploy? And who was leagued with him?

Who would support Melfallan's rebellion when it came? Revil and that madwoman regent of Airlie for certain, Mionn perhaps, but who of Tejar's other lords? Lim was inscrutable, as always, but not a fool to move quickly. Tyndale was senile and his odd daughter impossible: until the elderly count died and Tejar could replace him with a man of his choosing, that county lay neuter in any contest with Yarvannet.

And what of Briding? Tejar stopped in midfloor and pursed his lips angrily. Count Parlie was far too clever, too clever by half: Tejar had seen through his playacting years ago. But where did that cleverness lead? Was that quarrel with Melfallan tonight feigned or real? If feigned, and if Lim's bland face hid allegiance to Melfallan, this shari'a witch might be Melfallan's first move against Tejar, carefully chosen, aptly laid.

Tejar had not liked his reading of his lords at tonight's court, although he could not pin with certainty this word or that expression as cause. He had not liked Melfallan's defiance, but that, too, had its ambiguity. Did Melfallan merely defend a commoner beyond prudence, politically inept in his new rank as earl? Or did he suspect Tejar of Audric's murder, and feel frustrated by his inability to prove it—and so now laid a clever plot, using this girl?

But why take the risk of a witch trial in Tejar's own court? Unless the girl was not shari'a, of course—or unless she was? He paused in midstride again. Did it really matter whether she was or not? Tejar smiled grimly, admiring his enemy's deftness. If this girl was not witch, Tejar convicted an innocent girl and so Melfallan became champion of all innocents. If she was witch, Tejar used an outworn law too easily invoked against any of his lords, and so Melfallan became champion of the lords' right of rule. Either way, Melfallan won.

It was a brilliant plot, if it was plot. Yet it had a fatal weakness—did Melfallan know that? For either of his gambits, Melfallan needed the girl.

Tejar's small eyes narrowed as he considered that crucial fact.

A knock came discreetly at his door. "Come in," he growled, and sat down behind his desk.

Gammel Hagan entered the room, gliding like a menacing shadow in the black doublet and hose that he affected, but a menace Tejar still controlled, whatever his justiciar's prancing. "Sire, you summoned me?"

"I have instructions," Tejar said. "Sit down."

Hagan sat. Despite the man's arrogance, Tejar found Hagan the most useful of tools. Gammel Hagan would do anything Tejar asked, however depraved or foul, produce any evidence desired, marshal a desired prosecution through any means—so long as Tejar did not inquire too closely about certain other play in Hagan's den four floors below. Tejar considered the bargain quite fair.

"Tell me about this shari'a girl," he said.

"I have done only my initial examination, sire, a few questions, nothing more."

"Is she stupid or sly?" Tejar asked. Perhaps the girl herself was a clue.

Hagan paused, then smiled laviciously. "Ripe, sire. A woman who needs taming, but not very bright. She tried to impress me by hinting she has seduced Earl Melfallan: I've decided that was a lie."

"Why?" Tejar asked curiously. "Maybe she has. If Melfallan's had a taste of her but hasn't finished the meal, he'd resent Landreth spooning his plate. Maybe the other girls were once Melfallan's, too."

"I've read Sir James's document, sire. It's possible, but I doubt it."

Duke Tejar raised an inquiring eyebrow, then gestured for Hagan to continue.

Hagan lifted his narrow shoulders, let them drop. "Frankly, sire, Melfallan wouldn't be interested in this girl. She's thin and washed-out, not very pretty, very shrewish, too bold. With all of Yarvannet's garden to pick, and him a handsome man, he could have any girl he wanted. And I doubt she has the intelligence to be discreet, and I've not heard Melfallan is stupid. If there'd been a liaison, we'd have already heard of it from our spy in Yarvannet Castle."

"Then why is he protecting her?"

"Perhaps he truly believes she saved Lady Saray in childbed."

"With magic spells? Waving an invisible sword?" Tejar snorted his disbelief. "I don't believe it."

"But Captain Bartol claims it as well, I'm told. All of Yarvannet Castle believes it."

Tejar considered skeptically. "So?"

"It doesn't explain it," Hagan agreed. "He should have delayed answering your summons, gratitude or not. There must be something more."

"But what?" Tejar demanded.

"I don't know, sire. I can try to find out, if you'll permit the examination. The girl first, then Landreth."

Tejar shifted impatiently. "You've already done the preliminary interviews. The trial lords must meet before you can do more with her. And Sir James would have to be present at the questioning. It's her legal right as Melfallan's liegewoman. Melfallan's, too."

Hagan steepled his fingers. "But if she volunteered to the

guard that she wished to confess? Right then, without delay, despite the night hour?"

Tejar studied him. "Go on."

Hagan looked down and straightened a minute wrinkle in his tunic sleeve, then pursed his lips. "There is a great subversion afoot against you, my duke. A subversion abroad in Yarvannet. This girl has seen the wrong of her ways, but is terrified of Melfallan's threats that forced her compliance. Or perhaps he has become indifferent to her fleshly charms, enough to make her hate as a woman hates. Whatever her reason, she asks to see me alone, without Sir James."

"Hmm."

"To me she then reveals the whole of the plot and agrees to confess in writing, for tearful hope of mercy from you despite her crimes. If she recants later, we still have the writing."

"Interesting," Tejar said noncommittally. "What plot did you have in mind, Hagan?"

"Whatever plot you wish, sire," Hagan said blandly.

Tejar narrowed his eyes, considering. One of the ablest political gambits, his father had taught him, was to turn a tool on its maker, to be a knife snatched and thrust to fatal end. Could the girl be turned against Melfallan? If so, he wanted her. "I want no marks on her," he said firmly. "And no rape, justiciar. I'm warning you. Later, after she's condemned, you can play with her. Not until then."

"If I am limited in my methods, sire," Hagan said, obviously displeased, "I cannot promise success."

"No marks! If Melfallan can show obvious torture, her confession is worthless."

"And if she confesses and then disappears," Hagan said stubbornly, "Melfallan would have no bruises to display." He waved a long-fingered pale hand. "After confessing, she escapes by seducing a guard, and some weeks later her body is found in the forest, too rotted to show 'marks.' Her flight itself is evidence of guilt, and thus proof that her confession is true. Melfallan would have no way to prove otherwise, having no marks, as you say. Even if the other trial lords refused to return a verdict, they would always wonder." Hagan folded his thin bloodless hands into his lap and stared his insolence at Tejar, waiting. Hagan would obtain the confession, but he had also stated his price.

Tejar considered, weighing the plan, and thought again of Melfallan glittering at the duke's own soirée. He thought also of his coronet, and Melfallan's probable lust for it. He gave his justiciar a wintry smile. "I said no marks," he said, then waved his hand casually. "At least none that Melfallan sees."

Hagan drew in a sharp breath, and something unnamable, dark and roiled, leapt into his eyes. An instant later, he had stilled himself with an effort, becoming again the cool machine, the essence of control. Almost. Hagan licked his lips, his spade tongue flicking. "Very well, sire," he agreed. "Melfallan will see no marks when she's found."

"After this, Hagan," Tejar said, "I will own you completely, for this girl and the others I've let you have. Deliver this confession, and my favor will continue."

"With an earldom?" Hagan asked daringly, testing the bounds of Tejar's gratitude. "My mother birthed me without a named father—perhaps it might be discovered he was a lord. Perhaps I have as good a noble bloodline as Bartol—or have you someone else in mind to take Yarvannet?"

Tejar grunted. "You listen well at the right doors, Hagan, and I remind you that eager ears can be cut off when I wish it. I have someone in mind, but it won't be you, whatever your imaginary noble father. Accept that." Hagan shrugged. Both knew a duke had other rewards to bestow, if not as gilded. "Besides, you aren't a fool. The Count of Farlost believed my promises, and his stupid son is now in my dungeon." Tejar shook himself irritably. "The idiot. Sir James has an airtight case, and I will have the sentencing. I may castrate Landreth—or reprieve him and send him back to plague the Courtrays. I haven't decided. Prepare your recommendation after you've talked to him again."

"You can rely on me, sire," Hagan said. He smiled. "For either outcome."

"If it's the one over the other, I'll even let you wield the gelding blade," Tejar said sardonically. "Now, as to the content of the girl's confession." They discussed the details. As usual, Hagan had several useful suggestions and the instructions were soon clearly stated. When they were done, Hagan rose smoothly from his chair to leave.

"What will you do to her?" Tejar asked impulsively, then regretted the question as Hagan's eyes changed into shadows, giving him a window into Hagan's dark soul that he had not wanted.

Hagan did not immediately answer. Instead, he stretched his long arms sinuously over his head, moved his pelvis suggestively, then licked his lips, a long slow slide over both lips, a lizard's slide. He languorously pumped his hips again, lifting an obvious bulge. Tejar scowled with disgust at the display. "Do you want to watch?" Hagan asked with a smirk. "Or perhaps even help? You've not come to my den, sire, to see what I do with my young girls. Perhaps it's time you did. Rape in all its methods is an art."

"Beware of me," Tejar warned harshly. "I can crush you, Hagan."

"Sire, I am your loyal servant. I suggest only that you understand your tools. To know what can be done to persuade. To understand *me*." Hagan's smile was one of pure evil.

Tejar hesitated badly, and knew in that moment he would have to destroy this able justiciar. Hagan had no fear, not even of his master, and that, regrettably, was too dangerous a quality in a man a duke must trust with secrets. Already Hagan tempted his duke with his ploy for an earldom, his subtle defiance, his deferent threats, and now this obscene display of himself. Most important, Hagan would know the truth about the girl's confession, the only other who knew except Tejar himself, with an earldom in play. Did Hagan understand his peril?

Tejar gestured a casual dismissal. "Perhaps another time," he said coolly. "Bring the confession to me in the morning. See that the girl is gone by then."

"By nightfall," Hagan demurred in his arrogance, and sealed his fate. "I need time for my inquiries, sire."

"By noon, and no later," Tejar commanded, conceding that much. What did it matter? "Make sure she is gone by noon, not to be found for weeks, too rotted for marks. And her confession in writing. See to it."

"As you wish, sire." Hagan bowed low and left him.

Brierley woke suddenly in her bed and heard footsteps in the hall. *Hagan*, she sensed with alarm, jerking her head up. A moment later, a key ratcheted in the lock and the door swung open.

"You will come with me," the lean man in black growled at her. The jailer was not visible behind him. "Get up," Hagan ordered. He moved with quick nervous tension, his eyes glittering.

"Does Earl Melfallan know of this?" she demanded. "You have no right! Lord James is my justiciar, not you!"

He yanked her out of her bed, then added a shove in her back toward the door. "Move." An instant later she felt the sharp prick of a dagger against her neck. Hagan's arm slipped sensuously around her waist and he pulled her tight against his body, pinning her. "Don't fight me," Hagan said in her ear, his voice as light as a lover's. His breath tickled her skin. "I'll slice your neck if you do."

"Earl Melfallan—"

"—doesn't rule here. Duke Tejar does—and he wants a better statement from you. For the trial, you understand. A confession of your evils." The promise of trial was a lie, she sensed, a promise to lull her into docility. Tejar had no intention of risking a trial, and that fact now fueled Hagan's strange fervor. Why? Did Melfallan know of this? Hagan's dagger point bit into her flesh, and she felt a trickle of blood slide down her skin.

Brierley swallowed uneasily, knowing Hagan could kill her now, given excuse. "All right," she said. She bit back a cry as Hagan's hand fondled her breast through her nightgown, then slid downward to caress her, probing, then moving his forefinger enticingly. She writhed away from his touch with a disgusted moan, knife or not.

"Like it?" he breathed into her ear. "I thought you would. You can have more, once we're downstairs."

Hagan kneed her forward, then walked her down the hall outside, his fingers digging deep into her flesh, the knife still poised. When they reached the jailer's station, no one stood there, and she saw no one else as he hurried her down the stairs and past the small courtyard where Megan had dipped water. Again, she entered the small anteroom where he had questioned her before, but this time he unlocked the inner door and swung it wide, then pushed her through.

She stumbled into a wide room with stone-set walls and strange machines. In one end of a room, a wooden table stood in shadows, chains and manacles at each corner and a large wheel beneath it. Near it stood a tubby metal brazier, winking reddish flames through a grill on its front, with metal bars projecting through the grill and now heating a dull red. A table and a metal chair were caked with blood and darker substances; shelves were filled with flasks and knives and odd implements. Barrels of chemicals stood against the opposite wall, and a spill of paper covered a small desk in the near corner. A fire in a small fireplace heated the room, but did not ease the chill that snaked down her spine. She swallowed hard, trying to hide her fear.

Hagan shoved her hard in the back, making her lurch forward. She gasped as she lost her balance and went down hard on one knee, but caught her fall with an outstretched hand. As his bootstep trod behind her, Brierley quickly got to her feet and backed away. With great deliberation, Hagan took a key from his doublet pocket and locked the door, then pocketed the key again. He smiled.

He inspected her slowly from head to foot, lingering over the loose linen of her nightgown. "You don't look like much," he summed up casually, and leaned against the wooden door. "But then you wouldn't, to have survived this long. Where are the others? Concealed like you were?"

"Other what?"

"I will ferret all of you into daylight and end your evil once and for all," Hagan promised, sketching his vow on the air. "And I will sample each as I wish. Who are they?" he demanded. "How many? And where do they live?" When she kept silence, he smiled thinly. "There are ways to make you talk, mistress."

Brierley lifted her chin. "Why am I here, Gammel Hagan? Does Earl Melfallan know that you've sought another interview?" She bared her teeth at him. "Take care to meddle with witchery; it can seize you and burn you up."

He dismissed her threat with a shrug. "So you admit your witchery!"

"Not at all."

"How can you deny it?" he asked mockingly. "Half the nobility of Yarvannet saw it before their eyes, according to several accounts."

She returned his shrug, pretending a carelessness she did not feel. "I deny any witchery. Make of that what you will."

"Oh, we will, believe me. Captain Bartol has reported in full to Duke Tejar." Brierley did not cower at the news, and that annoyed Hagan. "As the principal witness, Saray is expected to describe your crimes upon her."

"Crimes? What crimes?"

"You tell me: I'd like to know the particulars—for your confession."

"I have nothing to confess. I demand to see Earl Melfallan!"

"I've already heard your insolent tongue, mistress; I suggest you curb it."

Brierley shut her mouth and kept it firmly closed. It amused Hagan, and he stared at her for a while, inspecting her again, letting his eyes rest overlong on her breasts, then moving lower to stare rudely. He licked his lips slowly, making small thrusting movements. After a few moments, he deliberately reached down and adjusted his hose beneath his doublet, his hand lingering there in slow caress of himself. It was his most excellent of threats, that sexual menace, and she kept her face expressionless, staring back without blinking.

"You're too thin," he drawled, "but the thin ones are often lusty enough. Have you bedded with anyone, or are you still virgin maid?" Brierley felt a slow flush climb her face, betraying her. "You won't say it aloud then. Perhaps I should find out," Hagan said, and made a show of considering. "A maid confides much after coupling, once she's given up her play of virtue and enjoyed a man's body. It will help my inquiry."

"You wouldn't dare!"

"Wouldn't I?" Hagan laughed at her. "If you tell, mistress, they won't believe you. Your word against mine on whether it was willing? A commoner's word against the duke's own justiciar?" He gestured vaguely upward, toward the upper floors and their rich suites. "Melfallan is no friend of yours, Mistress Mefell. He can't be, not for a shari'a witch. But I—I might be able to save you, if you pay me with the only useful thing you have, yourself. Spread your legs for me and I'll save you."

"I am not shari'a. You are mistaken."

"What you are or aren't doesn't really matter," Hagan said casually, his hand moving sensuously under his hose. He smiled and licked his lips slowly. "Nor does it matter if you consent. But I bother myself to ask. I don't want too much kicking and bleats, at least not to start. The bleating I want is quite different and comes later in the coupling." He bowed to Brierley mockingly. "I think you will bleat nicely, mistress."

"You had better not," Brierley said, and heard the quaver in her own voice. She clamped her jaw and glared at him, but too late. He knew she feared him now. I had not thought of rape, she thought in panic, in my innocence. I touch to heal: what would rape do to my witch's mind? Desperately, she fought to erase the fear from her face, and saw her failure in Hagan's slow smile of satisfaction.

He walked away to the mantel of the fireplace, and began to make much of stoking the fire. He watched her as he moved the poker sensuously in the coals, easing in and out in deliberate rhythm. "Are you virgin maid, Brierley Mefell? Have you had a man's best part inside you? No? A lack you need fixing, mistress." He moved the poker in and out of the coals, staring at her, and increased the pace of his stroking, his other hand caressing himself briskly. "There are many speeds for the thrusting, mistress, slow at first after the maidenhead is taken, faster as the bodies oil themselves with the galloping lust, and the hardest and best near the end." The poker jabbed down hard into the coals. Hagan mimicked a lusty moan, then sighed and licked his lips. "I like it best near the end. I think you will, too."

"You are a foul and evil man," she said with contempt. "Duke Tejar should hang you."

Hagan replaced the poker on its stand and turned to face her. "Oh, he won't," he said casually. "He can't. I know too much." He smiled confidently and pulled down the front of his hose, exposing himself. "Do you like its size, mistress?" he asked with a wider smile. "Others have." He stroked his rigid shaft, sliding his hand languidly up and down as he watched her face. Then, like a cat, he stretched his arms high over his head and his erection flexed in response. "Oh, yes. I think you will like its size."

"I know of an herb that will help you," she said.

"Indeed," he mocked. "Do tell."

"It makes men impotent for a month. The healer women in Yarvannet prescribe it for men like you, men with a sickness in their head about women."

"Shut up," Hagan said, his face flushing.

"Castration works, too," she added maliciously. "You might suggest it to the duke."

Hagan took a step toward her, his fists clenched, then stopped himself. "Over there," he ordered, pointing at the table with the wheel.

"No."

Hagen unsheathed his dagger and tested its edge on his thumb reflectively, then abruptly leaped at her. Brierley dodged around the table, eluding him. Hagan followed and grabbed, but missed.

"You can't get out," he said, "and I don't mind if you're damaged when I mount you." He shifted his grasp on the dagger and raised it in warning, ready to throw. "I have an excellent aim. I can slice any tendon I choose, prick any blood vessel, enough to spare your bleeding to death before I've enjoyed you. Not that it matters: I've had dead flesh, too, and liked it."

"I won't confess!"

Hagan grinned smugly. "Confess? Why waste time for that?" He nodded at the paper on the desk across the room. "Mistress, you've already confessed. I've written it out for you, ten pages with explicit detail. Later you can sign it, if you can sign anything by then. If not, I'll sign it for you. And then, mistress, you simply disappear. You'll run away, probably with a guard you seduced, or maybe with Melfallan's help."

"Why? What am I to Duke Tejar?"

"A chance to put Yarvannet in better hands," Hagan said and began to circle the table. Brierley kept ahead of him as they shifted position. "Your earl made a mistake tonight, gloating too proudly: it'll cost him his earldom. He should have killed you in Yarvannet when he had the chance."

He lunged suddenly and got hold of an edge of her nightgown sleeve. She recoiled instantly, hearing the fabric rip loose in his hand. They circled the table again, Hagan prowling for her on light feet. He was enjoying this greatly, his hunting of her, and intended to prolong it by giving her a useless hope of safety, of even escape. He lunged at her again, half-feinting, and she skipped deftly around the table, avoiding him again. Hagan shifted his dagger to his right hand and lunged with the naked blade straight at her throat, missing deliberately as she darted aside.

"I won't confess!" Brierley cried. "I've done nothing wrong!"

"Use your shari'a powers," Hagan taunted with a grin. "Can your witch's art make our coupling a gasping ecstasy? How, I ask? Tell me every detail, mistress. Tell me how you'll pleasure me, mistress, when I ride you."

"You don't believe in my powers, you liar."

"Women tell many lies." He darted again with his dagger, teasing at her. "I'll believe in yours, if you use them to pleasure me." He stretched out his foot and kicked over a bucket of dark fluid. "There. Run through that. It eats shoe leather—and feet. Later we'll put what's left of you into a barrel of it—unless you pleasure me, Brierley. Won't you pleasure me? I think you want to." His voice was a silken croon.

"Never!" Brierley cried and bolted uselessly toward the door. Hagan caught her halfway, tackling her hard and throwing her to the stone floor. The impact knocked the dagger from his hand and she fought him wildly, twisting and turning, as they both scrabbled for it. She reached it first and rose to her knees. Then, with all her strength, she raised the dagger high over her head in both hands and drove it down at him.

Hagan shrieked as the dagger sank into his chest. As his pain pierced her own heart, Brierley screamed with him, then cried out again as the Beast's darkness swept upon her. Its roaring filled her mind, blanking all thought with its terror. On a distant beach, she saw the Beast seize Hagan and tear at him ferociously, until Hagan's body slumped lifeless in its grasp, his head sagging, his eyes staring. When Hagan was dead, the Beast crooned and patted the emptied body with pleasure, playing with it a little, then slowly turned its great eye on Brierley.

She cringed, but the Beast was not interested in her, not tonight. It turned away into the sea, taking Hagan with it. She watched as its gas-bloated body floated easily through the surf, its tentacles shifting, then plunged from view.

The next instant, she was kneeling by Hagan's body, her breath coming in great gasps. She leaned a hand on the floor as her head swam unpleasantly, then felt a stickiness on her hand. He had not had much time to bleed, and already the small pool of blood was cooling, spreading no further. She wiped her bloody hand on her nightgown, then looked dazedly around her.

I killed him. Ocean save me, I killed the duke's justiciar. There'd been no time to think before it was done, no time for anything but keeping her life from Hagan's blade.

I didn't know if I could kill, she thought dazedly, even to save my life. Now I know. A line had been crossed, giving its own grim strength.

The only sound in the room was her own panting and a slow drip of water in the corner. Hagan had brought her here secretly, and she might stay secret for a time still. But what then? Most folk in the castle were fast asleep, but a few would soon stir, readying for the morning. It must be nearing dawn.

Her eyes fell on the corrosive oil Hagan had spilled on the floor, then saw the hardening drippings of the same dark oil on a nearby cast-iron barrel. Using the help of the table leg, she wobbled to her feet and investigated, lifting the lid to peer cautiously inside. *Put the rest of you in it*, Hagan had jeered.

Disgusting, she thought, and made a face. But what do you will, Bri? To be found in a bloodied nightgown by Hagan's body with a knife in his chest? Tejar would have no need of a witchery trial: the murder laws would suffice. She tightened her lips. She'd not gamble her life on this duke's manner of justice. Trust in Melfallan's fairness, yes, but this was not Yarvannet: Melfallan did not rule here.

She was vaguely aware of her lingering shock, but used its dullness to set to the task of dragging Hagan to the barrel. First she carefully removed the key from his pocket and set it on the table, relieved that she had remembered before, not after. Then, struggling with his limp weight, she lifted him and tipped his head and upper body into the barrel. The oil attacked his flesh with a bubbling fury, raising a cloud of acrid fumes that made her cough violently. She turned her face away and held her breath as best she could; then slowly eased Hagan's body forward as the oil took him. As his boot soles sank beneath the bubbling surface, she covered the barrel hastily with the lid, then backed away. The barrel plopped and fizzed for over a minute more, then stilled.

"Put you in it," she whispered.

She found a rag on a shelf and wetted it in the small water trough in the far corner, then wiped up the blood from the floor. She made a quick survey of the room, and picked up the papers on the side table. Her confession had indeed been written, she saw, its text even more vile than what Hagan had dictated two days before.

Now she had murdered dozens in Amelin and Natheby, not a few mere infants, and had even spelled the winter plague that killed nearly a hundred in Amelin five years before. Through her foul arts, she controlled Earl Melfallan, her lover, and counseled treason against the duke. Melfallan's son had no soul, for she had stolen it. Saray she would poison in time, as she had poisoned Audric, and then would marry Melfallan, turning that poor lord into a bed-slaved idiot. In time, when she had tired of him, she would kill Melfallan to make herself regent for Yarvannet's soulless witch-given heir. When Lord Landreth had discovered her plan, she and Melfallan had conspired against him with false charges of—

She scowled. So Hagan had talked to Landreth and heard a nimble story. Steal an infant's soul? She wondered which man, Hagan or Landreth, had thought up *that* deed.

At the end of the confession, there was a blank line for her signature, waiting to be signed by herself—or by anyone else, as Hagan had taunted. If she was dead, who could say the signing wasn't hers? And when witchery is alleged, even if unsigned, what lie cannot be believed?

"This is a foul thing," she said in disgust. She looked at the barrel, but could not bring herself to approach it again, not yet.

Carry away the confession? she asked herself. To show to whom and why? And if you're caught with it by the duke's guard, with Hagan's barrel still popping bubbles? She glared at the barrel as it made another soft noise. She steeled herself and a few moments later the confession joined its author in the barrel. Then, like a shadow in the night, Brierley cautiously opened the door and slipped through the antechamber to the hallway beyond.

At the courtyard with the well, she stepped into the shadows of a doorway and listened with both ears and mind. On the other side of the courtyard, the stair led upward to her tower cell, and she sensed that the jailer was not at his post. Should she return to her cell? When the lords inquired, she could look blank and stupid, admitting nothing, and explain the blood on her gown as her own. And consign herself to more waiting on these High Lords, until they decided what to do with her? Brierley rejected that option with an angry shake of her head.

What if she disappeared today, gone without trace? Hagan had suggested it, and she could choose it for her own purpose, not his. Indeed, it would be a mystery without solution: the duke's justiciar gone, Brierley gone, Brierley's clothes abandoned in her room, Hagan's own quarters as curious. The duke would have no convenient confession to plague Melfallan, and would not dare admit his own knowledge about Hagan's orders to get one. And there the trail would end.

She dared not involve Melfallan, who now slept several levels away in a suite of rooms. If Tejar's guards discovered him with Brierley, she handed Tejar accusations far too useful against Yarvannet and Melfallan himself. She paused, just for a moment, to listen to him sleep: he was dreaming of a boat, with himself pleasantly adrift in Tiol's harbor, although gomphreys lurked below, thinking. She smiled in amusement. The nonsense of dreams: at least his were pleasant. She felt a sudden longing for him, one last time to see his face, to hear his voice, before she vanished into new obscurity.

If I disappear today and don't see him now, she thought with a pang, I may never see him again. It would be best never to see him, best for him, best for Saray. She took a deep breath. He is an honorable and decent man, a kind lord to me, but you're not in love with him. Even if you were, Bri, you have a sensible heart. Use it.

Where would she go? And how? And what about Megan?

She hesitated another moment. Now is the time, she told herself. Now is the time you won't wonder later if you should have run.

Brierley circled the courtyard to the broad riser of steps leading downward into the kitchens. In the nighttime, the sea of mental voices in Tejar's castle had quieted into the mumbling of occasional dreams. She could sense those few who were awake, mainly Tejar's guards at their various posts through the castle. In his cell in a nearby tower, Lord Landreth paced to and fro, his thoughts tumbling between hope and despair. In another direction, in an upper suite, the countess Rowena sat reading in a chair, a lacy coverlet tucked around her knees, as was her habit. The sky had begun to lighten and soon the servants would be rising. Already a kitchen cook yawned in her bed nearby and thought to throw off the covers. She did not have much time. Like a wraith, she vanished into the darkness of the nearby stairway, moving silently downward toward the kitchen.

At the base of the stair, she turned right into a narrow passageway and drifted on bare feet past doorways, hunting Megan among the sleeping rooms of the kitchen servants. In the third low-ceilinged room, a dozen beds were ordered in rows, little more than thin mattresses on low wooden platforms, and she caught a whiff of a familiar dream.

On the high balcony of her castle, the high lady Megan sat at ease in a silver chaise, a jeweled salamander perched on her hand.

Brierley tiptoed into the room, listening intently to the sleeping minds in the other beds. A few drifted in their own dreams, and others lay in the oblivion of deep sleep. Behind her, beyond the passageway and a corridor and two large hearth rooms, the cook who had roused now lifted a pot from a shelf and yawned.

Brierley reached the small bed in the corner and knelt beside it. Megan slept beneath a tattered blanket, her hand curled under her chin, her dark hair tumbled on the pillow. If Brierley woke her too suddenly, she might cry out and wake the other sleepers. Brierley leaned over the child and listened, then projected an image of herself standing by Megan's dream river. She concentrated. *Megan—*

"Megan!" someone called from below, and Megan's salamander squawked and flew away. Megan sat up, startled, and leaned forward. Beneath the balcony. Brierley stood on the river sands, looking up at her. "Megan! Come with me!" she called, and beckoned urgently.

"Where are we going?" Megan asked, her voice high in surprise.

The woman laughed and spread her arms widely. "To find another river, child, one that's real. Come!"

Come— Brierley eased her fingers onto Megan's wrist, and the girl's eyes fluttered open at the touch. Megan blinked in sleepy confusion, then widened her eyes as she saw Brierley bending over her. Brierley caressed her hair and smiled, then held her finger warningly to her lips. *Come with me.*

"But—" Megan began, and Brierley shook her head. *No speaking. Come, Megan.* She pulled back Megan's blanket and held out her arms. Megan sat up, then hesitantly wound her arms around Brierley's neck. Brierley lifted her from the bed and stood Megan on her feet, then dressed her quickly in the daytime dress that hung from a peg nearby. She bent for Megan's small sandals. *Here: hold these, Megan.* Megan obediently took the shoes.

Brierley listened carefully to the sleepers again, then together she and Megan walked quickly out of the room. Megan's mind pricked with questions, but Brierley sensed that she seemed only half-real to the child, as if this were dream also. They had reached the steps leading up to the kitchen courtyard.

Where are the storerooms, Megan? Megan pointed to an open doorway beside the base of the stair.

At the end of the short hallway beyond the door, Brierley stepped into a long storage room, its walls lined with wooden shelves. As the dawn advanced, dim gray light now came through small rectangular windows near the ceiling. The air was cool and heavy with the scents of leather and grain, fabric dyes, dust, and the tang of drying fruit. Brierley found women's clothing in a large bin near the back and hunted a homespun dress for herself, then a petticoat and bodice and stockings. She found better clothing for Megan, too, and held up the dress to the girl to match the fit, then added a change of clothing for each of them, and better shoes for Megan. She found boots for herself which nearly fit and would do.

What else do we need? she thought, looking around her at the shelves. Take the time: you can't count on help on the journey, though it might come.

She took down two large leather saddlebags from a high shelf and loaded one with clothing and two warm blankets, the other with fruit and bread, a large cheese, dried fish in wrappers, a lamp and oil, two knives, flint and steel. Megan ran on light feet from shelf to shelf, helping, sometimes by Brierley's pointing, sometimes by her own choosing. And so Brierley's packs also acquired a trowel, a man's belt, a card of buttons, a ball of twine, a tattered doll, and a package of sticky candy. The bags packed, Brierley hunted again through the clothing bins, and found a warm hooded cloak in dark green for herself, a smaller blue cloak for Megan.

Come, Megan. Brierley ran a strap through the handles of the saddlebags and lifted it over her neck, then took Megan's hand. They had one chance for freedom, narrowly run through the servants of the castle. At least Megan was known to them, and could escape back into obscurity even if found in Brierley's company. Megan was yet not marked as witch. Brierley pulled the edges of her hood closer around her face. *Where are the stables, child?* Megan pointed again.

More people were waking now. Like bobbing line markers in the mental sea, Brierley felt the quickening of each mind as it awoke and set about the new day. Walking as silently as she could, Brierley led Megan onward. A guard stood near the end of one hallway; they took another hallway around his post. The cook bustled toward the large pantries: they waited behind a corner until she had passed them by, then slipped by the half-closed pantry door.

Another stairway, two corridors, and a massive wooden door exited into a straw-filled room, with several dozen horse stalls on one side, an array of saddles and other leather bindings on the other, each hung on sturdy pegs. According to Megan, who knew this area of the castle like a mouse knew every cranny of her barn, the wooden door on the opposite side of this long stable room led to a small courtyard, and from there to the city streets. This small stable was not the duke's own stable, nor even for the keeping of other noble horses, but a small establishment for the mounts of servants and the steward's messengers.

A groom sleeping on guard in one of the stalls roused as the inner door opened. *You see nothing*, Brierley sent quickly. *Sleep again.* The groom yawned and lay down again in his bed. Brierley waited until he fell deeply asleep, then looked over the half-dozen horses in the stable.

Megan pointed at a black mare in the third stall. *She is nicest.*

You've ridden her?

Me? Oh, not me. I hide here sometimes, with Friend. "Friend" was obviously the black mare. *She doesn't always talk much, but we know each other.*

The mare looked placidly at them both, her jaws moving

back and forth as she munched on a mouthful of hay. Megan clucked her tongue at the horse, and Friend swiveled her ears forward in interest, her calm gaze focused on Megan. She nickered softly, and seemed a pleasant beast.

Friend it is. Brierley quietly led the black mare from her stall. With a wary eye on the sleeping groom, she saddled the mare, then tied the saddlebags behind the saddle. Brierley had never saddled a horse in all her life, nor had Megan, but Friend knew what needed to be done. Brierley sensed the alert intelligence of the mare, but heard little meaning in her thoughts. Megan and Friend, however, could obviously carry on a very active conversation, and did so, with many hand-wavings and ear-twitches and giggles and friendly snorts. Wary of the groom still sleeping nearby, Brierley had to shush their noise twice, but through the odd tricorner conversation to Megan to Friend and back again, Brierley managed to saddle the horse to Friend's satisfaction. She dubiously checked the saddle straps one more time, drew a deep breath, and lifted Megan into the saddle.

Brierley mounted awkwardly behind the child and leaned around Megan to get the reins, but her fingers dangled uselessly inches short, even at the full stretch of her arms. She dismounted again and so learned to have reins in hands while mounting.

Riding a horse is tricky, Megan offered.

Hush, child, Brierley reproved, and suspected Friend thought it funny, too. Brierley tentatively nudged the horse with her heels, and the mare moved forward. It was a wonder.

How many times have I been on a horse? Brierley asked herself wryly. Why, hundreds of times—not in the flesh, of course, but hundreds. Every traveler who passed me by, each forester, each lady, each plowboy, all comfortable on a horse. She kicked the horse's sides harder and the mare moved faster toward the broad stable door leading outside. Brierley dismounted to lift down the bar and push open the broad doors, flooding the stable with light. She glanced behind her, but the stableboy slept onward, undisturbed by the dawn light.

The light is the same, she thought with delight, half-closing her eyes against the mellow pale brightness. The light is the same as it was on the beach that day I accepted the gift. She saw a wooden staff from among a half-dozen rough staves leaned near the door and took one, then planted its end firmly on the straw.

It is today, she thought. Today I refound the craft, as Thora bid me. Today I believe in dream friends and the future. For your sake, groom still sleeping. For your sake, Harmon and Clara and all others whom I love and will love. For Melfallan and his gentle lady. She looked at Megan perched high on the mare. And especially for you, my shari'a child, the jewel of my future. What else I found today, I'm not certain. But it is begun.

She laced the staff across the supply satchels, and then remounted. There was an echoing clatter as they passed through a bridgeway from the horse stalls to the cobbled square beyond, then the sharp report of the horse's hooves on the courtyard pavestones as Brierley emerged into the open air. She turned the horse's head slightly to the left and rode across the square toward the open gate.

She was a lady's maid riding out on an early-morning errand, nothing more, and would be little remembered by those who glanced at her. The gift would see to that. She keyed up her witch-sense to high vigilance, watching every mind in the square as the mare plodded, step by step across the cobblestones. The half-dozen people in the stable square were occupied with their chores and with the noise of a stamping mare who disliked her handler and resisted him. Brierley suddenly remembered another stamping horse, and Landreth's cruel blow, an age ago. When the angry hostler glanced in Brierley's direction, she clouded his attention. *A lady's maid, nothing more*. The hostler turned back to his contrary horse and cursed foully.

Halfway to the gate, she came within the view of the three guards standing on the upper walls above the square. All glanced at her, but without interest: an alarm about her had not yet sounded, a delay caused by the duke himself in his secrecies. She might hope for hours yet before the search began. Riding sedately, Brierley passed through the gate to the street and dared to glance behind her, but saw no one looking, not even the guards. Megan's head practically revolved in her excitement and she would have exclaimed at some marvel she spotted, but quieted at a touch from Brierley.

Not yet, child.

Brierley nudged the mare again with her heels and joined the early-morning traffic in the city street. They fell behind a passing carter's wagon and kept to his pace, as if they were children to him, older daughter and younger daughter, riding the family horse on a market trip to and from Darhel with their father. No one noticed her, not even the carter when he looked behind him.

Do not notice, she prayed of them all, carters and farmwives, horsemen and rivermen, a growing flow of people along the road, passing east toward the foothills and west toward Darhel as the Daystar rose steadily above the eastern mountains. Ahead of them, nearly a mile away through the city streets and buildings, she could see the shadowed tops of tall trees: that far to the forest. Beyond those first trees, the foothills rose steadily into the distant mountains—and to freedom. She rested one cheek against Megan's tangled hair and closed her eyes for a shuddering breath. One mile.

What's the matter, Mother? Megan asked. The girl yawned hugely and pulled the edges of Brierley's cloak closer around her for its extra warmth.

Nothing, child. Go back to sleep, if you wish. Megan turned her face into the enveloping pocket of Brierley's cloak and drifted to sleep, despite the wonders of a street and city Megan had never seen except from high windows. But, then, how much of what happened this morning seemed real to Megan, if anything? This child had practiced the art of denying the real.

I will need to do something about that castle of hers, Brierley thought. A few more years and Megan might have managed to stay permanently in her dream world, sane by a choice made only on her terms, though no one else's. It was one option for a witch-child abandoned in a surf of voices, just as Jocater's suicide had become the option for Brierley's mother. How many other witches, lost between impossible choices, had destroyed themselves?

She looked at the people on the road, and wondered if any other witches lived here in Darhel, or perhaps in the duke's counties of Airlie, Lim, Briding, or Tyndale. Bartol had encountered a witch sometime in his life to be wary of them—where had he met that witch? Probably in Darhel, but maybe not. Where had he spent his boyhood before he came to Tejar's court? It was a puzzle she couldn't answer, and could not safely ask, even if she and Bartol somehow met again.

Perhaps some witches dwelt even in Mionn, the eastern earldom, the oldest land of all the lands. Surely there were others of the gift somewhere, hidden in small towns or bywater villages—but not many, she expected. As a race, the shari'a might have flickered into near-extinction. Thora's cautions suggested as much.

In the foothills ahead, she guessed, numerous Allemanii folk lived as farmers and foresters, hunters and quarrymen. Each farm and quarry east and south of the city conducted a busy trade with the merchants of Darhel, as did the rivermen bringing their large catches up or down the large river that flowed to the north side of Darhel. Yarvannet's commonfolk had a similar traffic with Melfallan's port capital, but here the population was larger, the trade busier. The size of the city, its position as the duke's capital, and the ready river transportation created a bustling market. Some of the commonfolk like the carter ahead of them had spent the night in the town after a full day haggling at market, and now returned home, ten or fifteen or twenty miles distant, a long day's ride at mule's pace.

She could not stay in these Darhel uplands: they were too close to the duke's capital, with too much traffic and gossip passing up and down the road each day. What would the duke expect her to do, so that she might do the contrary? In what direction would he expect her to flee?

She did not know enough of the counties of Lim or Briding or Tyndale, and would not feel safe in any of the duke's lands in any event. But he would search west, just to be certain. She could not go south to Yarvannet, knowing full well Tejar preferred that choice. In Yarvannet, she would become the duke's weapon again, when he caught her.

But what of Megan, if he did?

She lifted her eyes to the high eastern mountains ahead, topped with snow and clouds. Halfway up the mountain, the carter knew, the road branched southward toward Airlie, Rowena's domain. The duke might expect that she go southeast to Airlie, troubling that land again with a witch. She had not sensed much of the countess on the docks, nor much more as she had passed silently through the castle this morning, but she had sensed a friend, a lady too rash at times, but powerful in her angers and intelligence. Perhaps later, in a year or two, she might pass through Airlie, and might send secret word to Melfallan that she still lived. She swallowed painfully. No. Don't count on that. Better he not know.

Beyond the fork south to Airlie, beyond higher passes that crossed the mountains, she knew, lay the fishing towns of southern Mionn. Perhaps there she might find safety. In those same passes also, though its exact location was now lost, lay the ancient caverns of Witchmere. She might seek out Witchmere, if she could find it, and disappear altogether from the world for a while, a long while. There would be time for Megan to grow older and stronger, time to look for answers, time to plan the refounding of the shari'a and how it might be done and what might happen to the Allemanii lands when it was.

If she could find it. Thora had bid her look for Witchmere, there in the mountains above Darhel. Her fingers tightened on the horse's reins. Step by step, the mare followed the carter's slow pace toward the forest edge.

12

Melfallan woke slowly in midmorning, reluctant to leave a pleasant dream of boats and Brierley waving to him from the shore. He became conscious of Saray's familiar warm weight beside him, and turned toward her drowsily, pressing his face against her fragrant hair. Still half-asleep, his hand wandered, caressing the long line of her hip, then settled on a warm breast. He opened his eyes and saw Saray looking back at him quizzically, inches away.

They were not the eyes his dream had led him to expect, but eyes that were fair enough. He sighed and took his hand off her breast. "It was too soon last night," he said. "It's not fair that you never think of yourself, Saray."

"It is my duty," Saray said proudly. Melfallan sighed, then rolled on his back and took her hand in his.

"Your duty be damned, wife," he said mildly. "Sometimes I wish you would be less dutiful. Do you think I want your interest always trampled, that what you wish be always set aside?"

"But—"

"I didn't want to marry your mother, yet sometimes it seems I have."

"Did you want to marry *me*?" Saray asked in a low voice, surprising him.

Melfallan turned his head on the pillow and looked at her

fondly. "Yes, I did," he said, and it was true. He smiled. "I didn't know you very well back then, but you were pretty and sweet. You still are, fair Saray," he added gallantly. "I'm sorry I've been cross lately."

"And I think you are feeling lustful, Melfallan," she said comfortably. "Your compliments always wax more brightly when you are."

He yawned and pressed her fingers. "Yes, I'm afraid so. I don't remember the dream now, but it was a lovely dream." He brought her hand up to his lips. "But appreciation of your beauty needn't have a motive, whatever your accusings. And it's too soon, and so we won't this morning. Say it, too. I insist."

Saray raised herself to an elbow and pretended to consider. "If I say it because you insist, isn't that being dutiful?" She wrinkled her nose, mischief in her eyes. It was a part of Saray he didn't see often, that mischief. "What if I were to say we will? What would you do then, my lord?"

Melfallan smiled lazily. "Well, then we're talking of a husband's duty to please his wife, and it won't please you if it hurts. True?"

"Who are you to define my pleasure?" Saray tossed her head grandly, posing for him. It was a direct copy of one of Rowena's favorite gestures, and her effort touched him. She obviously thought he wanted to be persuaded into more lovemaking, misreading him yet again.

And it isn't fair, he told himself, to compare Saray to someone who might do differently, to someone with quiet gray eyes, a pale lovely face.

"Saray—"

Someone pounded urgently at their bedroom door. "Melfallan! Wake up!" An instant later, the door flew open and Stefan rushed in. "Your grace! Duke Tejar has invaded Countess Rowena's chambers, and is accusing her of treason! He's going to arrest her! You must stop him!"

"Treason?" Melfallan asked, dumbfounded. "For not going to his soirée last night?"

Stefan gestured impatiently. "This is not a jest, your grace. You must come! The duke has soldiers in her chambers *now*!"

It was the open fear in his face that convinced Melfallan. He tossed off the coverlet, not bothering with modesty, and quickly pulled on the clothes he had discarded the night before.

"When did this start?" he asked Stefan hurriedly.

"Minutes ago. The duke burst in with soldiers and ordered them to search her rooms for the girl Mefell."

"For Brierley?" Melfallan asked in surprise. "Why? Isn't she in her cell?"

"I don't know, my lord," Stefan said frantically. "His guards are emptying the closets and throwing all her dresses on the floor, dumping drawers from her desk, even slashing the mattresses. 'Looking for proof,' the duke says. But proof of what? What does he think the countess has done?" He clutched at his arm. "Come quickly. You must stop it! I think the duke has gone mad!"

"Of course I will. Where is Count Robert?"

"I sent Tess to get him."

"Good thinking."

"Melfallan?" Saray quavered uncertainly.

He bent and kissed her quickly. "Get dressed, Saray, and wait here for me. I'll return shortly." Melfallan followed Stefan out the door.

Rowena's chambers were only two corridors away, and already a crowd of servants had gathered outside the outer door. Melfallan pushed past them and strode into the countess's private chambers. Rowena stood near the window, dressed in a satin robe, her head high as she glared with open fury at Duke Tejar. Stefan moved quickly to Rowena's side, ready to toss back any soldier who approached her.

The duke was calmly directing his soldiers as they ransacked her rooms. As Melfallan watched, two soldiers ripped open the cushions of a chair with their daggers. "I'm surprised, sire," he drawled. "You expect to find Mistress Mefell inside a cushion?"

The duke whirled and scowled ferociously at him. "Naturally you rush in, Yarvannet."

His tone accused Melfallan, but of what? What malicious wanderings in Tejar's mind had led to this outrage? "Of course I do," Melfallan threw back at him. "The lady Rowena is my aunt, and a noble lady of your lands. I trust you will pay for all this damage." He shot a glance at Rowena's pale face, and saw her smile tightly.

"Oh, he will," she vowed.

Tejar's finger stabbed in Rowena's direction. "You're a traitor!"

"I am no such thing," she retorted, tossing her head. "You are insane at last, Tejar. It has finally happened. Your plots have turned on yourself and scrambled your brains into mush." She stamped her foot. "You have *lost* your reason!."

"Quiet, woman!"

"I am not a woman," Rowena declared. "I am a countess."

At that moment, Count Robert arrived, panting, then looked wide-eyed at the demolished room. "What in the—?"

Melfallan folded his arms across his chest. "The duke *says* she's a traitor. The duke also says she's a woman, which she denies." Rowena wrinkled her nose and sniffed. "The duke *says*—"

"Shut up, Melfallan," Tejar growled.

Melfallan glared at him. "I will not. This is an outrage. *Have* you lost your mind?"

"Where is Brierley Mefell?" the duke demanded. "Where have you hidden her?"

"Nowhere," Melfallan shot back. "She's not in her cell? And why not?" He took a step toward Tejar, his fists clenched. "I have questions, too. Mother Ocean, what have you done with her? Has Hagan killed her?"

"No!" the duke protested. "I gave no such order. I would not."

Melfallan stared at him, not knowing if Tejar lied. The duke was a good liar, and quite convincing in the skill: Earl Audric had always said so. "Then summon Gammel Hagan," he demanded suspiciously. "You'd use him for the deed. Has Hagan examined Brierley, without Sir James present? When? How?"

"You forget yourself," the duke spat.

"I don't forget anything," Melfallan retorted. "I've earl's rank and I have the right to ask." The duke's eyes shifted uneasily, and Melfallan's suspicion leapt into certainty. "Where is Gammel Hagan?" he demanded. "Bring him here!"

The duke sneered. "Yes, where is Gammel Hagan? I'll be asking the Count of Lim that very question. Hagan was his man first."

Rowena made a rude noise and toyed with her lace sleeve. "Lim, too? Will you be arresting *all* your lords, Duke Tejar?" she asked sweetly. "Will every pillow and mattress in the castle be torn asunder?"

Abruptly Tejar snarled at his guards and stamped out of the room. When all the soldiers had followed him out, leaving their wreckage in their wake, Rowena sagged against the windowsill and looked around her chambers in despair. "What a disaster!" She quirked her mouth. "Fortunately, most of the furniture belongs to the duke, not me. I think he forgot that." She delicately picked her way across the floor toward Melfallan.

"Has Brierley truly escaped?" Melfallan asked her hopefully. "How'd you manage it?"

"Ocean believe me, Melfallan, I've not set eyes on the girl today," Rowena replied, dashing his hope. "I haven't hidden her, nor helped her escape." She eyed Melfallan and Robert in turn. "Did you? Robert?" Both men shook their heads, and Rowena sighed deeply, and leaned her hand on a chair. "Then the duke has killed her, Melfallan. Damn his foul heart! He could not risk a trial—and apparently the justiciar who did the act has conveniently disappeared, too. With what reward?" she asked savagely. "What?"

Melfallan stared at his aunt. "I don't believe it. Tejar wouldn't dare."

"Why else this frenzy? What else makes sense?" Rowena gestured broadly at the room and its destruction. "Why this outrage of arresting *me* for 'treason'? Why this noise and furor to cover up a truth? Next he'll demand a search of all the roads, and make you help with the searching." Rowena seized his forearm tightly. "Be careful of the party with which you ride, Melfallan. There is treachery here, but it isn't mine. He may strike at you now through another."

"I agree," Count Robert said firmly. "If he can kill a commoner girl, he might be tempted to other killings. You must watch your back, brother."

Melfallan stared at him incredulously. "She's not dead!" he shouted. "She's not! I don't believe it!"

Rowena's eyes filled with tears. "Oh, my dear one. You must be prepared for it—and watch your back. Robert is right." Melfallan bit back a curse, then gently guided her to a chair that still had its cushions, and helped her to sit. He straightened and looked at Robert.

"I'll make inquiries," Robert said, and left the room.

Where is Brierley? Melfallan asked himself in anguish, and a slow sinking horror grasped at his heart. While I lay in my comfortable bed, warm and lazy with my wife, what happened to Brierley in the night?

How could I fail her again? he asked himself in despair. How? Although his every wish ran to foolish hope, he thoroughly believed Tejar capable of Brierley's murder, as firmly as his aunt believed it. Why else this display in Rowena's chambers, as she had said? Why else this panic in a duke who used his very emotions as his cold-minded tools? Where was Gammel Hagan?

He ground his teeth, his own panic rising that Rowena's fear was true. And I thought myself so very clever, so artful at my politics! If she's murdered, I killed her with my cleverness by acting Tejar's fool. I brought her here to Darhel, and I gave her to Hagan, as surely as I had stripped her for the rape with my own hands, then handed him the dagger afterward.

He groaned and covered his eyes with his hands.

She trusted me. Ocean forgive me.

"Ho there, Jack! Pull hard now!" the carter cried and cracked his whip, urging his mule onward. The mule threw himself against his harness collar, pushing with his strong legs against the slope.

By midmorning, Brierley and the carter had reached the foothills and now climbed steadily up the mountain road, winding to and fro past the several homesteads hidden on the broad forested slope. Brierley kept her mare at the carter's pace, as she had all morning, not wanting to pass him and gain his attention, yet not wanting to slow and allow any following carters to see her face. When wagons passed them descending the mountain, she kept her head bowed, her face concealed within her hood. Uninterested in a mere carter's daughter, the passersby had paid her no attention. The carter ahead of her rarely looked around, content to mull his thoughts and occasionally slap the reins on his mule's hindquarters.

"Get up now!" he cried.

Wrapped warmly inside Brierley's cloak, Megan was hardly visible at all, and sometimes drowsed, sometimes watched the changing scene with silent interest, though likely the quiet forest road seemed as much a dreamland as her river castle. All her life, the child had lived among the kitchen folk in the duke's castle, barraged by the mental noise and confusion of the hundreds of minds all around her. Here in the foothills, that tumult had been left far behind, replaced by birdcalls and the wind in the trees. At the moment, Megan was sleeping again, warm and comforted within Brierley's arms.

Gently Brierley ran her fingertips across the child's face, feeling tiny flashes of pain from the bruises, then systematically ran her hand over the rest of Megan's body, hunting the injuries that hurt and might be eased. As her hand moved slowly from place to place, Megan relaxed even more against her. It was not the same as a healing, this slow movement of the hands: Brierley felt no draining of her strength, no hint of the Beast in the deep shallows. Perhaps she merely guided the child in healing herself; perhaps only the touch comforted, like all touches.

Where are you? Brierley asked, her thought a bare whisper.

Where? Megan's mental voice was drowsy, distant and alone. *Safe* . . .

Where are you? Brierley repeated, her hands moving slowly, retracing their movement from shoulder to back to face.

Mother Ocean,

Daughter Sea. . . .

Do you know the prayer, Megan? My mother taught it to me years ago, when I was a little older than you. Try it with me.

Safe. . . .

Megan sighed deeply and escaped back into her drowse. Brierley suspected a deliberate sleep by the child, perhaps a much-prized opportunity that had usually eluded her in the kitchens—to sleep away the day, to sleep forever, a wish always broken by a rude slap or pinch, by hands that hit, by the head cook's harsh voice. It was a healing sleep, Brierley hoped, and kissed Megan's hair. She cradled the child closer and sang the prayer in its little song into Megan's ear, then let her sleep.

Brierley sniffed happily at the mountain air. A shari'a is not meant to live in a city, she thought. We are creatures of sea and forest, we witches, solitaries who should wander the roads. She imagined a future of many daughters in her craft, not just one small child safe in her arms. She imagined her daughters each walking a quiet road in the forest, each a living flame of what the shari'a had once been—before the troubles, before the Disasters.

After the weeks of fear, and the dread that had never truly left her, this quiet ride up the mountain now calmed and soothed her. She took a deep breath and at that moment thought she could believe in all things, even a ghost's musings about a refounded craft. A hundred daughters—a thousand. And perhaps sons, too: was witchery only a woman's gift? If so, why? If not, why did Bartol fear witches and think himself maybe one of them? Questions, always questions. She wrinkled her nose.

The road bent to the left, beginning a slow climb back and forth up the higher foothills. They entered a tunnel of blue-tinted green, with tall trees on either side and the sound of a morning breeze moving in the leafy canopy. The carter neither hurried nor dawdled, but kept his large mule at a patient plodding upward. She smiled at his back from within the shadows of her hood. He was a solid sort, happy with his wife, content with the day, much like Harmon in character, but without as much wit. The gentle ones of the world, she thought. Bless you, man, for the aid you give me, if unwittingly.

At the next bend in the road, the carter turned off into a lane branching to the right. Just above the trees, a thin blue spiral of smoke wound into the sky, and his dogs began baying an eager welcome to their master come home. Brierley reined the mare to a halt and watched the cart vanish behind the screen of trees, then looked behind her. The next cart behind them had not yet turned the bend, though she sensed the carter who followed, and a second and third far behind. For these few minutes, however, she was alone on the road.

We must go faster, she decided, and go very far before we rest. "Come on, Friend," she murmured, kicking the mare's sides. The mare picked up her pace, walking more briskly, winding upward.

After a steady of climb of two more hours, they reached the first low-slung saddle of the mountains. Brierley allowed the mare to choose their speed, and grew accustomed to the gentle sway of the horse's walk. The animal knew her own stamina and, dimly, in her creature's mind, knew her best pace—and Brierley needed distance, not a foundered horse from a rider's abuse.

As she rode along, to her bemusement, Brierley found the mare was becoming strangely aware of Brierley in turn, as if she knew Brierley's kindness in deferring to the mare's better judgment. Though she lived in a rural countryside, Brierley had little actual experience with horses, though she'd seen them frequently. The mare was far more intelligent than she had expected. Perhaps one learned to talk to horses, Brierley thought, merely by the continuing acquaintance. It was not something her cave books had ever mentioned.

She knew that beasts had minds and their own curious kind of thought. Brierley had often watched sea larks spin above the ocean, touching briefly their tiny minds as they darted and flew, but she disliked most dogs and found fish boring. Apparently a few sea animals, like the star dolphin and gomphrey, bordered on a genuine intelligence, as if they were a beast-people with their own destiny and reasons for being.

Were they a people? she wondered. Were horses a people, too?

"Do you have a name of your own?" she asked the mare. "I mean, besides the name Megan gave to you?"

The mare plodded along, content with her lot and uninterested in names, at least those Brierley could comprehend. Brierley smiled at the mare's disdain. Perhaps horses had their own manner of knowing each other, she thought. Or perhaps Friend enjoyed being stubborn. Either seemed equally likely. But she was a good beast, patient and gentle. Brierley patted the mare's neck and kicked her sides lightly. "No matter. 'Friend' will do."

She looked behind her to the west, where the Daystar had disappeared from the evening sky, its setting stirring the gentle upslope winds and spreading the growing twilight over Darhel's river plains. Following the Daystar, four hours behind at this turn of season and now directly overhead, the Companion shed its own gentle blue light, touching every needle, every leaf with a faint blue glow, like jewels. In spring, the Companion would pass the Daystar in the sky, thereafter leading the brighter sun in a blue-brilliant dawning, longer and longer until midsummer's ceaseless days. Then, turnabout again, the Daystar would lead the Companion, with growing twilight in the evenings as the world fell toward winter. A thin cloud scudded across the blue sun, scarcely dimming its brilliance.

Brierley looked at the eastern sky, hunting other storm clouds. In Yarvannet, autumn brought chiefly clinging mist and high winds with a heavy surf, but Melfallan had said the autumn storms were worse in Ingal's mountains, and worst of all in Mionn's Eastern Bay. Today, however, she saw only a scattering of heavy clouds to the east.

She looked around at the dark trees and smelled the wind now blowing more lustily upward. It feathered against her face, cool and welcome, and tugged playfully at her hood, flapped her cloak edge, then rushed onward, bending branch and leaf, tumbling over the forest. Even if they catch me again, she told herself, I will have had this day.

"I am tired, Friend," she told the horse, trying to ease her sore muscles from the long day's ride.

"Me, too," Megan said suddenly.

"You? You've been sleeping most of the day."

"I like to sleep." Megan nestled happily within the folds of Brierley's cloak. "Sleeping is safe. Where are we going? Where are all the other people?"

"The other people are back at the castle. We are going into those mountains." Brierley pointed ahead.

"Why?"

"We're running away."

"Are we?" Megan asked casually, then yawned wide enough to split her jaws. "I never dreamed this place before. I like it." Megan yawned again, then fell asleep again.

"I like it, too." Brierley clucked her tongue softly and tapped her heels on the mare's sides.

After another hour, the twilight deepened, turning to dark shadow beneath the trees. The mare was tiring now, too, but still walked willingly. Friend twitched her ears and reached for a mouthful from a passing bush, then chewed slowly as she walked. Brierley watched her ears flip to and fro, bending toward a distant birdcall in the forest, flipping back toward a rustle in the nearby bushes. Friend ate more leaves, then lifted her head and sniffed at the air. Brierley looked in the same direction, knowing the scent that filled the horse's nostrils, though the mare could scent things far more distant than she.

"Water? We need water. Is it far off the road?" They had come some twenty miles, she guessed, and she hesitated about riding into True Night on an unknown road, a road as unknown to the mare as to herself. And Megan needed tending, and they all needed rest.

What is wise? She could hear nothing behind her, either by ear or mind, but riders could be coming swiftly in the morning, soon into range.

"Take us to the water, Friend," she decided. "I'm tired, too."

She turned the mare's head toward the brush at the side of the road, and let the horse choose her own way toward the stream. The mare picked her way patiently through the bushes, around a large tree bole, then into a small glen overshadowed by evergreen branches barely inches above Brierley's head. Brierley stopped the horse and listened to the forest, conscious of Megan's warmth against her body. All was quiet, with the peace of the trees disturbed only by the distant cry of a mock owl. Nearby she could hear the soft sound of tumbling water. She looked around her at the small glade, smelling the tangy scent of everpine needles, the dark richness of the earth. The pine branches shirred above her, moving slightly in the breeze that flowed over the mountain. It was altogether lovely, and missed only the scents of the sea.

"We will stop here," she told the horse.

Brierley dismounted awkwardly, with Megan cradled in her arms, then laid the child under a protecting branch of evergreen. She unsnapped her cloak clasp and covered Megan with its warm folds, then unsaddled Friend, tracing the straps several times with her hands to learn their arrangement before she unfastened the buckles in the dimness of the glade. She found a small leather pouch behind the saddle and explored its contents curiously, puzzled by several of the odd shapes of leather and tooled metal, then repacked them in the pouch to study tomorrow.

"Horses come with gears and wheels, it seems," she told Friend, who agreed with a congenial snort, then swished her tail into Brierley's face. "Hey!"

She wondered if she should tie the horse, then worried that Friend might be thirsty in the night, unable to reach the stream. The mare swung her head toward her, then bumped her nose into Brierley's shoulder, her dark eyes gleaming.

"You won't run away?" Friend stamped a foot, mildly offended, then dropped her head to gaze on the green bunchgrass. "Well, all right." Brierley patted the horse, grateful for her help. She hesitated another moment, then lay down beside Megan, her cloak warm around them.

When she slept, Brierley found herself again on the river sands in Megan's dream world. She looked out over the broad moving river, then turned and looked up at the spires of Megan's castle, a lovely structure with a wide oaken door, white stone and white mortar, and the hint of colored panes in the upper windows. Where was Megan? she wondered. She looked up as she heard the child's faint giggle from high overhead, dancing on the air. Brierley climbed the broad stairs to the castle door, opened it, and went in.

She stood in a cool flagged entryway. On either side, wide rooms were visible through doorways; ahead, a staircase led upward. She looked left into a dim and comfortable parlor, then right into a sparely furnished library. Where, she wondered, had Megan learned of a library?

She looked up as she heard a scurrying sound above her, a light footstep. Brierley mounted the staircase and climbed upward to the second floor, seeking the child. As she climbed, a cool breeze blew into her face from above, winding downward from the upper levels, and, behind her, dimly on the air through the open front door, came the cry of birds over the river.

On the next landing, Brierley encountered a hallway with several closed doors. What did Megan keep here? she wondered. She opened the first door and looked into a dank room, dripping with water and heaviness, dimly lit and peopled with ghosts. The sorrow lay heavily on the air of remembered griefs, not only Megan's own, but those griefs that lay deep-buried in other minds. There, the baker's lost infant, and there, the young soldier's keen disappointment at his own lacks in training, and there, the young noblewoman's hopeless love for an indifferent lord. Megan had absorbed their memories like a sponge, and kept them here within the walls of this room. Brierley drew a deep breath, her heart aching in response to the grief in the room, then withdrew. These were not her sorrows, and past mending.

In the next room, the air was half-ablaze and seething, a furnace of envy and malice. Flames of anger crept along the walls, sullen and flickering, flaring occasionally when a blast of heat shot into the air of the room. In midair, two swords danced, jabbing at each other, blood dripping from their blades. Beneath the swords' jerking dance, the bodies of the envied and hated lay crumpled on the floor, singed and blackened and unmourned. Brierley took another breath of the hot air and reeled, then backed out hastily.

In the third room, she found Death, with its lost emptiness and hollow footsteps. The Beast's odor of stagnant seawater and rotting weed lay on the air, its victims now conquered. Brierley stood in the doorway, her head up, listening to the defeats. Scholars taught that death was a doorway to a better life, where Mother Ocean welcomed her children to ease and comfort, gave answer to all questions, gave an end to care and want and need. Too deafened by the roar of the Beast when it triumphed, Brierley had never heard the Mother's gentleness beyond life's doorway—but perhaps it was so.

Across the narrow room, a door stood partly ajar, a faint mellow light issuing from the crack: perhaps behind that door lay the answer—

"*There* you are!" Brierley gasped in surprise and whirled. Megan stood behind her, grinning widely, and held her elbows as she chortled at Brierley's fright. "I surprised you!" she declared triumphantly.

"You certainly did," Brierley said. "And shortened my life by years, child. It's not good to frighten others."

Megan sniffed, unimpressed, then grabbed Brierley's arm. "This floor has only old things," the child declared with the disdain of the very young. "The next floor is better. Come and see!"

"What's in that room?" Brierley asked, resisting her tug. She pointed at the next door.

"I never go in there. That's where the hands live." Megan tugged insistently on her arm.

"Hands?"

"The ones that grab you from the walls. The ones that grabbed *her* and hurt her with that poking thing. Then they grabbed *me* and pulled me out of her and she died. Sometimes the hands get loose and move around the castle, inside the walls. You have to watch out."

Brierley's eyes widened. Did Megan remember her own

birth? And perhaps even her engendering? Or had she absorbed her mother's memories at childbirth or, more likely still, learned the knowledge from other minds?

"Come *on,*" Megan said impatiently, still pulling on Brierley's arm. "Or I won't show you."

"Show me what?"

"Come see."

Brierley let Megan tug her into a step, then obediently followed the child back to the stairway and climbed with her upward. As they ascended, the air subtly changed, filling with light and motion, and the sound of rushing river water far below. Sunlight splayed through a broad doorway on the next landing; a gull's shadow wheeled across it and was quickly gone. Brierley heard its raucous cry, aloft above the river.

"Come see," Megan said. "This is where I live."

Brierley followed Megan into the third floor's single large room, a wide and light-filled room that looked out on a balcony bathed in bright sunlight.

It was the best of rooms, Brierley thought, looking around at the sunlight and Megan's choice of perfect furnishings. No cares here, no fears—only sanctuary in a large room with a water-green couch, a table filled with sweets and fruits, a soft bed for sleeping warm and undisturbed. Within the confines of her own mind, Megan had found her version of Brierley's own sea cave, and had filled it with the toys of her imagining.

Brierley bent slightly to look into the jeweled eyes of a salamander perched on a nearby bookshelf. Its slim body shimmered with tiny plumes of fire, red and yellow and flickering blue. The creature sat up on its haunches and hissed at her, a long slender tongue flickering. On another shelf nearby, a tiny miniature bear sat hugging his toes, blinking at the sunlight, and on yet another shelf a group of colored blocks stilted to and fro on pipestem legs. Children's toys, perhaps modeled on the noble children's toys Megan had seen from time to time—only these were far better. As she watched, the animated blocks piled themselves into a tower and fell down with a tinkling cascade of high-pitched giggles.

Brierley smiled with delight. I never thought to do anything like this, she thought. How lovely!

The salamander hissed more urgently as Brierley leaned closer. Megan clucked her tongue chidingly and held out her hand. The tiny beast leapt onto her fist, then balanced itself neatly with tail and wings, preening. The salamander's fire flicked over Megan's skin as she held it, but caused no harm.

"What's its name?" Brierley asked.

"He hasn't told me yet," Megan said carelessly. "I'm not sure he has one, but we don't care. He's happy here. So am I."

"I can see that. Do you come here often?"

"Yes. This is my place, my best place. No one bothers me up here, not even the hands in the walls." Megan turned toward the balcony and walked out into the sunlight, the salamander balanced on her hand. Brierley followed and sat down beside Megan on the sun-warmed planks of the balcony floor. Together they looked out over the short railing at the river.

"In Yarvannet," Brierley said, "I live in a cave by the sea. It has a stairway to the top of the rock, shelves of books, and an Everlight."

"An Everlight? What's that?"

Brierley hugged her knees. "I'm not sure. It just is. It knows when I come and go, and somehow we talk to each other without words, just by feeling things. The Everlight is very old. I think once it lived in Witchmere, though I'm not sure of that."

Megan's eyes brightened in interest. "What's Witchmere?"

"A place where people like you and me used to live, long ago." Brierley sniffed at the wind. "Very long ago. Nobody lives there now, I think."

"You know lots of things, Mother. Old things always do." Megan's voice had the settled satisfaction of speaking a long-known truth.

Brierley looked at the child, and indeed felt ancient under Megan's guileless gaze. This dream-place held the true child, the one without anger and fear. Here angers could be locked up in another room, fears slipped into a box and held away. Here was rest and ease, pleasure and beauty, all created by Megan's wishing. No wonder Megan so often escaped away to this room: it made perfect sense.

In this high tower, Brierley could truly believe in a place that had no cares, few questions. Here the Beast had no power, banished by the wistful dreams of a witch-child and defeated forever. Here the shari'a were not feared and hunted, nor pain allowed. If only it could be so easy, she thought: if only Megan's imagining could change the world. The sun beat down on their faces, warming flesh cooled by the river breeze. Brierley took off her hat and let her hair blow free. "I like this place very much," she said.

Megan leaned her head on Brierley's shoulder and sighed. "So do I. Can we live here forever, just you and me? I'll share it with you, Mother. Can we—forever?"

Brierley sighed and kissed her forehead. "How I wish we could, you and I. Forever."

Brierley gently untangled a curl of Megan's dark hair, then studied the child's face so near to her own. In the sunlight, Megan's face was thin and worn. Long inky lashes shadowed the eyes, and she had a firm jaw, and a soft line to the cheeks and nose of her half-formed girlhood. Brierley looked for any resemblance to her own face, but did not see a similarity. Perhaps Megan looked more like her father, whoever he had been.

Are you my niece, child? she wondered. The age is right, if my twin survived in Darhel. Or are you other than Jonalyn's kin? Perhaps you come from another family here, another birth-line of witches. Perhaps. Who had Bartol met in Darhel, to think he knew witches? Will I ever know?

Thora had said to look for the shari'a in Darhel, but if Thora was the Everlight and could not hear across the distance, perhaps the Everlight also wished rather than knew.

Are not dreams the best of wishes? As Megan had wished herself to a place of safety and so found it, had the Everlight wished Brierley to its sea cave and so found her? And as Brierley wished when she dreamed of cockleboats and a wistful ghost?

What do I wish now? she asked herself, hugging Megan close to her. Melfallan I cannot have, and Thora is more ghost than real. She tenderly rearranged one of Megan's curls, then caressed her face. Megan wriggled, then sighed as she leaned her head onto Brierley's shoulder. They watched the gull swoop over the river, flashing white wings in the brilliant sunlight.

What do I wish? I wish for your health, child, for our future companionship, for the mutual exploration of each other as witch and friend. For that I will have to wean you, just a little, from this lovely castle. I must give you reason to live in the real world, if only sometimes. I shall be your reason, if I can—as you now give me new reason for living.

My beloved child. How I have longed to meet you, and now I have. She kissed Megan's forehead.

"You are safe, my Megan," she whispered. "I will build safety for you, my child, in all our worlds, your riverbank and my sea cave, this forest and that mountain. I promise you, Megan. I promise."

Brierley sighed, then drifted away to sleep among other dreams and other wishes.

Brierley opened her eyes to True Night. The Companion had set, taking its shimmering blue light from the world, and now tree and bole lay in near-total darkness. A cold draft shivered through the glade, and Brierley nestled beneath their warm cloaks, Megan wrapped in her arms. She listened sleepily to the forest all around her.

A mock owl hooted nearby, then slid on whispery wings across the glade. Brierley felt the stream of air through strong wing feathers, the buoyancy of the easy glide. Talons reached and grabbed for a narrow branch. Then, wings tucked neatly to sides, the owl bent its large eyes on the ground for a betraying rustle of life. In the shadows below, small terrified hearts beat frantically as instinct froze the tiny shrews into immobility. Panic, panic, beat the frantic rhythm, until one shrew could not bear the tension any longer and ran madly for its burrow. The mock owl stooped—

Brierley shook her head slightly, trying to ignore the delicate savagery of the mock owl's disemboweling of its prey. It swallowed the last morsel, then cast a still-hungry eye on the brush beneath its perch. The terror grew—

"Hey!" Brierley called out, startling the bird. The mock owl squawked and launched itself, gliding away from the unexpected intruder, then soared up the slope. Brierley smiled.

Little shari'a, came a deep voice into her mind, reproving her. *Death for some is another's dinner. She has owlets to feed.* Startled, Brierley's eyes roved the dark glade and, after a minute, she cautiously lifted herself to one elbow to look behind her. A movement in the tree branches above caused her to tighten her arms on Megan, and think to run.

"Who are you?" she breathed.

Was it smoke? A dark broad mist lay on the branch above her head, little more than a shadow against the darkness of the trees and night. She thought she saw a flicker of deep-set emerald eyes, then the vague outline of a reptilian head. The dragon smiled at her and laid its chin on the branch. Golden claws flexed into the wood, then stilled. *Who am I?* it echoed, and she sensed great amusement at her question. *I am many things, little sister, but tonight I am your guardian. Sleep again and take your rest.*

"Sleep?" Brierley whispered. "With you in that tree? Who *are* you?"

One of the Four, it replied casually. *Although you are sea witch, Brierley, and your child a fire witch, you are in my forest tonight, and so I take the watch. We Four still abide in shari'a lands, guarding the few shari'a who remain. Be at peace.*

"Sea witch?" Brierley blinked in astonishment, then looked down at Megan's sleeping face. "And—"

Fire witch, the dragon repeated, and shifted comfortably on its branch. *As I said. Although all the shari'a have mind-speech, some are given greater gifts. The Allemanii called them witches; the shari'a had other names for their adepts, before the troubles came and the Allemanii ravaged the shari'a lands. Did not your mother ever explain this to you?*

"My mother never explained anything, spirit. She wished only to forget. And my books never said the Four actually *appeared* to anyone, much less reclined on branches to have conversations." She eyed the dark shadow above her. "If you're real." The dragon's deep-set emerald eyes glinted in amusement. "I think not," Brierley decided. "I think I'm dreaming."

As you will, little one.

"Am I dreaming?" Brierley asked plaintively.

Aren't you?

"You sound like Thora when she makes least sense," Brierley complained. "Are you, aren't you, who can say?"

The Everlights seek patterns, my child; it is their nature. They especially delight in the sound and puzzle of words, even when it leads to the loss of sense. Thora's Everlight is no different, and is now very old. The love remains. It smiled at her benignly. *Sleep now: I will watch.*

Brierley wished more answers, but a deep lassitude came over her, relaxing her body, bringing a deep sigh and the closing of her eyes. Unwillingly, she slipped back into dreams, if in fact she had ever left them.

13

Brierley awoke just after dawn and heard the distant baying of hounds. Her eyes flew open and she listened for a paralyzed moment, then threw off the cloak and surged to her feet. The Daystar had not yet risen above the distant peaks, but spread its lightening grays in the eastern sky. She stumbled through the dim light to the saddle and lifted it onto the mare's back. Behind her, Megan sat up, her eyes wide and frightened.

Her fingers trembling, Brierley fumbled with the straps, not quite remembering how they had unfastened. The more she tried to hurry, the more the saddle straps confused her. She took a deep breath and studied the straps one by one, the wide girth strap, the forward leather strap that passed across the mare's front chest, a third narrower strap across the mare's haunches and under the tail. It was a ladies' saddle, she realized, without the filmy draperies and bright bells. She opened the leather pouch and pulled out a bell, one of the metal objects she had felt in the pouch the night before. Those she would not need. She thought to throw it into the grasses, then tinkled it gently. It has a fine mellow sound, fair on the morning air. With a sigh at herself and her fancies, she returned it to the pouch with the others and finished saddling the mare.

"I hope I have this on right," she told Friend. "Stop when it starts to slide off, will you?" Friend snorted.

She turned toward Megan and held out her arms. "Come, Megan. Bring the cloak. We must hurry." Megan didn't move, only stared down the mountain toward the sound of the dogs. Brierley stamped her foot. "You must help me now. Megan!"

Megan moved as slowly as shifting sand, but she did move, the cloak dragging behind her. Brierley lifted her onto the horse and swept her cloak around her own shoulders, struggled with the clasp, then stepped carefully into the stirrup. As she raised herself upward, the saddle stayed on the horse, to her relief. She threw her leg over the mare's back and settled into the saddle, then wrapped the cloak ends tightly around the child in front of her. With an sharp nudge of her heels, she urged the mare back to the road.

As they regained the dusty track, the sound of the dogs became clearer, bell-like tones lofted into the cold air. It was a haunting music that reawakened Brierley's oldest fears. Her books told of such dogs, when the lords urged them after a witch to the quick and bloody end. Megan whimpered, sensitive to her emotions, and Brierley hugged her reassuringly. With a good kick to the mare's sides, she nudged the mare into a trot up the inclining road. The mare went willingly, her ears pricking forward and back. Brierley looked behind her, half-expecting to see the pursuers burst into view around the last turn in the road, but saw only a dirt-beaten road and the forest on every side. The dogs caroled dimly in the distance. How close? She couldn't tell. A mile? Two miles? She had slept too long.

Ahead were more trees and the distant mountain peaks just visible through the treetops. The road seemed to grow steeper as it climbed. She urged the mare onward, until Friend's trotting jounced them busily up and down, enough to rattle Brierley's teeth. She kicked the mare again and she broke into a light canter, her hooves digging into the soft dirt of the road. Megan gave a little squeak at the alarming change in the horse's gait, and her fingers tightened on Brierley's arms.

"This is fun!" Brierley said firmly.

"Fun?" Megan asked. The child gasped as Friend fell back into a jouncing trot, then squealed again as a firm blow of

Brierley's heels pushed the horse back into a canter. Brierley swiveled in the saddle to look back, desperate to know how close the dogs were. Should she hide in the trees? Would the dogs find her? Were they hunting her? She knew nothing of hunting dogs and the noblemen who made a sport of the forest chase. What would they hunt in this season? In this land?

Like a flicker of a trout across a stream and as quickly gone, she touched Count Robert's mind as he cantered with a group of soldiers and another lord, all following two dog handlers running after their leashed dogs. How far behind me? She couldn't recognize trees in such a forest, not as to place and turning. Brierley bit her lip and cast her sensing again, and caught another flicker of the forest the count now passed, but, again, it looked too much like many stretches of forest she had passed—and that in the dark. But that she could hear him at all brought him too close, however her gift might hear farther in her fear. She kicked Friend's sides and pushed the horse to greater speed.

The road grew steeper, but the mare cantered onward, reaching out with her front legs strongly, pushing hard with her rear legs, taking them steadily upward, her breath steaming in the cold air as she snorted. She was a young horse and liked the exercise. Strongly she tackled the slope, legs sweeping in a steady rhythm. Brierley and Megan grew more accustomed to the rocking pace, and the child's death grip on the saddle horn grew less white in the fingers.

"Fun?" Brierley asked softly.

"Fun!" Megan now declared, and laughed aloud. The mare twitched her ears.

Oh, to be a child, Brierley thought. She tried to temper her own fear, and urged the mare onward up the steep road.

The narrowing road turned to the left and ran for a quarter mile, then swept right and upward, now a narrow dirt track through heavy forest. Heavy ruts in the center of the road showed the effect of rains, and the track showed little sign of being used, not like the road farther down the mountain. As they cantered onward, the light of the Daystar strengthened with the dawn, turning light gray and then into dawn colors of red and lavender, a shimmer of pale green. Brierley blinked, dazzled, as the next turn swung them due east into the flare of the Daystar, just visible over the peaks ahead.

After another mile, they reached the top of the next hill and the mare ran easily across its broad top, then plunged down the road on the other side. The sound of dogs fell away. As the mare swept into another turn and pounded up another ascent in the road, Megan laughed again, delighted with the speed of the horse. Brierley tightened her arms around her and felt Megan's fingers tighten on her arms in response.

"Run, Friend! Run!" Megan cried. Friend flicked her ears happily and cantered briskly.

They had gained another half-mile up the new ascent when the sound of the dogs bayed abruptly into the cold air, echoing across the valley behind them. Brierley looked back but could not see through the trees that screened the road behind them, and guessed that the pursuit had just reached the top of the last hill, closer than she thought—and faster than she expected. The mare pounded onward, her breath puffs of vapor in the cool dawn air. The brilliant dawn light of the Daystar dimmed as clouds ahead scudded across the sky, and the wind bore the scent of snow from the peaks far ahead. As they climbed, she saw lingering patches of older snow on the ground beneath the trees, and the air seemed still colder. The hounds bayed steadily.

A half-mile farther, the road ran across a broad meadow of drying grass toward a cliff face, a tall jumbled façade of yellow stone, cracked and pitted by harsh weather, with dwarf trees and tall brush clinging to its higher ledges. The cliff face extended around three sides of the broad meadow, but the road led straight ahead, plunging into a small grove at the cliff's foot and then winding through tree boles to a narrow track that climbed steeply upward along a narrow ledge. Brierley stopped her horse at the bottom of the trail and craned her neck to look upward, but the track disappeared into the trees. Is this the road? she wondered.

"Can you climb that?" Brierley asked the horse. Friend snorted and took a step forward, and Brierley shook the reins in encouragement, then leaned forward hard as Friend began picking her way up the steep path, step by step.

In some places, where the rock was slick, the mare's hooves sometimes slipped on the smooth stone, but Friend caught herself easily and labored upward, one slow step at a time. Brierley clung to the saddle horn, hoping again that her saddle straps had been fastened correctly. At this angle, imagining the slide off and down had good help from a glance behind her. Already they had climbed a hundred feet. The meadow disappeared behind a heavy screen of trees as they reached a turn in the narrow path.

They reached a small dirtslide where the track had collapsed, creating a soft ledge chest-high on the horse. Above the ledge, the track continued, hard-packed and stony. Brierley prudently reined the mare to a stop, and Friend stood patiently, snorting, her hooves braced on the soft dirt. Brierley studied the ledge, not sure of the horse's agility to make the leap, especially with herself and Megan on her back. The sound of the dogs grew louder as they broke into the meadow below. She heard the jingling of bridles and the creak of leather of the several horsemen who followed.

"Hold yourself right there, Friend," Brierley said softly. "I'm getting off." Carefully, Brierley swung her leg over the mare's hindquarters, trying not to shift her weight too suddenly, then jumped lightly to the ground. She helped Megan shift backward into the saddle. "Hold on tight, Megan."

She took a solid grip on Megan's skirt and arm, ready to snatch the child off if the mare slipped, then urged Friend to turn toward the ledge. "No, wait!" Brierley said as the horse bunched her legs to jump. "Let me take Megan off."

Brierley lifted Megan down and struggled up the three-foot break in the trail, then carried the child several feet up the track. As she turned to go back for the horse, the mare jumped the ledge, stumbling a moment to her knees as she landed, then quickly getting to her feet. The mare shook her head briskly and snorted, then trotted the few feet to Brierley, very pleased with herself.

"As you should," Brierley told her and patted her neck. "I think we'll all walk now." She took the mare's reins and got Megan to her feet and started up the new level of the track. The hounds were very loud now. Her heart began a slow panicked beat, and she heard Megan whimper in response.

"Mother," she said, clinging to Brierley's skirt.

"Shhh." Together with the horse, Brierley and Megan climbed slowly up the steep track, hidden by the screening trees as the horses and dogs swept up to the base of the cliff.

"Wait!" a man shouted, so close that Brierley stopped and crouched down, dragging Megan to the ground with her. Through the screen of tree branches below, she could see the sleek bodies of the hounds tumbling over each other, baying in confusion as their handlers jerked back on their leashes. Just beyond them she saw the brown flash of a horse's body, then other flashes of color of red and blue and black as the other mounted men stopped at the base of the cliff.

"My dear Lim," one man said, and she recognized the voice of Count Robert, Saray's brother. His voice rang loudly in the clear cold air of the meadow. "As I've told you, we are following the duke's courier to Mionn. He would take this road *and* his horse would smell of Darhel's stable just like hers would, if she took a horse. I agree with Countess Rowena: if she's alive, she went south to the sea."

The other lord snorted. "I don't believe the duke murdered her."

"Oh, you don't?" Robert said. "Well, I do, and so does Earl Melfallan now. Why else did the duke make such a show yesterday morning in Rowena's chambers? Ask Stefan here how it was. And why else did Tejar then accuse *you* of murdering Hagan, merely because Hagan was once your liegeman? It's absurd, but real danger to you, Toral. You can't sit the fence much longer, balancing the duke with Mionn. Tejar's after *you* now. How does it feel?"

"I don't believe the duke killed her," Toral said stubbornly. "Duke Tejar wouldn't do such a thing."

"Ocean's deep, you can shout that aloud and cry the morning, but it doesn't change the truth. The duke read his court, including you, and decided he might lose at her trial. And so she's disappeared and so has Hagan. And Hagan was your man first, just as the duke said. Where is he, Toral?"

"I don't know!" Toral shouted at Robert. "I know nothing of *any* of this! I've never even seen the maid, and Hagan left my service nine months ago! I want nothing of Melfallan's quarrels with Duke Tejar. Nor yours, Mionn! I say she rode east! If Melfallan thinks she went west, why does he search into Airlie?"

"He had to choose some direction, with Tejar demanding that all the High Lords join the search. And his aunt wanted fair conduct home."

"To guard himself, I'm sure. If he is found with that girl, the duke will accuse *him* of Hagan's murder—and have the proof of it in the finding."

"You'd like that, wouldn't you? Put yourself first, as always. But it's no use, Toral. The girl is dead, and Melfallan knows it, and so do you. All of this hieing around the countryside is the duke's fine show to make truth different."

"Truth? Where is Melfallan's truth, I wonder?" Toral sneered. The count's voice was tight with anger and dislike. "He and his aunt started this plot, and now have the ruins of it. Ask Stefan, you say. Well, I do. Who knows what she told Stefan in, say, an *intimate* moment?" Brierley heard Stefan react instantly with the quick sound of drawn steel.

"Stefan, put that sword away," Robert ordered crossly.

"I'll run him through!" Stefan cried. "How dare he insult my countess!"

"I'll insult whom I please!" Lim shouted. "It's not seemly how she fawns over you, and you nothing but a steward's son. And her widowed all these years but still comely enough to win a man to bed. Why not you, Stefan? You're comely enough yourself."

"Lim, shut up!" Robert cried. There was a busy stamping of horses' hooves as Robert maneuvered between the two angry men. "Stefan, calm down! He's just the duke's lizard, snide and jealous. He doesn't matter."

"*Lizard*, am I?" Toral cried. "Even as lizard, I'm better off now than your precious earl and countess. The witch's flight proves her guilt, and fortunes will fall with that, and more than Melfallan's. Look to yourself, Mionn, in whom you choose as ally!"

"You toad!" Stefan shouted. There was another great stamping of horses as Stefan tried to maneuver around Count

Robert, bringing all three closer to the cliff. Stefan's sword flashed brightly in the daylight.

"Stefan!" Robert shouted, blocking his way, then struck out at the flat of Stefan's blade with his gloved fist. The sword went flying toward the brush under the cliff-side trees, and Stefan promptly flung himself off his horse to retrieve it.

Brierley held her breath as Stefan's sword turned idly in the air, sailing high toward her, and crashed into the brush immediately below her ledge. The Count of Lim laughed, which only added more furious action to Stefan's plunge into the bushes. As Stefan reached the sword, he snatched it up and lifted it high, looking up as he did. Then he saw Brierley above him, and froze, sword still lifted, his eyes widening in shock. (*It's her! Sweet Ocean, she's alive!*) Brierley gasped softly and shrank backward, pulling Megan tighter against her.

Rowena's man. It was her only hope—would Rowena's man protect a witch?

Stefan stood frozen for another long moment, staring up at her, then threw a wild glance back at the two counts still occupied with their furious arguing. Then Stefan looked back up at Brierley, tossed her a wide grin, and with a flourish, brought his sword blade to his lips in a salute. Then he turned and stomped back vigorously through the brush toward the others.

Brierley let out the breath that had caught in her throat, and shuddered as her heart began to pound with a wild exultation. Stefan had seen her, and would tell Melfallan. Did he truly believe her dead? Did he grieve? What thoughts were in his mind at this moment, riding with his aunt into Airlie? But Stefan would tell him and, with that news, Melfallan could direct the search elsewhere, giving Brierley time to escape into the mountains, to hide herself in safety. And the duke would believe her dead, as did the other High Lords, when she was never found. In Mionn, in the southern towns far from the earl's northerly capital, she could build a new life with Megan.

A chance for life, truly a chance for life, far from the duke and his hatreds! A chance! Suddenly she wanted to dash and run, leap high, and shout to the hills. She wished to seize the stars and toss them still higher. She wanted to dance and leap and cry aloud.

On a distant beach, in another time and all time, an Everlight flickered in the gloom, and a young red-haired woman stood facing the sea's broad horizon, the suns' light warm on her face. *Good spirit, what can I hope for?* Thora had called, bereft and weeping. *The Disasters have fallen upon us and I am alone. All is ended.*

Soft with the slurring sound of tumbling waves, a Voice had answered her, rich, alive, acknowledging her: *My daughter, do not despair: I shall send an heir for you, another who can believe.*

Brierley bowed her head and choked back a sob, then hid her face against Megan's hair.

Beneath her ledge, the men's voices still contended, making the hounds nervous and quarrelsome. Their handlers struggled with the leashes, then finally backed them firmly away from the brush, behind the soldiers who stood waiting for orders. Brierley peered again through the screen of leaves, trying to see, but felt content that if she could not see well, neither could the men below see her.

"Put that sword down," Robert ordered, as Stefan stepped out of the brush.

Stefan made a show of sheathing his sword. "You are mistaken, Count Robert," he declared loftily. "The Count of Lim is toad, not lizard. But even toads are given life, as mysterious as Divine Ocean's reasons might be."

Count Toral made an inarticulate sound of rage.

"Enough!" Robert declared. "Both of you!"

There was a long pause, broken only by the creaking of a saddle and the idle stamping of horses' hooves as all apparently glared at each other. Then Robert cleared his throat. "I still say this is the wrong road."

"I agree," Stefan said emphatically.

"Duke Tejar wants all roads searched," Toral objected. "You heard him give the order yourself."

"Not *my* road," Robert argued. "This high track leads to

Mionn, and no one accuses me of any allegiance to this witch."

"Saray's your sister," Toral shot back.

"I'm talking about choice of road, you idiot, not my bloodline. The girl wouldn't come this way—and if she did, the winter comes early in these mountains. Clouds like those can blow into a storm in hours and drop ten feet of snow in a day. Trust me: I know these mountains."

"She might have come this way," Toral said stubbornly. "She was seen."

"A *woman* was seen," Robert retorted. "A commoner woman on a horse with a child. How many dozens of such women live in these hills? And why would she have a child with her? Whomever they saw, those witnesses, it wasn't Brierley Mefell. Brierley is dead. Let me say it again: dead. And none of your whining or excuses for the duke will make it any different, Lim. Tejar killed her because he knew he couldn't win against Melfallan, and then he killed Hagan because Hagan was the witness to the killing. I wouldn't make yourself champion of the duke on this matter, Lim, not if you wish to keep Mionn's friendship."

"Are you threatening me, Robert?"

"Advising," Robert answered coolly, "merely advising. A commoner woman has a right to justice and life, however innocently entangled in a High Lord's politics. Tejar denied her that. That's not right. But what does Tejar care? And who's next for the witch cry? Airlie? Mionn? *Lim*? He's already accused *you* about Hagan, enough to make you sputter and cringe and ride off on the hunt. Believe me, now isn't the time to straddle your fence, saying 'yes' to Tejar and 'maybe' to my father. You had better choose, Lim, and choose soon."

"I still say—"

"I don't care what you say," Robert said forcibly. "If she did come east, count, she'll die on this road. Winter is nearly upon us, and there's more snow in those clouds. You may have men to waste, but I wouldn't send any man of mine over the mountains this late in autumn. Not on this road. The courier will be lucky to make the crossing."

"But—"

"Have you ever wintered a High Trail storm, you fool?" The young count's voice rose to a bellow.

"But the duke said—"

"Oh, yes, 'the duke said.' He says lots of things, but a wallowing sow has better judgment than he does." Toral gasped in shock. "So now go sniveling to our good duke's ears and report that!" Robert declared. "Tell him my opinion of our stout fool. I'm no murderer of young women. Stefan and I are turning back."

"Leave the hounds," Toral ordered. "I'll need them."

"I take the hounds. They're mine, anyway, and I've told you I'll trust none of mine in the passes this late in the season, not even my dogs."

Robert wheeled his horse and shouted to his men, then thundered off, Stefan and half the company following behind him. The remaining men, apparently Toral's own soldiers, hesitated and looked to their lord. Brierley heard Count Toral's muffled curse, then his cry to his horse as he galloped after Count Robert, his men pounding along in his wake. The furious sound of their hoofsteps echoed across the meadow, then faded into the distance. Brierley sighed and laid her head on her arm.

Megan stirred beside her. "Are the men gone?" she whispered.

"Yes, Megan. They are gone."

Brierley rose to her feet and took a firm grip on Megan's hand, then tugged on the mare's reins. As quietly as she could, she led the horse and child up the steep track. When Megan stumbled, Brierley picked her up onto her hip and struggled onward, the mare following patiently behind. The wind grew colder as they neared the top of the cliff, and Brierley looked up apprehensively at the sky and its scudding clouds. She knew nothing of the weather in these mountains. Had the count spoken truly of the fierceness of the storms? Or had he exaggerated to goad and taunt Toral?

I can't go back, she thought realistically. If I was inconvenient to the duke before, I'm worse now. The search parties are covering all the roads toward Darhel. Can I go forward to safety? Yarvannet sometimes had light snows in deep winter, more often a bitter cold that laid a thin shell of ice on any standing water. But the count's words had suggested more than that.

The wind bit hard as they topped the cliff and found more sloping ground ahead of them and a dwindling track—but it was a track, heading east into the higher ranges, toward Mionn. Brierley stopped and stared at the huge mountains ahead, jagged heights of stone capped with snow and gray-slated rock.

But maybe there is shelter ahead, if I can find it. I can't go back.

She lifted Megan onto the horse again and mounted behind her, then kicked the mare into an ambling walk, giving the horse a small rest after the hard climb up the narrow track. Later they would go faster.

After another few miles, they reached a crossroads as one narrow track crossed another. Brierley stopped the horse and looked down the southeast track. It led into deep forest, on rocky ground, winding quickly out of view behind a granite massif. But it led downward, away from the snows that clung to the eastern peaks. But downward to where, to what sanctuary? To Airlie, she guessed, remembering the few maps of the northern lands in her cave books. Countess Rowena was likely a friend and certainly Melfallan's ally, but Brierley brought desperate peril to Rowena if she was found anywhere in Airlie's county, and through that peril to Melfallan also.

She frowned as she remembered Toral's taunts at Count Robert. Had her escape put Melfallan in more danger? How? That she had fled showed her guilt, well, that was an easy argument, one she'd rather not face in Darhel. What had happened when the duke discovered she was gone? What had happened in Rowena's chamber, and why did Melfallan ride with her back to Airlie? Count Robert said he thought her dead, but he would know Stefan's news soon. And what then? What would Melfallan do?

Oh, let me go, Melfallan, she wished him earnestly. For your safety and mine. Be content with Saray and your son and Yarvannet's sweet shores. Believe me safe, somewhere, anywhere, and let me go.

The mare shifted her weight comfortably beneath her, waiting patiently. Brierley hesitated, sorely tempted to take the downward track to Airlie, then bowed her head in defeat. Snows or not, she had to climb to the east. She clucked to the horse and nudged her ribs with her heels, reining her head to the leftward track.

The air grew colder as the narrow dirt road wound upward into the highland forest, where the trees grew larger, dominated by the hardy evergreens, row upon row. Sometimes they passed a small meadow with standing golden hay, another time a small series of pools with ice rime on the edges and quacking teal ducks paddling busily in the centers. Megan lifted her head when she heard the birds, and watched the ducks bob their heads and flap their wings.

"Blue teal, I think," Brierley said, and Megan started slightly at the sound of her voice, then craned her head to look up into Brierley's face. "Have you ever seen waterbirds, Megan?"

"They are following us," Megan said in a croaking voice. "The men."

"What men?" Brierley could sense nothing of a pursuit behind them, and wondered that Megan could. "How far behind?"

"Far?" Megan shook her head in confusion. "It's cold here. Why are the men following us?"

"To take us back to Darhel." Megan made a gasping sound at that and stiffened. "Not while I have say otherwise, Megan," Brierley said reassuringly, wishing she could promise more to the frightened child. "And I still have a say," she said firmly.

She kicked Friend into a gentle trot, and the horse went willingly, her ears flicking to and fro at the bird songs and rustling wood all around them. Her hooves made gentle plopping noises in the soft dust of the road. Brierley thought to move her over to the grassy edge on one side. Perhaps it might hide some of their tracks. Though she saw many tracks in the road, proof of its frequent travelers in a muddier season, apparently the men could tell one set from another. At least the hounds could.

Friend trotted around a wide turn in the road. The forest opened up a little into a small clearing, where the road again divided, one path heading east toward the Daystar's place of rising, the other southwest. Where did that road go? she wondered. Another track to Airlie? Or did it turn below and wind eastward again through another pass? Brierley rode into the crossroads and again looked down each fork, then decided on the more level way east along the upper terrace of this area of mountains. The new path seemed little-traveled, with grass overgrowing much of the track. Friend slowed to a walk to jerk mouthfuls of grass.

"Hungry," Megan said in delight, pointing at the horse's chewing.

"Yes, she is hungry. Are you hungry?"

"Yes," Megan said emphatically.

Brierley reached back to the saddlebags and found bread and cheese, then unstrapped the water bottle as well. Not much of a meal after a half-day of journeying, and the food she had taken from the castle's kitchen larder was limited. She must think of gathering food as they traveled, and now regretted passing by the waterbirds. Would there be winter berries? Were there snow hares in these upper reaches? She saw no sign of farmsteads along this higher road, but knew food could be found in the forest.

She and Megan ate their meal, watching the passing trees and the distant mountains to the east. The clouds had cleared a little and the Daystar shone brightly down, making crisp shadows off every branch and projecting stone. The snow still hung in sheltered pockets, and the air was now stingingly cold. The temperature seemed to enliven Megan, for she began to exclaim excitedly as new things came into view.

Megan pointed to a sparkling vein in a tall boulder on their left. "Look! It shines. Like the stars!"

"Yes, it does," Brierley agreed.

Megan looked to the right and pointed again. "Look! A red bird!"

"Yes, it is a red bird." The star cardinal plopped itself on a bush and sang its three-note cry, fluttering proudly. "It's called a star cardinal. They like pineland forest."

"Oh, look!" Now it was left to a squirrel sitting on a high limb, its tail jerking and brisk. "What's that?"

"A squirrel."

"A squirrel," Megan said with great satisfaction. "Is it real?"

"Yes, Megan, it's quite real. See? It's watching you." Brierley guessed that to Megan all this greenery might seem unbelievable. Well, the forest had never seen Megan, either, and the squirrel seemed properly agog at the event. It berated them angrily in its high squeaking voice, then vanished into the branches with a flick of its tail.

"What's that?" Megan pointed right and Brierley looked but saw only trees and a shaggy bush..

"I don't see anything. What?"

"It's not there anymore," Megan said, sounding puzzled. "It was there, but it wasn't. It looked at us, and then it didn't."

"Looked?"

"It didn't like us." Megan sounded solemn. "It had bad thoughts about us."

Brierley looked back at the place where Megan had pointed, mystified by the child's words. What could be there and not, could look and didn't? An animal? She remembered vaguely that the larger forests had predators to avoid, a large doglike animal, a dangerous cat, hints of still larger animals. But most of the forest animals avoided people, not liking their smell.

"Bad thoughts?"

"I don't want to think about it," Megan said firmly and nestled deeper into the folds of Brierley's cloak. Despite Brierley's gentle prodding, the child would not say any more about the "looker" who hadn't liked them.

They rode for another two hours under the warm light of both suns, with Megan pointing now and then to some new wonder, and finally they came to a wooden bridge over a small stream. Brierley walked Friend down the slight bank for a drink, then dismounted and filled their water flask. As she straightened, she looked under the bridge into a small grassy glade by the stream bank, several feet below the level of the road and backed by a wall of stone. She hesitated, then turned to Megan.

"Can you hear the men, Megan?"

Megan looked down at her and blinked, and then braced her hand on Friend's neck as she turned and looked back up the road.

"I'm not sure," she said. "I don't think so. Why is it so quiet?" She looked back at Brierley. "Where are all the voices?"

"The ones in your head?" Brierley asked. Megan nodded. "We're not in the castle anymore, Megan. There's only a few people up here, maybe just us and the men. Can you hear me when I think?"

"A little. You don't think very loud," Megan said carelessly, then threw her hands to her mouth, her eyes widening in sudden terror. *Don't tell! Don't tell!* Brierley reached her in a single stride.

"It's *all right* to tell me. I'm like you: I hear thoughts, too." Megan's eyes were blurring as she began to fall away into her river world, and Brierley took hold of her leg and pinched hard. "I was in your safe place by the river. Don't you remember?"

Megan hesitated, then stared at her. "You were there! Twice!" Megan sounded wholly astonished. "How did you do that?"

"Because I hear thoughts, too. I'm like you, and you're like me. We are the same, so it's all right to tell me. I already know. You don't have to run. You don't have to be afraid."

Megan considered this, and Brierley chuckled at her skeptical expression. In some ways, this child was far older than her young years. "So don't believe me. I don't mind. I think we'll camp here. Friend is tired and so am I."

She tugged on the mare's reins and led the horse carefully down the streambed under the bridge. When they reached the grassy bank, the cold wind had completely dropped away. There was even a hint of warmth in the dell from the Daystar's warming of the rocks. Brierley lifted Megan down from the horse, then lifted down the saddle bags and unsaddled the mare. She carried the saddle bags over to a young stand of everpine and started unpacking, helped by Megan.

She pulled out the blankets and constructed a rough lean-to with tall sticks. As she hunted deeper into one pack, she found the provisions she had hastily gathered in the store-room—dried meat and fruits, another loaf of bread, a tangy cheese wrapped in strong cloth, a box of tea flakes, even a packet of sweet sugar cakes, enough to last a few days. She gave a soft sigh of relief, assured of her meager treasures, then dug through the other pack for flint and steel to make a fire. In another half-hour, she had a small fire burning and Megan sat comfortably in her cloak under the blanket tent.

"Do you hear the men?"

Megan shook her head, then put her thumb in her mouth, her eyes roaming over the trees and water and cliffside.

Brierley took a short walk up the road and, after some investigation into some high grass, found several ground tubers for dinner. She picked some grains from wild barley stalks, found sweet onions and then some nuts beneath a rowanberry bush. With some of the dried beef from her pack, the tubers and grain made a good stew for their dinner.

Afterward, as the Companion shed its brilliant blue twilight into the forest, she sat with Megan's head in her lap, watching the child sleep. Friend dropped her head low and dozed, shifting her weight from time to time in a casual motion. All around them the forest whispered in the breeze, the treetops bending gracefully forward and back, like ladies nodding to each other in agreement. But it was still bitterly cold.

Yet lovely still, she thought with a contented sigh, thinking she would live a night like this forever, if she could stop herself in one moment of time, one precious moment like this. Last night she and Megan had met on a sun-drenched balcony, high above Megan's imaginary river. Here they sat in the real world, and the peace was the same. The tensions of the past weeks dropped away from her, borne away on the quiet night breeze, chill and clear. That Megan thought "men" still followed, that storms hovered over the distant peaks, that she had no idea of her direction: all that counted as nothing in the peace of this moment.

She had lived alone for years, but had not lacked companions in the whirling of the sea larks, the crash of the surf, the daily progression of Daystar and Companion. And, occasionally, as in Clara's kitchen, she had glimpsed the homely life of others with wistfulness. Of husband and family, she had not truly considered: she would not repeat her mother's sad mistake with Alarson. But then had come Melfallan and his lady, and other champions she had not expected. And sudden terror in Gammel's chamber, and sudden freedom. She looked around her at the night, drinking in the silence with all her senses.

If Melfallan were here, would he feel the peace? Does he ever stop and drink in the stillness, and find the quiet there? She thought so, though he had not mentioned such. It lay in his talk of fishermen and river snows, in his manner of deliberation: they had not had time to match such things, finding them in each other, but she thought they might be there.

And here, she thought peaceably, she found new friends in the trees and stolid expanses of rock, the skitter of animals moving through the night, and, in the distance, the lonely cry of the night falcon. She looked up at the trees, but did not see a forest shadow with emerald eyes. She sighed regretfully: a dream, lovely if it were true, but only a dream. Brierley kissed Megan's forehead and tucked the cloak more closely around the child. And you, dear child, especially you.

Megan was not the child she had expected, that wonder of girlhood and quick intelligence, of instant acceptance and love for Brierley, looking to her teacher for all that is worth knowing. Such children of wonder were rare in the world, she admitted, if they even existed at all. But *this* child, strangely fragile and in need, fit the same essential.

And now it begins, she thought to herself. Her confidence rose, fierce and hot in her breast. Now it begins.

What began, she didn't know. Thora bid her to great purposes, and where it would lead her, she could not foresee. But in this night lay a beginning, with this child sheltered in her arms, and this darkness all around them, shimmering with the light of the world's blue star. She sat motionless, alive to the night, as the Companion drifted slowly westward across the sky and descended to the sea.

~

In the afternoon of the next day, the snow began, steadily thickening as a storm crossed the mountains from the east. Brierley had watched with apprehension as the gray clouds thickened, but when the snow began, it fell lightly at first, huge lovely flakes that fell to the ground and clung, quickly melting under the Daystar's bright shining. As another hour passed, the snow fell more heavily, sheathing them in a scattering curtain of white, silent and cold, masking the sky. Brierley stopped and unpacked the blanket to wrap around Megan, then draped the other blanket over the both of them, shielding the mare, too. It grew steadily colder and the snow stopped melting in the day warmth, covering the trail with a thin coating of white, then adding more.

Friend walked carefully through the light snow, snorting often in the crisp air, but accepted the unusual day with equanimity. Stall-bred and used to a river climate, the horse found snow almost as much a wonder as did Megan, who watched the snowfall with innocent delight. Brierley kept a close watch for a sheltered glade, wary of the chill wind that played with the blanket edge and seemed to knife into any exposed skin, but saw only rising rock on either side and thinning trees. The road still led upward, taking them into scrub forest and more bare rock, whitish gray beneath white snow.

She wrapped her arms around Megan, who had begun to shiver, and the wind blew more briskly, snapping snow crystals into their faces and tugging harder at cloak and blanket. The mare, too, began to feel the cold as a tingling on her exposed hide, a coolness in the leg tendons as she plowed through snow nearly knee-high. The mare began to flounder in the snow, quickly tiring as her body chilled steadily. Brierley's concern now extended to the mare as well.

We have to find shelter, Brierley thought. But if we take shelter here, will we be buried by morning? I should have gathered more plants for food when I had the chance, or looked for fish in the streams. She thought of the remaining food in their parcels, enough for another three days, but what would they eat if they became snowbound?

It's all right. Megan's thought dropped neatly into her mind, clear and vibrant with the witch's touch. So the child had decided to be brave, speaking mentally, not with voice. It pleased Brierley. *I'm not afraid to die.* Megan avowed with childish confidence. *It's better than being hit.*

What do you know of death, child? Brierley reproved mildly.

What do you know? Megan retorted, then stopped in midthought as she caught the answering image of the Beast in Brierley's mind, her flashing memories of the bending over a sickbed, the healing of wounds, the shadows of fear. Megan's fingers tightened on Brierley's arm. *Is that what we are*? she asked, her thought tinged with awe.

Part of what we are. You are the only other one like us that I've found—but there might be others, somewhere. But it is dangerous to be what we are: other people do not like it and hunt us.

As they hunt us now?

Yes. It is why we don't tell. Who told you to not tell, Megan?

Megan's mind fluttered with fear. Then, very softly: *I don't remember.*

It's all right, child. She hugged Megan closer to her chest and wrapped the cloak and blanket more tightly around her. After a while, from cold or the rocking motion of the horse, Megan fell asleep.

As the snow piled higher, Friend began to labor still more in her walking, pushing aside the snow with an effort. Brierley peered ahead, hunting any shelter, but saw only towering rock on either side with no hollows or copses of trees. Ahead the gorge widened, with one cliffside falling away to the left while the cliff to the right climbed higher and higher. Brierley kept the mare near the cliff, for it gave some shelter from the rising wind, and belatedly realized, when the path suddenly dropped into nothingness ahead of them, that they had lost the road. Ahead of them, beyond a hundred-foot drop of stone, lay a deep valley buried in snow, with other cliffs rising beyond.

Brierley carefully backed the mare away from the drop, and backtracked up the cliffside, trying to find the road, then struck across the widening gorge to the other cliffside. As they crossed the open space, the wind gusted at them harshly, chilling the flesh. Where is shelter? Brierley thought, fully alarmed now. She could see nothing beyond a hundred yards, surrounded by the falling curtains of snow that piled higher and higher. Stubbornly, urging Friend to take every caution, she picked her way along the left wall and could tell by the slant of Friend's back that the terrain was now descending and growing steeper. Bring us trees for shelter, Mother Ocean, Brierley prayed, if you have any power here, so far from your coastlands. Please.

They passed a few scrub trees, barely the height of her mare's head, then more trees that reached higher. Brierley leaned forward, peering through the falling snow at the rock face, hunting for some break in the rock that might shelter them, some group of trees that might break the grip of the wind. The cliff wall turned to the east and she rode gratefully out of the direct force of the wind, then saw the dark gap of a small cave in the rock.

Mother Ocean,

Daughter Sea. . . .

Brierley's heart swelled with gratitude. She urged the mare toward the cave.

Next to the entrance a group of young evergreens formed a small windbreak, enough to keep the cave entrance clear of the deepening snow. When she reached the cave mouth, she found it not deep, only a dozen feet, but just tall enough for the mare, and just large enough for some shelter and a fire in the back. She lifted Megan off the mare's back and carried her into the back of the shallow cave, then unsaddled the mare and covered her with the other blanket, and made their camp.

A fire made a difference, although Brierley had to hunt beneath the few trees nearby for tinder dry enough to burn. With the wind whistling past the cave mouth and the dying day, the temperature in the cave was little above freezing.

Brierley hunted through the nearby undergrowth for makings of a larger fire, then brought in more wood to keep the fire burning through the night. She suspected the fire would mean their lives, and kept herself to the search for wood through the drifting snow among the trees, though her skirts were cold and clammy and her legs heavier with every step. When she had collected all the dead wood nearby, she hunted the hand ax in one of the saddle packs and lopped off green branches, not certain if they would burn, then chopped drier branches near the bases of the trees. Megan sat huddled in the far corner of the shallow cave near the fire.

Wearily Brierley dropped her last load of wood on the pile she had made near one wall, then led Friend around the fire to the back of the cave and heaped more wood on the flames. She dragged in several long limbs for a windbreak over the cave mouth, and struggled with their weight as she positioned them over the doorway, then struggled even longer in spreading a blanket over the piney branches. When it was done, she sat down between Megan and the mare, her leg muscles aching, her whole back aching, everything aching, and sank her face upon her knees. Already the cave was warming: she had won them that.

But it might not be enough, she thought with despair. I don't know these mountains. I've never seen snow like this. Will it get worse? And what will I do then? None of us will know what to do: a river-bred horse, a city-bred child, a sea-bred witch.

Would you rather have been murdered by Hagan? she asked herself. Or burned as a witch by Darhel's court? But what of Megan? Even a madwoman is often treated with kindness, as she might have been in Darhel—and Megan always had her river home, her safe place in her mind as her sanctuary. Who gave me the right to err this way and rob Megan of her life?

She felt Megan's touch, then the slide of the girl's arm around her waist. *I love you,* Megan said simply, her thought barely a whisper, and leaned her head on Brierley's shoulder with a sigh. Then, with an odd mental tone that prickled

Brierley's spine with its hint of madness, Megan asked: *Why did you go away, Mother?*

Brierley struggled to keep her composure, as if Megan's abrupt confusion of place and person were not alarming. Perhaps Megan, too, sensed an essential she had long been seeking, a mother she had lost and preferred to any stranger, however kind, and retreated to the familiar. What was real to this child, who had made up a mental world far more pleasing? *When did I go, child?*

A long time ago. Megan cuddled close. *I'm glad you're back, Mother,* she thought contentedly. *I missed you.*

Brierley patted Megan's arm. *I've missed you, too, my child. I won't leave you again.*

That's good. Megan snuggled still closer, and sighed.

Brierley wrapped her cloak around herself and Megan, and lay down with the child. Together they watched the fire as it slowly warmed the cave, and together they finally slept. The cold snow drifted downward beyond the cave mouth, muffling all sounds, covering the forest with a deep blanket of white, and filling all the world.

14

Melfallan had insisted that Revil return with Saray to Yarvannet, and the Jacobys and the other Amelin folk had left with them, taking ship early in the afternoon. Count Robert had gone to the east toward Mionn, and Rowena had sent along her liegeman Stefan with Robert without saying why. At his aunt's suggestion, Melfallan had claimed the road into Airlie as his share of the search, and had used that choice to conduct his aunt home.

One of Rowena's soldiers, abroad on a late-night errand, had glimpsed Brierley and Hagan pass in the courtyard below, and the duke had been hard-pressed to offer an explanation. Melfallan's prisoner had disappeared while in the company of the duke's torturer, and now the torturer was gone as well, no doubt paid well and sent into safety. Whatever Tejar's sputtering, the High Lords had not believed his different suggestion, and each would leave Darhel after a search for one all knew would not be found.

After riding easily through the day, Melfallan's party stopped for the night at one of Rowena's hunting lodges in northern Airlie. Wide and spacious, with many rooms, his aunt's lodge stood in a thicket of everwillow a mile off the principal road. Melfallan sat on the porch as the Companion set in the west, and watched the sky grow darker to match his mood. He felt suspended between belief and incredulity, first veering to wild hope that Brierley might still be alive and had made a clever escape, then to a pit of rage and grief that threatened to swallow him whole: easier that he *knew* she was dead, he thought. Grief can be met, he told himself, and eventually set aside in time. Or so he told himself.

When he was not caught between knowing and not-knowing, he thought of the manners and ways he could murder Duke Tejar. A dagger sent in the silky concealment of night, the assassin creeping the halls until the victim was found and dispatched neatly. Or combat by sword before a court of witnesses, with Melfallan the victor wreaking his justice. Or poison that burned the throat and dissolved the bowels, an agony of hours before Death seized. The last would be particularly fitting, if Tejar had had a role in his grandfather's death.

Poison is best, he decided. It will hurt Tejar as Hagan likely hurt her.

How had she died? he keened silently. Was she afraid, or was she valiant to the end? Did she hate me, just before she died, for failing her again?

Fool. You wretched fool.

He looked down at his wine goblet and foggily tried to remember how many cups he'd drunk of Rowena's sweet wine. Six, or was it seven? Her wine servant had offered the bottle often, coming regularly out on the porch as he quietly circulated the lodge, offering to lords and servants alike. Offered too often, Melfallan thought. I think I'm drunk. He leaned over his chair arm and let the goblet slip onto the wooden floor of the porch, then slumped lower in his chair. I'll rest awhile.

The door opened behind him, swinging open with the soft creak, and Melfallan heard someone step onto the porch. The steward again.

"No more wine," he said. "I've had enough."

"I wondered when you'd stop yourself," Rowena said. Melfallan looked around in mild surprise, then watched as his aunt crossed the wooden planking between them and seated herself in another chair, her skirts rustling. "That's good," she added, as if she congratulated him on prudence, or else worried about his obvious self-indulgence. Perhaps her solicitude meant neither, but still her comment bit at him, irritating his temper.

"I don't need that kind of advice, Aunt," he said roughly. "I rule well enough."

Rowena eyed him askance, and made a small show of arranging her skirts around her legs. "In other words, nephew, I should mind my own land and leave yours alone?"

Melfallan grunted. "More or less."

Rowena sighed. "Melfallan, if she is alive, I think she went east toward Mionn. It makes sense: she would look for obscurity again, and the eastern road would be convenient and fast."

"Is that why you sent Stefan along with Robert? I thought you were certain she is dead. Or so you've told me. Why send Stefan anywhere?"

"Your mind is still working, I see," Rowena observed with a smile, and leaned back comfortably in her chair. "It can still match facts and reach a correct conclusion. That is good."

Her tone mimicked her earlier comment, and she glanced challengingly at Melfallan, daring him to be irritated with her again. Melfallan declined with a shrug, and sank lower in his chair, then crossed his ankles. He thought about picking up his goblet for another swallow, decided not. Rowena clucked in exasperation.

"Melfallan—" she began.

"Please, don't," Melfallan said suddenly. "No games, Rowena. No arch opinions and sharp sallies, no comments and poses and pert observations. Not now." He swallowed painfully and looked away. "Maybe tomorrow, but not tonight."

Rowena placed her hand lightly on his forearm. "As you wish, my dear," she said quietly. "I know I am sometimes tiresome, Melfallan, but usually I don't care whom I inflict. I do care for you, and I worry tonight. Why did you send Saray home? She could be here to comfort you, to help you."

"Oh, Aunt—" He looked at her in despair. "Saray doesn't understand any of this. If she did, or thought she understood, which she couldn't, she might think that— Not that Brierley and I—" He broke off and stared at his boots.

"I see," Rowena said.

"I doubt you do," he told her bluntly.

Rowena laughed softly in her throat. "Oh, Melfallan, don't you know how much I loved Jonalyn? Don't you know I understand, even if Saray does not? I showed my love with my favor to her, as I show it for Stefan, and probably cause similar rumors. But my favor toward her was enough for Duke Tejar or Earl Giles to float rumors about us in Darhel, rumors without truth, of course—cannot one soul love another without rumors? Margaret of Tyndale can flaunt her affairs and not care, but I resent the taint to Jonalyn's memory."

"Earl Giles?" Melfallan asked, surprised. "Tejar would do it, just for spite, but Giles has always been friendly. He likes the duke no more than we do."

"Friendly to your grandfather, Earl Audric, and to you as earl, but he disapproves of me." Rowena shrugged. "I'm unfeminine in my speech and manners, he says—and not softly to spare my hearing. I think I should shrivel into a hag if I had to live in Mionn, endure that court of his. Which brings us back to Saray, doesn't it?" She looked at Melfallan calmly.

Melfallan shrugged and picked up his wine cup. "I don't know what I feel. But don't worry. I'm not going to set Saray aside. I wouldn't think of it. She doesn't deserve it. Now, if she were shrill, like you are sometimes, or impertinent, like you are often, or—"

Rowena raised her hand. "Please, I get the point. Saray is not Rowena—though perhaps you wish she might be. Hmm?" She tilted her head to the side. Melfallan waved her away, knowing she tried to cajole him, knowing her jokes were meant as balm, not prickle.

"Now, do not react to my suspicions," Rowena persisted, "such that you think I have, which I don't. You are not a fool, Melfallan, and love Yarvannet too well. I favored your match with Saray, as you know, and I do not regret my matchmaking. I am aware of your problems, and shared it in my own marriage, the lack of connection, the difference, the curtain of silence." Melfallan took her hand and lifted it to his lips. She did understand, and he was grateful to her that she did. He kept her fingers in his and looked out at the forest again.

"Ralf was much older than I," Rowena said reflectively, as if she spoke from a grief long resolved. "He had had a prior wife, one who had been young with him when he was young, one he still mourned, though it be ten years since she died. I gave him three children, all taken by plague, and then I gave him Axel, to be his heir. In truth, he required little more of me." She sighed. "But the nobility has a duty of state in its marriages, and Saray's connections protect Yarvannet, as mine protected Airlie. Indeed, it was Tejar's invasion of Airlie twenty years ago that prompted your marriage to Saray: the two earls had planned it that long."

"I'm not surprised. The two earls must ally against a powerful duke," Melfallan quoted, "to insure peace and justice in the lands." He sighed and squeezed her fingers. "I've read the text."

"I knew that you understood. My father taught you well, though much is native gift. Whatever his faults, Tejar is powerful—and seeks more power still." She shrugged. "And Giles had always liked you: you're the grandson of Audric and future earl of Yarvannet, an excellent match for his youngest daughter, whom he worried might not marry suitably. Saray might have been an embarrassment in spinsterhood, lingering in Mionn's court, a visible reminder of a woman unused, a father's ineptitude in crafting his alliances."

"Aunt," Melfallan protested.

"I only speak the truth. You're a man like he is: he assumes you share his attitudes, and rarely discusses women with you. Isn't that true? To Earl Giles, women are usually ignored, save for pleasure and handing off inconvenient tasks. Bed them for the children, give them tasks in the housekeeping, and otherwise let them shut up. Giles did not want Saray in Ingal's counties and hand to Tejar that influence: as you say, he has little love for our duke. You were convenient and pleasant and in good health and Saray liked you. And so the marriage was made."

"I hadn't known you disliked Earl Giles this keenly."

Rowena tightened her mouth. "My husband was in his final

illness when he heard new rumors spread by Mionn, and he died uneasy, however I protested my love for him, only him. There was nothing to the rumors, of course, only the earl's dislike of my forward ways. A woman who behaves like I do, forward and unseemly, is probably cuckolding her sick husband as well, to his thinking. And so he carelessly sent the talk about and Ralf heard of it. I will *not* forgive that hurt to a dying man, nor Mionn's indifference and contempt in the years since." Her eyes glinted in the starlight. "See what a vengeful woman I am, Melfallan."

"Nonsense."

"You're a dear boy to indulge me so. My point is to warn you. Do not assume that Mionn is a constant support."

"Is that why you sent Stefan? In case Robert hunts the right trail?"

"Not because of fear of Robert, but of Lim who rode with Robert. Another uncertain lord. But, yes: just in case."

Melfallan picked up his wine and took a sip. "She's dead, Aunt. Why else would Hagan have fled?"

"And what if she is alive?" Rowena asked. "What will you do then?"

He shrugged. "I don't know how I feel. I told you that. And I will never set aside Saray. I'm not that kind of man. Saray is not property." He quirked his mouth. "I'm not Earl Giles."

"Be aware that Giles assumes you are and might suspect you, should your affection for Brierley show as mine did for Jonalyn. Remember that Tejar wondered why you came so promptly to Darhel—and reached the wrong answer. You must learn flexible thinking, my Melfallan, even over a commoner girl."

"She's more than a commoner, and you know it," Melfallan said forcibly. "You said yourself you were in love with Jonalyn—oh, Aunt, calm down. I know it was never sexual, but it was obvious enough to lead to the easy accusations. At least Margaret doesn't care, but you still do. It taints Jonalyn's memory, you said, and you don't want any aspersion, anything but recognition of the wonder she was, the beauty she was. When Brierley sang to my son that first night, walking him up and down in her arms, her peace settled on the castle. I've never heard such incredible loveliness, never felt such peace."

"Perhaps you *are* in love," Rowena accused mildly, but did not look displeased.

Melfallan shrugged. "I don't know if I am or not. What is admiration for a remarkable person, and what is love for the woman? I've had my affairs with commoner girls, as likely you've suspected, but not for some time now. I never found the right one, and it was too dangerous, anyway. I don't want to hurt Saray. Saray is good and kind, and loves me in the way she knows how to love. I know that." He stood up restlessly. "Even if I did dare, I know what Earl Audric would say: A commoner girl? Are you mad, boy? You throw away the excellent alliances I've made to protect you from Tejar? You idiot! You simpleton! You—"

"He did have a fine command of language," Rowena agreed drolly.

"And you, Aunt, sit there and smile at me, and tip your head, and love me whatever I do, whatever my mistakes."

"Of course. You are my favorite nephew, and my hope to be our future duke."

"It's not that easy, 'of course.' I—" He stopped abruptly and stared at her. "What did you say?"

"A duke's coronet is not destined for only one head," she said, "not if the wearer rules unwisely. You have the potential, Melfallan. You have the alliances, providing you measure well your allies—and your enemies."

"I have no such ambition!" Melfallan told her furiously.

"Duke Tejar doesn't believe that," Rowena retorted. "And his disbelief may in time compel you to action that will make you duke. That is the irony of our politics, that he will engender what is not and earn himself what he most fears. Reality bites us, especially when we think ourselves clever. Can't you see that he suspected Brierley as your gambit? Why else would he order her murder? It wasn't a gambit, of course, but it led him into his error. Perhaps Duke Rahorsum made the same mistake: he decided that certain lords' alliance with the shari'a could not be borne. Not because of the accusations of foot rot and miscarriage and storms, but because of their talent, their gift, their treasure: I'm sure that was the root of how it began. Witches are dangerous, for they can be owned by someone else—or so the High Lords might think."

"Tejar doesn't believe in witches."

"Not yet. But when he does, if Brierley lives or another of her blood is found, and if the witch is yours, Melfallan, the balance Audric and Giles created through your marriage will be upset. Look ahead, Melfallan. Don't look to the immediate, and refuse your destiny." Rowena gazed at him sternly, all her arts and fancies absent in her earnestness. Her eyes were clear and strong, the essence of the woman. She meant her suggestion seriously, and had obviously thought about it in depth. How long had she nursed such ambitions for him?

"Why not Axel?" he asked curiously. "He has the Hamelin blood right, not me."

She shook her head and smiled. "My son is ten years old, dear one. In twenty more years he might be Tejar's match, as you are now, but Tejar can destroy the Courtrays long before then. No, the times choose the lord, and you are that lord, Melfallan. Trust in it."

"You are a remarkable woman," he said, admiring her.

"Consider it," she commanded.

"Very well." Melfallan turned back to the night and listened to the wind sigh through the pine branches. "I will consider it."

A touch of cold floated on the air, sighing down the mountain from the peak high above. Snow soon, he thought: winter grew nearer each day, disturbing the weather, and the cold bleakness would follow. He lifted his head as the dim staccato of a running horse echoed through the forest. He stepped to the railing and peered into the dark. A few second later, Stefan pounded into the lodge clearing, and rode his horse to a skidding halt by the porch stairs.

"What news, Stefan?" Rowena asked, her voice suddenly eager.

Stefan glanced around quickly, hunting any other listeners. "She is alive, my lady," he said then. "I have seen her."

Melfallan gripped the railing. "Brierley? You saw her? Where?"

"Yes, my lord." Stefan leaned toward him in the saddle, joy leaping into his face. "I have seen her, and Robert and Lim did not. She is taking the eastern track to Mionn, and has a little girl with her."

"A girl?" Melfallan asked, bewildered. "Who is she?"

"I don't know, my lord," Stefan replied. "But she has a girl with her, and a horse and a pack, with warm cloaks for both of them, though a storm is gathering in the high passes. Count Robert has returned to Darhel to sail home, and Lim likewise. I rode here as soon as I could to bring you the news."

Melfallan took a step away from the railing, and felt Rowena grip his arm hard, checking him. "Let her go, Melfallan," she said. "She will find her way."

"She doesn't understand snow," he said distractedly. "We don't have heavy snows in Yarvannet. She could be in danger, Aunt. And if she's alive, as Stefan says she surely is, I must see for myself."

Rowena's fingers tightened painfully on his arm. "Let her go, Melfallan," she repeated. "Please."

Melfallan pressed her hand, then gently loosened her fingers. "Aunt, I cannot—not yet. Perhaps later. If I can."

She drew in a sharp breath, but yielded to him. "You have heard my advice. I have asked you to consider."

"And I agreed to consider." Melfallan kissed her forehead. "I need a man who knows the High Trail and the weather there. We could intercept her by taking the southeastern track before the storm strikes in earnest."

"I can lend you Sir Niall, my Mionn courier. He rides the High Trial all seasons of the year, and is trustworthy. Stefan!"

"Yes, my lady." Stefan bowed low.

"Please find Niall Larson and tell him to come to me for instructions. I am sending you both with Earl Melfallan to search for Brierley."

"Yes, my lady!" Stefan bowed again, then hurried away toward the soldiers' quarters next to the stables. Melfallan smiled down at his aunt.

"No more arguments, countess?" he asked.

Rowena shrugged humorously. "None. I will even abandon my argument that Stefan and Niall don't need you to make the search, but I know you too well. Ocean speed your steps, Melfallan." With a swish of her skirts, Rowena turned and left him, vanishing back into the lodge.

The snow outside the cave stopped some hours later during True Night, and the wind died to a cool draft sifting quirkily around the windscreen. Near dawn Brierley got up again to add more wood to the fire, then peered out at the clouds that scudded across the stars. How many hours till dawn? How many hours until it started snowing again? The night lay still beneath a blanket of clinging white, and the air was bitterly cold. She turned and looked at her pile of wood and hoped she had enough if they had to stay a second night in this cave.

In the back of the shallow cave, Friend stamped sleepily and turned her head toward Brierley, then snorted softly as Brierley walked toward her. "You have been a good horse," Brierley told the mare, deeply grateful to the gentle animal. She hugged the mare's neck. "Thank you. I am glad you are warmer. I'm warmer, too."

Friend blew out a breath and lowered her head again, one hind foot cocked as she dozed. Brierley leaned on the mare's neck for a time, comfortable with the horse, then returned to the windbreak at the front of the cave and sniffed the cold air. Though the snow was peril to herself and Megan, she found something tantalizingly familiar in the high cold air, the faint creaking of snow on pine branches, and especially the stillness all around her. The night had a . . . flavor of sorts, a feeling, a manner of being that reminded her of the Everlight. Yet it was not quite the same, but as if she heard a voice through a wall, muffled and changed. She wrinkled her nose, intrigued by the mystery that hovered just at the edge of her witch-sense, yet came no closer.

Where are you? she called silently, hoping Thora might answer by stepping out of a dream into the real night. But the night did not answer, and no slender form appeared in the darkness. Yet, still, it seemed that Thora might turn her head at any moment and be suddenly there: the night lay hushed with the expectation.

There is something out there, Brierley decided, something more than Megan's not-there thing that I don't see. I sense . . . vast memory, and that memory is shari'a, although now quieted and silent. Its scent still lingered on the air, like the faint smoke of an extinguished fire, or the crisp tang of fruit fallen onto the grass.

It is Witchmere, she thought, and felt the hairs on her nape rise. She needed no map to know she neared witch-kind's ancient fortress: that knowledge lay permeated in the very rocks nearby, in the air she inhaled, in the sound of the trees creaking with their burden of snow. She sniffed at the cold night air and considered: not too close nearby, but in the preternatural hours of the night, newly palpable to her witch-sense.

Could she find sanctuary there? Or was Megan's hostile "not-there thing" a first warning, even to the remnants of the witch-kind who once owned its caverns?

Brierley's books placed Witchmere in these mountains above the Darhel plains, "two days easy ride from Iverway," Duke Rahorsum's ancient capital. After Witchmere's destruction, Rahorsum had moved his capital from Iverway to a new site thirty miles downriver, where Darhel now stood. All that now remained of Iverway, Melfallan had said, was a few broken stones, the grassy mounds, and the road that led to it: even the wall stones had been uprooted and rebuilt into Darhel.

Why had Rahorsum moved his capital? Brierley wondered, staring out at the cold night. Was it because of plague? Had the witches truly created the plague and loosed it at Rahorsum's capital, as some tales hinted, as the witches' last great act of spite and malice? Or had the shari'a other weapons that had ranged these high mountains, that had survived the witches' own deaths? Ghosts and evil essences, as Harmon relished in his tales? Or strange devices like the Everlight, which seemed strange only because their understanding had been lost?

Did we truly control the weather? she wondered, remembering other claims in her books. How? Did we build the plague and release it into the world? Why? Is one's own impending death enough to justify tearing down the world? To leave behind weapons no one could then control? Had some in Witchmere become that twisted? Or are all the witch tales a calumny of the dead, the rewriting of history by the victors? But if a kernel of truth existed in the legends, what was it?

Brierley leaned her face on the rough cold stone of the cave entrance, watching the night.

Did you once walk in these mountains, Thora? Did you smell the crisp air and sniff at the night? Were you once as innocent as I?

Shivering in the cool air, Brierley returned to her bed with Megan.

The Daystar's dawning brought little more warmth, and made a glancing snow-shine that struck at her eyes when Brierley stepped out of the cave. The sky still scudded with more clouds, moving swiftly westward, but for now the snow had stopped. Brierley decided to risk the weather: what other choice?

She bundled up Megan as warmly as she could and put her on the horse, then cut off an end of the blanket for leggings for herself. The snow had piled three feet deep in front of the cave and she tramped awkwardly through the drift, tugging at the mare's reins to make her follow. How much farther across this height in the mountains? She could not see any higher peaks to the east. It seemed they walked the top of the world, and she guessed that a path downward must lie nearby. In this tumbled area of ravines and cliffsides, she could not guess where, but she would hunt for it, and trust in Ocean's grace that they would find it.

In the day's bright glow, her witch-sense no longer touched whatever witch's mystery lay nearby in Witchmere. Though she felt tempted to search out the place, the press of another snowfall was not a wise time to hazard unknown mysteries. But I will come back, she promised herself. Once Megan is safe in Mionn and grows stronger, once I have the certainty of spring and summer's mild weather: then I will come back.

The Daystar sent its reds and greens into the dawn sky, its light steadily strengthening through a haze of hurtling white clouds. Within an hour, as the Daystar rose above distant peaks, they had reached the ravine's entry into the gorge. Brierley stopped and looked around the narrow valley, and saw how she had drifted off the track. Well, it had found them the shelter of the cave. But not again, she promised herself firmly.

To spare the horse, Brierley walked in front, stepping high as she floundered through the snow. The snow clung to her skirts, weighting down the fabric and melting into icy water on her legs. She had no map, and the trail markers were buried by snow, but the wider course led generally downward for a while, away from the high drifting snow behind them. When she reached a narrower passage in the gorge, she looked ahead and imagined she saw the glint of green trees far ahead, perhaps even a valley. She turned and looked at Megan.

"Hold on tight, dear one. I'm counting on you to stay on the horse."

"I will." Megan tugged down her scarf and smiled. "This is fun, Mother. Can I call you Mother? I'd like to." Megan seemed to have forgotten her fancy of the night before, and that she had called Brierley "Mother" for some days: did much ever seem real to this child? But Megan's smile was happy, lighting up her small face.

"Of course, Megan," Brierley said, and returned her smile. She squinted at the small girl on the tall horse, then looked at the arras of unbroken snow ahead of them, snow Megan could ride, but Brierley must walk. "Fun," she said with a sigh, and set off across the smooth snow, tramping down a path for the horse with her own feet. Maybe later she might ride again, after she was confident of sure footing for the mare on this guess at the road. The mare followed willingly, her warm breath a steam cloud in the crisp air.

They walked a hundred yards, a vigorous effort for Brierley, before they ran into uneven ground. Brierley dug down into the snow and found tufted grass, then stepped aside as Friend moved forward hungrily to graze.

"You wait here," Brierley told Megan and scouted off to the left, tramping down the snow, then bending to dig down. More grass. Where was the road? Was it overgrown here with greenery, as it was earlier? How could she tell track from meadow? She wanted a road, for a road led somewhere. She looked back at the narrower gorge, then south toward the hint of green, trying to match up a probable road. If the road even led into that valley: did it? Had she missed yet another turn during the storm?

"I need a map," she muttered, and looked south again. Well, it led downward and seemed fairly even, judging from the smoothness of the snow, if that was a guide. If she had to, she would walk in front of the mare all the way, a long exhausting day for herself, but safety perhaps in that. She could not risk injury to the horse, or to themselves if Friend slipped and fell on top of them. So she would walk. The day was bright and clear, with only a hint of more storm clouds. They might have time.

She tramped back to Friend and waited until the mare snatched a few last bites of grass, then together they set off again to the south toward the green. Every once in a while, when Friend nickered the suggestion, she dug down into the snow and let the mare eat a few more snatches of icy grass. A tiny stream filled her water bottle near noon. By mid-afternoon they had left the gorge a few miles behind them and had entered scattered trees, each laden with branches full of snow.

The Daystar glinted brightly off the snow, but not warmly enough to make much difference in the air's chilly cold. Brierley covered most of her face with her hood edge and checked that Megan wore her scarf over her nose, wary of the bitter cold. By noon they had come another mile, but the green valley looked no closer. Brierley stopped and uncovered grass for Friend, then tried to make a small fire with wet wood, a useless effort. Finally she and Megan ate bread and some of the dried meat from the packs, and Brierley pushed on.

Her teeth were chattering steadily now, and she sensed the cold working inward in her flesh. She was dimly aware that her judgment might be faltering, but kept tramping onward. More belatedly, she realized she had lost her witch-sense as her body focused on keeping warm. She had to turn her head to check on Megan, no longer certain through her witch-sense that the girl still sat on the horse, though of course Megan did, and was thankfully warmer from her heavy blankets and the warmth of Friend's own warm body.

The trees grew thicker, with uneven ground between. Twice Brierley tripped over a root and fell, covering herself with snow. She shivered from the damp cold of her wet cloak and dress, though sweat often ran into her eyes and prickled unpleasantly beneath her clothes. Her feet became harder and harder to move, but she concentrated on one step at a time, no longer looking up toward the valley below, only the stretch of snow immediately ahead of her feet. She felt oddly light-headed, as if the sunlight were stretched in strange ways, and spots danced in front of her vision, and she knew she was approaching exhaustion. Megan sat comfortably on the horse, although she now watched Brierley with anxiety.

"I could walk in the snow for a while," she offered.

"No, child," Brierley said, looking around at her. "Your task is ride the horse. You are doing that quite well."

"And I've never ridden a horse before," Megan said with pride.

"That is very hard to believe, that you've never ridden a horse before. In fact, I don't believe it: you ride too well." Megan's eyes crinkled above her scarf, then suddenly looked left.

"Look!" She pointed urgently.

Brierley swiveled and saw nothing but trees. "What, Megan?"

"It's the not-there thing again. It was there and looked at us, then it wasn't there."

Brierley stopped and swayed in exhaustion as she looked up at Megan. "The not-there thing?"

Megan looked down at her in frustration, half-angry that she might not be believed. "It was there!" she declared. "I'm not lying. Honest!"

"I believe you, child." Some of Megan's angry protest faded. "What did it look like, the not-there thing?"

Megan hesitated. "It was hard to see. I don't know what it looked like. But it was there, Mother. I saw it—and it saw us." Brierley turned and looked carefully at the distant group of trees. "It's not there now," Megan muttered. "It didn't like us."

"How do you know it didn't like us?"

"I just know. It doesn't want us here."

"Why not?"

"I don't know. But it was there, and it looked at us."

Brierley nodded, perplexed. She could sense the child's truthfulness, but could gather nothing from Megan's mind that explained what a "not-there thing" might be in form or shape—though its intention seemed to have more definition. A deer? Perhaps a forest warden—but belonging to what lord in this deserted place, in such a snowfall? And what kind of deer or warden was a "not-there thing"? Witchmere, perhaps.

"Was it a round object with a light in the middle?" she asked Megan, thinking of the Everlight's boxy shape.

"No," Megan said promptly. "It was different than that."

"How was it different?"

Megan's eyes filled with tears. "I don't *know*."

Brierley patted her hand. "It's all right, Megan. You watch around us and let me know if you see it again."

Megan nodded mutely. Brierley clucked her tongue to the horse and began breaking more trail through the snow. After another hour, she had begun to stagger again and had to rest, but pushed on until her stagger threatened a fall.

"Mother—" Megan called worriedly.

"Ride the horse, child," Brierley muttered, her teeth chattering with cold. Megan fell silent.

The ground seemed more even, Brierley thought to herself, and looked up to see a wide clearing ahead, surrounded by a margin of trees. Beyond the other side of the meadow, only a few miles away, a green valley sparkled under a thin diamonded frost, with a hint of open water and brown fields. Brierley stamped forward with new energy, breaking down the crusted snow with her feet, the horse following behind.

A hundred yards across the meadow, the snow grew deeper and Brierley floundered and fell. As she lifted her hands, she saw blood staining the snow and found ice cuts on her hands from a deep rime of hard ice. She got awkwardly to her feet, and tried a few more steps, then fell again. She whimpered low in her throat, despite herself, and managed to get to her feet, though she swayed off balance. She knew she wasn't thinking clearly now, if she was thinking at all, and held only to her purpose in crossing the meadow.

It is so cold, so very cold.

"Mother!" Megan cried, but Brierley only shook her head dazedly. She hadn't much left, but to fall here and not rise would mean death by freezing. She tried again to walk and managed a stagger. Then, with a jarring thump, she sat down on the snow and looked up at Megan. Her head swimming, she glanced behind the horse and saw, far behind them on the slope above, black shapes moving on the snow. She squinted against the snow dazzle, trying to see more clearly.

Megan turned and whimpered in fear. "The men! It's the men!"

Brierley gawked at the child. "What men?" she demanded.

"The men! The men!" Megan shrieked hysterically and tried to kick the mare's sides, urging her onward. "Run! Run! It's the men! They're coming!" Then she screamed.

Megan's scream was a horrible agony, from a memory not her own. It was the worst of memories in the swords' fiery room, a memory that pierced the walls into Sorrow and Death. Surely not Megan's own memory, but it was a witch's memory, nonetheless, perhaps passed from Megan's mother, and that, too, not the mother's own, not in her short life. Whatever its source, it was a heritage that now seized on Megan and possessed her.

"Megan! Megan, stop!" Brierley cried. The child covered

her ears with her hands and shrieked in uncontrollable terror, jerking back and forth in the saddle.

"Go to the river!" Brierley commanded. "Go to the river castle and be safe! Megan!" Megan's eyes rolled upward, showing only whites, and she collapsed forward over the pommel. Behind the mare, the black shapes of the pursuit moved closer down the slope.

"No!" Brierley screamed at them. Infected by Megan's terror, she saw in that pursuit the hunt she had always dreaded—and the pyre to come. The old tales in her books blended into the present, creating her own waking nightmare. She turned and plunged onward into the snow, jerking the mare's reins to follow. She was panting within a few steps, but fought hard against the deep snow. Desperately, she dropped the horse's reins and beat at the snow with both feet and hands, trying to clear the way for the mare. She struggled another three yards, then three yards more, and found herself again waist-deep in snow. She sobbed in frustration and hammered at the snow with her hands.

It became a nightmare of fighting the snow, moving one foot, an arm, another foot, pushing the snow aside. She felt the slice of the ice rime on her legs, her hands, drawing more blood, and dimly sensed a similar pain in the horse when the mare stepped incautiously after her. In the end, her world shrank to a single necessity of defeating the snow, step by step.

She heard Friend snort in alarm, then a stamping close behind them. She looked around wildly. A tall rider on a well-muscled horse loomed up close behind the mare, his face concealed by a scarf. His stallion scattered the snow to either side as he leapt forward toward her.

"No!" Brierley shouted and plunged forward. A moment later, she heard a horse whinny and the creak of a saddle, then felt strong arms close around her. The man lifted her easily, letting her kick the air.

"Brierley!" he shouted in exultation, in Melfallan's voice. "Ocean praised, you're alive!"

Melfallan. She sagged against him in relief.

He set her down on her feet and turned her around to face

him, then tugged down his scarf. His eyes sparkled, and she could not mistake the sheer joy in his face at finding her. Then he shook her finger at her. "You sweet fool!" he said. "You can't cross these mountains when winter's almost here. Look at the snow, and with new storms coming! Oceans, Brierley, you're a sea lass! What do you know of snow?"

"As much as you, Yarvannet," she retorted weakly. "What do you know?"

He laughed and hugged her tightly to him. She leaned into his embrace, grateful for the support of her legs which now slowly collapsed beneath her. He swung her up into his arms and carried her to his horse. "I found you!" he exulted. "How I feared I would not!"

"Stefan told you he saw me?"

"He did. He told me where, and we climbed the other road from Airlie to intercept your trail. No one travels this pass during this season, Brierley: it's too dangerous."

"I heard Count Robert say that to Count Toral," she responded dully.

"And came this way, anyway?" Melfallan's eyes flashed with anger. "You little fool!" Brierley found enough strength to glare at him, but feared the effort was pallid at best. "Look at you! You're covered with snow, and chilled clear through." Without asking her permission, he swung her up onto his horse, then vaulted up behind her.

She saw Stefan and another man waiting in the trail, still mounted on their horses. She caught a flashing sense of Stefan's relief: he had been desperately anxious for her, too. Had her choice really been that stupid? Apparently it had been.

Melfallan stopped his horse beside Megan and the mare. When Megan did not rouse, he touched her leg and then shook her gently, without response. Megan slept onward, safe in her sun-drenched castle. "Is she ill?" he asked with concern.

"She has found safety from her terror," Brierley said. "She escapes in a different way."

"Good. I am not an ogre," Melfallan huffed. "I don't frighten little girls—at least not intentionally. Now Stefan might, with his looks." He tossed a grin at his friend. "Who is she?"

"My daughter." Brierley shivered.

"Indeed? Well, there's a story there, I'm sure, but you can tell me later. Stefan, come take the child before she falls off." Stefan rode forward and gently lifted Megan from Friend's saddle, then wrapped her snugly inside his cloak.

As he did so, Brierley's shivering built into waves, chattering her teeth, shuddering through her body, as if she had a palsy. Her exhaustion hit her fully then, draining all strength and turning her body into leaden uselessness. Weakly, she leaned against Melfallan, and felt his lips press against her hair.

"There is a rock wall over that way, my lord," the third man said, pointing west. "I saw the bluff from upslope. We might find shelter there." He gestured at the cloudy sky. "We'll need it. There's more snow coming in."

"Fine. Will you scout ahead, Niall? We need a fire. She is perishing with cold." Niall saluted and cantered away, his horse tossing up snow in billows. Stefan followed him more slowly with Friend on a lead, Megan secure within his arms. Melfallan nudged his stallion forward to follow.

"I found you," he whispered into her ear and tightened his arms around her. "Ocean be praised, I found you."

"I'm g-g-lad you d-d-id," she said through chattering teeth.

He laughed softly. "I thought I'd find you dead today, Brierley, if I found you at all, your body frozen hard as ice, with blank eyes staring, gone forever to Ocean's deeps. But here you are, alive and warm, taking one breath after another, perfectly naturally, and talking to me, if somewhat with a stutter."

"Alive, yes, w-w-warm, not much." She tried to control her teeth, but they rattled onward.

Melfallan snorted. "You've no one to blame but yourself, young woman. These snows are dangerous."

"And what other d-d-direction was I supposed to g-g-go?"

"Well, true," he acknowledged. "But how did you escape? Where is Gammel Hagan? Who is that child? You have much to answer, mistress."

"The Lord of Lim said you are in p-p-peril," Brierley said, "and that my escape was p-p-proof of my witchery and would cost you Yarvannet."

"Did he?" Melfallan said wryly. "Ah, Stefan didn't tell me that part. Toral's wishes aren't necessarily easy truth, but I admit your escape didn't help matters. You promised to trust me, Brierley, and not do something like this."

"Hagan was going to k-k-kill me," she said simply. "And y-y-you were not there."

She heard the sharp intake of his breath, and immediately regretted her careless words. "Melfallan—"

"Don't take it back," he said roughly. "Don't offer me that gentleness. It's true. I can only promise to try harder to not fail you again. And I do promise," he said. Brierley shook her head mutely, too tired to contest further with him. Melfallan pulled her closer, binding her round about with his arms, and tucked his cloak snugly around them. "I'm here now," he said into her ear. "Here, with you, Brierley."

"Yes. Yes, you are." Gratefully, she leaned against him as they rode out of the meadow.

15

The snap of Melfallan's cloak end in front of her face woke Brierley suddenly. An impenetrable white cloud sifted all around them, with the touch of snow sharp on her face as needles; her body trembled with cold.

Brierley sensed her sleeping child somewhere ahead, beneath overtones of Stefan's attentive care. Megan still slept in her river world, where all was brilliant sunshine. A light breeze shivered the reedbeds, and Megan sat on her balcony watching the river, her salamander preening on her hand. Brierley shivered and envied Megan her warmth. The two other men and their horses were invisible in the snow ahead, so intensely did the snow whip around and past them, and the wind bit with real teeth.

"Megan?" she said aloud.

Melfallan tightened his arms around her waist and leaned forward to bring his mouth next to her ear. "Did you speak?" he asked, but his words were immediately torn away by the wind.

Brierley gestured at the whirling snow. "How long did I sleep?" she shouted.

"Soon," he shouted back, not understanding her. The wind caught at her cloak edge and flapped it away into the air. Brierley grabbed for it and snatched it back. Then her hood snapped back, loosing her hair and whipping it into Melfallan's face like a lash. She struggled to resettle her hood, loosing the cloak ends again, and Melfallan brought his cloak firmly around both of them. His body trembled with cold at her back. Brierley felt a small prickling of new fear, and knew Melfallan shared it.

Ocean, had this gale caught me in the open! she thought. Would I have reached shelter? Not likely. It was truly a rescue, then, by Melfallan and his men—and true foolishness by herself to attempt this high pass in nearing winter. Surely Melfallan would tell her so later. He had that intent to tell her, she sensed, and would make sure she listened, he avowed. She was not sure she liked his protective attitude: he was a man accustomed to giving commands and having them obeyed, as if all the world were his to order. Well, an earl would think that, she thought, wondering if she indulged too much in her fondness, but she far preferred this restless earl who worried beyond reason to Duke Tejar's cold cruelty.

The wind rose still higher, lashing at them with hard-driven snow. As Melfallan's powerful stallion struggled through the snow, he nearly slipped to his knees. Melfallan called encouragement, his hands firm on the reins, and the horse plunged forward with new vigor, splashing the snow around them. A good beast, Brierley thought gratefully: are all horses of one kind, all good? She wished so. As the wind lashed at them, Brierley hid her face inside her hood, and desperately wished for warmth.

Suddenly the wind fell to near nothing. Brierley looked up and saw the looming shadow of a cliffside. High above, the snow blew a horizontal white curtain across the cliff top, but its tug was fitful here, baffled by the encroaching rock. The horses and their riders picked their way along the cliff face in single file. Riding in the lead, Niall rose in his stirrups and turned back toward Melfallan, then gestured broadly to the right. Then the man turned his horse's head and abruptly vanished from view.

Megan! Brierley called again. Like a sleeper turning over in bed, Megan shrugged her off and dreamed onward. It was time the girl roused from her dream world, if only to calm Brierley's fear that Megan might get lost in it. *Megan!*

What? Megan's answer was sluggish—and quite unafraid, as if her terror of "the men" had never existed. Had she stored it in one of her castle rooms, to drift there with other fears, the child untouched? Likely so. Brierley envied the child such a gift.

Wake up, Megan, she said firmly.

I am awake, Megan answered, and abruptly she was. She looked around her and noticed the snow. *Why is it white?* she complained, then realized she was on a horse and someone sat behind her, his arms holding her securely. She turned and looked up at Stefan, and saw his unfamiliar face smile down at her. *Who is he?* Megan thought, and then asked Stefan himself. A moment later she giggled, and then laughed aloud as he said something else. *You're silly, Stefan*, she told him.

Why is he silly?

He says he's Sir Stefan Quinby, the Lord Protector and High Guardian of the Lady Brierley Mefell—and of me, if I like. Do you have a High Guardian, Mother?

Not that I'd heard, child.

He's nice, Megan said with satisfaction. She patted Stefan's arm and snuggled closer to him. *My name is Megan,* she told him. *Why is it white?* Brierley wished she could have heard Stefan's struggle for an answer.

Stefan and Megan also turned aside and disappeared, Friend following on her lead, and a minute later, she and Melfallan reached the same turning found by Niall and entered a low-ceilinged cave in the cliffside. The cave entrance was narrow, barely wide enough for a horse with its rider, and low enough to make Melfallan duck warily. The cave was a good thirty feet wide and nearly as deep, amply large for their party, with walls heavily veined with sparkling minerals and a splash of darker material near the ceiling. The icy air teased into the cave from the entryway, and breathed coolness across Brierley's face.

Niall had already lit a lantern and a torch for light, and was unbuckling one of the packs on his horse. Stefan dismounted and lifted Megan down from his horse, then set her on her feet. Brierley awkwardly swung her leg over the stallion's neck and slid to the stone floor of the cave with a painful jar, and Megan ran to her. Brierley sank to her knees and gathered up Megan in her arms, hugging the child close, then closed her eyes and sighed.

"Horse!" Megan declared and pointed at Stefan's horse. "Stefan says I can ride him anytime. Now I have *two* horses, Mother." She sounded as if nothing more were needed for contentment in all things.

Brierley looked down at Megan, mildly exasperated. Gone were all traces of fear that had possessed the child earlier: all that existed now for Megan was Stefan's horse. Perhaps it was Stefan's magic in cajoling witches, if such he had. Why Stefan's horse was such a prize eluded Brierley, but Megan clearly thought it so. Perhaps Megan's father had been a horse tender sensitive to such differences in horseflesh, she decided. Other things might come with one's blood besides witchery. She tugged the girl's cloak more warmly around her, turning Megan toward her with the straightening. Abruptly Megan threw her arms around Brierley's neck and clung.

Mother! she sent joyfully, as if Brierley were new-sprung from the stone floor of the cave, long-missed for days. Brierley hugged her back, and sighed again. The child's delight in seeing Brierley exactly matched her delight over Stefan's horse, flattering to Brierley, true, but not reassuring. What fractured view of the world did Megan truly possess, to confuse mother with horse, and Brierley with mother? Megan's mother had died at her childbirth: how could Megan remember her mother?

For that matter, how could Megan remember the pursuit of another witch she'd never met, if indeed her freak in the meadow came from such a memory? At times, Megan had recoiled from Brierley as from a stranger, then mixed her memories enough to invite Brierley into her secret castle. Did anything seem real to Megan? And if not, how could there be a healing?

My child. Brierley kissed her. Megan patted her shoulder happily, then turned and looked around again at Stefan's horse, totally entranced.

"She really likes my horse," Stefan said, amused, then winked at Megan.

"That I can see." Brierley held out her hand to him. "Thank you for bearing word to the earl, Stefan. I had not realized our danger."

"You are welcome, sweet lady." Stefan took her fingers, then raised her hand to his lips in a lord's courtly gesture. Melfallan cleared his throat and gave Stefan a reproving glance. Stefan grinned, quite unabashed. "I can't help it," he said. "It's part of me, as you know."

"I'm glad your wife understands that," Melfallan said, and turned back to his horse.

"Oh, she does." Stefan shrugged comfortably. Niall snorted skeptically as he lifted the pack down from his horse and began to undo the buckles. "Well, she does," Stefan said, turning toward him. "And don't you pretend she doesn't, Niall. I give her the same courtesies, even more, and she says she likes them."

"She knows the price of a courtly husband, I suppose," Niall allowed. He glanced around the cave, assessing, then looked at Melfallan. "It seems a good shelter, your grace. We may have to wait out the storm here, with the way the snow's blowing. Early for a hard snow, but it happens some winters." Then he bowed to Brierley, with even greater grace than Stefan. He was an older man, dark-haired and sturdy-bodied, with a short dark beard and a prominent nose; she liked his calm gaze, his air of competence. "Lady witch," he said, "I am Sir Niall Larson, Countess Rowena's courier to Mionn, and your guide now. Good greeting to you."

"I am not a lady, Sir Niall," she said diffidently, but let him kiss her hand, too, wondering if she'd grow to like it. Probably.

"Every shari'a witch is a lady, to my thinking," Niall said, "and I'll not change my mind, I warn you." He smiled and pressed her fingers, then turned back to his horse.

The wind howled outside, only slightly muted by the echoing hollowness of the cave and its narrow door. Beyond the cave mouth, the snow drifted steadily down, already filling up the gullies made by the horses' passage. Melfallan dislodged the snow that clung to his boots with a vigorous stamping, then looked around the narrow cave thoughtfully.

He took the torch and went exploring back into the recesses of the cave, the shadows leaping.

"It doesn't go very deep," he said when he returned. "The cave leads to a short tunnel of some kind. Could it be a snow leopard's lair?"

"No bones or scat," Stefan argued, not liking the suggestion of snow leopards. "Do leopards hunt these higher mountains, Niall?"

Niall scowled and looked uneasy. "And other beasts. It's said this part of the High Trail is haunted, and few travel this valley in any weather, fair or foul. I take another pass, lower down, on my rides to Mionn. I'm not that familiar with this track."

Haunted? Brierley wondered, remembering Megan's "not-there thing." Brierley peered into the back of the cave, but sensed only a curious blankness.

Melfallan walked back to the cave mouth and squinted out at the driving snow. "Well, as you said, Niall, we're stuck here until that storm subsides. Can we make a fire?"

"Yes," Niall said, "and we'll need one, I'm sure. Both the lady and the little one are chilled to the bone, as am I, if you don't mind my admitting it. There'll be dry branches nearby under the everpines. Stefan, you can help. It's about time you did some useful work, you prancing dandy." Stefan made a show of indignant sputtering, but it was obvious the two were fast friends despite their difference in age. "By your leave, your grace," Niall said courteously, then left the cave with Stefan to get wood.

When they returned, Niall began making a fire, and Stefan joined Melfallan in unpacking the horses, laying out the supplies along one wall—lanterns, packets of food, warm clothing, bedding. Brierley had tried to help, only to be ordered sternly by Melfallan to sit down by the wall. And so she watched seated with Megan wrapped in her arms. When Melfallan took off Friend's saddle, the mare walked over to Brierley and nudged her shoulder with her soft nose, her dark eyes gleaming. Brierley petted the mare's silky neck, smiling as Friend snorted contentedly.

A simple life, to be a horse, Brierley thought. Subject to

the whim of masters, true, but still with small spaces of peace and pleasure. The mare sniffed at the wind that bit through the cave entrance, then turned her head and looked idly at the back of the cave. *What is there*? Brierley asked her, wondering if the mare knew. Friend twitched her tail, but showed no alarm—nor answer, either. A stubborn horse, Brierley thought, who said what she would and nothing more. But no leopards here. The mare was sure of that.

She thought to suggest again she help with the unpacking, so vigorously did the men work at the task, but seemed strangely unable to move, her body leaden and still cold. Instead she watched, light-headed and oddly remote, as the men unrolled bedding and laid out comfortable beds against the wall. Then a tarp was stretched across the cave entrance and hammered in with metal pegs, and the horses staked with loose leads to other pegs nearby. Her head sank toward her chest and she drifted.

She started slightly as Melfallan touched her shoulder. "You're half-asleep, Brierley. Come lie down and be warmer."

Obediently, Brierley and Megan lay down on the comfortable padding of a bedroll, and Brierley lay unmoving as Melfallan covered her with a blanket, then added another. She shivered, and Megan cuddled closer to her with a sigh, already asleep. Brierley listened for a time to the murmur of the men's voices, uncomprehending their sense but comforted, then fell softly into dreams.

She dreamed of vaulting spaces, dark and echoing. In the blackness, she and Megan descended a broad stair, cold air sighing all around them; water dripped hollowly in the far distance. Megan walked confidently in the lead, her salamander flickering on her shoulder. The tiny beast turned its head to look at Brierley, its golden eyes intent. *This way*, it said. *We must go this way.*

Why? Brierley asked.

To remember.

The dream fragmented, and Brierley drifted in her cockleboat, watching the sea with Megan in her arms. As they floated over the water, a cloud drifted across the Daystar high above, shadowing them, suddenly cooling the air. Slowly the cloud descended from the sky, misting the sea, and enveloped them in a looming darkness, stalking them.

The scene shifted again, and Brierley was writing in her journal at her table in her cave. Megan wrapped her arms around her neck and peered over Brierley's shoulder at what she had written, then giggled into Brierley's ear, making some mischief or another. Brierley smiled and patted the child's arm, then resumed her writing. Far above the beach, deep in the forest, a shire wolf howled, its eerie voice strangely multiplied by echoes. Brierley looked up: she rarely heard the wolf's voice this close to the coast, but the howl was not repeated. With a sigh, Brierley wrote onward, but water dripped in unseen places, and a metallic scrape sounded on stone. Brierley looked up again and frowned at the unaccustomed noise, but it was not repeated.

Then, in the next heartbeat, Brierley stood with Megan on a beach, a different beach than the shoal near her cave, yet not the timeless beach of the Beast. Dark shadows of everpine climbed a gentle bluff, and the wind blew briskly, stirring the waves hard against the brown sands. Above their heads, the Daystar and Companion competed in their colors, tingeing all with blue and gold. Megan held up a large white jewel, and showed it to Brierley.

See, Mother? It is the keystone, she said. *It remembers.*

What does it remember, child?

Megan looked at the jewel, sparkling in the suns' twin light. *This—*

Brierley gasped. They stood suddenly in a broad underground corridor, dimly lit by Everlights. The heavy air was filled with hoarse shouts and screams, reverberating against the stone. A woman dressed in fine velvet rushed toward them, a bloodied knife in her hand, a maddened soldier on her heels. She whirled and slashed at her pursuer, striking him across the eyes, then plunged her dagger into his chest. The man gave a low moan and staggered, his sword dropping from nerveless fingers, and fell. The woman stooped toward him, slender fingers nearly touching his face. "Forgive me," she whispered, then straightened and turned, the corridor light falling full on her face.

"Thora," Brierley breathed.

Thora's gray eyes, wide with terror, did not see her. Thora looked right and left in panic as other shouts came closer, and her pale face shifted from horror to anger to fear as a man screamed in agony. "Out!" she cried aloud, her voice ringing. "The Beast stalks us all!" With a single graceful movement, she stooped and picked up the soldier's sword, then took an Everlight from the wall and cradled it against her chest. She brushed past them and vanished into the shadows of the corridor.

Megan shrank against Brierley's skirts. *What is this place, Mother?*

Long ago, Megan, when the shari'a died.

Megan looked to where Thora had vanished into the gloom. *Who was she?*

The beginning, after the end came here, Brierley said sadly.

Brierley looked down at the soldier's contorted body, knowing that this death had haunted Thora the rest of her life. No matter that Duke Rahorsum's soldier would have killed her and counted it a blessing to the world. No matter that Thora had no choice. As I had no choice with Hagan—ah, Thora, it is not something I wished we had shared. Death has a keenness to its hunt once a witch takes a life. She took a shuddering breath.

This young man, was he evil? Likely not, not in the manner such judgments are weighed. A duke's duty, a soldier's violence. Did Hagan, being evil, deserve death? Did he? He would have taken my life without a question. I think Hagan deserved death for all his crimes, not just his intent against me, but this soldier did not.

Is the Beast sometimes a sword of justice? Does Death have value? Rahorsum had thought so, when he struck at the witches for the illness of his son, for the evils he thought the witches made, for all the unnamable reasons he had to slaughter the shari'a this day.

We should go, Megan said, holding up the keystone again. She pointed down the corridor from which Thora had come.

Why? Brierley asked.

I hear my salamander. Megan strode onward on her short legs, the keystone clutched in one hand. Brierley followed cautiously, looking to the left and right into richly appointed rooms, some already looted by the soldiers, others bearing shadows of several cowering victims, both men and women, all grievously wounded and now dying. *Come!* Megan ordered. *He is calling.*

They reached a winding stair and began to climb, and ahead Brierley saw a faint flutter of leathery wings, a flickering flame glimpsed ahead for an instant at each turn of the stair, round and round. The stair ended at a wide room filled with glowing machines where soldiers now used their swords to darken every light, slashing with a great pounding and shattering of glass. Several women lay heaped in one corner, limbs contorted, eyes glittering with the glaze of death. Megan scurried through the room, not looking at either soldiers or bodies, and vanished through a dark doorway.

Here!

Ahead, at the end of a broad corridor, daylight glowed in a bright rectangle. Brierley ran after Megan to the doorway and stepped out onto a broad porch that overlooked a wide valley. Tall evergreens rimmed a stony bluff that curved to a pass beyond, and a waterfall tumbled a hundred feet between two dark-needled giants nearby. Flowers were scattered through a wide meadow, bright with spring and sunlight, and in midvalley Duke Rahorsum stood glittering among his soldiers and lords, visored and armored on a proud black horse. He gestured vigorously, ordering more soldiers into Witchmere, then rode forward himself, his brightly clad noblemen riding behind him. Brierley and Megan watched as the horses clambered upon the broad stone staircase leading to the porch, then saw the soldiers pass within, their footfalls echoing on stone.

"I want this fortress emptied," Rahorsum ordered in a harsh voice. "I want them all dead and this valley cleansed forever."

"It shall be done, your grace," a nobleman responded. With a shiver of sounding metal, he drew his sword and spurred his horse through the gateway. *He wears Yarvannet's livery,*

Brierley realized with a small shock. *The Earl of Yarvannet was here, when the end came.* She looked at the other lords, in their array of bright colors, recognizing other standards. *They were all here. All joined with the duke in his slaughter. Why? What did we do to deserve death?*

Rahorsum reined up his horse and looked up at the stone façade, his mouth twisted with hatred. His black eyes glittered through the eyeholes of his visor. "All," he muttered. "Every one." With a convulsive motion of his heels, he spurred his horse onward and clattered into the darkness.

A great lord, Megan thought, very subdued.

He thought himself so, Brierley replied, sensing the Beast within him, a Beast Rahorsum had not welcomed, not in the beginning, but in grief and rage and sorrow had nurtured. I would rather him evil and unalloyed, Brierley thought sadly. I would rather these be deaths unjust beyond question.

Did we steal children? Did we loose the plague on Iverway? What were shari'a here, in this place, in this time? Brierley looked around the peaceful valley, then up at the bright spring sky where the Daystar approached Pass with the Companion. Why did we bury ourselves in caverns, away from the sunlight? Why?

Megan's salamander fluttered to her shoulder and gave a small cry of distress. *I like my river more than this house of buried stone*, Megan said and stroked its neck. *Shall we go there?*

Not now, Megan. Take us back to Earl Melfallan.

I like the earl, Megan said simply. *Stefan, too.*

Brierley looked down at Megan's small face. *So do I. They are both ours to guard. It is our craft.* Megan nodded soberly, then looked at the jeweled-eyed creature on her hand. The salamander preened, fire shimmering along his slim body as he moved in the sunlight.

He agrees. Megan looked up at Brierley and smiled.

Take us back now.

Yes, Mother. Megan raised the keystone and the mist rose again, but did not take them to the shelter of the cave. To her surprise, Brierley sat again in her cockleboat with Megan.

"What is that?" Megan asked in alarm, and pointed at the shadow moving toward them across the waves.

Then, in another quick shifting, they were in Megan's river world. The clouds rumbled and flashed bright crimson, bringing menace into Megan's sunlit high tower. "Mother!" Megan cried in alarm, and the salamander shrieked and took sudden flight. A shadow descended from the sky, looming closer, afflicting all dreams.

And struck—

Brierley woke abruptly, conscious of a weight crushing upon her, a quick movement, and then Megan's shriek of surprise. She sat up and, in the dim light of Niall's lamp, saw a bulking shadow retreat across the cavern, a kicking bundle in its grip.

"Megan!" she cried in horror.

At the sound of Megan's shriek, the men had tumbled from their blankets, swords quickly in hand.

Niall charged the shadow, shouting, and a razor-bright shaft of fire bolted across the cavern, missing him by scant inches. A second fire flashed, like lightning in a night sky, and she heard Stefan's cry as he threw himself aside. "No!" Brierley cried, and struggled free of her blanket. She leapt to her feet and seized the lantern, then plunged after the shadow that had taken Megan.

"Wait, Brierley!" Melfallan called desperately.

Brierley ran into the tunnel at the back of the cave, and nearly stumbled on the stone. Ahead, she saw the shadow slip from view around a far turning, a flash of darker shadow against the near-black. She ran after it. "Megan!" she cried.

"Motherrrr!" She heard Megan's thin wail ahead of her.

"Brierley!" Melfallan shouted again behind her. "Wait!" His bootsteps pounded behind her.

Brierley ran down the rough stone floor of the narrow tunnel, the lamp held high to show her path. After the first turning, the tunnel turned left through a square passageway, then right, sweeping in broad curves. She came suddenly to a wide staircase chiseled downward in the stone, the walls on either side climbing in height as she descended the long stair, again winding left and right. What place was this? she wondered with awe. She slowed her pace, cautious of her footing on broken stone, and listened anxiously ahead, but heard only a distant dripping of water, the echoing stillness of a hollow in the mountain.

"Megan!" she called out, and winced as the name ricocheted from wall to wall, fracturing itself into the depths ahead of her. She hurried onward, listening, and came to a division in the tunnel, both stairs descending. Which way?

She hunted a few steps into the left passageway, then retreated into the right, listening with more than ears.

Megan! she called silently, urgently, her call powered by her own fright. *Megan*!

Here . . . came the answer, weakened, beyond fright now, on the edge of consciousness. *Mother, help—*

Brierley gasped as the slender contact was snapped clean. Without hesitation, she plunged into the right stairway, her lamp held high, and behind her heard the heavy tread of Melfallan's boots, pursuing her as she fled onward.

"Wait, Brierley!" came Melfallan's voice, ringing against the stone. "Wait!" She heard him curse vividly as he stumbled, then tried to hurry all the faster. Reluctantly, Brierley slowed, then stopped and looked back up the stone stairs.

At the curve above, a torch's glow strengthened, then suddenly flashed, silhouetting Melfallan's figure. She heard him sigh in relief as he saw her, and watched him clamber down the stairs, fast enough to risk a bad fall, until he reached her. Melfallan looked back up the stairs with a scowl.

"The others were following, I think," he said. "Ocean, we'll all be lost inside this mountain." He looked at his torch, which was near guttering, and set it down on the floor. Their light would last as long as the fuel in Brierley's lamp.

She pointed downward. "This is the right way."

"Your witch-sense, I suppose," he grumbled. "At least we have some guide in this darkness." As she started downward again, he caught her arm and stopped her. "We should wait for the others. A lamp and a sword aren't much protection against whatever beasts wait down there."

"It took Megan!"

"And we'll find her, I promise you. But be prudent, mistress. It will do Megan no good if our rescue ends abruptly with our own deaths." He was right, though she felt wild anxiety to follow Megan. Melfallan looked back up the stairs impatiently, then pressed her arm. "Wait here." He took a step and then turned back. "You will wait, won't you?"

"I will wait." Brierley pressed her hands together anxiously.

"On second thought, come with me. I'll not have you run off without me again." She set her jaw and glared at him, and he read her expression rightly. "Please?" he cajoled. "It won't take long. Be sensible, Brierley. We must have the others with us, for that better safety."

Brierley peered anxiously down the descending stair and hesitated. A cold breeze flowed past her from the depths, tainted with moisture and the heavy scents of mold. Her lamp made a small yellow circle of light, sending shadows dancing into the heights above her as the stair descended, lower and lower. She could hear nothing—no sound except her own breathing, preternaturally loud in the stillness, no rhythm except the pounding of her own heart. But she *knew*, without knowing how she knew, Megan's direction, a direction that shifted slowly to the right. Whatever had taken her was still moving.

She lifted her chin slightly as something whispered in the far distance, like the brushing touch of a spiderweb, the tickle of a spring breeze. She strained her ears, then realized it had not been sound, but a thought.

Where are you? she sent with her witch-sense, expecting Megan to answer. *Where?* But the whisper came again, a tumbling nonsense of rushed words, then silence—and not from Megan. She swiveled her head as she sensed a second ghostly whisper from a different direction, down and to the right. *Megan?*

The rushed mental voice began again, babbling disconnected words, and then faded into the distance, briefly echoed by another. Her spine prickled. *Who are you?* Brierley demanded. The shadow? Could there be more than one menace in these depths? *Answer me.* Nothing replied.

"Brierley!" Melfallan insisted, and took her arm. Reluctantly, she followed him back up the stair, glad that he hurried. They reached the turning beyond the top of the stair—but found a wall of blank stone, not the doorway she remembered into the cave. "Where's the door?" Melfallan exclaimed. "Niall! Stefan!" Brierley placed her palms on the rough stone surface, as confused as he.

"This is the right way," she insisted, asking his reassurance. "There were no side tunnels to lose our way."

"No, there weren't. Where did this wall come from?" Melfallan pounded on the stone with the hilt of his sword, with no effect. "Stefan!" he shouted. "Niall!" He paused to listen, but they heard nothing. "I can't see any seam, if it's a door."

"That closed shut behind us? There was no door when you looked earlier, but the shadow came through a door."

Melfallan stepped back. "It must be a door that opened—"

"And closed."

"Do you know how to open it?" he asked, as if he expected her to know all things, as perhaps he did by now. She bit her lip.

"No, I don't!" She tried pressing her fingers into small recesses in the stone wall, hoping for a hidden key, but the wall did not move. Melfallan pried with his sword edge on each side, but could find no purchase to pry open the massive stone. Finally he grunted in defeat and stepped back.

"Stefan!" he shouted, making the echoes boom. "Niall!" Neither answered.

Brierley leaned her hands on the stone and cast with her witch-sense but, to her surprise, realized she could not sense Stefan and Niall beyond the stone wall. She tried again, but heard only blankness. She hammered futilely on the stone with her fists, and winced as the stone bruised her hands.

Melfallan seized her shoulders and pulled her away from the wall. "You're only hurting yourself. Don't beat stone." He stared at the blank stone wall, his hand flexing on the hilt of his sword, then let out his breath in a gust. "Well, there's no helping it. Lead on, Brierley. A sword and a lamp is all we'll have."

She smiled at him gratefully and turned back to the stair. They descended again, the stair winding through one flight after another, always descending. "What is this place?" he breathed in awe.

Brierley reached back for his hand. "Niall said this trail is haunted. By what? What ancient evil lived in this pass?" He looked at her blankly, confused. "That Rahorsum slew?" she prompted.

Melfallan's eyes widened as he finally caught her meaning. With a start, he looked down the stairway to the echoing depths. His fingers tightened hard on hers. "We're in *that* place?"

"Apparently. Where else would stairs reach into the depths, truly? You're pressing too hard on me, Melfallan."

"Oh." Melfallan promptly eased his grip. "Your pardon, dear heart," he said absently, not noticing his own endearment. "Then what took Megan?"

She shook her head. "I don't know. I only saw a shadow and bolts of fire. But it is still moving, and she is in that direction." She pointed unerringly, down and to the right. "And there are voices in the depths!"

"Voices?" She had Melfallan thoroughly alarmed now. For a man determined on the clear light of reason, the touch of old tales did not please. She bit her lip, then felt surprised by his chuckle.

"I am doomed to be enmeshed in witchly affairs," he said. "It's not your fault, sweet witch. Perhaps in time I'll get used to it. Let's go find Megan, armed with your lamp and my sword." He sounded resigned.

She gripped his arm gratefully. "Thank you, Melfallan."

"It's not so much," he said ruefully. "I won't leave her in danger, either, and—" He pointed at the stair above them with his sword. "What else to do?"

"Still, I am grateful."

He smiled. "Lead on,witch. I will follow. Let's hope we see the Daystar again sometime in our lives."

"A door in means a door out," she said.

"If we can find it—after we find Megan."

"Yes." She raised her lamp, and together they began their descent into Witchmere, hunting the shadow.

16

The stairway descended in broad sweeping curves, falling and falling into the depths. After they had walked several minutes, the wall to the right suddenly vanished. Brierley stopped in midstep and shrank against the remaining wall, startled by the sudden void beside them. Melfallan raised her lamp, which made little headway into the looming open space. Beneath their feet a ledge plummeted into gloom, without apparent bottom.

Brierley pointed out into the darkness. "It went that way. Straight across."

"Across the open air?" Melfallan asked, stunned. "How?"

"I don't know. A cavern bird?"

"No bird looms that large: It was man-size at least."

"At least no bird we know." She ran her fingers over the stone wall, then quested further, exploring the crevices another yard farther as she walked her hand over the stone for balance. "There must be a way down and around, perhaps by this stair."

"You still know her direction?"

"Oh, yes." She pointed again across the void. "That way. And it has stopped moving," she added, realizing it was so as she spoke.

Megan! she called with her mind, and heard a faint response of river wind and reeds. Wherever the shadow had taken Megan in these caverns, the child had fled from it to her special place, and it could not frighten her there. At least Megan had that comfort. It did not help Brierley find her, but at least she had the direction. In a city or town, Megan would be lost in the sea of other thoughts, but here, save only the ghostly voices and a faint dripping of water, the silence was total. In her sea cave, the ocean beat at the rocks, filling the air with sound. Here was only emptiness.

An emptiness of three centuries—and no witch had walked in these depths since.

Melfallan leaned cautiously to look over the edge of the abyss. "If we could sprout wings, we could follow."

"Feet must do, but be careful of your footing as we go. Some of this stone is crumbling." She raised her lamp, peering down the stairs ahead. They stretched into the far shadows, still descending beside the void. "This way."

In an alcove just beyond the next few steps, her fingers found a familiar boxy shape, but the Everlight did not respond to her touch, did not hear her, not now. It had been too long since a witch passed here. She caressed it another moment, then withdrew her hand, knowing now with certainty this place, and why Niall had called this high trail haunted. The Everlight proved it. Although this Everlight's voice was silenced, something else lived in these depths and had seized Megan. But what? What haunted the trail above, watching travelers as Megan's "not-there thing"? A device? A guardian? Her books in the cave had not spoken extensively of Witchmere—if indeed the later witches had even known the place. Likely they had not, no more than Brierley.

But Thora had mentioned guardians, she remembered, and had warned of them.

Melfallan peered curiously at the Everlight she had touched. "What is it?" he asked. "A device?" He reached out tentatively and tapped the Everlight's casing. "Cast metal—or porcelain, I think." He reached for her lamp and held it closer to the small alcove. "And finely crafted," he added, with obvious admiration. "This was cleverly made, indeed. What is it?"

"A guardian," she said softly. "Silenced now. It has been too long."

"Guardian? You seem to recognize it." The statement was a partial demand.

"Guardian of a shari'a place, I think. I have one in my cave in Yarvannet, though I never knew what it really was. Thora's book called it the Everlight. It was just—*there*, and did not answer questions, nor speak much at all."

"Cave in Yarvannet?" Melfallan prompted.

"There are many things you do not know," she said with dignity, "even though you be an earl."

"And?"

"Can I repair the impossible? No man, even an earl, can know all things." She looked at him, her mouth firmly closed. She was grateful for all Melfallan had done for her, grateful beyond words, but still she felt cautious, even with him. For too many years she had believed in the hue and cry that killed a witch, of the fatal certainty of a High Lord's attention. Melfallan eyed her impatiently for a long moment, then gave a short bark of laughter. He gestured her onward down the stair.

"As you will, witch. But I will persist, I warn you."

She gave the Everlight a last caress, and walked onward, descending the stair carefully, one hand on stone, though as quickly as she could. The stairs had deteriorated in this section, with water seeping from cracks to pry at stone. She stepped carefully, but felt stone shift slightly beneath her foot.

"About your cave," Melfallan said as he followed. He was not paying proper attention to his feet, wishing instead to talk to her. "What other witcheries did you keep in it?"

She relented a little. "Only the Everlight, and the writings of the cave witches. I had a journal, too. I used to write to my future child, whom I hoped to meet one day. Someday, I thought, I would meet the child, the daughter like me. I never expected to meet her in Darhel. I always thought someday, as I was walking down the road, or strolling through Amelin, I would see her suddenly, and she would see me, and—"

"Or never meet her at all."

"You catch the problem nicely. But I always watched for her, whenever I walked the roads."

"I had wondered why you had the child with you."

"Blood speaks to Blood, my lord: I'm not mistaken that

Megan is also witch-kind. Perhaps she is related to me: my mother was born in the north, although I don't know where. Perhaps my mother was kin to Jonalyn, but I'm not certain of that, either. But of Megan I'm sure, and I brought her out of Darhel—into this place." She bit her lip and glanced around at the shadows.

"I think you have been very lonely," he said.

"Not really," she said. "I had my books to read and I had my friends like Clara and Harmon."

"Whom you could never tell what you are."

"Well, true." She looked back at him and quirked her mouth. "That has certainly changed. Now I prattle on endlessly, especially to you."

"For which I'm honored." He paused. "I think you trust me a little more than you used to."

"I trust you more than that," she said simply, and she heard him take a sharp breath of surprise and stumble lightly on the stair, but it was true. She smiled. Melfallan had more than earned her trust, this young High Lord who risked so much to defend her, a sea-shine lass he hardly knew when he took up his championing. He could have set down his champion's sword at any time, and not defied the duke and not pursued her into mountain snows. And now? His first thought, when she had run after the shadow, had been of her. She sensed that he was troubled by his attraction to her, and he, too, recognized the bonds that held him elsewhere.

She stopped and turned back around to face him. He stopped short on the stair above and eyed her back, not certain of her intentions. "What's that smile for?" he asked warily.

"For you." She spread her hands. "And you must focus on your footing, dear lord, not on talking to me, or you will tumble headlong into that void, and what would that solve?"

"Duke Tejar would think it solves much," Melfallan said wryly.

"Who cares about the duke, as you surely do not? Megan is sleeping now, and is not harmed, but we must circle this void to get to her. The stair likely worsens ahead, and we'll be of no use to her if we tumble off the edge."

"I like to talk to you," Melfallan said comfortably and

leaned on his sword, looking at her. "Especially when you tell me what I want to know about you. There hasn't been much opportunity to know you, not with my prudent rule about keeping away from the dangerous witch, which unfortunately applied to me, too. Are you dangerous, Brierley?"

"Of course I am. In the meantime, please—" She waved at the stair. "It *is* urgent."

"I hear you." He smiled and straightened, then gestured with the swordpoint downward. "Lead the way, mistress."

They continued the descent, with the silence of Witchmere broken only by the sound of their boots on the cracked stairs and, far in the distance, the steady *plink-plink* of water. The ghosts whispered from time to time, causing Brierley to lift her face toward them, but still spoke no sense.

Why had the shadow seized Megan? Was it Megan's not-there thing? A guardian? A predator? Brierley was witch also: why did it ignore her? Why take Megan? Because only Megan could sense its presence? Could this guardian, this not-witch, cloud minds to conceal itself, even Brierley's? Her books had never described such guardians: what other crucial information did she lack? This was a shari'a place and she was shari'a, yet she peered as uncertainly down the winding stair as the Allemanii lord who walked behind her.

After several minutes of descent, they reached a level platform, and the enclosure of walls on both sides, and left the abyss behind them. Brierley raised her lamp and peered ahead. Ahead, blocking the corridor, stood a closed door with a great ring in its center, shadowed carvings mounting each jamb and lintel. Above the door and to either side, a great plinth had been broken away, to lie in its fragments on the floor.

Megan! she called, and caught a touch of Megan's sunlit balcony, reassuring her. Whatever had taken Megan had not yet harmed her—but might. Brierley set her lips firmly. Megan was *her* daughter, not theirs, whatever they were.

Brierley walked up to the huge door, and bent to pick up one of the small stones from the rubble at its base. She saw engraved letters dimly visible on the stone, and raised her lamp to peer at them. With a small shock, she saw that it was not Allemanii script, but a different alphabet, more cursive and blended, yet clearly writing. A different language, she realized—shari'a language. Until that moment, she had never suspected the shari'a had had a different tongue, for it was one Brierley didn't know at all. Like the rest of Amelin and Natheby, like all the cave witches, she spoke Allemanii. All the books in her cave were written in Allemanii; it had never occurred to her to question it. Thora's book must have been translated, she thought, sometime since the Disasters. And those older books on the higher shelves, the ones she hadn't dared touch lest they crumble? Had they borne the older script?

The Allemanii took even our words, she thought sadly, and then we even forgot the taking. How much had been lost? How much forever? If there were books here, how would she read them? She tightened her fingers around the carved stone and looked up at the massive door.

Melfallan pulled at the door ring with one hand, then put down his sword and braced his feet on the floor to pull again with more strength. The door shifted slightly with a grating sound, then stopped. Melfallan pulled steadily for another minute, straining at the weight, but the door would not move.

"It's too heavy," he said, panting hard.

"It's the way through. Let me help."

"You? You're not exactly muscled, Brierley."

"I'm stronger than I look. Here." She placed her hands above and below his on the ring, and together they strained at the door. It grated another few inches and then stuck again.

"Heave!" Melfallan cried. They pulled hard, straining backward, and won another few inches. Now the crack was two full hands' breadths wide, enough to allow a faint breeze that blew into their faces from the other side, rich with the smell of water and old dust. Through the crack, Brierley could see a broad corridor running straight ahead, seemingly without end into the far distance, and dimly lit by lamps on the wall. Lamps? she wondered. How could lamps burn for three hundred years?

Melfallan dropped his hands from the ring and shook his

arms, trying to relieve the strain. "At this rate, you might slip through after another heave but I won't."

"Then we'll heave twice. It's the way through."

"And stuck badly." He leaned over, his hands braced on his hips, and breathed deeply. "I'm not a fisherman who hauls nets all day. I'm a pampered lord, asked now and then to carry a saddle a few feet to my horse, but only if my groom is busy."

Brierley smiled. "You're strong enough."

"Oh, I'm not apologizing, mistress. I'm just stating a fact." He straightened and winced as a back muscle twinged. "I like facts, if you haven't noticed. Unfortunately, that door is a fact, too."

"We must get through the door," Brierley insisted. She leaned a hand against the doorjamb and sighed, suddenly exhausted by the broken sleep, the rush down the long stairway, the emotions of the night.

Megan! Where are you? On a sunlit balcony, a salamander flickered, its eyes gleaming. It stretched its jaws in a lazy yawn, then snapped them shut. Its head sank to its forepaws, at peace.

How much more time did Megan have? Did Brierley have?

"Let's try again," Melfallan urged. They took hold of the door ring and braced their feet, then heaved. The door moved several inches with a heavy grating of stone and a fine sift of dust. "And again!" Melfallan cried. They hauled again at the door, gaining a few more inches of movement before the door stuck. They strained a moment, then desisted.

"Again, my lord," Brierley said cheerfully, and planted a foot on the wall beside the jamb. "And pull!"

"Pull!" Melfallan cried, and they hauled at the door ring. Stone grated again. A cold breeze issued through the foot-wide crack, stirring the dust on the floor, then strengthened as Melfallan and Brierley added another handspan to the opening.

"Stop a moment," Melfallan said, puffing, and rubbed his hands on his tunic. Brierley slipped to the opening and put her face into the opening, then tried to squeeze through. "Ah, not yet," Melfallan protested. "I'll want to come through, too, and I'm not a reed-slender witch who can no doubt thin herself through any obstacle." He demonstrated with his hands, sliding a normal-sized witch into a staff-thin shadow.

"I cannot 'thin' myself in any such fashion," Brierley said irritably. "Don't you listen to your own nonsense."

"Nonsense!" Melfallan huffed. "I like that."

"You should," she retorted. She stepped back as they seized the door ring again and, with much puffing, slid open another foot, enough for witch and lord to pass. Brierley slipped through the opening before Melfallan could stop her and heard Melfallan mutter a curse as he hastily followed. He caught her elbow.

"No running off," he commanded.

"You will amend that order, my lord." she told him briskly, lifting her chin.

"Must I, indeed?" He paused and eyed her a moment. "Oh, dear mistress, please wait for me! How's that?"

"Better." He grinned.

"Are we closer to Megan?" he asked then, more soberly. He noticed the lights that lined the corridor ahead, a beaded string that extended on one wall into the distance. "How in—? Perhaps someone still lives down here? After all this time?"

She shook her head. "I don't know. This place is as strange to me as to you." She nodded at the corridor. "But that is the right direction."

"Then lead on, witch." He took her hand and they set off, walking miles and miles, it seemed, down the long corridor, each stretch of corridor like the last: blank walls, closed doors, and the glowing globes on one wall that shed light into the gloom. Dust puffed from the floor as they walked, silting small clouds as it drifted a foot to settle again. The air seemed heavy, but bore no scent except the ever-present dust.

Finally Brierley's feet began to drag, her legs aching. When she nearly stumbled, Melfallan firmly brought her to a halt and made her sit by one wall, then sat down beside her with a slide and thump. Brierley put down her lamp beside her and leaned back her head against the stone, then listened to her leg muscles twitching. It wasn't the distance, she decided, but the stairs—that and floundering through the snow all the day before. Yes, it must be that.

"I need a rest," Melfallan said, sagging against the wall. "How far have we walked?"

"At least two miles." He paused. "I'd say it was the long way around to find Megan. Flying is better."

"I agree. Next time we'll fly."

He put down his sword, and he took her hand in his, and they sat for a time, simply breathing. Finally Brierley stirred and got to her feet, and tried not to stagger as she set off again. Melfallan followed, sword in hand.

After another hundred yards, the stairs began again, descending steeply and curving to the left, then reached a crossways. Brierley lifted her lamp and gazed down the long hallway to each side, the farther reaches masked by shadow. "That way," she said, and pointed down the dusty hallway lined by doors, some wooden, some stone, some of a shiny material that sounded a high tone when tapped. None stood open, and Melfallan tested the latches on a few as they passed. In this hallway, the wall lamps were spaced farther apart, and they needed the additional light from her lamp to see their way clearly.

"I had heard Witchmere was a great castle underground," he said with awe. "How far does it extend?"

"I don't know," Brierley said wearily.

"Brierley, we'll find her, your witch-child. Merely lead the way."

Megan! Brierley called, without response. She tried to hurry her feet, only to fall back into her plodding. They reached another crossways, and she again bore to the right.

Megan! she called. They were very close now. *Megan!*

Megan responded at last, stirring from her heavy sleep. *Mother!*

Megan's eyes flickered open and she saw a dark shape looming over her. Startled, Megan screamed and cowered backward, still caught halfway between her two worlds, one a dream, the other real. Into Brierley's mind struck the sudden image of Megan's castle, now surrounded by the coils of a great serpent. The creature snapped viciously at Megan's salamander as the creature dove at its head, then licked its long tongue into Megan's balcony. *No!* Megan cried, staggering away from its touch. In terror, she ran to the stairs and vanished into the fears and torments of the castle's second floor. The serpent probed its tongue downward, hunting her.

"Megan!" Brierley called and ran down the hall.

"Wait! Wait!" Melfallan cried behind her.

Brierley burst into the next chamber at the end of the hall and saw Megan crouched in the far corner, her hands hiding her face. A metal box, a creature man-high and bristling with metal arms, floated in front of the child. One of its appendages plucked curiously at Megan's hair, and it hummed to itself, with sparks jumping in its crevices and joints. Along the far wall stood a row of tall compartments filled with other shadowed boxy shapes. As Brierley appeared, its domed head swiveled toward Brierley and it jerked up an arm.

"No!" Megan shrieked. "Don't, don't, *don't*."

Brierley dodged to the left as a jagged flame issued from the machine's arm, splashing through the doorway against the wall beyond. An edge of the flame washed into Melfallan, burning into his shoulder and chest: she heard his choked scream of agony as he fell heavily to the floor, the sword clanging. She gasped, tears springing to her eyes, as the Beast began to roar in the distance. Not Melfallan! Not him! The machine moved toward Brierley, hissing faintly.

"*Don't!*" Megan shrieked again.

Brierley slowly drew herself to her feet and faced it squarely. She could not run: the guardian's fire could lash at her in an instant. But it hesitated and did not attack further: perhaps it still knew the shari'a it had once guarded. Perhaps.

Brierley lifted her chin defiantly. "Do you not hear the child?" she said to the machine. She deepened her voice and glared at the guardian. "*We* command here."

The machine shifted slightly to the left, but still did not lash again with its thrown fire. Even at this close distance, she could not sense its thoughts, though it obviously considered her, obviously thought and planned. Brierley took a step toward it. "We command," she repeated intensely, reinforcing the thought with her witch-sense. The machine drifted warily aside.

Megan was watching her with open mouth, her panicked eyes flicking from Brierley to the guardian. *Help me, Megan,* Brierley ordered.

"We command," Megan said obediently and rose to her feet, bracing herself against the wall. The machine turned slightly toward her, responding to her voice. Suddenly, the child spread her hands ecstatically. "All this place. *We* command." Megan glared at the machine. "You will obey me," she spat.

Ocean alive, Brierley wondered, what witch's self has Megan borrowed now?

"*Li-masib raayih hasabat,*" the machine said hesitantly, its voice metallic and cracking. *"Li-masib?"* It whined faintly, then clacked to itself. Then: "You command," it said in quite understandable Allemanii.

"I command!" Megan exulted wildly. "I *command*!"

"You command," the guardian agreed, and slowly floated backward into one of the compartments, clicked itself into place, then settled to the floor with a soft thud. Its lights flickered fitfully, and it flexed its arms once, then stilled.

Once settled, the guardian did not move further. Four of the other compartments were dark and the guardian stilled forever, but three others flickered with faint life, waiting. Cautiously, her eye on the guardians, Brierley crossed the few steps to Megan, then stooped to her, drawing the child into her arms.

Megan was still focused on the guardians, her eyes fixed and staring. Brierley compelled Megan to look at her with a firm hand. "Megan," she said, sensing the child was suspended over a gulf, one that might fall deeply into madness, never to rise. These machines were not sane and had somehow touched Megan, heard her as she heard them. *Megan*! she sent.

Megan blinked and seemed to awaken from a dream. "Nasty thing," she said suddenly, her voice quite normal. "It killed the men."

"What men?" Brierley asked, confused. Had Stefan and

Niall been murdered above? That was not the sense of Megan's thought. Men from another place and time, she guessed, as Megan again tapped into old memories. She glanced again at the other guardians, then drew Megan out of the corner. "Come out of this dangerous place, Megan. Come with me."

Dreamily, Megan complied, though she looked back over the shoulder at the guardians, and her expression became far older than her years, harder and more confident, used to power. "I command," Megan whispered, gloating with the knowledge of it.

"Come, Megan," Brierley cajoled.

As they reached the doorway, one of the guardians moved slightly in its compartment, stirring to life.

"Tell it to stop," Brierley whispered urgently to Megan.

"Stop!" Megan cried. "Do not follow us!"

The machine did not answer, and it did not stop. It moved slowly forward, floating on the air, and flexed its arms like some unlikely insect.

"Stop!" Brierley shouted at it. "You must obey!"

The other boxy shapes now stirred, perhaps roused by their common thought or by Brierley's voice or both. Even the guardian that Megan had commanded to silence now moved. Whatever temporary hold Megan's command had worked, it was slipping.

"Come, Megan." Brierley picked up the child and stepped toward the doorway. Another step, and she ran into the corridor, Megan in her arms.

Melfallan lay sprawled on the floor, his tunic fabric charred into the flesh by the machine's fire. Megan squirmed from Brierley's arms and ran to him with a cry, then tried to help as Brierley pulled him to his feet. Melfallan groaned deeply, but managed to stand.

"What happened?" he asked, then staggered. She caught him from a fall with an arm around his waist, and felt the fire of his agony sheet through him as she jostled him. He gave a wild moan of pain, then bit it back.

"Don't speak," she said. "Even witches have a narrow edge with guardians so old—and I don't think these are sane. Come, Megan!"

Melfallan tried to match her hurried pace, though every step jarred agony into his shoulder and chest. They reached a turning and she led them to the right, toward new stairs leading upward.

"Megan, can you hear the not-there things coming?"

"Not yet," the child answered in her piping voice. "I don't know," she added, confused. "One of them wanted to eat and the others agreed, then one got a headache and stopped. I don't think they remember us, but they might later after they finish sleeping."

Sleeping? Brierley pursed her lips, then let that all go. "You listen for the not-there things, Megan," she said. "Tell us if one is coming."

"Yes, Mother."

"Not-there thing?" Melfallan asked dully.

"Later," Brierley answered frantically, and struggled to climb the stair as Melfallan leaned heavily upon her. "Climb, Melfallan. Don't faint."

"I am sincerely trying not to," he mumbled.

Megan gave a little shriek of alarm. "A not-there thing! It's following us!" She pointed into the shadows of the stair behind them.

"Quickly," Brierley said, and hauled at Melfallan's awkward weight.

"It is coming *now*," Megan cried.

They reached the top of the stairs, and Brierley pulled Melfallan into the side corridor just beyond the landing, where a stone door hung on hinges, carvings again above and around the doorway. Beyond the heavy door, another corridor continued onward in darkness, perhaps upward, perhaps down. She braced Melfallan against the wall on the other side, then pushed at the heavy door, managing to close it halfway. She strained as the door stuck, then managed a few more inches. A whirring sound echoed faintly on the stairway, and Brierley retreated to the wall beside Melfallan, out of sight, then pulled Megan to her.

The whirring approached the half-open door. "It is coming!" Megan whispered.

"Stop!" Brierley called out. The guardian ignored her and whined closer.

"Listen to my mother," Megan cried, suddenly enraged. "You listen to her, right *now*." Megan stamped her foot and would have charged the doorway if Brierley hadn't pulled her back. "*Now*!" Megan shouted.

Brierley saw a darker shadow hover just beyond the doorway, then the glint of glass and metal in the gloom. Megan moved forward again insistently, and Brierley let go of her hand, anxious that she did so. Whatever Megan had tapped in this place to guide her, she remained a child, and a child for whom little was real.

Megan planted her feet and stared through the half-open doorway. "I command," the child said malevolently. "And you are a bad thing."

"I guard," the guardian answered her, its tone insolent. Melfallan's eyes widened as he heard the machine's voice. "I kill intruder."

"Your friend attacked my mother," Megan accused. "You killed people here. And now you follow me when I tell you not to. Go back!" Megan lifted her chin proudly, tension in every line of her small body. Brierley watched her with amazement, sensing that Megan again drew from some other source outside herself, a source blocked for Brierley. Her books had said nothing about such witch-spelling, if spell it was.

"I guard," the machine repeated and moved closer to the doorway. "You are witch, but those others are not. Move. I will erase the danger."

"I am *not* in danger. You are wrong. Obey me! Go back!"

"No danger?" the guardian asked uncertainly.

"No danger!" Megan shouted.

The machine whirred, then suddenly began to babble to itself in singsong lilting words Brierley could not understand. Its voice grew more urgent as it muttered, as if it argued with someone else, perhaps even itself, then rose to a painful shriek. *"Li-masib! Li-masib!"* it shrieked. *"Danger!"*

"No danger!" Megan shouted. "Go back!"

"Danger!" the machine cried.

Megan gasped in outrage, and Brierley dragged her back the instant before fire erupted through the half-open door, a torrent of flame that splashed against stone. The machine clanged itself against the door, and Brierley threw herself against its weight, forcing the door nearly closed. The machine tried again to force the door, but its body was too wide, its force too small to widen the opening against Brierley's determined denial. With a whine, it suddenly retreated down the stairs.

"It won't listen to me," Megan said in outrage.

"Hush, child," Brierley said urgently, and went to Melfallan.

Melfallan flinched as she touched him, his chest and arm sheeted with agony. He blinked at her groggily, then moaned in relief as her touch eased the first of his pain. Gently, she eased him to the floor, and ran her fingers lightly over his arm, taking the pain into herself. They cried out together, and she moved closer to him, her hands sliding restlessly over his arm and chest.

"What?" he said in confusion, and tried to push her away.

"Rest easy, Melfallan."

"Hurts," he moaned, dazed by the pain.

"Rest easy."

Gently, she pulled away the charred fabric of his tunic, then lifted the rest of the shirt over his head, helping him to raise his arms. Her hands brushed over his bare chest, easing the pain, restoring the flesh, until only a faint covering of soot remained where the flame had lashed. Her own flesh was on fire now and she bit her lip, stifling a moan. Hearing it, Melfallan reached to comfort her, then pulled her close to him. He caressed her, his touch as gentle as her own. She drew back, disturbed by his response, but he rose to his knees and pulled her against him even more tightly, and she swayed into his embrace. Without intending it, she entered more deeply into another's soul than she ever had before, until her very spirit resonated with his. She trembled and felt his answering shiver, then somehow could not find her breath. His hands swept up her back to her head and he lowered his mouth to hers and kissed her deeply. She clung to him.

Finally, with a sigh, she pushed him away. Melfallan sighed deeply in turn, his eyes closed, then blinked and looked at her, half-stunned. He touched his chest gingerly, and then looked down at himself and could not believe his eyes. "It's healed!" he exclaimed.

"I am a healer," she replied dazedly. "And you weren't supposed to kiss me, Melfallan."

"Why not? I thought it was wonderful." He grinned, then caught her hand. She shivered at his touch. "You are a marvel, Brierley Mefell!"

She closed her eyes and sighed deeply, for her breath still would not quite catch. "What's wrong?" Melfallan asked with sudden concern, his voice jangling unpleasantly in her ears. The Beast roared in the distance, adding its own oppression.

"I went too far, I think," she answered vaguely. "You're not supposed to— And the Beast—" She tried to take a deeper breath. "Will you watch over Megan? For a little while?" She lowered her head and the Beast roared again in her ears, and she could not catch her breath properly, not at all.

"Brierley!"

She did not hear him. In the next moment, she stood again on a sandy beach and faced the Beast. It laughed at her and shifted quickly through the waves, coming closer. Brierley lifted her chin defiantly.

I will destroy you, the Beast promised.

Never! Brierley smiled grimly and crafted a sword from the air, then leveled its point at the Beast. *Come, Beast, and be defeated again.*

You thieved his soul, witch, and that is not permitted: I am the penalty. It rose from the waves, and sent its foul stench billowing toward her. *Breathe deeply and die.*

I stole nothing. He is unharmed.

You think so?

It laughed again, jeering, and then rushed at her.

17

Melfallan caught Brierley as she slowly collapsed forward. She hardly seemed to breathe as he laid her gently on the floor. She had looked much the same the night she healed Saray, and he guessed her faint was similar, and for the same reason. Part of the price for a healing, he supposed, although Brierley had never actually said so. He realized now that she had actually said very little about herself, probably a habit of all her life, particularly with a High Lord. He cudgeled his memory to remember what Marina had done for her. A blanket for warmth, but he had no blanket, no cloak—they were all back in the cave with Stefan and Niall. Even his shirt was gone, burned to tatters by the machine. Well, if he was comfortable bare-chested, she would not be chilled.

Megan knelt down by his side and gripped a fold of Brierley's skirt. She looked up at him fearfully. "She's fighting the Beast," Megan whispered.

"Beast?" Melfallan asked. He looked around him quickly and saw nothing but an empty corridor, dimly lit by a lamp, a nearly shut door. Where? But the Beast in Saray's birth chamber had been invisible, too, yet Brierley had surely fought one there.

"The Beast that comes," the child said obscurely, and made a brushing movement Melfallan did not understand.

"Can you help her?" he asked anxiously.

"I don't know how!" Megan said, and screwed up her face in distress. "I would if I knew how. She helps me in my castle, and she's my mother." Suddenly Megan whimpered, then made a low moan of horror that raised the hairs on Melfallan's neck. "It's attacking! Help her! Help her!" Megan threw her hands to her face and screamed, then abruptly folded on herself, kicking frantically.

Brierley's own body jerked in a sudden fit, then flopped to the side. Her face spasmed, and she jerked again, as if something had hold of her and shook her viciously. It hadn't been this way before. After Saray's healing, she'd only fallen asleep. Asleep!

"It's roaring!" Megan shrieked and covered her ears with her hands. "Mother!"

Brierley twitched and grimaced, caught in her silent battle against an invisible foe—for his sake, he knew. For healing him? Not this! Not this! Then he stared in disbelief as Brierley's body was suddenly lifted by unseen hands and flung back to the floor, hard enough to bruise. Then again, harder still: bones could break if it struck at her any harder. Melfallan caught his breath in a sob. He was seeing her battered before his eyes, by something invisible he could not stop. He rose to his knees and punched wildly through the air above her, trying to grapple with whatever afflicted her, but hit only air.

"No, please," Brierley murmured weakly, and abrupt tears filled Melfallan's eyes at the sodden pain in her voice, a voice emptied of strength. "No." She moved sluggishly, and threw up her hand as if to ward off another blow.

Impulsively, he caught the flailing hand in his, and held it tight. "I'm with you!" he said desperately. "I'll protect you. Show me how! I'll always protect you, Brierley!" Brierley's face twisted and would have pushed his hand away, but Megan's small hand rose to join his grip.

"I protect you," Megan echoed, her high voice ringing with assurance. "I guard! I guard! You will not take her!" Megan gave a high shriek of defiance, then snarled like a snow leopard, a bloodcurdling sound that rolled with real menace. Melfallan eyed the child warily, but did not let go of Brierley's hand. "I do not permit!" Megan shouted and shrieked new rage. "Call to her!" she commanded him. "Call now!"

"Brierley!" he shouted, and clung to Brierley's hand. "Mother!"

At that moment, Brierley's pale face suddenly relaxed, and then lost all expression, becoming utterly blank. Her body stilled its jerking and lay unmoving. Anxiously, Melfallan bent over her, and saw her chest rise and fall in a deep breath. She still breathed, thank Ocean. Her fingers slid their grip on his, going slack, but she still breathed, another breath, then another.

Megan gave a great sigh and buried her face against Melfallan's shoulder. "It's over," she said with relief.

"Will she be all right?" he asked the child anxiously.

"She's sleeping." Megan raised her tearstained face to his, looking small and vulnerable. "I *hate* the Beast," she declared. "I hate it." With a sniffle, Megan pulled her hand across her face, then stuck out her lower lip in a pout. "Hate it."

"I do, too," Melfallan said fervently. Every time she healed? This was the cost? He felt appalled.

Megan sniffled again. "She did it for you. It is her craft."

"And honor to her for it, Megan."

"As long as you *know* that," Megan said fiercely. "You should be grateful." A small finger poked at him. "You better be."

"I am." He gave her a quick hug, and saw her small face brighten. What a sprite she was, he thought: how had Brierley found her? "What would you do to me if I wasn't?" he teased.

"Something awful," Megan promised darkly.

Melfallan looked at the witch-child beside him and shivered despite himself. He believed her. It *would* be awful, whatever it was, and worse than what the Beast had done to Brierley. Megan would see to that.

"So long as you know," Megan murmured, satisfied, then curled up on the floor beside Brierley and closed her eyes. She fell asleep in a breath.

He knelt there for a time, watching them sleep, and did not know what to think, or what to feel. He knew how badly he had been burned by the creature's blast. Had he not died from the shock and inevitable infection, which was likely, he would have been disabled for life, unfit as earl with all that attendant loss. Yet Brierley had merely touched him, then caressed him to take the pain, and healed. He trembled at the memory of her caresses, then sighed deeply. It had not been sexual, but almost as intense, building to a peak as exquisite as orgasm, as if for a brief moment their very spirits had touched, then fading gently and ending in his kiss. He looked down at his shoulder and saw only slightly reddened skin, a slight pucker of scar along the muscle, and felt a dull aching in his shoulder and chest, nothing more. It was a marvel.

And she had almost died because of it: he knew that as certainly as his own breathing—and her breathing now. He smiled ecstatically as she breathed once more, lying quietly by him, and treasured each breath that came after, soft and sure. Breathe, Brierley, dear heart. Breathe, sweet witch, breathe. And another. And another. That's it. Precious girl, breathe. He closed his eyes with sheer gratitude to Mother Ocean that she breathed, then opened them in a sudden panic that she might have stopped breathing. But she breathed again, and he sighed with relief. He would watch through the night to make sure she did.

He slumped to a sitting position and crossed his aching legs, and had to pull at one ankle to get the leg settled. He'd had more exercise in the last two days than the past two months, sad to say, and everything ached. But not his shoulder, not his arm: she had taken that pain. Did she hurt afterward, maybe for days? he wondered. The pain had gone somewhere, he suspected into her: he had sensed that drawing—was that the word?—when she first touched him, but not afterward, only the growing intimacy of their closeness. But how? How did she replace flesh burned to char? Witchery, she called her gift. Were all the shari'a gifted like this? And did they have other kinds of witchery? What kinds?

He looked around at the neatly laid stone of the walls of the corridor, the wall lamp that still burned after three centuries, the faint drifting of dust on the floor. He thought of the strange machine that had stolen Megan, machines that talked, and obeyed—sometimes. He quirked his mouth. Can a machine turn too old? Become senile? Why? And why obey Megan and not Brierley? He guessed Brierley had been just as perplexed by the machine's obstinacy: some things were mystery to her, too. Apparently her books hadn't told her everything.

What books? he thought irritably, reminded of her earlier dodging. What cave? You have answers to give me, little witch, and how easily you elude me every time I ask. I'm the earl of Yarvannet: I'm supposed to be told these things so that I know. He smiled, guessing how she would answer his peremptory demand, something that would tilt her hat brim to shade her eyes, something to follow a vexing secretive smile—and, whatever his bluster, he would end up with no more information than before. Elusive witch. He reached to brush her cheek with his hand, feeling the warmth there. She sighed in response to his touch, and his breath caught again. He carefully withdrew his hand and for a moment didn't know what to do with it, then finally rested it on his knee.

I'm a practical man, he told himself firmly. Grandfather and Sir James have seen to that, surely. A touch is a touch, no more: it doesn't shiver up your spine and steal your breath, and it doesn't change burned flesh to new— He looked down at his shoulder again, and remembered how it had been burned. But she had touched him, and he had responded, drawing her into an embrace, to be embraced in turn, until for a moment, just a moment, two were one. He sighed again and then made himself take a deep breath to clear his head. It still resonated in her touch.

Does it wear off? he wondered, and realized how much he didn't know, an entire sky of not-knowing. Does it? He smiled. I hope not.

He could imagine Sir James's face as Melfallan tried to describe a touch that shivered the spine, and had no doubt of his practical no-nonsense justiciar's reaction: he'd doubt Brierley's sanity for claiming it, and Melfallan's for believing it. And Melfallan knew just exactly what his grandfather's old friend would say. Something pithy and to the point, and then Sir James would stomp out to get help.

Had others that Brierley healed felt what he had felt, that

union? Did her touch afterward shiver the spine, catch the breath away? Nothing Saray had described to him sounded like this: until the child had started to come, Saray remembered only vagueness and a frightening dream. She now dismissed all that with a flirty wave of her hand, calling it stuff and nonsense from hitting her head on the stair. He knew Saray thought Brierley little more than a gifted midwife, and certainly no real witch, though she had immediately understood Brierley's peril from the shari'a laws. But to believe that a slender sea-lass used her witch's power to cheat Death? That the invisible sword had been real, the Beast real? To truly *believe* all that? Never.

Stuff and nonsense. Had to be.

He appreciated now why improbability had been Brierley's true shield, her one protection. It had protected those shari'a who had escaped Witchmere but, one by one, during the centuries since, the High Lords had hunted them down. How many still survived? He looked at his sleeping ladies, and wondered sadly if he saw the last two.

Duke Rahorsum had slaughtered hundreds like Brierley when he destroyed Witchmere, then had made laws to insure that any shari'a who survived his malice met a similar end. And the Allemanii lords had enforced his laws for three centuries, until so few shari'a remained that even their memory seemed a legend, the stuff of tales for children. He felt a wash of shame to be a High Lord responsible for such laws: if Brierley had not healed Saray and won his gratitude, would he have let political expediency send her to the pyre? Blessed Ocean, he hoped not. He hoped he had more decency than that.

Like the other lords of his time, he had not truly believed in shari'a witchery, no more than he believed Ennis's claim about gomphreys thinking. Yet he had been there at Saray's healing, had heard the peace Brierley sang into the night. But then Brierley had lulled him, with her sweet face and voice, naming herself witch but seeming nothing of the kind. Witchery? An overblown legend for matters explained away as fancy, old tales. A sweet girl's innocent pretending to herself, honest but deluded, a silly fancy easily forgiven for the sweetness. And so he had spun his political sleight-of-hand in Darhel against Tejar, intent on saving an innocent girl from Bartol's absurd claims.

But witchery was real. He looked down at the young woman and child sleeping near him, and knew that both were now utterly precious to him. They were his to protect, because only he truly believed, only he knew. Yet the shari'a laws still existed, and Tejar and others saw those laws and their victims as a political tool, to Brierley's peril. How to protect her and her child? How?

By making myself duke, he answered himself quietly, and knew it was true. Nothing else would be sure. He narrowed his eyes thoughtfully.

As the night hours shifted slowly toward morning, he thought solemnly on the means, and weighed his alliances, and thought about what he would do.

Brierley woke slowly and clung to sleep, reluctant to stir from her sifting dreams. Finally she opened her eyes and saw Melfallan watching her, with Megan curled asleep on her other side, a warm comforting weight. She blinked and closed her eyes again, then sighed.

"Are you awake?" he asked quietly.

"Not really." She heard him chuckle.

"Are you well?" he persisted.

"I think so." She opened her eyes and forced herself to sit up, then looked at the shadows beyond the half-closed door, then turned to look up the hallway. "No guardians," she said with relief.

"I heard one come to the door again an hour ago, but it went away. Are they still hunting us?" For some reason, she noticed, Melfallan sat very still and watched her intently. Brierley reached up to smooth her hair, wondering if it stood in spikes, but it seemed in order. She glanced down at her clothes. Nothing awry. Her witch-sense had deserted her again, as usual after a healing, and offered no further clue. Oddly, she remembered very little of the Beast this time. She tried to remember, only to have her mind shy away like a frightened bird. "Are they?" Melfallan repeated patiently.

"Megan would know," Brierley replied. She reached and touched Megan's curls, then wound one around her finger and tugged gently.

"Let her sleep," Melfallan suggested. "If those creatures could get to us, they'd have done so by now. Not that I'd be much use if one did. We seem to have lost my sword." He grimaced. "Not that my sword made much difference, of course."

"You expect too much of yourself," she reproved. "You always do."

"Perhaps." He shrugged casually, and did not seem bothered by it.

With care not to disturb Megan, Brierley rose to her knees and gently touched his shoulder, testing the healing. He shivered in response and she quickly withdrew her hand, surprised by his reaction.

"If you do that again," he warned, his voice trembling, "I can't be responsible."

"What?" She sat back on her heels and looked at him, bewildered.

"I said I can't be responsible." Then he grinned, surprising her. "I kissed you before. I'll do it again, I warn you."

"Is that a threat?" she asked, amused, and wondered if he would, and if she should let him if he tried. Odd. The world seemed strange, about to tilt on its side. She looked around vaguely at the walls.

"Or a promise," Melfallan said. "But I disturbed you, witch, in your testing. Touch me again." He smiled at her brashly. "I dare you."

"I will not," she answered firmly, then eyed him. "You are in a strange mood, my lord."

"It's been a strange night," he muttered, and looked away. He swore softly to himself for some reason she couldn't fathom, then swore mildly at her when she smiled. When she reached to caress his arm, he froze to immobility, his eyes widening. When she then brushed her hand slowly down his chest, letting it linger, he stopped breathing altogether.

"It seems well healed," she said calmly, removing her hand. "I am pleased."

"And you just got thoroughly even for my teasing," he noted, and took a shuddering breath. "Do I get to kiss you now?"

"Later." She giggled at his sour expression. "I have a book you'd love to read, Melfallan. It's all about womanly arts, how to make men flutter. Marlena had a dozen noble suitors, all following her around in a pack."

"Is that so? All an *earl* has to do is beckon with an eyebrow, and they fall into his arms. I've proved it," he added smugly.

"Nice to be a lord," she observed. He seemed to have no shame in his boasting.

"Indeed," he said.

But his banter still seemed forced, as if he hid deep worry. About her? Why should Melfallan worry? She lifted her hand to her face and touched her lips, her eyes. Still there. "What is it?" she asked, confused.

Melfallan's face contorted strangely. "Nothing, dear one. Nothing at all."

What was wrong? she thought, greatly bewildered. Her heart fell as she thought of the reason. He had once seen her wave an invisible sword, true, but had seen her since as nothing more than a normal lass, whatever her odd claims of witchery. Now he'd seen the true witch, must have in the healing, and was afraid of her. Now all would turn strange and be divided, and trust would fade, dislike build. Tears filled her eyes and she turned her face away.

With a sigh, Melfallan reached for her and pulled her into his arms, then kissed her, a light touch of his lips on hers, little more. "Now, not later," he amended softly. "Why the tears, Brierley?"

"You're afraid of me?"

"Why would I be afraid of you?" he demanded.

Brierley blinked through her tears, then shook her head. "I don't understand you," she said helplessly.

He harrumphed and took time to arrange her carefully in his arms, then kissed her forehead. "There's plenty of time for understanding. You are very vague this morning, sweet girl; it worries me, but no more than that." He moved his lips to her hair and lingered there; she sighed.

"I'm sorry," she whispered.

"What in Hells for?" he asked in surprise.

"I erred, Melfallan. I was too exhausted to answer a Calling and should not have tried, but what could I do? I went too far. I didn't mean to harm you."

"What harm? Dear heart, you're not making sense."

"The Beast said I harmed you. That what I did was not permitted."

He studied her face, perplexed. "Well, you sailed beyond me there, but I don't agree with your Beast. I do not believe—I say I do *not* believe—that you would ever harm me, nor anyone you healed. You have a rare gift, sweet lady, and a gentleness that suits it well. There is peace in your voice, and healing in your hands. And even if you do blunder, if you did, it is not a fault that can be resented." He sighed and closed his eyes a moment. "You gave me a closeness to you beyond words, and I will always cherish that. And I will protect you as your lord and you will *not* worry that you did anything harmful to me." He glared down at her. "Do you hear? I forbid you to apologize for what you are."

"Hmmm."

"More than that," he demanded.

"The world tilts when you kiss me."

Melfallan laughed. "I like to kiss you, too, sweetling. And you are a little silly this morning, so just rest there awhile. There's no hurry. I doubt the Daystar has even dawned."

She yawned and rested comfortably against him, and listened to his heartbeat against her ear, slow and measured. When Melfallan moved his hand down her arm in slow caress, she shivered. He stopped.

"You, too?" he asked softly. "Do you know why, Brierley? Is this the way it is after you've healed?"

"No, never." She stirred restlessly. "I went too far. That's the harm, I think."

"I like it," he decided. "It feels delicious, like a keen wind."

He trailed his fingers back up her arm, and laughed softly to himself when she shivered again.

"Stop that," she said crossly.

"So get even and do it back. No, don't sit up. I'll stop, I promise." She hesitated, then settled back against him, and he did stop, content merely to hold her. After a time, his head began to nod, and she persuaded him to lie down beside her. Safe in his arms, her own arms around Megan, Brierley lay unmoving on the stone floor, conscious of Melfallan's chest rising and falling against her back, of Megan's small snores between her sleeves. All around them lay the empty shadows of Witchmere, as silent as a tomb.

She awoke a few hours later when Megan sat up.

"Where are the not-there things?" Brierley asked.

Megan stretched her arms over her head and yawned. "Eating. They forgot about us."

"That's a relief."

Megan looked down at her and smiled. "I helped you." She touched Brierley's face, and then caressed it with more confidence. "I helped you, Mother."

"Thank you, child."

"Don't try to remember the Beast," Megan said casually. "Maybe later. I'm hungry, too. When do we eat?"

"I'm not sure. Do you know the way out of here?"

Megan pointed at the ceiling. "Up."

"Up?"

"Up." Megan looked at her as if she were mind-sifted, and it made Brierley smile.

Melfallan gave a small grunting snore, disturbed by their voices, and woke. With a great creaking and groaning, he sat up and rubbed his back, then stifled another groan as he pulled up his legs. "Good morning—if it is morning."

"Good morning. Megan says we must go up."

"Up. That's all?"

"Up," Brierley said. She received another pitying look for the mind-sifted. Moving carefully, Brierley got to her knees, and then to her feet. She held out her hand to Megan. "Up." Melfallan got to his own feet in a series of cautious movements, with pauses between, then managed to stand.

"I need to go potty," Megan informed them.

"So do I," Melfallan muttered. "Do we use the wall?"

"Well, we don't know where a closet is," Brierley said reasonably. "What's wrong with you?"

"Just sore." He flexed his shoulder to reassure her, moving it easily. "Arm's fine: it's the rest of my body that's complaining, and sleeping on a stone floor didn't help. And you?" He studied her intently.

"I'm fine—truly," she asserted when he looked skeptical. "And I suppose the wall is all there is, unless one of these doors will open." She tried the nearest door, pushing her fingers into the recessed slot that seemed proper for the purpose, but the door did not move. Brierley helped Megan hunch down to relieve herself, and Melfallan turned his back to urinate against the other wall.

"Doesn't seem exactly respectful," Melfallan said lightly as he turned back around, retying his hose. "Our mark on Witchmere."

"Very funny," Brierley said and wrinkled her nose at him.

"It's too early to be properly witty. Later in the day I'll be my usual wonderful self, but I'm always a slow starter in the morning." He slowly bent forward, stretching his back muscles, then squirmed uncomfortably as they twinged. "Ocean, I ache. I think you do, too," he suggested.

"I'm fine."

"Why don't I believe you?"

"I can't help that," she retorted. "Up, Megan said."

They walked along the narrow corridor and found a flight of stairs at its turning, then climbed. One stair led to another, and they ascended steadily several flights and entered another hallway.

"Where are the not-there things?" Brierley asked Megan.

"One is waiting for us by the great gulf." Megan pointed behind them, down and to the right toward the broken door and the long stairway beyond. "It thought we would go back to the cave." She wrinkled her nose. "It's sleepy and hungry, and is tired of waiting."

"Hungry?" Melfallan asked. "Those things eat?"

"It goes into a box and eats," Megan said carelessly, "like

the other not-there things." Brierley and Melfallan shared a glance.

"How does she know all this?" he asked. "If it's true, that is."

Megan's small face abruptly clouded. "I don't lie!"

"I didn't say you did, child," Melfallan assured her.

"Didn't you?" Brierley asked and quirked her mouth. "It's witch-gift, my lord. She has an affinity for those guardians and so *knows* things. Don't you, Megan?"

"I *know* things," the child promptly parroted.

"I stand corrected," Melfallan said dryly.

They came to a crossturn in the hallway, and Brierley glanced to the right, where the corridors led back to the dark abyss and a closed doorway. She looked left and saw another stairway rising upward, far broader than the others, with deep shallow treads. She blinked in sudden recognition. She had seen this particular stair in Megan's dream. High above, beyond other stairs and echoing rooms, they would find the great gate where Duke Rahorsum had waited on his day of victory, when the suns' light had streamed down upon him.

"That way," she said, nodding.

They climbed and climbed, turning right, then left, one stairway after another, and the air grew lighter, fresher. They passed through a great hall, where darkness spread in all directions, warded only by the dim spheres of the wall lamps. They hurried across the flagstoned floor, catching glimpses of color and jeweled sparkles in the tiles, the gleam of metal plaques on the walls. At the far side, they reached a blank wall and hunted to one side, then the other, for the exiting doorway. Another corridor, another stair, winding steadily upward. Megan's steps slowed and Brierley lifted her to her hip for a while. The child leaned her head on Brierley's shoulder.

"Do you hear any not-there things, Megan?" Brierley asked.

"No, Mother." Megan yawned. "I'm thirsty."

"Yes, child."

At the next level, they found water flowing in a channeled stone trough at waist height along a wall. The cold water gurgled as it ran, and filled the air with the scent and sound of tumbling water. Melfallan tasted the water gingerly, spat out his mouthful, and then tasted again.

"It's sweet," he judged. "And I know you're thirsty."

"Yes." Brierley bent her hand into the water and drank a handful. The water had a faint taste of moss, not unpleasant, but dusty like all else in Witchmere. She offered to Megan, and the child drank thirstily, dipping her own hand into the trough. When Megan was done drinking, Brierley put her down on her feet. Megan looked up at her with a smile, dark eyes shining in the wall light. "You are a wonder, child," Brierley told her.

"I am a wonder," Megan said contentedly.

"Where did you find her in Darhel?" Melfallan asked curiously. "Your infant witch." Megan yawned and put her thumb into her mouth, her other hand clasped fast to Brierley's skirt.

"In Tejar's kitchens," Brierley replied. "As I said before, I think she might be a relative, but Megan doesn't remember. Her mother may have been my twin."

"You had a twin sister?"

Brierley smiled. "According to Thora, the ghost in my Everlight, I did." Melfallan's brows promptly lowered into a scowl, and she laughed at him. "It cannot help but happen, lord. You stray into witchly affairs, and you hear witchly things."

"I am content," he said gruffly. "I merely ask that your gaps, some of which be chasms, are eventually filled in. Unlike Witchmere's guardians, I can't float across a void." Brierley wrinkled her nose at him. "Do you know where we are?" he asked, gesturing at the stairs.

"There is a great gate—and its exit into the valley—in that direction." She pointed upward to the right. Melfallan nodded doubtfully but was determined to be polite. He obviously yearned to ask how she knew. "I dreamed it," she helped.

"Really?" He grimaced, then gave a short laugh. For a lord who liked facts, Brierley's witchery tested him sorely.

"Yes, I'm sure."

"A month ago," he observed dryly, "I believed all witchery to be a mere silly tale, and utterly irrelevant to me, High Lord though I am. In fact, I told my portmaster, the very day I met you, that the last thing I needed was a witch in Yarvannet."

"A spoken truth," she said. "And the last thing I needed, I was certain, was a High Lord's attention. Indeed the last thing, for your attention meant my certain death." She smiled. "Neither of us achieved what we expected."

"Indeed."

They looked at each other, until she sighed and looked away. "Yes, indeed. I have spent my days asking one question after another: you have added to my number, Melfallan. And my answers are no wiser."

He bent to kiss her lightly, then eased her against him, his arms tightening as the intensity grew. Their touch made them both tremble, a result of his healing she still did not understand—and thought a cause to worry. She thought to resist his kiss, then thought to yield, and ended up doing neither. His eyes looked his own question, and she pushed him gently away.

"This is dangerous," she said, reproving him. "You tempt yourself unfairly, and me—and we both know it's impossible. You are earl and I am witch."

"I am Melfallan," he amended, "and you are Brierley."

"That, too," she said impatiently. "I can see you are as unhappy with first answers as I am, wanting others. What we wish does not rule the world, either as witch or lord, however lords may deceive themselves."

"I'm not Tejar," he retorted. "You confuse your lords."

"You stubborn man!" She put her hands on her hips to glare. "Will you not listen to prudence?"

Melfallan glared back. "You are precious to me, Brierley Mefell, and I don't care about prudence. I want to bed you, I admit it—that's what such kisses should lead to—and I can't help it, and I already know everything the whole world would say about it, but there it is. And it's more than just wanting that, and you know other things came first. Shall I name them? A friendly liking for a sea-shine lass I just met, my lord's duty to his own when she had need of me, awe and gratitude for your healing of Saray, amusement at your eluding my questions, concern, determination, grief, fear for you. Is that enough?"

"I don't want to quarrel," she said unhappily, and looked away.

"Then don't lecture me like some old grandnanny about what is proper and prudent. What do you want me to do? Pretend as if there's nothing between us, that I hardly know you, and you hardly know me? Pretend we could part without a pang from the leaving?"

"I like him!" Megan announced then, meddling.

"See?" Melfallan pointed triumphantly at Megan. "She likes me."

"Don't involve her," Brierley said crossly.

"Why not? Why can't she be my daughter as much as yours, in all the ways it counts? I know I'm married and I'll stay married. I'm earl of Yarvannet and I won't walk away from that. I can't walk away, no more than you can walk away from your healer's craft. But does that mean we must be nothing to each other?"

"But what *can* we be?" she asked in despair.

"At least let's talk about it, dear heart." He kissed her cheek, then brushed his lips across hers. They both shivered at the touch, and he smiled. She sighed, and that made him laugh softly. "Later, when there's time worthy for it."

"Maybe it wears off," she said resignedly.

"I hope not. For now, I want us out of this place with its floating guardians who don't stop when told and spurt fire to show their displeasure. I want you safe, and our Megan, too. Then we can talk about prudence, mistress—or the lack of it."

"You are a vexing lord."

"So long as it pleases you." He laughed at her expression, then spread his hands to Megan. "Will you not let me carry you, young mistress? To spare your mother for a time?" Megan consented to let him lift her, then wrapped her arms around his neck. With a sigh, she laid her head on his shoulder and blinked sleepily. "See?" Melfallan gloated. "I have an art with witches, even the infant ones."

"And boast too much about it, too," Brierley said.

"I'm sure you'll improve me in time."

They climbed another broad stair to another hallway and walked onward. As they passed one room, this one without a door, Brierley stopped short, her eyes widening in sudden recognition. "Wait!"

She stepped through the doorway and saw Thora's library before her—the same shelves, although now laden with dust, but the same cabinets, the stone bench against the wall, the same gleaming panels of the Four. The patterned wall tiles climbed dizzily up into the gloom of a tall ceiling, and the lamplight glinted off brasswork high above. Brierley walked to the center of the room and turned in place round and round, amazed. It was exactly the same, in every detail.

"What is it?" Melfallan asked from the doorway. Megan squirmed to be put down and then ran to Brierley.

"I dreamed this place," Brierley said in wonder. "It was a true dream, but I never knew it. She *does* live in the Everlight. Oh, she does!"

She half-expected to hear Thora's step in the shadows—then wondered if the Beast of her recurrent dream also lingered here, half-alive in the hidden corners. But of death she sensed nothing here: Death had passed through these halls centuries before, and had not lingered to await other prey, not after so many dusty years, after such a glut of death when Rahorsum's soldiers invaded Witchmere's caverns.

"We can't stay here," Melfallan said uneasily, glancing behind them into the shadows. "We must try to get above ground while it's still daylight. There's a way-station cabin at the end of this valley. I saw it when we climbed the pass to intercept you. Shelter there—and water and food. And no floating guardians."

"The not-there things go into the valley," Brierley said absently.

"Really? That's wonderful."

She crossed to one of the bookcases and caressed its wood, then carefully pulled a book from the top shelf. Its leather crumbled under the pressure of her fingers, and she hastily replaced it. "I forget the years," she said. "When Thora knew this place, all was new." She looked around the room again at the hundreds of books, some enclosed in glass, others visibly disintegrating and spreading their rot to their neighbors. "Can any of these books be touched, much less read? After three hundred years?"

"There are means," Melfallan said. "We need a bookmaster to aid us, someone who understands paper and leather." He stopped in front one of the four mosaic panels, where a golden dragon stooped from the sky, lightning in its claws. "Magnificent artwork. How are the stones set?" He touched the portrait curiously. "Why a dragon?"

"Bookmaster?" She turned toward him, surprised by the unfamiliar word.

Melfallan shrugged. "We haven't one in Yarvannet: my grandfather had the library recopied and rebound in his early years as earl, but never replaced old Nason after he retired. But aging books need a master, and Tejar has a bookmaster on his staff. So do most of the High Lords. A few years ago, Count Parlie discovered an archive in a forgotten basement vault and borrowed Tejar's bookmaster for a year. It's a rare art, but old books can be saved, Brierley." He looked around at the shelves, then walked over to the one of the cases and carefully removed a book that appeared to be in better condition than others. "And we must save these, for what they can tell us." He opened to the first page and promptly frowned.

Brierley lightly caressed a dusty shelf, then ran her finger lightly along the spines of the books. "Answers," she said wonderingly. "What answers are here, to be found and known? And what new questions?"

"This is odd," Melfallan muttered.

"A different alphabet?"

He turned to her. "You knew?"

"Not until I came here. There were words carved on that broken lintel. All my books in Yarvannet are in Allemanii, like yours, but the shari'a apparently had other words, words I don't know." She gestured at the many books on the shelves. "Answers—but how can I know what they are?"

Melfallan closed the book in his hands and reshelved it, then peered at the bindings on the others. "Maybe there are some books in Allemanii. Maybe even a dictionary that compares words. This is a scholar's library, and the learned are careful about such things. And the shari'a had reason to study us." He ran his fingers down the spines, then stooped to look at a lower shelf. Brierley followed his example at another bookcase, hunting for letters more familiar than the cursive shari'a script. Beside her, Megan mimicked Brierley by stilting her fingers down the books at her level.

"Ah!" Melfallan said, and pulled a slim red volume from a shelf.

"What is it?" Brierley hurried to his side. Taking great care with the book, Melfallan sat down cross-legged and balanced it on his knees. She knelt beside him eagerly, and leaned forward to see. He opened to the first page.

"*A treatise for the Count of Airlie*," he read aloud, "*given in friendship by Valena of Witchmere, a scholar and air witch, written in his own language for his greater understanding*."

"Friendship?" she asked, surprised.

"Things settled down after we invaded, as I remember. After you turned up in Yarvannet, you witch, Sir James and I scoured through my library. According to the histories, the Allemanii landed our ships in Briding, then spread out into the countryside to establish the counties. There were some clashes with the shari'a, but the invasion was largely peaceful, whatever happened later. Lots of room, after all. We built towns by the rivers, but the shari'a preferred their forests and hillsides. The two peoples lived peacefully side by side for nearly eighty years before Rahorsum. Time enough for friendship." He ran a finger over the script. "It appears Airlie has a tradition of favoring witches. My aunt will be pleased."

He turned the page. "*On the Nature of Witches*," he read, then smiled beatifically. "*Know then, good count, that the shari'a adepts are of four kinds—*"

"Four!" Brierley exclaimed.

"That's what she says. *—four kinds: alchemist, healer, stormcaller, and guardian. The forest witch, beloved of Amina, is given the gift of alchemy, that is, knowledge of the substance of things and their sympathies, and of the ways of* *beasts and plants, and of the patterning of life.*"

"Lorena," Brierley murmured with sudden insight. He glanced at her inquiringly. "One of the witches who lived in my cave," she explained. "I've studied her journal many times for its lore. She knew substances and herbs, and used them to heal, but never wrote about the Callings."

"Callings?" he asked.

She shook her head impatiently. "What more does it say?" she urged.

Melfallan read on. "*The sea witch, beloved of Basoul, is given the gift of healing, that is, the power of touch to ease injuries and pain, and knowledge of the inner heart, and of the peace that abides between people.* That's you," he said smugly, as if only Melfallan had possessed that fact before this moment.

"More than one gift? I never knew that!" Melfallan was greatly enjoying her reaction, she noted, more than she really approved. She craned her neck to read over his shoulder, prompting him again.

"*The air witch,*" he continued, "*beloved of Soren, is given the gift of weather, that is, knowledge of storms and winds, of clouds and rain and mists, and of the ether between the stars. Finally, rarest of all, is the fire witch, beloved of Jain, who is given the gift of memory, that is, knowledge of the people of the past, and the power to preserve, and the control of the guardians of Witchmere.*" As one, their heads turned to Megan.

"I'm a *fire* witch," Megan exclaimed happily, and hugged herself.

"So you are, child," Brierley said, amused. She remembered that the forest shadow had named Megan as fire witch, and wondered again if she had merely dreamed it—or had actually spoken that night to a shari'a spirit.

"What are these odd names?" Melfallan asked curiously, peering at the page. "Beloved of so-and-so?"

"They must be the names of the Four." Brierley's eyes moved to the panels between the cabinets. "See? There's a shari'a word at the bottom of each panel. Maybe they say those four names."

"The Four?" he asked, confused. "Four what?"

"The shari'a spirit-dragons." She pointed to each panel in turn. "Forest, sea, air, and fire. The shari'a worshipped those elements, and believed these spirits were their essence. Allemanii faith looks only to Mother Ocean and Daughter Sea, probably because you were originally a sea people." She turned to stare at the portrait of Basoul. Shimmering with blue scales, eyes a brilliant aquamarine, the sea dragon coiled on a dark sea stone above a crashing surf, a healer's cup between its talons. "You were there that day?" she whispered. "When I chose to heal?" The sea dragon's eyes gleamed in the lamplight, but did not answer.

"Spirit-dragons?" Melfallan asked dubiously.

"Different language, different religion." She glared at him. He pretended to ward her off with his hand.

"Sorry," he said. He closed Valena's book and set it carefully on the floor. "We take this one with us. Let's try to find others we can read." He got up and went to one of the cabinets; Brierley went to another, Megan following like a shadow. After a half-hour's searching, they had found a dozen books, four of them histories. Melfallan hefted one in his hand to look at the binding. "*Duke Rahorsum's Reign*," he read. "From whose point of view, I wonder?"

"The tales say we stole children, and spread foot rot and affliction, and created the winter plague."

"The tales say lots of things, and omit most of the truth." He picked up another book from their short stack. "And you found a dictionary, praise Ocean. It's the key to the others, Brierley."

"But what shari'a books do we translate first?" she asked, looking around at the hundreds of other books on the shelves.

"Your choice, sweet witch. I think we can handle two more."

"Witchery doesn't apply to book-picking, Melfallan," she said helplessly, and circled in place to look at all the shelves once more. What two? Of all these books, what two?

"Let Megan choose," Melfallan suggested. He smiled down at the little girl. "Mother needs two books, Megan, ones in good shape so they don't fall apart. Which should they be?"

Megan hesitated. "Books?" She looked at Brierley, then back at him.

"Two books for Mother," Melfallan said.

"Melfallan, you're confusing her."

"I don't mean to. Megan has been very patient with our silly adult preoccupations this last half-hour, and I think she should choose. Don't you, Megan?"

"Books!" Megan said enthusiastically.

"Two books. Choose for Mother."

Megan went to the nearest bookcase and selected a blue book, then a heavier book with a water-stained cover. "Books!" she announced and held them up to Melfallan.

"Thank you, sweetling. Your two books, Brierley."

She looked at him uncertainly. "Are you mocking me?"

"Not at all. I haven't a clue what to pick, either, and if your witchery can't tell you what books we should add, we might as well look to random chaos—that's you, Megan—and then *you* won't have to fret later about making wrong choices. See how I know you?" He raised an eyebrow. "So?"

"Well—"

"And when the dictionary informs you that Megan chose books about the habits of snow leopards and the seventeen ways of wall-building, then you can comment. How about that?"

Brierley laughed and spread her hands. She looked around the library once more. "I wonder if Thora left a book here," she said wistfully.

"Who was Thora?" Melfallan asked. "You've said that name before."

"The first of the cave witches in Yarvannet. She left a part of herself in my Everlight and advised me in dreams. My dearest friend and guide. As Megan is my child, so I was hers." Brierley looked around the small library again. "This was a place special to her. Perhaps her own compartments were nearby, near this place of study. I dreamed of this library, guided by her."

"If she was like you, she must have been lovely," he commented. "Later you can explain more about Everlights and dreams and guides; I'm still badly adrift. And I'd like to hear more of your Thora, too; it'll help me understand you better." Melfallan stooped and picked up the stack of books, then handed half to her. "And we must leave, dear heart, before the daylight's gone. I want us safe by nightfall."

"I agree." She accepted the books and tucked them in the crook of her arm, then held out her hand to Megan. "Where are the not-there things, Megan?"

"Sleeping."

"Good," Melfallan growled. He led the way back to the hallway, and they continued their climb to the daylight.

18

Their climb upward required another hour, and Brierley's feet felt like lead near the end, but the lure of the end of the corridors drew her onward. They passed room after room, some empty, some filled with shadowed cabinets and furniture. Witchmere far surpassed Darhel's ducal castle in size, even without the tunnels leading to its secret exits. The air moved slowly but blew fresh and clean, especially as they neared the upper levels. Sunlight sometimes glanced in from high shafts, creating pools of shimmering gold on the dusty floor.

"It would take months to explore properly," Melfallan commented, looking around him with intense interest.

"And what other secrets would we find?" she wondered aloud.

"And what secrets would we not? As inclined as I am to admire witch-kind, given the company I share, I doubt even Witchmere had answers to all questions, Brierley, even yours."

"Perhaps. But what questions did these shari'a ask?"

"Indeed."

They finally emerged into the Daystar's pale light onto a porch overlooking a snow-buried valley. Once Duke Rahorsum had waited on this porch, confident of his justice, vigilant in his defense. She took Megan from Melfallan's arms and arranged the sleeping girl comfortably on her hip. Megan sighed softly and wrapped her arms around her neck, and Brierley caressed the curls around her small face.

It was near noon: they had walked all of the morning. The Daystar shone brightly in the sky, masked by streamers of clouds. In the east, another bank of clouds loomed, promising more snow. Melfallan sniffed the wind and squinted at the sky.

"The storm has blown itself out, but I smell another one coming." He looked up and down the valley. "This is the same valley we climbed earlier," he said with relief. "I know where we are." He looked above them at the great weathered face of the tall bluff above the porch, then pointed southward, where the meadowland turned westward and disappeared behind the bluff edge. "The way-station cabin should be in that direction."

"It is cold," she said.

"It will be cold until spring now. Or so I remember Airlie's high mountain passes. Even so, I admit my own knowledge is only slightly greater than yours, and that usually limited to Airlie summers. Niall knows better than I."

They walked down the broad stairs, now heavily weathered and overgrown with weeds, and reached the broad meadow. Sheltered by the surrounding cliffs, the snow was not deep, with easier walking than the upper passes, and they found sure footing on a ridge of stone swept nearly clear by the wind. As they rounded the end of the bluff, the ground fell away even more rapidly, descending into a green valley shadowed with everpine. Brierley glanced behind them and stopped abruptly.

"You can't see the porch!" she exclaimed. She gawked at the bluff that now looked like all other bluffs nearby, yellow-white in the early sunshine, cracked and pitted by winter colds and summer heat, one bluff among a few dozen.

"I'm not surprised," he said. "Witchmere has been lost for three centuries, though foresters sometimes hunt these mountains and the couriers travel regularly over the passes. Besides, everyone knows Witchmere is only a matter of rumor, not fact. Legend and nonsense—like you." She wrinkled her nose at him comfortably. He looked up at the cliff face with its tumbledown broken rock that concealed the porch. "I'll hazard the guardians dispose of anyone who chances upon that doorway—as they might still dispose of us. Let's move on." He shivered in the cool air. "I'm half naked without my tunic, and I'm feeling it."

They made their way steadily downward across rock and thin snowdrifts, then entered a scattering of trees that thickened into forestland. After an hour, Brierley had set Megan on her feet and encouraged her to walk to keep warm, but Megan soon wheedled Melfallan to carry her again, since Brierley would not. Brierley carried only her own precious books and tried to read in one of them as she walked, nearly tripping herself for the effort. With a sigh, she shut it up and concentrated on walking the uneven ground.

The Daystar sank lower in the sky, its brilliant light glancing down into the gaps between the trees, but the wind did not grow warmer. Brierley shivered and stamped her feet vigorously.

"We'll reach shelter soon," Melfallan assured her, his teeth chattering. She could guess his fatigue—Megan was no easy weight—and her own body sent its twinges and warnings. Roused at midnight, chased by guardians, walking half the night up endless stairs, and now this tramp down a cold valley: with the ease of tension, her body seemed to grow palpably tired with every new step, though she carried only a few books.

"You are tired," she said. "So am I."

"Soon."

"Don't be stubborn to the point of stupid," she said irritably.

"Stupid, am I?"

"Let's quarrel," she agreed. "We can stop and talk to each other, and so rest our legs. It might even invigorate us, such sweeps of emotion and rage." He did stop and eyed her suspiciously. She stared back. "See?" she said. "I'm not a wholly lovely creature, to be adored at every moment. I can be unpleasant."

"For you, this is unpleasant, I agree. Others manage better."

"I am tired."

"And cross." He put Megan down on her feet.

"And hungry," she added.

Megan promptly sagged to the cold grass and curled up to sleep. With a sigh, Melfallan stooped and picked her up again.

"We're nearly there, Brierley. It was a half-day's ride through this valley."

"Ah," she said and squinted at him, then at the sky.

"Are you thinking at all?" he asked, bemused.

"No."

"Ah," he said back.

"Lead on," she said, although she sighed. They set off again, the carpet of everpine needles crunching softly beneath their feet.

They trudged another two miles, less than she had dreaded, and there found the small cabin Melfallan remembered. Built of sturdy logs and a solid plank roof, the wayfarer cabin stood in a small glade surrounded by tall everpine, with a long porch across its front and a lean-to stable attached to one side. Melfallan carried Megan into the cabin and laid her on one of the narrow beds, shut the door behind Brierley, then began stamping his feet and swinging his arms in the cold air of the room. The cabin was not large, little more than a single room with a wide hearth, a table, an iron stove for cooking, shelves and cabinets for stores, and straw-tick bedding, but it was shelter.

Brierley sank down on a mattress beneath the front window and looked out through the panes. Already the wind blew colder, bringing the first few crystals of new snow drifting down from the sky. Though at a lower elevation, the cabin would be drifted in snow by nightfall. Where were Stefan and Niall? Were they safe?

"Will we be snowed in?" she asked, not really caring much if the answer was yes or no. She sagged against the windowsill and closed her eyes for a moment.

She started as he was suddenly there beside her, easing her back onto the mattress, and tucking a cloak around her. A blanket followed next, warm in its woolly folds, with her feet lifted to tuck in its ends. Behind him, she saw a log fire burning on the hearth, popping and cracking, and already the chill had begun to lift from the room. He lifted her shoulders and brought a cup to her mouth, then encouraged her to drink. She sipped at the hot cup, then bit into the hard roll he offered. He sat down on the mattress beside her, then shifted around her to sit against the wall. He had found a tunic for better warmth, though it was a trifle small across the chest.

"Food," she said stupidly.

Melfallan bit into a second roll, then reached for another steaming cup on the windowsill. "Not much, but some. Some dried meat, some waybread, wood for fuel. If the storm lifts tomorrow, I'll try to set some snares for small game. I saw wood-pigeon tracks in a drift or two." He quirked his mouth. "I'm used more to hawking for sport than real hunting, but we'll manage for a few days. If Stefan and Niall are safe, they'll come down this valley and find us."

"There might be berries still on the vine, and ground tubers." She drank from her cup and felt the warmth seep into her body. She lifted her head to peer at the other bed. "Megan?"

"Sleeping. Lie back and rest." He yawned.

"You'll fall asleep sitting up," she advised him comfortably, then poked him in the chest as his chin sagged lower. "Melfallan, you're falling asleep now."

Melfallan jerked up his head and blinked at her, then put his cup and roll on the sill, placed what remained of hers beside them, and wearily rearranged himself to lie down next to her. Wrapping his arms around her, he sighed deeply, and fell asleep within a few breaths.

Drowsily, she watched Melfallan's face as he slept, and studied the curve of his cheek and brow, the feathering of his eyelashes. Did Saray sometimes watch his face as he slept? Did she treasure the rise and fall of his chest as he breathed deeply, the relaxation in his face as he rested? Her witch-sense stirred and she sensed Melfallan slip into dreams, fragmented and uncomfortable, then fall into deeper sleep, where true rest lay and dreams did not disturb.

Outside the cabin, the wind continued to rise as the eastern winds brought a new storm into the mountains. A breath of cold air slipped through the window casement and caressed her face, then tickled at her hair. She nestled closer to him. We could almost be a forester couple, she thought peaceably, resting in this wayfarer cabin during a journey, with our child sleeping nearby. He would be liegeman to a count, perhaps a forest steward, scouting the game in the hills and inspecting the lord's stands of pine. I would keep house for him and tend our daughter, and watch for his return every evening. I would see his face light as he saw me, and I would call out in joy to see him, though we be married all these years and growing older each day.

She reached and touched his face gently, tracing the curves from nose to mouth. If he were not lord. The fault lies there, I fear. As witch, I might find my own Harmon someday—or Melfallan in a commoner guise—and live a divided life as my mother attempted. Perhaps I might even tell my husband of my secret self, a privilege my mother never found in Alarson. Perhaps.

And as witch, I might even choose a lord, to be his lover and never wife. But as lord, Melfallan cannot choose me, not openly. Saray is daughter to Mionn, an ally he needs—and Saray is innocent, even greater reason.

I was too late in meeting him, she thought sadly, if such a meeting ever had hope at all. She sighed and curled her fingers behind his neck, feeling the warmth of him, and closed her own eyes.

The sharp rattle of the windowpane awoke them both with a start. Outside the cabin the wind howled, whipping snow against the windows in a slithering icy sound. The storm had struck again. Brierley blinked dazedly at Melfallan, their faces only inches apart. She lifted herself on one elbow, then craned her neck to check the fire. It had burned low on its load of wood, but still glowed with hot coals. Megan slept oblivious on the other bed, warm and safe in a deep sleep.

Melfallan's hand rose to touch her hair, then caressed her face. She shivered and he laughed softly. She smiled in response and took his hand, then turned it to kiss his palm. He shivered, too.

"I don't understand this," she said. "What did I do?"

"Whatever it was, don't stop." He stretched and then relaxed back against her. "Do we talk before or after?" he asked lazily. "I'd rather after, in case talking leads to shouldn't and we don't even get to after."

"My, are you confident!" she exclaimed. "Before or after?"

"I approve of after," he said comfortably, "and boldness suits a lord." He slid his hand down to her breast, taking liberties, though his heart rose to his mouth as he did it, with an anxiety that he had offended her. He hesitated badly, thinking to remove his hand, thinking he might not. "You certainly won't start it," he accused.

"Are you so sure?"

He laughed softly and pulled her closer to him. "I dare you to kiss me, witch," he whispered. "I dare you." And so she did, thoroughly enough to leave them both breathless. By then Melfallan's hand had undone her bodice and fondled her breast, teasing up the nipple with his fingers. In retaliation, she unlaced his tunic, making a slow game of it, and saw his expression change to surprise. "Hmmph," he said, and stifled the first four things that sprang to his mind. He suspected she was virgin maid, and so expected that gentle trouble and not at all what she was doing.

"Should we talk?" she asked in delight.

"No," he growled and pulled her hard against him, his lips moving firmly from neck to bared breast. "After," he mumbled. She laughed, and he laughed with her, and she yielded to the sweet pleasure with him, and he yielded in turn, warm beneath their blankets, heated flesh pressed together, the shock of the joining, the frenzied passion of their coupling, safe from the storm, safe in each other's arms.

They lay next to each other long afterward, saying nothing, listening to the wind. Melfallan slowly caressed her as he drowsed, and she caressed him in turn. It *was* delicious, she decided. In time, his caresses intensified and he sought her lips again. As the Companion's dusk fell into True Night and the wind blew furiously against the panes, he took time to pleasure her with his lovemaking, his own desire partly satisfied by their first coupling, and now completed by a long lazy hour. They drowsed together and then fell asleep in each other's arms, still joined in every sense.

In the morning Megan woke her up, demanding food and attention. Brierley kissed Melfallan as he slept, rearranged her clothing, and then slipped out of bed to go to her.

"You're all warm," Megan said, glaring up at her.

"Is that your word for it?" Brierley asked. "Were you awake, more than I realized?" Megan's eyes sparkled with irritation and suspicion, a reaction Brierley easily recognized from her own childhood. She had no trouble in guessing the cause. "Haven't you heard lovers coupling before, Megan? Surely you have."

"I don't like it!" Megan declared.

"Neither did I, when I was your age. It's hard not to listen, Megan, but it's part of what people are to each other. He is a good lord, a fine man, and your friend, too." Megan's face clouded still more. "Don't be jealous, sweet child."

Megan put out her lower lip and decided to sulk, though it was a narrower choice than Brierley expected, barely tipping against them. Brierley smiled and cuddled her for a while until Megan slightly eased her anger, then got up to find water and a meal for the child.

As Brierley reached for the teakettle on the shelf above the stove, she gasped. Megan's salamander perched on the teakettle handle, flames sifting along its scaled sides.

"Well!" Brierley exclaimed in surprise. The tiny beast opened its jaws and showed her small white fangs. Then it made much of cleaning a claw. "Can I have the teakettle, please?" Brierley asked dryly, wondering if she'd lost her wits. The salamander obligingly moved aside and settled on another part of the shelf. When Megan hopped off her bed and walked over, it crooned at her happily.

"Do you see something?" Brierley asked the child, and received a puzzled gaze in answer.

"Only my salamander. Why?"

Brierley looked down into the guileless eyes. "Never mind, child," she decided.

Megan chirruped to the beast and coaxed it onto her hand, then walked back to her bed, where she sat down to wait patiently for her breakfast. Brierley fetched water from the cistern to fill the kettle, and then started a fire in the stove, eyeing Megan and the salamander all the while. The salamander yawned casually, baring its needle-sharp teeth, then looked vastly amused at Brierley's expense. Megan giggled.

I am Jain, the salamander announced.

"You're the fire dragon?" Brierley asked skeptically, remembering that name from the book, one of the Four.

What is reality? it offered casually. *What is dream?* Then it laughed at her outright, a fiery hissing sound like water on coals. When it was done with its amusement, it gave a delicate shrug of its shoulders. *The little one needs me today in the waking world. The lord will not see me.*

As if on cue, Melfallan stirred in the other bed and turned over onto his back, then stretched hugely. He gave her a smile and clutched at his blanket as he dressed, then went outside to relieve himself. Brierley continued making breakfast. He was shivering violently as he returned and had to force the door shut against the wind, then joined her by the stove. Megan scowled ferociously when he kissed her, and Melfallan noticed.

"Is there a problem?" he asked Brierley. Megan promptly stuck out her lip.

"I never liked listening to my mother and stepfather in their bedroom, either," Brierley answered. "Lovemaking has an intensity that frightens a child. It's easier when it might be an emotion shared: once I became a woman, the terrors eased—but I still didn't like hearing it." She turned to look at him, then winked at Megan. Megan flung herself facedown on the soft mattress and screamed.

"Ocean alive," Melfallan exclaimed. "It's that bad?"

"Yes, it feels like that." Brierley took hot water to Megan and cajoled her to take bread and a little dried meat she had warmed on the stove. Melfallan stayed away on the other side of the room, eyeing them both. After she had eaten, Megan got on her knees to peer out the window, then blew the ice crystals on the pane to water with her breath.

"I think someone else is jealous, too," Brierley commented when Melfallan persisted in his eyeing and staying away.

"I am not," he declared. He leaned against the wall and crossed his foot across his other ankle, the portrait of casual unconcern. She snickered at his posing. "*She's* upset, you say. I'm not used to witnesses, and hadn't realized we had one." He colored slightly and looked around the one-room cabin. "It's too cold to put her outside—"

"I'm *not* going outside!" Megan exclaimed indignantly.

Brierley soothed her. "Of course you're not, dear one."

Melfallan shrugged helplessly. "I just don't know the rules."

"Don't you? I think we both know the rules, quite well." She kissed Megan, and then went to him, winding her arms around his waist, and felt his arms come around her. The contact tingled and she laughed softly, then rubbed her face against his shoulder. "I can't return to Yarvannet and you must."

"Not forever," he protested, tightening his arms around her. "I'll find a way to bring you home, I promise."

Brierley shook her head. "But not yet."

He sighed his acquiescence. "I suppose we have to talk now," he said reluctantly.

"After breakfast," she suggested. He pressed his face against her neck, breathed in the scent of her skin, then released her.

"After," he agreed.

"If I become duke, Brierley," he said earnestly, "I can change the shari'a laws. There was peace before, in those eighty years until Rahorsum was duke and attacked Witchmere. We can have that peace again. The knowledge in Witchmere can benefit both peoples, yours and mine."

"But *why* did Rahorsum attack the shari'a?" she asked. "What happened in those eighty years that went awry? I suspect there were mistakes made, something the shari'a did." She raised her hand to forestall his protest. "I know that the shari'a have cause to hate Rahorsum and think him wholly evil. I've read such assumptions in my cave books, but I've always wondered why he began to hate, Mefallan. Why do the tales say that we stole children, and that we crafted the winter plague? Perhaps some of those ideas had a kernel of truth in their beginning. Legends often do."

"I don't believe the shari'a did any such thing."

"That's because you're besotted with me, sweet man. In one of my books, the author boasted that she poisoned Yarvannet's earl."

Melfallan's head came up sharply. "Recently?"

"No, not at all. That was truly Landreth. This was long ago, maybe four generations or more. Most of my books are undated, and I'm not sure of the order except by the age of the book—and that is complicated by some recopying. But this witch claimed that she taken a position as healer in the castle, and then she poisoned the earl out of spite. I wonder if she was my type of witch, although certainly a healer witch could misuse her power. There are hints of that in other books." She nodded toward Megan, sound asleep across the room. "Rather, I think that witch might have been a guardian like Megan, one of the fierce ones who protects with revenge, even if the cause be centuries old. She *gloated* that she had killed him, Melfallan. Her book stops shortly afterward, and I think she was killed by the Beast. Or perhaps the earl caught her. Do you know?"

He shook his head slowly. "If the earl caught her, it was for murder, not witchery. I didn't find any reference to that in the histories we examined, but it might be in the judicial records." He frowned. "You're saying that the shari'a aren't always sweet and lovely and precious as you are." He reached to caress her and she dodged him.

"Pay attention," she said severely. "It's time to talk."

"After," he insisted. Megan was taking an afternoon nap, her salamander coiled against her side, and Melfallan had been thinking about opportunities. His thinking had led to her thinking, to their severe distraction.

"Now." She pushed his hand away and looked at him fiercely. He chuckled, then relented and sat back in his chair. "You are a vexing witch," he announced.

"You are worse."

Melfallan grinned, then reached out his hand. With a sigh, she slipped her fingers into his. They both shivered, then sat contentedly together, their two hands clasped on the tabletop. The fire popped and fizzed in the fireplace, a homely sound. Outside the cabin, the wind howled and complained, and smattered snow against the windowpanes.

"Do you think that you and Megan are the only shari'a left?" Melfallan asked.

She shrugged. "I don't know. I honestly don't. There is no one in Amelin or Natheby or I would have found her by now. There might be shari'a somewhere else in Yarvannet, in those places I haven't been, or in the other counties, in hiding as I was. Until the laws are changed, it is too dangerous to expose them."

"Hmm."

"Melfallan, the shari'a have managed to survive for three centuries. We can continue to survive, even the laws are not changed. You should consider your obligations to Yarvannet—"

"Dear heart," he interrupted, "I would probably have moved on Tejar, anyway. Not this soon in my rule, but later. My aunt has already urged it, and the other High Lords are restless, too. A duke rules by consent of the other lords, especially the earls—at least in theory. The reality is backed up by alliances and soldiers and wealth, of course. Duke Selwyn is deeply missed, and Tejar's misrule suffers in the contrast." He shook his head again. "What kind of duke employs a man like Gammel Hagan? A justiciar always suffers from sifting rumors, but Hagan's reputation had grown foul too quickly. What kind of duke murders a young woman for political advantage? A High Lord sees that kind of knife employed by the duke, and he knows such a knife can turn just as easily toward him."

"I wasn't murdered," she pointed out.

"*They* don't know that, so there's little difference. What did happen to Hagan, by the way? You still haven't told me."

She looked at him levelly, then took a breath. "I killed him. He intended to rape and kill me, and I killed him first. Then I put his body into a barrel of acid that ate him."

"Did Tejar actually order your death?" Melfallan said tightly. "And the rape?"

"Probably the death, maybe not the rape. I wouldn't have been the first; I suspect Hagan killed several young women in his dungeon. He boasted as much. But how do you prove Tejar ordered it? Likely I dissolved your only witness." She shifted uncomfortably on her chair, remembering how the barrel had popped and fizzed.

He smiled and misread the reason for her discomfort. "Am I supposed to gasp that you killed somebody? I'm glad you did, if the choice was his death or yours. To become duke, I have to kill Tejar. You never leave the former duke alive, not if you're smart, and I may have to kill his sons, too, for the same reason. When my grandfather put down Pullen's revolt, he killed— Well, Sadon of Farlost was the only local lord left alive. It's a bloody business, being an earl." He grimaced.

"That's why I said—"

"I'm not going to argue. As I said, war was likely, anyway. Tejar has pushed his dislike for me too quickly and too hard: I've been earl only six months. Everyone knew he disliked my grandfather, but he never pushed this hard at Audric. He thinks I'm weak, and so has started something in motion."

"Or he envies you."

"What for?" he asked, mildly startled.

"Oh, Melfallan, you are a silly fool. He is middle-aged, you are young. He is fat, you are handsome—"

"Am I?" he teased. "Say it again. I like to hear it from you."

"Calm yourself, lord. Harmon told me that Tejar has always been despised, enough to warp him since boyhood, and that's why he hates you. Harmon doesn't like Tejar, not at all, never has."

"And Harmon is your weather vane in all things?" His voice had a faint edge to it, and she smiled, amused.

"Are you jealous? Of Harmon, of all people? Harmon *was* my weather vane on lordly affairs until recently—when the duke gave me my own reasons for dislike. But men can be dishonorable, even evil, and the world still makes a space for them. Your grandfather managed for years to keep Tejar at bay. Can't you?"

"Perhaps, but my grandfather didn't have a witch problem." He winked at her.

"That's what I mean about thinking of other loyalties."

"I will—but you are one of the loyalties to consider. That's final."

She eyed him, then sighed.

He shrugged. "It may be years before I can make any definitive move. Did you know that Tejar promised Amelin to Bartol? Parlie brought me that little tidbit, garnered from a spy who talked to a cook who talked to the guard standing outside the duke's private door. War is merely the obvious threat, Brierley. Trade wars, spies, and treachery are others, and Tejar has already encouraged poison to remove an inconvenience. My baby son will tempt him badly, if he can't get at me. Without a son—well, you know what that meant. Without a son, all is at risk again, and Tejar knows that, as do I."

"I'm sorry," Brierley said, appalled by his dangers.

"Sorry that I live in such a world? Believe me, dear heart, I'm amply paid for it. I'm an earl. All the wealth in my earldom is mine. My wife can have jewels and fine clothing to her heart's desire. My son will grow up rich. I live in a fine castle, richly appointed. Men bow to me, and defer to my every wish, and seek my favor. If one of them has a dagger hidden in their sleeve, well, that's part of the price. Everything that is worth having has its price. I have my politics; you have your Beast. Which of us is the most afflicted?" He smiled at her gently.

"I worry for you," she said.

"I know—and I for you." He pressed her fingers. "Well, we've settled lord and witch. Now the hard part of our talk—Melfallan and Brierley." He paused wistfully. "Can't you say 'after' and smile at me coyly? I would dearly love that."

"Avoidance won't solve the problem."

"On the contrary, avoiding solves lots of problems. Tejar tried to avoid you by giving you to Hagan. Saray avoids things every day."

"You should be more patient with her, Melfallan."

"I *am* patient, but I'll try harder because you ask. Can a

man love two women, maybe in different ways, but love both truly?"

"Of course he can," she said. "But only one can be wife."

"If you had the choosing, would you be my wife? And know your sons will be hunted by assassins? That the length of your life and our children's lives are measured by mine, and mine alone? And you're a shari'a witch. Imagine what a political knife you could be as my wife, mine to direct whom to heal, whom to allow to die. The duchess is dying now: imagine my weapon if the duke knew of your gift and thought I controlled it."

"Perhaps that's the answer, Melfallan, why the Disasters happened, how it began. What if the Witchmere shari'a dared such power with the lords?"

"Indeed." After a long pause, Melfallan stirred restlessly. "Have we resolved anything?"

"No," she admitted. "Maybe there's nothing to resolve."

"Now, *that's* helpful," he growled and stood, pulling her up with him. "Megan is still asleep. Come to bed with me, Brierley. I want you, and our time together runs out with this storm. Then I must go to Yarvannet, and you must go into safety elsewhere." He kissed her hungrily. "Who knows how long until I see you again?" he whispered, and moved his face against her hair. "Help me not to think about it, dear heart, I beg you."

She clung to him, and he sighed deeply, then carried her to their bed.

The storm began to lift the following morning, and Melfallan hunted for her with snares, catching two rabbits. She accompanied him on the brief walk in the forest, digging tubers from the cold ground and finding a last smattering of berries on everholly bushes clinging to the boles of trees. Melfallan could not supply much in an outing of a few hours, not in the stinging cold and the threat of more snow, but the cabin stores had enough food for some weeks if Brierley was frugal. Melfallan promised to send up more supplies from Airlie, as soon as that could be done secretly. As Melfallan and Brierley foraged, Megan skipped and ran through the snow, the salamander sporting the air above her.

Then, at noon the next day, Niall and Stefan rode down the valley and found them safe at the cabin, to both men's open joy. As Melfallan walked out to meet them, Brierley stood on the porch steps and watched.

"I didn't know what to do, Melfallan," Stefan cried. "The tunnel closed up and we couldn't find you anywhere. Are you truly well?"

"I was going to bring up a search party from Airlie," Niall declared. "What happened, your grace?" Both men dismounted with a great creaking of leather and Melfallan clasped their hands happily.

"It's a long tale," he said, and clapped Stefan on the shoulder. "It's good to see you both. I worried about you, too. Did you have a hard ride through the snow?"

"Not hard, your grace," Niall said, "but there's another storm on its way." He pointed at the eastern sky, where new snow clouds were piling.

Brierley pulled her shawl closer around her shoulders and turned to check on Megan. The child had run to Friend the moment she saw the mare, shrieking a wild welcome, but the placid horse had borne it well. Jain had flipped and twisted in the air above them, sharing Megan's joy, and Brierley wondered idly if Friend could see Megan's secret companion. So far the horse showed no sign. Certainly Melfallan had not seen him, despite the beast's antics inside the cabin, nor had Stefan or Niall blanched death-white when Megan ran by. A clue there: the salamander was truly invisible—when he wanted to be.

Jain landed on a nearby everpine branch and set it to waggling, but none of the men saw that, either. Brierley sighed.

Just as a shari'a is invisible, he commented blithely, *when she's a sea-shine lass in the shade. Isn't that what Harmon always called you?* He pushed snow off his branch, and landed it with a thud on the ground. Nobody noticed—except Brierley, of course, and then only because Megan was busy with the mare. She quirked her mouth. *Do you* want *them to see me?* Jain asked, all mischief in his eyes.

No, she said firmly. *You'd be far too hard to explain.*

The dragon snickered.

The following morning, Brierley and the three men sat around the cabin table, the remains of breakfast before them. "She should go down farther with us into Airlie," Stefan argued, waving his spoon. "She could spend the winter at an upland farmstead or village, and no one would be the wiser."

Niall shook his head. "It's not safe for her there, Stefan, even in Airlie's upper reaches. You do not know it, mistress," he said to Brierley, "but your resemblance to Jonalyn is quite striking, enough to be noticed by those who knew her. I certainly did when we met. Better to stay here in this cabin for the winter, then go elsewhere in the spring, probably to Mionn. I know several fishing villages where you could hide yourself, at least until it's safer. Don't you agree, your grace?"

Melfallan nodded and sipped at his hot mug, then kissed Megan's forehead as the child sat comfortably in his lap. He put down his cup and set the child on the floor; Megan promptly wound her arms around Brierley's waist and clung. "I'll send up supplies as soon as it's safe," Melfallan said, "enough to last the winter. Sir Niall should stay here with you, Brierley. As my aunt's liegeman, Stefan would be missed, but Niall is Rowena's courier and is frequently gone from court, so we'll say that you're in Mionn, Niall, caught by the storms. Make sure she's protected. I'll tell Countess Rowena I said so."

"Yes, your grace." Niall bowed to them both from his chair.

"Then we should be going," Melfallan said and stood. "That storm is lowering fast." He turned toward Brierley and hesitated. "Hells," he muttered. He bent over Megan and kissed Brierley soundly, taking his time to do so. "Forgive me, dear heart," he said with a smile as he straightened. "You now get to explain *that* to Sir Niall." He drew on his heavy gloves. His eyes locked with hers. "I'll send you word," he promised.

"Yes," she said in a faint voice. And then, with a tramp of boots and a slide of cold air from the door, he and Stefan were gone.

Sir Niall cleared his throat, but said nothing. Brierley sat in her chair at the table and caressed Megan's hair as the girl pressed against her. Megan then kissed Brierley with a smack and ran off to her bed to pounce on the tattered doll Brierley had unpacked from Friend's saddlebags. Another instant friend. To Brierley's amusement, the salamander had sulked jealously, and Megan had not yet taken the time to wheedle at it. She was too busy with the doll. The fire at the hearth crackled, spreading its warmth into the room, and already the wind outside was rising.

"Do you need an explanation, Sir Niall?" Brierley asked, turning her head to him.

He smiled and shook his head. "When I was fourteen, dear lady," he said comfortably, "I met the love of my life. I knew it the moment my eyes saw her. She was lovely beyond compare, and her name was Jonalyn, but she hardly knew I existed, that being the fate of boys and their first loves. I've never forgotten her. You never do, you know." He lifted his cup and took a long swallow. "When I was thirty-four, meaning just before I left Airlie some days ago, Countess Rowena told me to become your liegeman, if I could, and to place your interests above all others, even her own. I always follow her orders." He paused for another swallow from his cup. "From what I've seen, and I haven't much as yet, I admit, you could be Jonalyn's twin in spirit as much as in face. And so I don't need an explanation for anything, and never will. All that matters is that I am your liegeman." He stood up and bowed to her solemnly, then reseated himself in his chair. "Lady witch," he said with satisfaction.

"I'm not a lady, Sir Niall," she objected.

"With respect, lady witch, I do not agree." They smiled at each other.

Brierley went to the door and stepped out on the cabin porch, then walked to the railing that looked down the valley.

Stefan and Melfallan had ridden nearly out of view, descending toward Airlie along the forest track. She watched until they vanished at the turning of the trail, and waited a while longer in case he came back. He did not.

Megan watched her solemnly from the cabin doorway. Brierley turned and looked at her, and saw the corners of Megan's mouth turn up in response.

"We are the last flame, my Megan," Brierley said. "And the first of the beginning. I swear it." She held out her hand. Megan brightened immediately and came to her, and wound her arms around Brierley's waist.

Brierley bent to kiss her daughter, and together they watched the snow begin again, its lacy petals drifting lazily down from the sky into the narrow valley. A silence lay on the everpine forest that surrounded them, a silence built of expectation and memory, of fulfillment and longing, of terror and peace. Opposites contended in the air, the faint lingering traces of nearby Witchmere as it had been—and might be again.

Will I rebuild our shari'a fortress? she wondered. Will my daughters then challenge the High Lords and bring down the destructions once again, with no rising after? Or is there a different answer? She looked upward at the gray-washed sky. Will we sail the stars, we lords and witches?

"It is a beginning," she whispered. "But of what? And who will do the choosing?"

"Mother?" Megan asked in confusion.

She looked down at Megan with a rueful smile. "Questions are a witch's lot, Megan. There's no escaping them." Brierley turned toward the cabin door and the warm sanctuary that lay behind it, where her liegeman waited patiently, seated at the table. "Come, my child. It is cold and will get colder. We should go in."

1

As the Daystar set and dusk settled over the land, the Companion, the world's second sun, ruled the short twilight of the cool winter evening, edging every grass blade and tree leaf with a shimmering blue light. Countess Rowena Hamelin rode through a sea of blue shadows and silvers, dusky blue under the occasional forest canopy that shadowed the road, brilliant silver in the open meadowlands. For the day's travel, she had dressed warmly in a long woolen riding habit, with a skirt that swept half to the ground, warm underbreeches and tunic, stout riding boots, and a furred cloak with a hood that kept the chill off her ears. The tang of the cold air chilled her face deliciously, and she could smell snow in the air. Beside the road they traveled, the broad Essentai River sparkled in the muted light.

Her heart lifted at the familiar sights of her beloved Airlie, the county that marriage to Ralf had given her and which, over the years, had steadily supplanted in her heart the Tyndale and Yarvannet of her youth. This land she now guarded for her ten-year-old son, for the time when Axel became count in his own right. This land she guarded in all its beauties and its folk, as the counts of Airlie had always guarded their meadowlands. A mere woman, certain High Lords would sniff—a mere woman as regent? Nonsense! But Rowena had defied them all, and dared any to diminish her Airlie in any manner, any threat.

Two days before, she had resumed her journey home from the duke's capital of Darhel to her own Airlie capital, Carandon, with a small company of her marshal, two lady-maids, and a dozen soldiers. The first day they had advanced a good twenty miles, then had quartered in a village by the river, her folk coming out to meet her and apologizing for the simple lodging they could offer, which was all they had. She had spent a pleasant evening at the headman's house, with her folk craning through windows to watch her as she took the children into her lap and talked to her village folk, at ease with them. As Airlie's regent, Rowena must flatter her Airlie lords to keep their sure loyalty, but among her commoner folk, who had chosen to adore her since she first arrived in Airlie as Ralf's young girl-bride, she had no such purposes. And so she had smiled at them as they shyly told her their news of simple things, fish and grain, a fine foal to drop in the spring. She teased them until they dared to joke with her, and then ate a hearty meal and matched glass for glass of wine with the headman, and so paid with a solid headache the following morning. The village folk had gathered in the road as she left, waving after her, and Rowena had waved back. My Airlie, she had thought happily. My heart and spirit, all in you.

She breathed in the crisp cold air, remembering, and watched a few isolated snowflakes twist down from the sky. A gathering storm over the mountains had threatened snow all day, but the racing icetrails had never thickened as they rode gently along the river road. When the road crested to overlook the long descent into Airlie's southern meadowlands, Rowena saw a herd of winter fawn run leaping across the grass far below, long-legged and graceful. The blue twilight gleamed on their dappled hides. She reined her horse to a stop and watched them run.

"Good hunting, my lady?" her liegeman Stefan suggested, eagerness in his voice. Roger Carlisle, the young captain of her soldiers, turned around in his saddle, adding his own look of sudden interest. Stefan and Roger no doubt found this placid ride through forest and meadow a bit thin in adventures. Roger had that lean look she liked so much in Stefan, and she felt fond of him, as she felt so often fond of the fine young men now entering her service, one by one.

She eyed both of them reprovingly. "Are you tired of riding guard on me, Roger?" she asked. "I think my soldiers are never bored in my service, whatever I ask of them. Don't you agree, Lord Heider?" She turned to her marcher lord, and saw his grin.

Lord Heider of Arlesby had joined them with a troop of his soldiers near midday a few miles beyond the village, wishing, he said, to guide her through his borderlands as courtesy. Stout and flaxen-haired, Heider had a wicked wit and eyes that saw farther than most. Rowena highly doubted Heider had ridden forth from his comfortable manor into this winter weather, breathless for the sight of herself, and, indeed, he had another purpose, as Heider usually did. During their ride through the afternoon, with grace and not enough to annoy, Heider had steadily probed her with questions about her nephew, Earl Melfallan Courtray, the new earl of Yarvannet. She had warned Melfallan that the more astute of the Allemanii lords were watching him, and Heider's overt interest confirmed her suspicions. When a young falcon rose into sight, the huntsmen below always took special note.

Heider bowed in his saddle. "Of course, my lady," he said smoothly. "How could they dare?"

Perhaps hearing a reproof in Heider's tone, Roger promptly saluted. "I never argue with my countess," he avowed.

"A prudent young man," Rowena said. "Stefan could learn from you." She looked at her liegeman, and earned herself only an impudent grin. She had become too indulgent, it seemed: these pleasant young men rarely feared her now, as was proper. She frowned warningly at Stefan, and only made his smile grow wider. Her lapse was confirmed by Heider's chuckle, but, sadly, one could not glare properly at Airlie's principal marcher lord.

"Winter fawn are good eating, my lady," Roger ventured, then put his hand on his breast, all innocence, when she looked at him. "I dread border rations and cold camps without a fire. Winter fawn have to be cooked, and cooking means a fire and that means warmth." He pretended a shiver and rubbed his arms briskly. Rowena glared, but Roger was undented, no doubt learning his manners from Stefan: they were close friends.

"Winter is settling in, countess," Stefan chimed in. "I could freeze my breeches off tonight. And there's this, too: if I froze my breeches, so might you, and your liegemen must always think of your comfort and safety." He bowed genially in his saddle. "Don't you agree, Lord Heider?"

One of the soldiers behind them chuckled, too audibly for prudence. Rowena turned in her saddle to glare at him, and got wide grins back from the lot. Yes, she had badly slipped in her rule. None of her folk feared her: this would not do.

"Good eating," Stefan said.

"Warmth," Roger added fervently.

"What an outrage!" Heider declared, now laughing outright. "Already your authority is slipping, my lady. Listen to them!"

"I will think of something suitably vile for punishment," Rowena promised. She glanced sidewise at Heider. "As I foully punish all my Airlie lords, usually for nothing important."

Heider grinned. "Oh, I've noticed that, my lady. That's why all your Airlie lords love you, and would have no other lady to govern them." He bowed in his saddle, as neatly as Roger. "Winter fawn *is* good eating," Heider suggested.

Rowena turned back round in her saddle, and considered the leaping shapes racing across the meadow. "Hmm."

"It wouldn't take long," Stefan said with sudden hope flaring in his young face. He obviously hadn't expected her to consider it.

"Horses can't outrace winter fawn," Rowena countered.

"Neither can shire wolves, but they catch them." Stefan tapped his blond head. "Strategy, my lady. Sometimes winter fawn don't out-think a pack."

"And you can go whooping along with your pack, you and Roger racing your pretty mares at top speed as you love to do—whether you catch a fawn or not."

"Well—" Stefan grinned, abashed—how incredibly young they were! He glanced hopefully at Roger, and they traded an eager look before both young heads swiveled back to her. "But it's for your sake, countess," Stefan said fervently, pressing his hand to his heart. "For good eating and a fire." His eyes danced with laughter, and Rowena smiled fondly at him despite herself, and saw her Airlie in his handsome face.

She snorted. "All right, then. For my sake—but don't take too long. And don't take too many of my soldiers for your pack, Stefan."

"Yes, my lady," Stefan said eagerly. "Walter, toss me your lance. You—you, and you," he said, pointing randomly at three of their soldiers, "come with us. My Destin will leave you all in the dust of her heels, but you can try to keep up, vain as that hope is."

"So you say, Stefan," Roger retorted stoutly.

Stefan laughed, and he plunged off the road and raced down the grassy slope toward the distant herd, the others in instant pursuit.

"Do we ride much farther tonight, my lady?" Lord Heider asked her courteously.

She shrugged. "We probably should," she said. "I wish I had more villages along this stretch of river; I prefer sleeping in a bed, pampered by my lady-maids." She smiled at Tess, whose nose was pinched red with cold, bundled although she was to her eyebrows. Tess was not an outdoors person, never had been, and the new one, Natalie, was obviously even less: both her maids looked miserable, good training for Natalie but not entirely fair to Tess. "Do you believe that lie, Lord Heider?"

"I will believe anything you want me to, countess," he avowed.

"Of that I'm sure," she retorted wryly. Rowena stood in her stirrups to stretch her legs, then sniffed the cold wind blowing up the slope. In the distance on the road ahead, she saw the dark speck of an approaching horseman—but, no, there were two such specks. Somehow her marshal had acquired a companion, and she idly wondered why. She nodded to Heider absently and heeled her gelding forward.

Sir Godric had ridden ahead to find a suitable camping place alongside the river road, for they had no convenient town or manor for tonight. Fifteen miles farther, for tomorrow night's stay, lay Lord Effen's rivertown, where he guarded the major river ford in central Airlie. Tonight, however, she would sleep beneath the stars and sky, a cold snow camp, surely, but a change she always relished. As a girl in her father's Tyndale castle, Rowena had grown up restless and active, more interested in racing along the river-shore and other boys' games than in proper activity for a noblegirl. She loved hunting, choosing hound over hawk for its wilder ride through forest and dell. Under the tutelage of her father's castellan, she had learned good skill with the sword, and had been an able horsewoman since the age of eight. Indeed, long after acquiring solemn dignity as awesome countess and ageless mother, she had once astonished Axel, then eight himself, by climbing the courtyard tree to a dizzying height. She smiled to herself at the memory, of which she still felt ridiculously proud, as silly as that was.

To her surprise, and even more so to Heider, Godric's companion was Heider's castellan, Sir Alan Thierry. Another excellent man, Sir Alan had served Count Ralf for years before taking up his post in Arlesby, and he had grown gray-haired in Airlie's service. Alan had been her close friend during the early years of Rowena's marriage, as fond of Rowena as she was of him. Of all her senior servants in that time, Alan alone had truly understood the gaps in Rowena's marriage to Ralf, and had offered his quiet understanding. How blessed I am, she thought suddenly, as she nodded to him with genuine pleasure.

"What brings you away from Arlesby, Alan?" Heider asked brusquely. "Is there trouble?"

"No, my lord," Alan assured him. "I had heard that a courier had arrived from Darhel with a message of some importance. I rode to see that you had received it."

"I did," Heider growled, his displeasure with Alan quite obvious, enough to make Rowena wonder why. She looked at him curiously, then back at Alan.

Alan smiled and bowed low in his saddle to Rowena. "Then it's my good excuse, my lady, to see you again."

"How are your wife and family, Sir Alan?" she asked.

Alan grinned broadly. "Six grandchildren now, my lady: they keep my good wife busy. Hmm. Seven, maybe." He squinted. "Yes, I'm sure it's seven."

"Ocean bless you, Alan, you should keep better track."

"I'll hazard you'll have the same problem, countess," Alan said comfortably, "when you're my age and have grandbabies to count. They do swarm so."

"I suppose they do." She grinned at him, then made a show of tsking, to be paid for her effort with another of those wide grins that had been greeting her all day. Alan wasn't afraid of her, either. She sighed.

"Will you be coming to Arlesby in the spring, my lady?" Alan asked. "My wife would love to see you again."

She shook her head, with some regret. "No, I'm afraid not. Melfallan's son will have his Blessing Day next month, and I won't task Sir Godric this year with two grand journeys." On the baby's Blessing Day, Melfallan would acknowledge his new son as his heir to his earldom, continuing that Courtray holding in Yarvannet. It would be a high occasion for the Courtrays, one to strain even Sir Godric's considerable talents at organization. Already a worried line had settled between her marshal's eyebrows, and he sometimes walked into doorjambs in his daze, or so she teased him. In truth, the tease was only half-false, and Godric's preoccupation would worsen as the event approached. She only hoped she could restrain his impulse to empty Carandon Castle for a sufficiently large party to match the occasion; they should leave behind at least a few soldiers for defense, should Duke Tejar use the lapse to invade her county. "In fact—"

"Shall we ride on?" Heider prompted impatiently. "I presume you found a campsite, Sir Godric?"

"Yes, Lord Heider," Godric replied and turned to point along the road. "Another mile or so, in a stand of trees." Rowena could see the shadow of the everpine grove ahead, barely visible in the growing darkness.

"Then shall we continue, my lady?" Heider asked. Rowena nodded, nudged her horse into motion, and they rode on.

"So you've definitely decided you'll go to Yarvannet?" Heider asked.

"Yes, Baby Audric is my grand-nephew, and my presence at his Blessing is important politically. I should take Axel, too, although I worry about the hazards on the road." She grimaced. "These are uncertain times, Heider, and I dislike lessening his protection. In Duke Tejar's mind, I'm too obviously Melfallan's ally, and a blow against me would be a telling blow against him." She scowled, likely showing more worry than she should. "And this duke remembers too well that his Kobus grandfather overthrew a Hamelin duke, and so sees plots where none lie."

"You think he'd strike at Axel?" Heider asked, affecting surprise. She gave him a sharp look: Heider was not obtuse about Tejar, and she wondered why he now pretended otherwise.

"Tejar would strike at anyone," she said, "if he thought it brought him advantage. A ten-year-old is a tempting victim when a full half-dozen claimants would clamor to be Airlie's count if Axel dies. Airlie in contention would be weakened, with opportunity for a duke to meddle to his gain." She shrugged. "Yarvannet isn't the only Allemanii land that hangs on the slender life of a child. At least Melfallan can have more children to protect his succession. A widow cannot, at least not without great scandal." She winked at him. "No, I must wait until Axel is safely married and producing heirs of his own. Then I will feel easy for my county, Lord Heider."

She clucked to her horse and eased him into a slow trot. The others heeled their own horses, and the troop, both Heider's and her own, fell in behind them with a jingling of reins and the quick scattered rhythm of horses' hooves.

The wind was cold, plucking with icy fingers at cloak edges and exposed skin. In the spring, when all was green and new, she liked riding about her lands, stopping at the manors of her Airlie lords to stay a week or two for feasting and hunting, for parties, and fine banquets, with each of her Airlie lords determined to do her the highest honor. In the beginning of her regency, a few of the older lords, Heider chief among them, had grumbled about being ruled by a woman. After eight years of good governance, her Airlie lords now accepted her as their countess, genuinely so, not with a false smile and mutters behind the hand, but with appreciation, a liking she returned. It was something she had earned in her own right, not given her by her father's rank or her accident of beauty, nor by fact of marriage or motherhood. It was something she had accomplished herself, and so she greatly enjoyed her lords' flattery, perhaps more than she should. As Melfallan had warned her, vanity was too easy a fault.

He always was perceptive, she thought fondly, even as a boy. She easily remembered Melfallan in his youth, quick, active, ready for any challenge, always the leader of the pack of boys who ran with him. Melfallan's inventive mind had lent vigor to his boy's pranks, to her frequent dismay when she discovered the risks he'd taken—breakneck horse races over the meadows, climbing on the roofs of Carandon's tallest tower, swinging from trees. She had not berated him for his madcap adventures during his boyhood summers in Airlie, when for a brief few months Melfallan was free of his grandfather's stern eye. Indeed, Melfallan thought she had never known of his escapades, an illusion she had not corrected.

Her father, Earl Audric, had been overcareful with Melfallan after plague had taken both of Rowena's brothers, all too conscious of the single frail life that ensured the Courtrays' future holding of Yarvannet's earldom. He had restrained Melfallan, lecturing him against unnecessary risk, weighing him down with too early an awareness of his duty as heir, checking impulsive fun that Audric disapproved. And so Melfallan had become solemn too early, and too prone to doubt himself when measured against Audric's high standards, standards that Audric himself did not always meet. It had complicated Melfallan's character, a useful gift for any High Lord enmeshed in Allemanii politics, but had made Melfallan too complaisant in Audric's choosing of his wife. Rowena had played her own role in that, one she now regretted.

Her father had chosen Saray of Mionn more for alliances than any thought of Melfallan's happiness—not that Earl Audric considered happiness a higher good than a deft move against the new duke he despised. In hindsight, Rowena now believed Melfallan's happiness had been more important than her father had realized, for happiness in his marriage would have encouraged Melfallan's personal gifts as a High Lord, lessened his doubts, given him purpose.

Most of the Allemanii High Lords quested for power and, once they had achieved it, often used their power to rule well, as had her father and Earl Giles of Mionn. Other lords, more rarely, drew their strength of rule from other sources—a sense of commitment, of duty accepted, of love for one's folk as sufficient in itself, for commoner and noble alike. Melfallan was one of those others. She suspected that Earl Audric had little understood his grandson, and so had never seen the inner boy and the man he would become.

Perhaps Brierley Mefell, the young midwife Melfallan had chosen to champion against Tejar's accusations of witchery, might change that now, although she did not wish Melfallan the risks. After a duke's man had accused Brierley of witchery, Melfallan had been forced to take her to Darhel for trial. Although Melfallan had only hoped that a trial could clear Brierley's name, if Melfallan could arrange certain High Lords as her judges rather than others, the duke had imagined another gambit in Melfallan's obedience to his summons, and so had ordered his justiciar to murder Brierley in secret. The young woman had defended herself, killing Gammel Hagan in turn, and then had fled into the mountains east of Darhel.

Two nights before, Melfallan had stood before the fireplace in her bedroom at the lodge, still cold from his long ride down from the mountains where he had left Brierley in the safety of a wayfarer cabin. The shifting light of the fire had illuminated the clean line of his jaw as he stared down into the flames. Perhaps he saw there a face, with large gray eyes, gentle curves to the cheeks, long hair curling to frame that face. Rowena, too, had loved a shari'a witch twenty years before, but had failed to save her. Perhaps now Mother Ocean offered a second chance. At times, their Allemanii goddess seemed indifferent to one heart's ardent hopes, choosing instead Her wider vision of all lives, all times. But not always: at other times, even solitary hopes might be answered, sometimes unexpectedly.

When Rowena had risen from her chair to join him at the fire, Melfallan had started slightly as she touched his sleeve.

"Where did you go?" she asked him. "Have you fallen into fire-staring, to the loss of your wits?"

"Probably," he said, turning to smile at her.

"You need to practice not thinking about her," Rowena said, and saw his mild surprise. "Soon you'll be home with your wife and son, Melfallan. And Brierley is supposedly dead, not safe in hiding, and pining is not grief." She eyed him. "Stefan and Niall will watch over her. So shall I."

"You shouldn't go up there," he warned. "I know you want to meet her, but you are certainly watched."

"I wanted to meet her in Darhel, but she acted too quickly in escaping Tejar's dungeon."

"Aunt—"

Rowena waved her hand dismissingly. "I have sense. I won't try. But, I, too, have my wistful moments. I do wish I had met her before you hid her away."

"Someday you'll meet her," he promised. "Sir Niall says she resembles Jonalyn, 'enough to be noticed,' in his words. They might have been related."

"As the child is related? Megan—is that her name?"

Melfallan nodded. "Her niece, Brierley thinks. She talks about dream castles and Everlights as the reason she thinks so, but she's probably right. She told me she had waited years to find another shari'a like herself, aching years. I can't imagine that kind of loneliness, having only yourself and no others. She was convinced that if we High Lords ever discovered her, she'd be killed." He snapped his fingers. "Just like that we burn her, because she dared to exist. No matter what healing she had given to others, no matter what lack of blame for being born shari'a. Duke Rahorsum's law is a vile thing. Do you think any other shari'a survive?"

"If so, how do we find them? They have reason to hide."

"True. But I wonder where to look."

"There are none in Airlie, Melfallan. I *have* looked. Twenty years ago I made myself Jonalyn's champion for all to see, and I had hoped it might encourage one of the others to make themselves known to me. But in twenty years I've found not one other shari'a. We Allemanii have been very good at killing witches." She grimaced.

When the Allemanii had come to these shores three centuries before, they had lived in peace for a time with the native people, the shari'a. During the third Karlsson duke's rule, however, Duke Rahorsum had suddenly attacked Witchmere, the shari'a capital, with a great army, and had murdered all he found there. The duke had then enacted the shari'a laws, proclaiming all shari'a witchery as foul and evil, and had condemned to death any surviving shari'a witch, should she be found anywhere in the Allemanii lands. Although no High Lord had found and burned a witch in nearly two centuries, those laws still existed.

Melfallan sighed. "Brierley says there are none in Yarvannet, either. But surely Megan and Brierley aren't the last two—only two, Aunt. I won't believe she has that slender of a hope. How do you rebuild a craft with only yourself and a six-year-old child?"

"Is that what she intends? What craft?"

"I'm not sure she really knows. What is this Everlight she keeps talking about? She says Thora Jodann's spirit lives inside it and sends her dreams, as if a woman who lived three centuries ago somehow can take new life. How does an Everlight, whatever that is, send dreams?" He shook his head and laughed softly at himself. "I mean, what is the procedure? How is it done? And how can a ghost live inside it? How is that explained? I mean, aren't there supposed to be rules?"

"It depends on whose rules," Rowena replied with a smile.

"That really helps," he snorted. "Rules are rules, dear aunt: we don't have separate sets, please, one for us and one for them. Otherwise the world is chaos, right? But why are there four kinds of witches? And—"

"Four kinds?" Rowena asked, startled.

"We found a book—"

"A book?" Rowena said eagerly, pressing his arm hard with her fingers.

"I'm here for the night," Melfallan said irritably, "and you'll hear the whole tale, Aunt—if you'll let me tell it." Rowena tossed her chin, but gestured for him to continue. "She talked about dragon-spirits that the shari'a revered. In the library in Witchmere, there were mosaic panels of—" He stopped as Rowena opened her mouth with another question, then chuckled as she firmly shut it again. "Ocean, how to tell it in order? Theirs is an entirely different world, Aunt, hidden away, that might now flicker out of existence—and we never even knew it was there." He paused, gazing at the flames for several moments, then shook himself slightly. "I wonder if the Founders had that same puzzle when they met the shari'a after the Landing, and if any of those Allemanii ever really understood the shari'a before they tried to destroy them."

"As they nearly did, nephew, and Tejar might attempt again—not for fear of the witches, but of you. To change the shari'a laws, you must become duke. Don't shake your head, but listen to me. In that goal I support you, and I would have urged it even if you had not found Brierley. Tejar is an evil man in an evil house, and I don't say that merely because his grandfather overthrew a Hamelin duke. Our Allemanii politics are difficult enough without wise rule, and Tejar's sons will be no better than he."

"To become duke, I'd have to kill Tejar, and I haven't accepted that I must." He scowled down at her. "Or his sons."

"Tejar has no such difficulty about killing you, nephew. Accept at least that. Tejar scents the wind changing, as we all do. That's why he struck imprudently at Brierley—and at you. It is time for the coronet to change heads again: all the High Lords feel it, and most are looking to Yarvannet. You must accept that, too. It is expected, now that your contention with Tejar is out in the open."

Melfallan tightened his lips. "I appreciate your advice, aunt—"

"—but you have a wider issue. I know. I am my father's daughter, dear one, enmeshed in my political plottings, my devious considerations of whom to manipulate, whom to kill, whom to let live. Believe me, I know exactly what I am. Your grandfather never saw an issue beyond politics: to him, that was the highest of all affairs. But I knew Jonalyn, as you now know Brierley, and I, too, wonder about your other shari'a world we've nearly extinguished. It seems it was a gentler world than ours, one of grace and lightness, of marvelous powers, where ghosts could walk in dreams, and a mere touch could heal. I wonder what other wonders they worked with their magicks, and what they thought about themselves, and how deeply we earned their hatred by our butchery at Witchmere. I, too, think of many things besides ambition."

Melfallan smiled. "I love you, aunt, however bloody-minded you are."

"If I am such, you can be less of it. True?" She smiled back at him, then waggled a finger. "But not too much less, Melfallan. Savagery of thought will keep you alive. Ask Duke Tejar. Ask any of the other High Lords."

"I will do as I choose, savage or not. I don't accept murder of whole families."

"But you must consider its necessity. That is all I ask."

"I think Brierley would hate it," he said slowly, "that I would do such a thing to save her. She's a healer, and healers never accept death as a necessity."

"She lives in a different world, dearest, her shari'a world where all that matters is healing with a touch, and the gentleness of a quiet day, and the care of her child. You must live in your world, to protect hers."

"Perhaps," he said stubbornly. "Must you meddle in everything?" he asked and tried playfully to disengage her arm from his. She resisted, tugging at him until he staggered. "Meddler," he accused.

"Yes, I must meddle. It's a fact of your being, Melfallan. Live with it." She smiled, then disengaged her arm and seated herself in a chair, beckoning to him. Melfallan sat down at her feet and leaned back against her knees. Rowena caressed his hair, as she had done when he was a boy and he had sat at her knees in her chamber, comfortable like this. The wind sighed down the chimney, raising a shower of sparks. "Your face is still cold," she murmured, touching his cheeks. "My Airlie winters can be too harsh."

He rubbed his face against her hand. "I'm warmer now. Don't worry about me." And she had bent to kiss his hair.

Yes, perhaps in Brierley, Rowena now thought as she rode through the crisp winter air, Melfallan has now found his purpose as High Lord—and his happiness as well. His defense of the shari'a witches, for Brierley's sake, would turn

Allemanii politics on its ear, and perhaps ultimately give the lands a new duke, a different kind of duke, one who ruled for more than power, as the Kobus dukes had always ruled. Perhaps. She knew she had not convinced Melfallan of the necessity—not yet.

They had entered the long wood, deeply shadowed. Many of the trees had dropped their leaves, but everpine and thorn-trees grew thick beside the road, their needles gleaming in the Companion's blue light. Rowena heard the soft hooting of a mock owl in a nearby tree, then the howl of a shire wolf, miles away. Its fellows joined in its wavering cry, beginning a hunt of their own. A cool wind shivered the needles of the everpine, surrounding them with a sibilant murmur. Down the slope, the voice of the forest rose and fell, a sound similar to the surf that had dominated Rowena's girlhood in Yarvannet. She narrowed her eyes and listened, remembering the sea. Yes, perhaps she would stay in Yarvannet for a little more time than needed, if only to hear the sea again, murmuring in all of Mother Ocean's quiet voices.

The Companion now neared the crest of the distant coastal mountains, and its twilight had deepened into lavenders and deep blues. They might ride another two hours in the twilight, but Rowena felt the fatigue of the day's cold ride seep into her muscles, and the wind had seemed to grow colder. She welcomed Godric's choice of an earlier camp, this pleasant glade beside the road with overarching branches to keep away the snow.

As the soldiers unsaddled the horses, Rowena climbed a small rise beside the road and watched the twilight deepen over the grasslands. Far below, Stefan and his companions were dark specks racing over the grasses in pursuit of the herd of winter fawn. Rowena smiled as the prey easily eluded the pursuit, and eventually both fawn and riders disappeared over a low hill. She turned back to the camp and settled herself near the small fire, then accepted a cup of hot soup from Tess. Tess sat down beside her with a sigh and pulled the edge of the blanket over her head, then shivered for effect, knowing that Rowena would see it. Rowena patted her knee in sympathy.

"Cold," Tess said with a chatter of her teeth, then sipped at her own mug.

"Yes, it is. You've been very good today, Tess."

"Thank you, my lady."

"Does Natalie give you trouble?" Rowena asked.

"Not that I can't handle, my lady," Tess said confidently.

Rowena sighed. She mildly regretted taking Saray's lady-maid into her service, despite Melfallan's pleading. Already she disliked the girl, and not only for the bit of byplay she had seen at a distance between Natalie and Brierley on the Darhel docks. Rowena knew Natalie's type well. First came careful deference to the high lady, until she was wheedled sufficiently into an indulgent good humor, then a bit of over-reaching, taking a bit more than one deserved, then presumption, waxing ever greater as time passed, and perhaps, near the end, outright contempt, even if kept safely out of earshot of its target. Rowena had no doubt that Natalie had passed through all four stages with Saray, lending an edge of desperation to Melfallan's hinting, and so she had relented. After thirty years of dealing with lady-maids in her service, first as favored daughter to an earl, then as countess, Rowena was quite familiar with Natalie's tactics. She also knew what to do about them. For now, however, Tess could cope.

Rowena reached for an extra blanket and gave it to Tess, who accepted it gratefully.

"Cold," Tess repeated. "I far prefer our castle with its roaring fireplaces. Even a headman's cottage would be better. You have a hard service, countess."

"In a moment I'll be pitying you. That won't do." Tess laughed softly.

The soldiers cut branches from the nearby everpine and built rough mattresses on the ground, and three of her Airlie troop had sat down on their own beds to eat a trailside meal and drink from their water bottles. They noticed her watching and smiled, then might have got up from their comfort if she had not waved them off. Other soldiers, both Heider's and her own, were tall shadows in the nearby trees, keeping the watch, and two had stationed themselves at the edge of the forest to watch the meadows below. Eventually, Roger's sergeant appeared before her and saluted. "My lady, Lord Heider asked me to report that the watch is set."

"Thank you," she said with a nod. He marched off to his own station.

Rowena looked toward the road. "And where are my eager young men?" she asked, annoyed. "Hasn't it been enough time for their futile chasing?"

She got to her feet and walked over to the road's vantage again, then looked down into the meadows below, then along the river road behind then. The twilight filled the meadows with blue shadows. In the far distance, the dark shapes of winter fawn were leaping across the grasses as they raced up a broad hill, but she did not see any horsemen in pursuit.

"I should not have let them go," Rowena said as Sir Alan joined her. She tightened her lips with irritation. "Why do I indulge them?"

"There's likely some cause," Alan said soothingly. "A lame horse, a throw—or even a winter fawn caught. It would take time to gut the carcass."

"I suppose you're right." She bit her lip, then turned back to the fire. "Sometimes, my dear Alan, I find life annoying, and I worry like a silly old woman."

He smiled. "You, old? Not yet, my lady."

"It will come in time, I'm afraid," she said with a sigh, "and sooner for me than others. I envy Stefan and Roger their youth. I even resent it. Ah, to be twenty-four again! I can hardly remember how it felt. And that in itself shows me turning old." As she settled herself on her bed of soft bracken, Sir Alan stooped to spread a blanket across her shoulders. Tess had curled up under her own blanket, already asleep. Natalie was nowhere to be seen. Likely she had wandered away into the trees to flirt with one of the soldiers. Rowena frowned, then let it go.

Across the glade, Lord Heider emerged from the shadow of the far trees, sword in hand, and walked toward her, smiling. She smiled in response, then something about his stance, the edge to his smile, made her pause. Two other soldiers in Heider's livery appeared behind him, then three more, all with swords drawn. The soft metallic sound of Alan's sword being drawn brought Rowena quickly to her feet, and in that same instant Heider made his charge.

"Alarm!" she shouted as Alan lunged in front of her, his sword raised in her defense. "Alarm! To Airlie! To Airlie!" Heider slashed out at Alan, his face convulsed with rage, and steel rang in the glade as Alan's blade met it in midstroke. "Step aside, Alan!" Heider roared.

"Never!" The marcher lord struck again at Alan, shouting curses when the man would not yield way.

Alan's quick defense had won her time. Rowena ran to a nearby horse, where a sword scabbard hung on the saddle. She drew the sword with a shivering clang, and turned just as one of Heider's soldiers reached her at a dead run.

She hadn't time to set her feet, nor even raise her blade, and so she dodged his swinging blow. The blade whistled past her and sank deeply into the horse's haunch behind her, and it screamed in shock, then reared, striking out with its hooves at its attacker. Blood spurted from its flank, a mortal wound, and its hind leg collapsed beneath it, but not before strong teeth had ripped into the soldier's shoulder, dragging him upward as the horse tried to rear again, staggering as it screamed. Rowena thrust upward with her sword, striking for the heart, then skipped backward as both soldier and horse fell heavily to the cold ground.

"To Airlie!" she shouted. "To Airlie!" Rowena ran around the kicking horse and retreated toward the trees as two more of Heider's soldiers menaced her, trying to box her in as one circled to the left. She raised her blade and dropped into a sword-fighter crouch, watching ahead and behind. She heard a piercing woman's scream among the trees, then shouts and the angry metallic clash of swords, but all her Airlie soldiers were still too distant to give her aid. His teeth bared, one of Heider's men swung his sword, and she parried neatly, then met his next blow with ringing force, enough to force him backward. Off balance, his sword swinging wildly, the soldier staggered and Rowena put her sword into his throat. He gasped, his eyes bulging, and threw his hands to his throat to stop the blood that gushed from him. As he staggered and fell, Rowena whirled to meet the other man who swiftly pounced on her, and fought fiercely against the other's longer reach.

"You would murder your liege lady?" she demanded. The man's mouth twisted but he said nothing, and only strengthened his attack. This soldier was not as careless as the other, and nearly outpointed her in his furious assault. She prudently retreated, matching blow for blow.

Her own soldiers had almost reached her when Rowena's foot, hampered by her riding skirt, misstepped on a buried root and she stumbled, falling backward. Knowing her danger, she twisted as she tried to rise, and an instant later felt steel pierce her right shoulder, striking agony as it bit deep and through. With a cry of triumph, Heider's soldier ripped back his blade, tearing open the wound still wider, and raised the sword high over his head. Rowena flinched, seeing her death in that coming stroke.

"To Airlie!" an Airlie soldier cried, and the next moment he plunged his sword into the man's chest. He pushed Rowena roughly to the ground and straddled her, his blade raised against other men who rushed down on them. Another Airlie soldier joined him, then three others, making a ring around her. A moment later, she heard the hammering of horses' hooves on the road, and Stefan burst into view at full gallop, the others at his mare's heels. There was a shout and suddenly the battle turned as Heider's men fled into the trees before Stefan's furious assault.

As their safety was rewon, Rowena pushed away her soldiers' hands and staggered to her feet, then moaned from the pain in her shoulder, nearly falling again at the sheeting of it, the slicing edge of it. She grabbed at her arm and staggered. No spurting of bright blood, she noted, with far more detachment than she expected. I've more than a few minutes to live. It seemed a distant question, hardly important. Odd.

And then Stefan was there beside her, lifting her up in his arms. As Stefan turned toward the fire, she saw Sir Alan, panting heavily, standing over Heider's body. "Rowena!" Alan cried as he saw her wound, shock in his face.

"She's taken a blade in her shoulder," Stefan shouted and carried her to the fire. Then Tess was there, bending over her, and then Sir Godric, her marshal, and the others crowding around her. Rowena's head swam and blackness picked at the edges of her mind.

"I'm all right," she insisted, and struggled to sit up.

"No, you're not," Stefan said and pushed her back again. "Will you not listen to me? Lie down!"

Rowena hesitated and then relaxed against him. Dear Stefan, sweet youth on the morning. But then Sir Alan had pushed Stefan aside, and ripped her sleeve from her gown and put a cloth to the wound. "It's deep," he muttered. "Can you move your fingers, my lady?"

"With some trouble," Rowena said faintly, and then closed her eyes against the agony that it caused when she tried. "Hurts," she whispered, and blinked furiously as the world shimmered with tears. The blade had passed cleanly through her shoulder, penetrating the seam of her sleeve: a lucky thrust combining the soldier's sword-skill and Rowena's own stumble. I should have worn mail like Melfallan does, she thought dazedly. Wise Melfallan, wiser than me. Oh, Ocean, keep him safe! Keep my Axel safe! Blood now gushed from the cut, cascading down her arm and soaking through the cloth in Alan's hand.

"Hurts," she murmured again and her face twisted as Alan's fingers probed her wound in the inadequate firelight. She struggled against her own daze, to do what must be done, to protect—"How many are dead?" she asked faintly.

"Five of our soldiers," Sir Alan answered, "six of theirs, and your other lady-maid, countess. Apparently she and one of the soldiers were in the trees—" He shook his head impatiently. "The rest of the Arlesby men have fled."

"And Heider? He's dead?" She hardly recognized her own voice, so weak it sounded.

"Yes, and rightly so," Sir Alan growled. He pressed her hand urgently. "Countess, you must know about the message that came from Darhel yesterday. The courier would not put it in my hand, only in Lord Heider's. He seemed too lofty a man for a mere courier, and Heider was ill-tempered and silent after he left. Then, suddenly, this decision today to join you. I was worried, my lady." He bared his teeth. "Ocean bless me that I chose this time to act. I served the Hamelins before I served Arlesby—and I still serve you."

Rowena squeezed his fingers. "My thanks that you did, Alan. Dear friend, dear—" Rowena's voice failed her as the world began a slow turning, bringing down the blackness from the night sky.

"She's bleeding badly," Stefan exclaimed from a far distance. "How far to Effen's town?"

"A good fifteen miles," Alan's voice answered far above her. "A hard hour's ride, too rough for the wound, Stefan."

"Then we'll ride at less speed." Rowena felt Stefan's lips press against her forehead, and then felt herself being lifted gently in his arms. As he carried her to his horse, her head sagged weakly against his shoulder. The darkness of the night shimmered in black waves, pressing down on Rowena, merging with the pain. Her head spun, and her breath seemed harder to draw. She could no longer move her fingers in that hand, however she tried, and she felt the blood slowly pumping from her shoulder. To end like this— It wasn't right. It wasn't right, to die by a traitor's murdering, although she'd faced its possibility all her rule. Axel, my son—

Melfallan, guard my Airlie— Rowena yielded at last to the darkness.

Stefan lifted his countess onto his horse and swung into the saddle behind her; then, muttering an anguished curse, he heeled his horse forward into the night.

"Break camp!" he bellowed. "Leave the bodies where they lay! We ride!"